Philip Gilbert Hamerton

Round my House

Notes on Rural Life in France in Peace and War - Vol. 2

Philip Gilbert Hamerton

Round my House
Notes on Rural Life in France in Peace and War - Vol. 2

ISBN/EAN: 9783337188221

Printed in Europe, USA, Canada, Australia, Japan

Cover: Foto ©Andreas Hilbeck / pixelio.de

More available books at **www.hansebooks.com**

ROUND MY HOUSE

NOTES OF RURAL LIFE IN FRANCE
IN PEACE AND WAR

BY

PHILIP GILBERT HAMERTON

AUTHOR OF "THE INTELLECTUAL LIFE," "A PAINTER'S CAMP," "THE SYLVAN
YEAR" ETC.

Quid potes alibi videre, quod hic non vides? Ecce cœlum, et terra, et omnia elementa
nam ex istis omnia sunt facta. —*De Imitatione*, Lib. I. Cap. XX.

BOSTON:

ROBERTS BROTHERS.

1888.

PREFACE.

THERE are two kinds of books about foreign countries, those written by passing travellers and those written by fixed residents. Each of the two kinds has its peculiar merits, and neither of the two can escape its peculiar defects. This book is of the latter species. The fixed resident is certainly the person who ought to write about a foreign country, because, unless he be singularly unobservant, he will know much more about it than the passing traveller, and yet there are peculiar difficulties in his case. Habit, in course of time, makes things seem matters of course to him which would strike the passing tourist as interesting from their strangeness or delightful for their beauty. Every one knows that in course of time we all positively cease to see the pictures and furniture in the room which we constantly inhabit, so that a stranger will have a far livelier sense of their merits and defects than we can possibly have. This is the great obstacle to writing about what we see continually—the freshness of the eye is wanting, it is gone for ever, and cannot be recovered. It is perhaps for this reason that almost all the books which are written on other countries are the result of, at most, a short residence. After a few months in a place we write about it, after many years we feel a disinclination to write, because we know it too well, and yet feel that we ought to know much more before publishing results and conclusions. In many cases there are also reasons of delicacy for not publishing what concerns the manners and customs of a place that one has lived in. Every author is aware that people have a passion for recognizing themselves and their neighbours in print, a passion which goes to the most astonishing lengths, for people will select some character as unlike themselves as possible, and then complain of the unfaithfulness of the portrait. The author of the present volume, like everybody who has written a novel, has had some experience of this. The *one* occupation of all his friends and acquaintances appeared to be the recognition of his characters as portraits, and the same character in the novel was detected by the cleverness of several different correspondents as a likeness of several different originals. Some correspondents even went so far as to recognize themselves in the literary picture, to acknowledge that the satire was deserved, and promise amendment, although the author had not once thought about them during the composition of his work.* Now, if

* I am not sorry to take this opportunity of observing that this nabit of readers is based upon a completely erroneous conception of an author's mental processes. It is quite true that most fictitious characters have been *suggested*, in some remote way, to begin with, by a living person, but no author with the least imagination stops at portraiture. His imagination plays with the first suggestion and develops from it something entirely different. It is narrated of a certain painter, celebrated for the beauty of his Madonnas, that he had no other model for them than a wrinkled

people seek and find portraits of themselves and their neighbours in novels, how much more ready will they not be to discover such portraits in an avowed description of the manners and customs of the particular locality in which they live! The author, it is true, might have recourse to certain artifices, not affecting the substantial truth of his descriptions in matters which it concerned his readers to know, and yet shielding individuals. He might, for example, allowably describe a man so as to put his neighbours on a wrong scent, by making the fictitious person live in a new house when the real person lived in an old one, or by giving him red hair when nature had given him black. Still, however skilfully this might be done, it would be better not to excite popular curiosity about people whose privacy ought to be respected. This consideration would of itself make a writer hesitate, in certain circumstances, before publishing a book in which there is so much painting from nature as there is in the present volume. It would be wrong in a Frenchman to publish a work of this kind about an English neighbourhood, because his book would be read in the neighbourhood itself, where people would recognize, or fancy that they recognized, the originals of his descriptions. When M. Taine wrote his " Notes on England " he had this inconvenience continually in view. But we may use much greater freedom in describing a French neighbourhood where there are no English residents, when the

old man-servant. This is a very perfect instance of the working of imagination. It needs some suggestions from the world of reality, but a very remote suggestion is enough.

book is addressed to English and American readers
only. France is very near to England, but England is
as remote from France as some province in the heart of
China. A book written in Chinese, or in Egyptian
hieroglyphics, or in Babylonian cuneiform characters,
would have quite as good a chance of being read in
this country "round my house" as a book written in
English. It is, therefore, impossible that any persons*
alluded to in the volume should be identified by any
one. The English reader cannot identify them because
the originals are unknown to him, and those who know
the persons are ignorant of the language in which they
are more or less accurately portrayed. It is as if an
English neighbourhood were to be described in Chinese,
with the right of translation reserved. The Chinese
author might go into detail without hurting anybody's
feelings.

These observations have appeared necessary because
so few English readers are likely to realize the wonderful remoteness of England from rural France, and some
might be disposed to accuse me of a want of delicacy,
when in reality I have been at great pains so to manage
matters that no private person alluded to will ever be
identified, whilst if such identification were possible, the
worst consequence of it would be to reveal some fact
which everybody knows, as, for example, that such a
gentleman's establishment consists of one woman-servant and two men, or that *déjeûner* is his principal

---

* Except the bishop, but it so happens that I was able to paint
him as he is and yet observe the rule of *nil nisi bonum* without
ever thinking about it.

repast. The general impression which the book will produce in England and America will be favourable to my French neighbours, who, whatever may be their faults, have qualities which will bear to be painted truthfully. I offer it as a small contribution to what ought to be the great work of international writers in our time, namely, the work of making different nations understand each other better.

It was originally intended that this volume should be illustrated by the author, but as a set of etchings would have greatly increased the price, and as, after many experiments, I remained dissatisfied with the processes which produce blocks to be printed cheaply, the idea of illustrating was at last abandoned. It is likely that the purchaser of the book has lost very little by this decision, but as it happened that my American publishers announced it some time ago as "illustrated," I thought something ought to be done to compensate my American friends for whatever little disappointment they might feel when the text reached them without any graphic accompaniment. I have, therefore, given them fifty or sixty more pages of text than the quantity originally intended. There is, I think, nothing to regret in this arrangement, for the book does not need illustration, and the sketches of a landscape-painter could have added but little interest to its pages.

CONTENTS.

———o⊙o———

ROUND MY HOUSE.

CHAPTER I.

IT happened a good many years ago that my wife and I set off on a tour in search of a house. I wanted a fine climate, or at least a climate in which I could count upon fine summers, and scenery interesting enough, and sufficiently varied, for a landscape-painter to work happily in it without going very far from his own home. My wife, on her part, though quite willing to let me have my way in the choice of climate and scenery, had also requirements of her own with regard to house-keeping. We had lived together in a very beautiful but very out-of-the-way place in the Highlands of

B

Scotland, where we were literally twelve miles from a lemon, and forty from the nearest hairdresser ; whilst at certain seasons of the year there was not (in activity at least) such a functionary as a butcher in the whole county. Here we had learned the lesson, which nobody ever does learn except from actual experience, that a too distant retirement from the conveniences of civilized life, far from being favourable to projects of economy (as the inhabitants of large towns sometimes imagine), is on the contrary a cause of incessant expenditure, as unsatisfactory as it is unavoidable, unless, indeed, you choose to submit to the privations of a Highland shepherd, and live upon oatmeal and diseased meat. I was the more willing to conform to my wife's house-keeping requirements, that I had observed for my own part how a life far from conveniences invades and breaks up the time of the master of the house, how he has always to be looking after details which a lady can scarcely attend to, and has to sacrifice time in frequent journeys to the distant town, all which may be rather pleasant than otherwise for men who are without occupation, but is vexatious in the extreme to the artist or *homme de lettres.* In a word, the sort of life which we were determined to avoid was what may be called the *colonial*—that life which is led in its full perfection by the holder of a sheep-run in New Zealand. On the other hand, I had never been able to share the spirit of resignation with which so many landscape-painters submit to pass their days in the streets of cities, without ever seeing a blue or purple hill in the distance, or having any more direct impression of sunset splendours than what is to be gained by observing that the chimney-pots of the opposite houses look somewhat redder than usual. Nothing in the lives of landscape-painters whose biographies have been written appears to me more pathetic than a sentence in that of Chintreuil, when, in his penniless student days, literally suffering from hunger, he exclaimed, "Oh, if I had but 150 francs to go and live two months in the real country!" Yet not all "the country" is suitable ground for a landscape-painter, and what is rich in material for one will be barren land for another. Neither is it the place which seems to him the most strikingly beautiful when he is travelling which will be the best for him to live in year after year. There are so many things to be considered in choosing a place for a long residence! Some places have a strong dominant feature of a special kind, which is very interesting when the coach stops at the way-side inn and you have half an hour to go and look about you, but which would be either indifferent or tiresome to a fixed resident. The valley of Chamouni, for example, would be a very bad place to choose, because Mont Blanc is far too dominant there; you cannot get out of its way; you must either think of hardly anything else in landscape, or else become indifferent to landscape beauty altogether, as the Alpine peasants are. There are natural objects which interfere with the individuality of a painter who lives too near them, and it is as difficult to work independently in their presence as it would be to pursue intellectual labours in the continual presence of some overwhelming human potentate, such as the Czar of Russia, for example. Another great objection to a place is, not to be able easily to get out of it. A perfect country is one which, in a day's drive, or half a day's, gives you an entirely new horizon, so that you may feel in a different region and have all the refreshment of a total change of scene within a few miles of your own home. There are very many places in the world where this is quite impossible, some dominant characteristic of the landscape pursues you wherever you go, for thirty or forty miles, and you must undertake a serious journey to get under other influences. There is a house in the middle of Glen Coe, about equally distant from its two extremities, which seems a very undesirable place of residence, for it is only just possible to get out of the glen and come back again in the course of a summer's day, whilst every excursion, in either direction, must of necessity be in the same scenery. So I suppose that on the plateau out of which rises the great white cone of Chimborazo you may travel for many miles, whilst, for any variety of scenery that you get, you might as well remain quietly under the shadow of one cactus, if a cactus gives any shadow.

It is a very amusing, yet at the same time a very fatiguing business, to travel in search of a house, especially when you are not tied down to a limited extent of country. We had the whole of eastern France to explore, south of Sens, and our impression at first was that our only embarrassment would be in having too many delightful residences to choose from, but we soon perceived our error. The house was to be a *maison de campagne,* and the difficulty of finding one to suit our tastes and **purse** at the same time will be better understood when I have explained what a *maison de campagne* is.

The reader will please observe that I leave the words in the original tongue, without any attempt at translation, and the reason for this is, that a translation would convey quite a wrong idea of the habitation to be described. *Maison de campagne* does not mean " country house," nor anything like it. It answers much more to the English shooting or fishing lodge or cottage. It generally belongs to somebody with a moderate income, who lives habitually in a town, but likes to have a little place in the country on his own estate, where he may go and spend a few weeks at a time during the fine weather, and hear the thrushes and the nightingales, whilst his children may run about in the fields. A very well-to-do Frenchman told me lately, that he was going to build a *maison de campagne*—a " château," as he laughingly called it—on the most beautiful site on a very beautiful estate which he inherited last year. He has planned it all himself in the most original manner. There is to be a large hall as the general living-room, with cells and cupboards round it, and the hall is to open on a terrace with a glorious view over a rich expanse of country. The dwelling is not to have more than one story. The owner and deviser will arrange everything exactly according to his own fancy, and not at all in obedience to any kind of fashion or conventionalism, so that every time he goes there he may feel as free from the tyranny of " social pressure " as Robinson Crusoe in his castle. This is exactly the Frenchman's idea of the *maison de campagne.* He thinks of it as a place where life is to be rather rough, where he is to sit on cheap chairs, or a hard form per- haps, and sleep anyhow, in a cupboard or on the floor, or at best in a little cell ; but where, as a compensation, he may wear any kind of old clothes, and work in his garden, or roam about in his woods to his heart's con- tent. The reader will at once perceive how difficult it is to find a *maison de campagne* fit to live in all the year round as one's principal or only residence. There is, indeed, another class of country house—the *château,* which is often roomy enough, though seldom particu- larly comfortable ; but you will not often find a château to let, and when you do it is likely to be encumbered with land and gardens, which are a source of expense rather than either pleasure or profit. The sort of house we wanted did not belong to either of these categories. We required more space, and better arrangements, than are found usually in the first, and wanted our house to be more compact and less expensive than the second.

Our tour began on the line between Paris and the Mediterranean. I did not intend to go so far south as to get into the dreadfully long, arid summers of Pro- vence. Avignon, for example, was too far south for our taste, though we knew that neighbourhood well. All that Provençal country is delightful before the dry heat sets in, and it is a very rich country for an artist, especially if he has a hearty appreciation of old build- ings, rugged bits of foreground, and clear mountainous distances ; but in summer it is better to be farther north. My first plan, therefore, was to choose some locality south of Lyons, yet north of Montélimart, in the immediate neighbourhood of some town upon the Rhone. Of all the French rivers the Rhone is, at the same time, that which is best worth illustrating, and that which has been least exhausted by artists. It was also the river towards which I felt the strongest per-sonal attraction, which is of the very utmost impor-tance for the interest of artistic work, as no artist can ever interest others in subjects which do not interest himself.* My artistic scheme was, therefore, to have easy access to the whole of the Rhone scenery, and in this I counted much upon the assistance of the rail-way line from Lyons to Marseilles, for the railway always keeps within a moderate distance of the river, and so gives access to many points of interest, whilst the interval between one station and another, or be-tween any station and the river, could always be easily traversed on foot, or in the common conveyances of the place. Another great advantage of the railway was, that if I chose to descend the river in a small boat, the railway would take charge of it on my return. Besides this, an artist living close to the Rhone would have the advantage of the Rhone

---

* Amongst the innumerable doctrines about what artists ought to do which are doubtful and uncertain (their uncertainty being proved by the success of artists who disobey them), a few appear to be confirmed by the general experience, and this is one of them. An interesting picture is always a picture of something which the artist has either passionately loved or at least cared about in earnest. But it is not by any means so sure that the converse is also true. The strongest affection for a place will not enable us to paint it in an interesting manner.

steamers, which would stop and land him anywhere at his convenience.

If the reader will kindly enter into this project from the artistic point of view, he will at once perceive how much was involved in it. A landscape-painter may be said—in a peculiar sense, ·of course, yet to him at least in a very real and intelligible sense—to possess the land he lives in, so far, at least, as he can appreciate its beauty ; just as a student who lives near a public library possesses the library, or at least so much of it as he can use and understand. And the longer I live, the more profoundly am I convinced that this kind of pos session is the truest and most satisfying kind of owner-ship ; nay, even that it is the only ownership, which being infinite in its nature, is adequate to our infinite desires. To me, a house by the Rhone, near a railway and steamboat station, meant the possession of the Rhone itself, with all its crags, and castles, and ·pic-turesque old cities, and those leagues of lovely or noble landscape which lie between one city and another.

If the reader will glance at a map of that part of the country through which the Rhone flows, he will find that, for part of its long journey, it passes between the departments of the Ardèche and the Drôme. The railway follows it all along, on the left bank, and from this great main line there are now two lines to Grenoble, one from St. Rambert, and the other from the Isère, both in the department of the Drôme. Between these two branches, and about fourteen miles north of Valence, there are two little towns exactly opposite each other, with the Rhone flowing between

them ; that in the Ardèche is Tournon, that in the
Drôme is Tain. Now it seemed to me that to live
somewhere very near there, would be in the highest
degree favourable to certain artistic projects, for I
should, at the same time, be close to one of the noblest
and most interesting rivers in Europe, and have easy
access to the most magnificent mountain scenery, by
the help of those lines of railway.

So the first place we went to was Tain ; that, at least,
was the station, but we went to the hotel at Tournon,
and that hotel must be mentioned here because it had
a very important influence on our destiny. If that
hotel had been clean, we should have stayed there
patiently and explored the country in every direction,
the end of which exploration might possibly have been
the discovery of some suitable dwelling ; but the hotel
was *not* clean—indeed it was so exceptionally dirty,
that it required great courage to stay in it a single
night. What floors ! what walls ! what a staircase !
and what servants ! There was space enough, the
house was not badly built, there was no especial difficulty about being clean, and as for water, the Rhone
flowed swiftly by ; but the place was given over to
uncleanliness, as if it were a foretaste of Italy or Spain.
It is scarcely too much to say that the floors inside
the house were like the flags in a Manchester street
when a fog has saturated the soot ; the walls had not
been papered, nor the paint washed for years, and the
women were in a state not to be described without an
intolerable realism. There was one apron especially—
but let me refrain ! It is many years since then, and

that **apron** is now purified. It has passed into a higher
state of existence ; it has become paper, perhaps the
whitest and smoothest of papers in some rich man's
library, in an *édition de luxe.*

Just opposite Tournon rises the world-famous hill of
the Hermitage, where the noble wine is grown. As
every inch of the ground is of almost fabulous value,
the hill-side, which is very steep, has long been artificially cut into terraces supported by walls, which spoil
its beauty entirely. Behind Tournon, the road leads
up a hill ; we followed it from curiosity, and soon came
upon a magnificent view of the course of the Rhone
and the snowy Alps of Dauphiné. That was a sight
to compensate for the ugliness of the vineyards by the
river. But there was no house up there, and if there
had been one, the situation would have been particularly inconvenient. After much seeking, we discovered
at length a genuine " maison de campagne " on the left
bank of the Rhone, and a wonderful little building it was.
How miserable it looked ! It had the honour, indeed,
of being a detached residence, but this only made it
look the more wretched as it stood alone in its desola-
tion and its nakedness. It was all out of repair, and
not a door nor a shutter fitted. I rather think there
was a pepper-box turret, which made the owner call it
a château, and ask an absurd rent ; but the fact is that
all the rooms were so small that the whole mansion
together would have gone into a good-sized studio.
Then we saw reason to suspect that, during the inundations which display so much energy on the shores of
the Rhone, the lower rooms had the advantage of being

under water; and we observed also that in the heat of
summer, which in those parts is sufficiently intense, the
inhabitant of the mansion had not a tree big enough
to shelter him, but would have to set up an awning,
or a big umbrella, like a negro king. In spring he
would be disquieted by his neighbour the Rhone ; and
in summer he would dwell in the full glare of a
southern sun in a desert of burning sand. The mere
idea of living in such a place brought on feelings of
depression which made the whole neighbourhood seem
dreary to us, and we were in such great haste to get out
of the dirty hotel that we were rather glad not to have
found a dwelling-place. We received an impression
that we were too far south for cleanliness ; and this was
confirmed by another remarkably unpleasant hotel at
Vienne, where the rooms were stifling and dark, and
looked out upon a horrible little yard. I confess to
being excessively impressionable by the aspect of
places—indeed I am so to a degree which far transcends
the limits of what is reasonable. The unpleasant
southern hotels really had very little to do with our
project of residence, for we did not intend to live in
them ; yet they discouraged us, and put us almost into
low spirits. The dwellings which we had examined
seemed to offer sufficient accommodation for a bachelor
with one servant and a cat, but as for lodging a family,
and finding room for a library and a studio besides,
there seemed to be no way of accomplishing it except
building. Still, when I think of that Rhone project,
which seemed so magnificently attractive when first
indulged in as a dream, I am even yet surprised at the

facility with which it was abandoned. We had ex
amined very few places, we had spent very little time
in seeking along the river, when we retreated north-
wards, as fast as the train would carry us, with a sense
of relief, as if we had escaped from danger, or at least
avoided committing an imprudence.

There were three departments, some distance to the
north of Lyons, in which we felt much more at home
than in the Ardèche. We had friends in the *Côte d'Or*,
and my wife's father had been connected politically
with the departments of *Saône-et-Loire* and the
Doubs, having been a representative for the first and
prefect of the second. It does not require very much
to determine a preference amongst places one knows
very little about, so this bygone political connection
gave us a sort of reason for examining these departments rather more particularly.

We began with Mâcon. Lovers of art will remember
it because of Turner's beautiful picture of the vintage
there, an admirable ideal work, which does not bear the
slightest resemblance to the place. Nobody, however,
who knows how Turner worked, how he used nature
as a suggestion merely, and not as an original to be
copied in fac-simile, will ever be so far misguided as
to place the least confidence in him as a topographer,
nor will he ever feel disappointed because places are
not so poetical as Turner represented them to be.

Our impressions here were more encouraging than
they had been at Tournon and Vienne. We had
spacious rooms in a rather large and airy hotel over-
looking the river, the servants were clean and attentive,

and we felt ourselves approaching more nearly to the regions of comparative cleanliness. Here, at any rate, were space and air. The broad Saône flowed slowly beneath our windows, with stately regiments of tall poplars on the other side—rather too orderly to be very entertaining to the eye—and beyond the poplars stretched the plain that goes to the foot of the distant mountain lands of Jura and Savoy. The weather was hazy during our stay at Mâcon, but it added greatly to the glory of the rooms we occupied to believe the lively landlady when she told us that there was a fine view of Mont Blanc from those very windows. If the reader will only bring himself to believe that Mont Blanc is visible from his own window, he will find that this faith communicates a certain grandeur and dignity to his room, which are well worth having, however illusory. Years afterwards I found that Mont Blanc, under peculiar atmospheric conditions, was indeed visible from Mâcon, and more impressively than from nearer places. It is wonderful to see that dome of rosy white suspended in the sky like something that is not of this earth. It seems as if it were a satellite of our planet, like the moon, and one expects it to rise higher and higher as the moon does, till it sails alone amongst the stars, detached from everything terrestrial.

All about Mâcon the country has a certain largeness and openness of aspect, the exact opposite of snugness, but very appreciable also. The reader will at once understand what I mean by snugness in landscape, but I may give an example of this character in Rydal Water a Grasmere, where it is to be found in the fullest perfection. The opposite character is often very admirable too, as at Mâcon, and from that town southwards along the Saône. Everything is large and tranquil. The slopes of the vine-lands are vast in extent, and gentle in declivity, unlike the abrupt terraces of the Rhone-side, where the hills are cut into huge stairs. The river is broad and quiet, spanned by a bridge of twelve arches. The plain beyond the river is so broad that it seems to have no limits, and when the dome of Mont Blanc is visible it is so remote that, instead of setting limits to the distance, it only makes it more appreciable. The town is on the sloping bank of the river, and the upper houses have wide panoramic views. One of these was to be let, and we went over it. The building was tall and narrow, like a tower, with a number of sham windows painted on the walls, and a strange little stair going down into the garden. Those sham windows are a characteristic of the south, and they begin to prevail on the Saône. As you go southwards, you find more and more sham architecture painted upon the stucco—Italian cornices, pilasters, medallions, festoons, brackets, balustrades, and other abominations, all in the most frightful colours that were ever mixed by the ingenuity of a house-painter—intolerable pinks and buffs that would make an artist sick to look at them. Here, however, the evil is in a mild, incipient form, not much worse than I have seen it in some parts of England, where a window would be represented by a slab of stone in place of the glass, on which stone the house-painter would do his worst, and represent, on a black ground, a sash half open, with curtains and tassels visible through the imaginary glass, and (supreme triumph of his art !) a vase of flowers in the middle, which no gust of wind would ever dash to the ground, nor any sunshine fade. This tall, narrow house at Mâcon had, however, other charms than its painted windows. It belonged to the new class of French houses, the neat and tidy class, *à l'instar de Paris*, in which the old provincial notions of abundant space and the most awkward arrangements, with an incredible roughness in everything, have given place to the most unexceptionable neatness and finish, with such a rigid economy of space that there is scarcely room to turn. The polished oak floors were certainly very pretty—much too pretty to be walked upon in strong boots—but the rooms were so small, and the stairs so narrow, that it was like being in some tiny Parisian apartment. By way of compensation, the garden was very large, and in the most beautiful order. This set me against the genteel residence at once. I have a hearty dislike to gardens of all sorts,* and the only quality which could ever reconcile me to a big one, is its close resemblance to a wilderness. I saw plainly that the owner of the residence was one of those un-fortunates who are afflicted with the garden-madness, and the sequel proved this, for when we began to talk about terms, he asked an absurdly high rent, in the first

---

* Supposing anything better to be accessible. There are places so ugly that a garden is very precious, and there are places so shadeless and so poor in foliage that a few trees in a garden are a priceless luxury in summer. But a mile of wild trout-stream is, to my feeling, worth the gardens of either Chatsworth or Versailles.

place, and in the next made it a condition that I was to
keep on two servants of his, to take care of the place,
whether I liked them on farther acquaintance or not!

As we could hear of nothing suitable in the neighbourhood, we decided to look at some apartments in
the town itself, more to satisfy our conscience than for
any result to be expected from such an exploration.
The wonder in those old French towns is, how the
people can endure to be lodged so badly. There were
generally two decent rooms and a sort of kitchen somewhere, after which we asked in vain for the bedrooms.

Not quite in vain, perhaps, for the person in charge
always answered, with the greatest decision, that nothing
was easier than to show them, on which he or she began
opening a series of recesses called alcoves, and here and
there perhaps some tiny closet, generally quite dark
and deprived of all possibility of ventilation. In a
word, the " *appartements* " in question were admirably
adapted for a bachelor's lodgings, especially if he had
his meals at the hotel, but it would be difficult in the
extreme to establish a family therein, except as people
do in very little yachts, where the same space has to
serve both for day and night, and any berth is big
enough which enables its tenant to go to sleep. The
most wonderful of all these dwellings deserves to be
mentioned separately. There was a fine *salon* of course,
(there always is,) a pretentious drawing-room with gilt
mouldings and glistening flowery paper, and alcoves to
hide the beds in, and a marble chimney-piece and the
rest—a place in which a good deal of vulgar furniture
might have been displayed to great advantage. There

was also a kitchen, a miserable little hole, so gloomy that the poor cook would lose the use of her eyesight in it before long ; and close to the kitchen there was the dining-room, a place presenting as cheerful an appearance as the vestibule of a solicitor's office in Lincoln's Inn Fields, about eleven o'clock at night. Not only was it dingy and mean, but it was dark, so dark that the inhabitant could not eat in it at mid-day without a lamp. We asked if the tenant was expected to take his *déjeuner* by candle-light, it being just noon at the time of our visit. The answer we received was an answer never to be forgotten. "Unfortunately," said the guide, "you have come two hours too late ; but I assure you that at ten o'clock, which is the proper time for *déjeuner*, a ray of sunshine darts into the room as if on purpose, and illuminates it most agreeably." On this I asked if the sun were so good as to come back at dinner-time too.

The dining-rooms in these habitations are often nothing but a passage or entrance, but the inconvenience is not much felt, as even in the poorer middle class in France the dining-room is never inhabited, except during meal-times. In England, as the reader knows, unless he is some very exalted personage who has never been in a middle-class house, it is a very common custom to pass the evening in the dining-room, which accounts for its superior comfort. A Frenchman will dine anywhere if he has only a cheap chair to sit upon, and four bare walls to keep the wind out, but he does not like sitting in an eating-room. I think that in this the Frenchman is quite right. The essential quality of a *salle à manger* is, that it should be used for that purpose and no other.

It is astonishing how uncouth **were** some of the *appartements* we visited at Mâcon, and what dismal look-outs they had. One of them, consisting of two or three very big rooms, looked out upon a dingy old back street with a stagnant *ruisseau* in the middle of it, or in other words an open sewer, and after this we had enough of seeking, for the present. One of us proposed a voyage on the Saône, from Mâcon to Lyons, as a steamer passed every day, coming down from Châlon. So we got on board and left behind us the city of Lamartine. The steamer was very long and very narrow, and the deck was so encumbered with merchandise that it was hardly possible to stir. There were also numbers of peasant women with produce for the Lyons market. We sat on a box, and soon forgot the discomfort of the boat, in the lovely river scenery which now passed continually before us.

The Saône is a particularly tranquil stream between Châlon and Mâcon, and also for many miles further south. As you go down it on the steamer, it seems as if you were boating on a long pond which opened into another long pond, and so on, endlessly. The scenery is of the kind which is often described as uninteresting, but, in truth, it is exquisitely beautiful in its own quiet way. I think that scenery is always interesting if only it is in one extreme or another. The mountain-river is delightful (the Orchy, for example, which passes by Dalmally, and enters Loch Awe at Kilchurn), but the broad river of the plain is delightful, too, in its sleepy

reaches, where the tall and graceful trees reflect themselves in the smooth broad water. You have not here
the excitement of the mountains, but what a sweet
repose! You have scarcely any grandeur, except here
and there the grandeur of some noble tree or some
huge cumulus cloud that sails slowly across the plain,
and reflects its whiteness in the broad water ; but you
have beauty, serenity, and a sort of dreamy infinity, for
it seems as if such scenery could never have an end.
A hundred pictures compose themselves and break up
again into fragments as the steamer steadily advances,
till at length the mind accepts the illusion that it must
be so for ever, that the river will flow on in a boundless
plain, infinite as the sky.

Our voyage, however, came to an end—and to an unexpected end. After we had steamed for several hours,
when it was late in the afternoon, the river began to
conduct itself very differently, and the land was no
longer the same. The banks rose steeply now, and to
a great height, all covered with vines and villages—a
rich land. The broad river began to wind about like a
mountain-stream, and to ripple and run over its shal-
lows. One of the most poetic impressions I ever received was the view of Trévoux from the river, an old
town with a mediæval castle ; the town on the slope
of a steep hill with a curve like an amphitheatre, the
towers of the castle on the top, the river flowing at the
bottom, and all in the mellow glow of a late afternoon
sun, which bathed the rich confusion of old buildings in
a warm, strong light like that in the pictures of Adrien
Guignet. It was a painter's scene, under a full pictorial

effect. After that the hilly character of the scenery continued, and at length, when within eight miles of Lyons, we came to a swift rippling shallow in a sharp curve, just such as you will find in any trout-stream, but on a much larger scale, the long steamer ran aground, and our voyage reached a sudden and unexpected termination.

This was very like canoe-travelling in the running aground, but it was not at all like canoe-travelling in the difficulty of getting afloat again. The canoeist jumps out, gives his little vessel a shove, then gets in again and paddles away merrily, but our long steamer was not so easily dealt with. The men got very long poles and pushed as hard as they could, the paddle-wheels revolved and churned the shallow current into foam. As for the peasant-women who were going to the Lyons market, they showed no sign of alarm, but quietly began to eat their own apples, having evidently no expectation of any immediate deliverance. In tidal estuaries, such an accident is of little consequence, because the captain knows that the tide will come to deliver him, and the almanac foretells the hour of his liberation, but in a stream like the Saône the only increase of water occurs in rainy weather, and when we ran aground the barometer was *au beau fixe*. A hawser was sent to the shore and tugged at by a crowd of people—they might as well have tugged at a church. As the steamer was simply immovable, the captain came to us very politely and expressed his regrets, say-ing that we should do well to leave the boat at once, which we did accordingly. There was a railway station very near, but we had an hour or two before train-time, and spent the interval in exploring the beautiful neighbourhood of Fontaines and Collonges, which are to Lyons what Richmond is to London, but not nearly so populous, for one of these villages has but a thousand inhabitants, and the other rather less. All this part of the Saône is hilly, and from the heights on the right bank you have magnificent views, bounded by the Alps of Savoy. Many rich people at Lyons have houses between this place and the city, either on the banks of the Saône itself, or in the lovely valleys which come down to it. The region is quite a noble one, but we were discouraged for the present in our house-seeking, and did nothing but enjoy the beauty of the place as simple tourists till we returned to Mâcon. As for the steamer, we left her where she grounded, and what became of her I know not. The captain would no doubt discharge a part of his cargo to lighten her, and let us hope that the peasant-women of La Bresse* got their apples and cheeses to market.. They were all the more interesting for that very funny, but not altogether unbecoming, costume of theirs, with its especially remarkable headdress. The reader may perhaps have noticed the one-legged stool which the Alpine herdsmen carry fastened behind them when they go to milk the cows on the mountain-sides; well, the headdress in question is very like that stool wrong side up, with its one leg in the air, the large round disc being flat on the head, with four curtains of black lace hanging from it,

* La Bresse is the plain between the Mâcon country and the Jura.

two on each side, and a narrow valence of the same material all round it. The pinnacle, too, is decorated at the top and also close to the disc. Odd as it looks, this headdress is a good invention for a country where the summers are very hot and glaring, and it often saves the women the trouble of carrying an umbrella as a parasol, which they very commonly do elsewhere in the great heats. The rest of the costume is quaint and picturesque, and has a pretty coquettish look when it is new, with the short petticoats, neat aprons, and broad bands of velvet on the bodices. Add to this the perfect whiteness of the linen, with its pretty embroidery or plaiting in collar and cap, and you have a traditional dress which may gratify the female anxiety to look nice, whilst, at the same time, it effectually prevents the disastrous vanity of copying the upper classes.*

* It is expensive in itself, however. My fellow-traveller, who is a much better judge of these things than I can pretend to be, tells me that in no single instance did she ever detect a bit of imitation lace on one of these headdresses, whilst the gold chains are at least as costly as those worn by ladies, and the costume is not complete without chains. But, however expensive a traditional costume may be, it is far cheaper in the long run than the changing frivolities of the Paris fashions; and, besides this advantage, it prevents women from thinking incessantly about their dress and studying the gazettes of fashion, such as *Le Printemps* and *La Mode Illustrée.*

CHAPTER II.

THE great wine-district of Burgundy had few attractions for me as a place of residence; indeed I know few regions of equal interest to the passing tourist, which seem so little desirable for permanent habitation. Every traveller who has gone by railway from Dijon to Châlon will remember how the great plain of Burgundy is bounded on the west by a steep and lofty bank of land, precipitous here and there, and almost interminably long, covered with vineyards, and with many rich villages at its base. That steep long bank of stony ground is the famous *Côte d'Or*, where the grapes are grown which fill so many cellars with wine and so many pockets with gold. It is a region of well-to-do people, a region where the perennial flow of grape-juice, always easily transmuted into money, has made all but the imprudent rich. It is a country of good living, where excellent cooks have transmitted their science from generation to generation, improving it and adding to it incessantly. The inhabitants are manly, frank, hospitable, and good-tempered, though rather hasty ; and as for intelligence, it is not easy to find a region in all Europe where men's wits are so keen and lively. But, notwithstanding all these recommendations, the *Côte d'Or* is not a land where I should care to live. You have the *Côte* and the plain, the plain and the *Côte*, two great things, but likely to become very wearisome in time. There is no water, with its pleasant life and changefulness ; no hills are visible but the steep *Côte*, except on a very clear day, when you get a sight of the distant Jura, like a pale mist far away ; there are no trees, or hardly any, so precious is the land for the wealth-producing vines ; and your only refuge from the wearisome monotony of the scenery is to go up one of the dry narrow rocky gorges which, happily for the inhabitants, penetrate at intervals into the elevated land, where, after winding for a little distance like true valleys, they come suddenly to an abrupt termination at the foot of an inaccessible precipice. We stayed with a friend in this region who possessed a very pretty châlet-like house (much more convenient than a real châlet), and therefore we saw the country under a more cheerful aspect than if we had stayed in one of the rough inns ; but my first impression remained unaltered, in spite of all that hospitality could do to make things seem agreeable. A vine-land is very

splendid in autumn, for the autumnal colour is beyond
all description glorious ; but in summer the dull green
is sadly wanting in variety, and in the dreary blaze of
unchanging sunshine the low vines offer no shade.
Besides, one has no sense of liberty when looking on
a French vine country, for it is not a pleasant land to
walk over, in the narrow paths between the sticks. In
short, the vines may be an agreeable sight for those
whom they make rich (most disagreeable, however, even
to these in the bad years, which occur so frequently); but a
landscape-painter, who likes to surround himself with an
abundance of natural beauty, does better to avoid them.

During our stay in the wine-district, we were taken
to see different places in the neighbourhood, and I remember one of them which was so thoroughly French
in character, so unlike anything you will ever meet with
in England, that a short description of it may possibly
be read with interest. The place was a château belonging to some old noble family, a wild and lonely
mansion far above the level where the vines grow, surrounded by broad dreary fields, which, in their turn,
were entirely hemmed in by the densest forest. From
the windows of that house nothing was to be seen but
this opening of rough pasture, with the ring of close
dark forest all round it ; no other human dwelling was
visible, nor any landscape save one or two slight undulations of the forest-land. The house itself was
surely the roughest place ever inhabited by a gentleman.
There was not the faintest pretension to finish in any
part of it. Even in the interior the floors and stairs
were composed of rough-hewn blocks of stone, which

looked as if they just came fresh from the quarry. A certain wild picturesqueness about the place gave me a sort of grim satisfaction for an hour or two. It was full of character, with its big stables, and dog-kennels, and everything necessary for a French hunting estab- lishment. One could easily imagine it filled with men —jolly strong fellows, spending their days in the chase and their evenings over the wine-flagons on the rude oak table in the dining-room ; but no stretch of fancy could imagine ladies there as inhabitants—the place was too rough for them. The floors were made, as it seemed, for big strong boots, and not for pretty thin dancing- shoes. It is not possible to imagine any dwelling more utterly opposed to the sentiment of the modern draw- ing-room. It was not a Philistine residence, not *bourgeois* in the least—from that vice it was safe indeed, it was thoroughly and grandly *barbarian*—a place where you might utterly ignore and forget the modern world, with all its refinements and aspirations, and live only to hunt boldly, eat with a hunter's appetite, and drink like a rich Burgundian. As for that dreary, sad sentiment which appeared to reign about the lonely place, no doubt some feeling of that kind would invade the mind of any delicate lady or thoughtful gentleman who might live in such a situation alone for months together, but the merry huntsmen would bring with them another temper to the place. To them the dreary forest would be nothing but so much excellent cover for the deer and the wild boar—to them the cheerless- looking rude old halls of the castle would be gay in the evenings with their own gaiety. I can even fancy just so much of art about the place as this—I can fancy some painter of sylvan sports setting up his easel for a month or two in one of the big uninhabited rooms, and painting there some picture of a stag-hunt or a boar-hunt that he had just recently seen and shared in. Or, on the other hand, I can well imagine some novelist dwelling there through the wild months of winter, when the wolves come out of the forest, and composing some fearfully tragic story, enough to make every reader shudder, and cause his own blood to run cold as he sat imagining and writing it. Indeed, so strongly impressed was I with the appropriateness of the château as a scene of tragedy, that I communicated the idea to the friend who had taken us there, and he answered—not in the least to my surprise—"There is no need to imagine any unreal horrors for the place, since what really occurred here is enough."

"Has there been a murder here, then, really?"

"You see that small pool of water on the terrace just before the *perron* at the front door. Well, the house was inhabited by two brothers, who suspected their sister and the gardener of a mutual attachment, so to put an end to it they simply went and drowned him in that little ornamental pool, holding him down in the shallow water till life was quite extinct."

So this is what the barbarian sentiment of the place had led to, and quite in recent times! These two young noblemen had been leading the true barbarian life there, slaying every day in the wild forest, and quite beyond all civilizing influences; so the mere apprehension of a possible *mésalliance* made them capable of anything to remove the danger. They might have dismissed the gardener, but such a course did not seem so effectual as that little plan of holding him down in the shallow water until he breathed no longer. Passion and self-will develop themselves very freely in the noble barbarian life. The reader may remember the case of a young nobleman in Brittany who murdered his own brother from jealousy about a servant-girl. All this is in the true middle-age spirit, which lingers still in the old families—that spirit which looks upon inferiors as its natural prey, and removes whatever comes between a desire and its accomplishment.

When we got down again into the comfortable money-making wine district, the change from that half-savage château amongst the woods was like passing from the fifteenth to the nineteenth century in a single afternoon. How rich, and safe, and prosperous everything looked there! The snug mansions of the wine merchants and growers (most of the growers are merchants also), the great clusters of buildings belonging to the rich peasants, all slept in the sunshine surrounded by their vines and gardens. Along the broad good road which passes from hamlet to hamlet, from village to village, you would meet at that time hardly anything but great long carts with enormous wheels, and barrels piled to a giddy height above, held tight by cords stretched with a windlass, or else the safer-looking four-wheeled waggon, laden with the same inevitable barrels. That was in the piping times of peace. In the winter of 1870 the same region was the scene of the most furious fighting in Burgundy. We were staying at a house very near the famous Clos Vougeot, and I remember going on foot one day to the little town of Nuits, having a pleasant walk, enlivened by an occasional chat with some peasant on the way, and with the shopkeepers in the place, where everything seemed so sleepy and quiet that the wonder was how the shops ever found any customers. I like an intensely dull little town, where the people never seem to be in a hurry, but can lounge and gossip in the evening about their doors, or stay inside when the sun is hot at noon. Such a place was Nuits, at that time ; but when the war-tide rolled over the country it so happened that this cosy little place was the scene of one of the bloodiest battles fought during the whole campaign. In its one street there occurred a hand-to-hand struggle with bayonet, sword, and revolver, which quite literally covered it with dead or wounded men. And then the hostile forces took to fighting in the houses—men stabbing each other in staircases, and fighting duels in narrow passages and amongst the furniture of bed-rooms. It is difficult to imagine anything in warfare more terrible than a conflict in houses. It is like a massacre, and much of it is sure to be little better than downright murder. Either in the town itself or along the line of railway, near the station, the Prussians alone lost a number of men equal to twice the population of the place. Amidst all these horrors occurred one very ludicrous incident. A cowardly *mobile*, wishing to get out of harm's way, hid himself in a closet, but a frag-ment of shell burst through the door and wounded him rather severely.

The monotony of the district, and the absence of water, had decided me against it from the first, so we took the train for a much more beautiful region—the valley of the Doubs above Besançon. We made that city our head-quarters. My wife had rather a tenderness for the place, from pleasant recollections of the time when her father had been prefect there, and of the kind sympathy of the inhabitants when he resigned the prefecture for reasons of political honour, and quitted them. I suspect, too, that there may have been lingering sentiments of regret for certain charming and very tasteful rooms at the *palais*, which is one of the handsomest in France. We had leisure to walk about the town, which I had not before seen, and although ladies are not generally very accurate topographers, my guide showed me everything of interest. Our plan was not to take anything within the walls of Besançon, yet, by way of precaution, we looked at every possibly suitable tenement that was to be let. This was a repetition of our experience at Mâcon, with the difference that at Besançon the *appartements* were better-finished and more showy than at Mâcon, but less roomy. I remember one of them especially, with a particularly well-finished *salon*, just like a large *bon-bonnière*, the good taste of which was very pleasing to me ; but then there was nothing else except closets. In an English country town you would have had a con-venient house with good bedrooms for the same rent. The patience with which the French submit to unen-durable inconveniences about their dwellings is another thing which still surprises me. though I ought to be

used to it by this time. We were recommended at
Besançon to go and see a very eligible apartment with
a good view of the hills, and when we got there we
made the discovery that the only way of getting in and
out would be through a public *café.* Who would put
up with such an intolerable inconvenience as that?
Certainly no Englishman would unless he were absolutely forced to it, but in France it will not prevent the
owner of the building from finding some respectable
tenant.

To any traveller who is not house-hunting, Besançon
must appear a very well-built city. The houses look
very roomy and substantial from the outside, and are
strongly constructed of good stone. There are plenty
of picturesque old houses by the river-side, which an
artist would be glad to paint, with all their ins and outs
of gables and odd corners faithfully reflected in the
Doubs ; but if he were wise he would be sorry to live in
one of them. Picturesque old mediæval buildings are
a great attraction to sketchers, but they are not salu-
brious, and the modern town-councils are excusable
when they clear them away. Besançon is situated on
an elevated piece of land that is all but islanded by the
Doubs, which flows almost entirely round it. The town
is grimly guarded by very strong forts on neighbouring
heights of rock, and has altogether the rather prison-
like aspect which makes all fortified towns undesirable
places of residence, unless, like Paris, they are so big
that you can forget all about the fortifications.

We went up the valley of the Doubs as far as Belfort. It is not a long journey, yet quite long enough

to carry the traveller from one set of national habits to another. Near Belfort we passed a building which, though it was called a *château*, was in reality a German *schloss*, and when we got to our hotel, we were charmed with a degree of cleanliness very different from the state of things which had put us so completely out of humour with the Rhone. The floors of the rooms were prettily arranged in squares of white wood, bordered with dark, and as clean as possible, so that the two kinds of wood (white pine and walnut) showed the contrast of their natural colours to perfection ; in the south they would have been confounded together under one uniform crust of dirt. The people, too, were cleanly and agreeable, so that, during our short stay at Belfort, we could see things with unprejudiced eyes. The great fortress there is apparently one of the strongest in France (in modern fortification the strength is not always apparent to a civilian) ; and I distinctly remember how we said to each other what a terrible struggle the siege of such a place would be—little thinking that so short a time would elapse before the bomb-shells would be shattering themselves against those mighty ramparts, and the heroic defence of Belfort would be one of the very few bright pages in a gloomy and disastrous chapter of French history. Little, too, did we think that all the stretch of country visible to the eastward would so soon become Prussian territory, and Belfort would only be preserved to France by the patriotic obstinacy of one old man passionately pleading before an irresistible conqueror, for ten hours at a time. He had his reward later; there in Belfort itself, when the people gave him such a reception as any sovereign might envy, but only the most beloved of sovereigns could command.

Here, however, it was plain that we had either gone too far to the eastward, or not far enough ; that we had left behind us the beautiful valley of the Doubs, and had not yet gone far enough eastwards for the interesting scenery of the Upper Rhine, especially that portion of it which divides Baden from Switzerland, the country of Rheinfelden, Lauffenburg, &c., beloved of Turner. All that lay due east of us now, and not at any great distance, but it was out of France, and my wish was to keep within the frontier. We therefore determined to explore the valley of the Doubs more in detail, and see if some suitable house could be found there. All that valley is beautiful down to Besançon. The lines of the hills are especially graceful, and well worth studying. At that time my great interest in landscape was in the beauty of mountains, so that a region of this kind was rich in the material that I most desired to study. The river, too, charmed me by its purity, and a sort of tranquil grace appreciable even from the railway, but which would no doubt have been infinitely more delightful from a boat on the river itself, and this I very well knew. The most beautifully situated place in the whole valley appeared to be Beaume-les-Dames, so we stayed there to explore. Here we established ourselves at an inn kept by an elderly lady, who immediately took the most maternal interest in both of us, treating us with a degree of kindness which made us inclined to believe that she must be an unknown aunt of ours,

D

or grandmother, if such a thing were possible. Beaume-les-Dames is celebrated for a particular kind of goody made from quinces, a sort of sticky paste served at dessert, and which certainly does (when it is properly made) retain all the perfume of the fruit This *pâte de coings* was in perfection at our inn, and my wife praised it, to the delight of our affectionate land· lady, who must needs teach her to make it. Our search for a dwelling interested the old lady exceedingly, and she did all in her power to help us. Am I heart-less enough to laugh at her for her kindness ? Certainly not. We could not help being a little amused by it, because it was unexpected and incongruous, and so entirely undeserved ; but we were not ungrateful. What a difference between that good-natured interest in our proceedings, that eagerness to teach us to make quince paste, and the icy indifference of the "adminis-trateur" of a huge hotel, who does not care whence you come or whither you go, provided only that you have money in your purse !

There was one point on which the superior practical sense of my fellow-traveller more than once preserved me from error. I have a weakness for antiquity and the picturesque in houses, and should like very much to nestle in a corner of some dilapidated old mansion or castle, and gradually get the rest of it into a state of simple repair (not fanciful "restoration" of that which had never been) ; arranging perhaps two rooms every year, till the whole building became habitable once again. This would be my fancy, but I have always been happily prevented from carrying it into execution

by the practical spirit of my fellow-traveller, who cannot endure untidiness in any shape, and could never
bear to feel responsible for the half-ruinous state of an
old building. Her ideal of a house is that it should
be just big enough for convenience, yet not too big to
be easily kept in order; that it should be perfectly
"distributed" so that all the rooms be just where they
are wanted, and that there should be every imaginable
facility for carrying on smoothly and regularly that
mysterious and very comprehensive business which is
called "house-keeping." She became rather seriously
alarmed, however, at Beaume-les-Dames, because I manifested that dangerous passion for a romantic habitation
which so recklessly sets aside every consideration of
utility. There was one old house with a crumbling
tower in the courtyard, excellent for a sketch, and we
ascended to the upper apartments by a genuine Gothic
corkscrew stair, like the stair in a church steeple. One
or two of the rooms were wainscoted with old oak that
had been painted grey, but then how easy it would be
to remove the paint and repair the carving wherever
necessary! I felt a certain attraction to this ancient
dwelling, which looked as if it were haunted by the
ghosts of former generations. The owner of it lived
up on the hills, so we took a carriage and drove to his
habitation. During our journey the driver volunteered
an account of the man we were going to see, and a contemptuous account it was, but the effect of it was very
different from anything that the narrator intended, or
was capable of imagining. The more contemptuous
he became, the more sympathy and respect did I feel

for the owner of the old house. His history in brief
was this: Instead of adding franc to franc, and field
to field, as the small French proprietor generally does,
by denying himself all liberal life and culture, this man
had narrowed his fortune in the pursuit of knowledge.
He had travelled much, bought books, indulged in the
habits and tastes of a cultivated man, and so neglected
his pecuniary interests, until he had finally reduced
himself to a mere pittance. I am far from wishing to
imply that men ought to ruin themselves in the pursuit
of knowledge, or even that they can do so blamelessly,
and I much more warmly approve the conduct of those
who manage to conciliate culture with frugality, for
they add to their intellectual strength the moral
strength of self-denial ; but the passion for knowledge
is so rare in the provincial mind—it is so rare to find a
provincial proprietor who will give five francs to know
anything, that when we do meet with such a passion,
even in excess, we cannot but feel for it a certain grave
respect, a deep and earnest sympathy.

I shall never forget the meeting with that lonely
man. It would be difficult to imagine loneliness more
complete. On a dreary table-land, high up in the Jura,
in a little hamlet inhabited by illiterate peasants, in a
thatched cottage with the usual puddle at the door, he
lived with the remnant of his books. The old ruinous
house at Beaume-les-Dames was the only source of
income left to him, and it was not easy to let. I was
welcomed with an eager politeness, as a possible tenant.
The reader will suspect me of inventing for artistic
effect when I describe the inhabitant of the cottage,

but the description is simply faithful. I found him studying a noble old folio volume, with other such goodly
companions lying on the plain deal table before him.
The student himself looked grey and worn, the surroundings were those of an anchorite, and without the
books I know not what must have become of him.
Day after day, night after night, from year's end to
year's end, he lived with these, and had not a soul to
speak to who could understand him. I knew from the
driver's contemptuous tone what the people thought
of the strange solitary being who lived amongst them.
A fool who had spent his money, a useless wreck of a
man who was always idling over books—this was the
popular decision. Had he been born irremediably
vulgar, with a natural keenness after money, hardening
into avarice in early manhood, the neighbours would
have respected him.

He returned with us in the carriage, that we might
examine the old house together. My fellow-
traveller, as the reader knows already, was not
enthusiastic about the house, but regarded it rather
with a cool disposition to criticize, from the utilitarian
point of view. The owner, on the other hand, had
much to say in its favour. His eloquence seemed to
remove every difficulty. All inconveniences vanished
before his description of changes which were not only
possible but delightfully easy. When the workmen had
been in the place three weeks we should not know it
again. There was one rather large wainscoted room
which I fixed upon as the future studio. It had a fire-
place which looked very capable of smoking. We

inquired if it smoked. "Yes, it does," was the frank
reply. "I admire your candour," I said; "you are the
very first house-owner I ever met with who would admit
that a chimney smoked." "I confess the truth. The
chimney *does* smoke, but only one day in the year—the
twenty-ninth of March!" We laughed very heartily at
the idea of the chimney which kept an anniversary, but
why it had fixed upon this particular date, whether from
some political motive, or some private grief, we were at
a loss to imagine. I suggested that if the chimney had
chosen the twenty-ninth of February as its smoking-
day it would have been still more judicious.

Utilitarianism carried the day against romance, and
we sought elsewhere. Then we found a perfect paradise
of utilitarianism—a mansion built quite recently, with
all modern conveniences. Every floor in it was of the
neatest oak parquetry, waxed and polished; every
chimney-piece looked as if it had come from Paris; not
an inch of the whole house was out of repair. There
was plenty of room in it, too, and it was "distributed"
on scientific principles—the passage and staircase just
in the middle, and rooms most neatly arranged on
each side, with two stories above the ground-floor, and
commodious attics. There was a very tidy garden too,
excessively *bourgeois*, and easy to keep in order. "Is
not this perfection?" I asked, rather sarcastically. "It
is perfection from a housekeeper's point of view." We
should certainly have taken this convenient residence if
the rent had been rather more moderate, but the owner
had spent a great deal upon it and wanted interest for
his money. There is a grim satisfaction in knowing

that a place you only half like is just beyond your
means, because that ends your doubts and settles the
question.

So we went back to Besançon, having gained nothing
by our expedition except the art of making quince
paste. At Besançon we heard of a country-house by the
Doubs, a few miles above the town, and so drove to see
it. The back of this house was near the road, just as
Abbotsford is near the road on which you drive from
Melrose ; but between the house and the river was a
large well-arranged lawn, very English in appearance,
with plenty of finely-grown trees for shade, and the
lawn ended on the margin of the beautiful river itself,
which flowed quietly by in all clearness and purity—the
very ideal of a river to swim in and boat upon. Beyond
the river were the picturesque heights on the other side
of the valley, and behind the house was a delightful
rocky ravine with a mountain rivulet in it, coming down
from the lofty pine forest. All this suited me exactly,
for it was exactly adapted to the work and play of my
life. I could write and paint in such a house as that all
day long without being disturbed by noise ; for even
the road behind it was but a country road, little frequented, and the smooth river swept by silently. In
summer I could work happily in a shady bower near
the water, or find some nook in the wild ravine behind.
But the garden seemed attractive, even to me who dislike gardens, for it was merely a sort of very smooth
meadow with beds of flowers and clumps of trees
scattered about it. For physical health and recreation
there were the river, one of the loveliest in Europe, and

the noble hills with their recesses of inexhaustible beauty. As for convenience, we had Besançon within easy reach—Besançon with its fine public library and museum, its good shops, and its society. The rent of the house was moderate, the size of it sufficient, so fancy and utilitarianism were of one mind about it, and it was quite decided that this should be our future home. The owner of the property was a noble lady, but she confided her interests to a gentleman in Besançon, whom I saw. There appeared to be no difficulty whatever, we could have immediate possession, "nevertheless," said the lady's representative, "I think I should like to consult the owner herself, and get her answer before giving up the keys; it is just possible that she may have changed her mind." On being consulted, the lady began to hesitate, thinking that possibly at some vaguely future time it might be pleasant to her to have the place for little summer excursions. During the next two days her hesitation increased, and the end of it was that she decided not to let.

Here was a vexatious ending to our quest! the annoyance was that the house so exactly suited us, and (now that we could not have it) seemed more beautiful and more desirable than ever. We had fixed our home there, mentally, already. Imagination had outstripped the slow advance of time, and had already taken possession, with her furniture in the rooms and the keys in her pocket. And now, poor disappointed Imagination had to be turned out. The consequence was that we took a sudden disgust to the whole neighbourhood, and quitted it. Ever since then we have reverted with a regretful feeling to that house by the beautiful river ; but consolation came at last, in the war-time. That lovely valley was not a pleasant residence for anybody in the winter of 1870. Between the fortresses of Belfort and Besançon—one of them in the heat and fury of conflict, the other with guns shotted and gates closed, expecting the enemy daily—a country house was very like a little yacht that finds itself by ill-luck in the midst of a naval engagement—with the difference that the yacht can move, and the house is unfortunately a fixture.

These three tours on the Rhone, the Saône, and the Doubs (I omit the wine district, as that did not suit us from the first) had left a general impression of dis-couragement. During all our wanderings we had only found two habitations that suited us, and only one that suited us in all respects. It is so difficult to combine several different conditions, especially when one of them is moderation in expenditure ! The critical reader may think that we were difficult to please ; but it was not much a question of pleasure, we wished to combine the convenience of practical life with convenience for the studies of a landscape-painter ; and nobody who has not tried it knows the difficulty of such a combination. Most places which seem pretty at first sight are sure to be exhausted in one summer. It is true that a land-scape-painter *may* live anywhere ; he may live even in the heart of London or Paris, and work always from sketches taken during his excursions—many do so, and paint very good pictures ; yet, even when you do not care to paint directly from nature, it is an immense con-

venience to have good and abundant natural material
within your reach for immediate reference. It is like
the convenience of living near the British Museum for
a student of history. He does not wish to copy the
books word for word, but he likes to be able to refer to
them whenever his work requires. And here it may
not be out of place to say something about the value
and utility of a neighbourhood as a book of reference
for a landscape-painter. When once he has learned the
art of using nature, he is no longer bound down to the
unintelligent copyism of the scene before him, but
acquires the power of extracting the knowledge which
he needs from material which does not show it obviously
on the surface. I can make this clearer by an example.
Suppose the case of a painter of Venetian subjects,
obliged by circumstances to live, let us say, in Lancashire. There is no town in Lancashire with the peculiar
beauty of Venice, and it may be thought that our
painter, amongst the unlovely seats of the cotton manu-
facture, would find no material for study which could
possibly strengthen him in his art. Yet a clever artist,
so situated, would be able to get very much help and
teaching out of the Leeds and Liverpool canal, with the
factories on its banks, and the barges on its muddy
waters. The light strikes a factory or a barge exactly
as it strikes a gothic palace or a gondola, the reflections
of bridge and boat in the canals of Lancashire are
exactly the same as those in the equally impure canals
of Venice, and there is not a town in Lancashire so
ugly that a painter might not acquire much knowledge
of Venice there, provided only that a canal passed

through the middle of it. It would be easy to give many other illustrative examples, but this one is enough to show how material, apparently most different from that which an artist is actually painting, may be full of instruction for him if he has the opportunity of constantly referring to it. And this is why I like to be so situated, that I may have easy access to several different things from which knowledge is to be gained. A river like the Doubs is not, for me, one river only, for it contains many elements which are common to all rivers; one good group of poplars can give poplar knowledge generally; one fine old French city can teach you how to paint other cities of a like character, and when there are variations, you note and remember them easily if one good type is thoroughly well known to you. But the difference between having access to your teachers, and being separated from them by distances involving long railway journeys, is the difference between making your reference and not making it.

CHAPTER III.

IT being apparently impossible to find a suitable house, the only solution of the difficulty seemed to be the camp. "Let us set up the old painter's camp," I said, "in some pleasant valley, and hire a field for it by the side of some crystal rivulet, and dwell there in perfect peace, far from the haunts of men and the vanities of the world!"

But my fellow-traveller cannot be brought to see the merits of tents, and does not feel their poetry. She says they are hot in the sunshine, and chilly when evening comes; that the canvas walls are always flapping in the wind, and so produce headaches; that the ground is damp, even through the floor-cloths; that creeping things get in; that vipers *might* get in; and that the meanest cottage with four stout walls and a thatched roof is better than the pavilion of an Indian prince.

This view of the subject entirely leaves out of the question the peculiar delightfulness of camp life, the ineffable charm of its near association with nature, and the healthiness of being so much in the open air; still I admit and confess that it is the sound and practical view, especially for a reading and writing creature that must needs have a waggon-load of books.

Another plan remained to us, without relying upon the camp. We were incompetent to find a house for ourselves, so why not entrust the task to another? A friend of ours in Burgundy said, "Let me try and find a house for you;" then he asked what we wanted, and made a note of it. The conditions seemed rather numerous, but they did not daunt him. "You want a river, of course, being an aquatic Englishman; and you want a picturesque neighbourhood, being an artist; then you must be not too far from a town, for supplies—some picturesque old town if possible—and you want a habitable house, with a sufficient number of rooms, and a garden, and so on." All these things being duly noted, our friend actually got into the train, travelled a long distance, and came back to us after an absence of some days. "I have what you want," he said, and then gave us a description of his discovery.

We went to see the place, and after a long journey by rail and diligence, arrived at an ancient city, built on a hill which rises between a much steeper hill and a flat plain. All round the plain is a circus of hills, the highest of which are about 2,500 feet above the level of the sea, and 1,500 feet above the level of the enclosed basin. The basin itself is about

fifteen miles in diameter, and appears very nearly circu-
lar.   There are some pretty estates in the plain of about
two hundred acres each, and every one of these estates
has a house upon it, in some cases with the style of a
small château adorned with an old tower (one of them
has two such towers, with the inevitable pepper-box
roofs), but others, more modest, are still habitable
enough.   It happened that the most beautiful of these
estates belonged to a man who lived at a distance, and,
consequently, that the house upon it was uninhabited.
A charming trout-stream ran through the property, and
another smaller stream, derived from it, bounded the
garden, which was large and shady, with broad walks,
terraces, and bowers, and a wood of its own with
winding paths, and rustic seats in nooks so retired that
nothing was to be seen from them but wood and
meadow, and nothing heard but the ripple of the swiftly-
running clear rivulet.   The house was like a shooting
or fishing lodge on a small scale, but the space in it had
been economized to the utmost, and the rooms were
cleverly arranged.   There was stabling for eight horses
(much more than we needed), and the only inconvenience
was that the farm buildings were too near.   The farm
was let already to a respectable old peasant, so that we
had no trouble with land, an encumbrance which I have
neither time nor inclination to undertake.   Farming is
a noble and necessary work, but it is not for students
and artists.   Only the farmer can farm profitably, and
in France he manages it by incessant toil and a wonderful sobriety, frugality, self-denial.

It was sweet to me to be once again in a land of

hills and trout-streams, and my fellow-traveller approved of the little house ; so we took it, on a short lease, which has been renewed since more than once. Afterwards we migrated to another house on the same estate, larger but more prosaic, and farther from the . stream.

Our geographical position was in many respects favourable enough, though London friends wondered that we could live in such an out-of-the-way place. In a single night we could reach either Paris, or Lyons, or Geneva. It was possible, also, to dine quietly in the evening at our own house, and to dine the next evening in London. Since then the Mont Cenis tunnel has been opened, and brought us very near to Turin, from which Milan and Venice are easily accessible. With all these cities and their art-collections so near (if you reckon distance by time), we were not precisely in the position of emigrants to the antipodes. The finest natural scenery was also very near to us. In a single night we could arrive either amongst the mountains of Switzerland or Savoy, of the Jura, or of Auvergne. For water, a single night would take us either to the lake of Geneva, the lake of Neuchatel, or the smaller lakes of Annecy and the Bourget ; and in the same space of time, or less, we could be on the banks of the Saône or the Doubs, the Rhine, the Rhone, or the Loire. I think that this short list of accessible places is enough to prove that our geographical situation was not injudiciously chosen. Certainly there is no spot out of Europe from which so much that is interesting in art and nature can be reached in a single night ; and even in Europe itself, I think that there is hardly a place so truly central, if both art and nature are to be taken into consideration. There is not an American or colonial reader of this book who will not envy such easy access to what is best in the old world : and even in Europe itself there are many places (Berlin, for example) which, however busy and populous they may be, are much more remote from what is most beautiful and most sublime.

Let us not forget, however, in choosing a house, that the importance of what is accessible increases enormously with its nearness, and that the surroundings which chiefly influence the daily life and thought lie within a radius of twenty or thirty miles. I soon discovered that the neighbourhood of our new residence had one very valuable characteristic in great perfection, namely, variety. There was nothing in it very striking at first sight, but we had a little of everything. An old inhabitant, who knew the country intimately, and loved it, said to me, " *Ce qui caractérise notre pays, c'est que nous avons un peu de tout.*" His observation has recurred to me a thousand times since then. He had precisely hit upon the secret charm of the region which makes it so good for permanent residence, and at the same time so insignificant to the passing tourist, fresh from the valley of Chamouni, or from the boulevards of Paris. When I think over the great variety of things which may be reached in a pony carriage in the course of a morning, I doubt whether any other place I know can offer so many different specimens of what is interesting. Hardly anything is transcendently magnificent or striking, but everything is just big enough and important enough to occupy the mind agreeably. To begin with architecture and antiquities, we can still find some fair specimens of Roman work, a temple and two Roman gateways, erect and strong after their eighteen centuries. These are visible to everybody, and so is the Roman wall, still continuous and very strong, to the west of the city, with all its towers. But antiquaries, who look to the ground itself, see much more than this. In certain streets the huge stones of the Roman pavement are still in their places, and the modern peasant drives his oxen over them, little thinking how long they have been there or what mighty· conquerors laid them. The foundations of the theatre and amphitheatre are still well above ground. Discoveries of Roman work are not infrequent. One day not long since a man deepened his cellar, and found a great mosaic below which extended under the adjoining house. The city has, in fact, been a mine of Roman antiquities for generations, which, instead of being kept to enrich its own museum, have been carried off to Paris, or else sold to the dealers in such things. I confess, however, that remains which deeply interest the antiquary, are often of little importance to anybody else. It is enough for most of us to know that a Roman city has been in such a locality. A visible building interests us, but, unless we have the true antiquarian instinct, the tracing out of foundations, the finding of fragments in pottery or bronze, do not affect us much, though we are glad that some industrious and observant person should be there to take notes for any

F.

light which may be cast by them on historical studies.
It is something, however, to have great Roman walls and
gateways, for it is impossible to see them without being
brought nearer to Cæsar's time, and made to feel that it
was a reality. As this neighbourhood contains *un peu
de tout*, we can follow architecture from the genuine
Roman work of t .e gateways down through Romanesque and Gothic to the Renaissance, and so to modern
work, either in the ancient city itself or in the immediate neighbourhood. You can, in fact, teach a boy
all the elements of architecture from real examples
without going more than a few miles. The cathedral
is a mixture of Romanesque and Gothic, and has, I
believe, the most magnificent Romanesque portals in
all France, besides one of the most beautiful Gothic
spires. As on the western side of the city the walls
and towers are all pure Roman work, so on the
southern side they are all Gothic, and as picturesque
here as the middle-age fortifications of the old Swiss
cities, such as Fribourg or Lucerne. Amongst the
remnants of the middle ages there are still some
substantial hotels, and a good many smaller houses.
In Renaissance work there are a church, a fountain,
and one or two fine châteaux in the neighbourhood.
Turning from architecture to literature and painting,
we still find the pervading principle "a little of
everything." The city possesses one masterpiece of the
modern classical school, in a kind of classicism which
leaves me perfectly indifferent, but this picture is a first-
rate specimen of it. Then there are a public gallery of
pictures and a public library, neither of them rich, and

yet an agreeable addition to one's limited private pos-
sessions in literature and art.

I shall have much more to say about the inhabitants
in a future chapter; but for the present this may be
noted, that as there are a few specimens of architecture
and painting, so there are a few specimens of that very
rare bird, the cultivated human being. So far as I
have been able to ascertain, there are at least five or
six of these in the whole *arrondissement*, which has a
rural and urban population of about eighty thousand
souls; the proportion is not large, it must be confessed, but it is very nearly what I had already observed
in the north of England. Unfortunately there is a
peculiar evil in the condition of these eccentrics.
Each of them studies something which the five others
know nothing about, so that, although he is vaguely
respected by them, he cannot talk to then about his
own pursuit, and is practically almost as much isolated
as if he lived in the Arabian desert. Happily, he can
get to Paris in a night, and call upon some fellow-
labourer there, and so relieve his mind. Another cause
of separation between cultivated people, which operates
very strongly here, is difference of social position,
involving often great difference in politics and religion.
We have a bishop, for instance, who is a cultivated
person; but how can you talk reasonably with a man
who is accustomed to be addressed as *Votre Grandeur*,
and to be venerated continually? We have also an
intensely proud nobleman, who is said to be a really
consummate scholar; but no agreeable intercourse is
possible with a man who stares and frowns at you if

he fancies you are not deferential, and who lives in
an inflamed state of chronic antagonism towards the
modern spirit. All these social matters, however, I
leave for fuller consideration at another time. It is
enough for the present to note that there are cultivated individuals in the land, but not any cultivated
society. There is nothing exceptional in this, for in
the present low state of the general mind the great
capitals are the only places where you can fill a
room with people capable of talking well together
about any important subject.

Men are always rather unsatisfactory objects of
contemplation, however interesting, so let us turn to
nature. We have no mountains here, but an abundance of hills, one of which shall be described later
in 'detail. The little valleys are as beautiful and varied
as anything on that small scale can be. Each valley
has its little stream, often running clear and swift in
the greatest heats of summer, through green meadows
with shady trees. All these streams fall into one
river, which is a tributary of the Loire. The general character of these watercourses is the same, they
are full of good pools for bathing, and (except when
the water is very low) are navigable for a canoe;
they are also rich in a particular kind of beauty, and
not spoiled in any way, for even the occasional villages,
or watermills, or old châteaux upon their banks, add
to their interest and charm. There are no lakes in the
country, but there are a great many ponds, which are
often just as good as lakes for purposes of study.
One of these, containing about two hundred acres, is

so happily situated in the midst of striking hill-scenery, that it has quite the character of an English or Welsh tarn; another, of nine hundred acres, is large enough to give many of the effects to be studied on the lochs of Scotland, or at least to remind us of them when we have known them intimately in former well-remembered years. This lake is surrounded by bare and rocky hills, and has no trees near enough to reflect themselves on its surface, but other lakes or ponds are in the richest woodland.

Owing to the considerable height of the region above the sea, the flora is that of England and Scotland. This may not appear a matter of much importance, but it is wonderful how much, for an Englishman living abroad, the presence of the plants of his own country diminishes the feeling of exile. To me the presence of birches, and heather, and Scotch firs, all of which grow within a hundred yards of my house, is infinitely more welcome than would be the stateliest palms or the sweetest bananas. Whatever may be the poetry of warmer countries, and of that tropical vegetation which so delighted Kingsley in the West Indies, I would not part with our poor northern flora for all the wealth and the glory of it. Why, the old English and Scottish poetry would lose half its meaning for a reader severed from the northern plants! Think of the refrain,—

"And the birk and the broom blooms **bonnie**,"

and of this other,—

"As the primrose spreads so sweetly;"

and of all the thousand allusions to the flora of the
north which fill what is most touching and most tender
in our literature! And have we not associations too
which touch us more than these, and lie much nearer
to our hearts? It is not the written poetry which
affects us most, but the unwritten poetry of our own
youth, and mine is all bound up with heather and fern,
and streams flowing under the shade of alders.

There is, however, a peculiar advantage, from the
botanical point of view, in living so far south as this.
We are in the latitude of Bern, a latitude quite southern
enough for vegetation not to be found in the north of
England. Being about a thousand feet above the sea-
level, our flora, just here, is as nearly as possible that of
Surrey, but, on climbing a little higher (which is easy)
we find ourselves in Lancashire or in Scotland. It is
just as easy to descend a few hundred feet, and then we
find ourselves in the flora of the Swiss valleys, amongst
gigantic old chesnuts ; a little lower still and we are in
the vineyards of central France. The variety of climate
within a few miles is so great that we can choose
amongst these different regions for a day's drive ; and in
the spring we can go three weeks backwards or three
weeks forwards at pleasure. I once left our garden in
May, and found that up amongst the hills the country
was still at the beginning of April ; at the same date
the plain of the Saône was very nearly in our June.

People who have always lived in countries very well
provided with roads are seldom fully alive to their
value. I found that out some years since—not in
Lancashire or Yorkshire, of course, for there the roads

are good and abundant, but in the West Highlands where they are few, narrow, and laid out by a military man, who had very imperfect ideas of what is convenient to a civil population. I well remember hiring a carriage for ourselves and some guests to make an excursion in Argyllshire, and being compelled to send the carriage back again because the road was so bad that it turned out to be useless. There are houses on Lochaweside which cannot be reached in a carriage, and in many of the lonelier parts of the Highlands, when there is no water communication, the glens are accessible only to horsemen, pedestrians, and perhaps (if there is a road at all) to a light strong two-wheeled cart going at a slow pace. This part of France was exactly in the same condition within the memory of the elderly inhabitants, but it happened most luckily that just before the railway system was introduced, the Government (that of Louis Philippe) was seized with an enthusiastic passion for road-making, which conferred upon the land one of the very greatest blessings of a civilized country. Had this been deferred a few years longer the railways would have been made first, and then the grand highways would never have been made at all There would have been little narrow roads from town to town, from village to village, but the railways themselves would have suffered from the absence of the great feeders, and the country people would have communicated less easily and frequently with the market towns. The state of the roads forty years ago was such that a load of wood could not be taken from my house to the town in winter with less than three pairs of oxen, which dragged it by main force through the ruts and holes. To-day, one pair of oxen will take a load of wood six times the distance easily, and the road is so broad that three waggons can travel abreast. There still remain, in the upper regions of the hills, perfect specimens of what was understood by road-making in the middle ages. These are still used by the peasants with their carts drawn by oxen—vehicles so strong, and animals so patient, that they can be taken anywhere. In order to understand what the difficulties of communication must have been in former times, one has only to travel a few miles on one of those ancient roads. I know one of them where it is scarcely possible even to walk after sunset without a lantern. Ribs of rock cross it frequently, and after passing each of them the cart-wheels drop suddenly from six inches to a foot. Massive blocks of granite lie in the way, undisturbed, and the carter must steer his oxen amongst them as he can. There are holes full of soft mud two feet deep, into which the wheels sink to the nave, till nothing but a great effort can get them out again. If two carts meet, one of them must go into the wood or amongst the broom or heather to let the other pass. Even travelling on horseback can only be done at a slow pace, and with a sure-footed animal ; a rider who wanted to go fast would quit the road and gallop across country, unless the road led through a forest, and then there would be no help for him. Such were the means of communication before the great road system was created. The feudal times knew nothing better, the monarchy of the Renaissance time created a few great paved highways, on which lumbering vehicles jolted along. The road system at present existing consists of three distinct kinds of way—the great highway, which is called *route royale, route impériale,* or *route nationale,* as the government may be royal, imperial, or republican ; the lesser highway, which is called *route départementale ;* and, finally, the country road, which is not called a *route* at all, but only a *chemin, chemin vicinal,* and is to a small neighbourhood what the *route départementale* is to a department. Of these three classes of road the first two are thoroughly well made all over France, and the project is so far completely realized, but the third class, that of the *chemins vicinaux,* is not nearly so complete yet. Towards the end of his reign, Napoleon III. conceived the idea of gratifying the peasantry and associating his own name in their minds with a network of country roads, but he did not remain long enough on the throne to carry the project into execution. The cost of the war against Prussia would have made plenty of country roads, but in the present unintelligent condition of the public mind it is impossible to get up any national enthusiasm for the works of peace. A nation will allow its rulers to drain its purse for the most unnecessary war, but it begrudges a tenth of the expenditure for works of utility. Had Napoleon III. felt his throne secure, he would have done much in the interior of France, for he had a liking for great useful enterprises, and always strongly favoured their development ; but he knew that these could not consolidate his dynasty, and that a successful contest with Prussia would ensure the transmission of his crown

The newspapers laughed at the scheme of *chemins vicinaux*, yet it would be difficult to suggest any more useful work, or any work more worthy of a government which cares for the general welfare. Even from the financial point of view, a government can scarcely find a better investment if you consider the indirect results, the increase in the value of property, and the economy of a nation's time. Such as they are at present, the *chemins vicinaux* are fairly good country lanes, kept in order by the *maire* and common council of each little commune on its own account by means of a tax on the inhabitants, which may be paid either in the form of labour or of money. It may be observed, in passing, that the lane by which the *maire* himself communicates with the high road, is always sure to be in excellent condition. "What a good road you have!" I said to a functionary of this description; on which he ingenuously replied, "*Vous savez; c'est le chemin du maire.*" The objection to these roads is not so much that they are badly kept (for you may drive on most of them at full trot), as that they are not sufficiently numerous and not intelligently planned, being merely the result of hap-hazard engineering and old custom. The consequence is that they often take you a great round, and in hilly places they are sometimes dangerously steep. I remember one of them which was a sort of shelf or ledge on the face of a precipice, and the road actually sloped to the *outside*, so that the sensation in driving over it was always that of considerable peril. A few yards farther, the road ran down an excessively steep hill without any sort of protection, and at the bottom crossed a little bridge at a right angle—a blunder for which any road-maker ought to be severely punished, for it is like planning accidents beforehand. On the other hand, I may observe that, when a *chemin vicinal* is planned by the scientific engineers of the present day, it is admirably well done. I know one such, in a very steep and dangerous gorge, which is so well laid out that carriage horses can trot down it all the way,.and take the turns of the zigzags at the same pace. It seems to me now that the only great public improvement which is needed in rural France is that the scheme of communal roads should be fully carried out. Even in its present half-satis-factory condition the country is as well-provided with .anes as most English counties that I have visited. Nothing can be prettier than these lanes in our neigh-bourhood, for the growth of the hedges is most luxu-riant, so that in spring they are covered with flowers, and in late autumn with berries.

All the fields in this part of the country are divided by hedges as they are in England ; but however beauti-ful a hedge may sometimes be in itself, it is a terrible spoiler of landscape. In a land divided in that way we can never realize the beauty of the earth's surface, with its delicate undulations, or far-receding flats. A hedge eight feet high will conceal miles of perspective. Two or three such hedges hide a flat landscape completely, and ruin all the beauty of its distanges. The peculiar grace of the landscape, in many parts of France, is often visible only because there are no hedges to spoil it.

The transition from roads to the vehicles which run upon them is a natural one, so I may say something about them in this place.   In these regions almost all the heavy work is done by large cream-coloured oxen, only the very poorest peasants using cows of a, smaller breed.   Horses are employed by the farmers for speed only, in light spring-carts, and many of them have very swift strong horses indeed, which they drive at a great pace.   The vehicles drawn by oxen are of two kinds, the *char*, and the *tombcreau*.   Both have been used from time immemorial, and are very strong and simple in construction.   The four-wheeled *char* is long and narrow, with removable sides of open rail-work, inclined to each other like the sides of a capital V when seen from the front or back.   The front wheels only turn a little (like the high wheels of an American phaeton) and soon catch the side of the waggon ; the two pairs of wheels are held together by no body except a single stout tree in the middle.   The *tombereau* is the two-wheeled ox-cart.   All the organic parts of it are very strong and heavy, but the removable sides are light and open. Both *char* and *tombereau* have immensely heavy, square poles (like beams) fastened to the wooden yoke which lies on the necks of the oxen behind their horns, and the yoke is fastened to the horns by long leather straps wound about them many times.   These vehicles are generally made at the farms themselves by a journey-man wheelwright from wood grown on the spot, so that they cost very little.   Not the slightest care is taken of them in any way.   They are never painted, and never even partially housed under a shed, but are left in the farm-yards exposed to the weather all the year round, so the sun splits the wood in summer, and the ice in winter ; but a peasant argued with me that it would not pay to build sheds for them, as they are not worth the cost of preservation. One of the many signs, however, of a coming change in the customs of the peasantry is, that for some years past the more well-to-do peasants have begun to order their *chars* and *tombereaux* of cartwrights in the towns, who turn them out with a much higher finish and give them a coat of paint, so that they look worth preserving. It is interesting to see a long procession of ox-carts going, let us say, from the wine district to the hills of the Morvan, laden with great casks full of the cheaper sorts of Burgundy. The drivers, like true Frenchmen, associate together for the sake of sociability, and have many a pleasant chat, whilst the oxen all follow the first cart steadily, and need no more looking after than the links of the chain that a land surveyor drags behind him in the grass. In the middle of the day the caravan halts for an hour or two where there is open grass by the roadside and the shade of some old oak or chestnut. The drivers of wine carts are never unprovided with gimlets, so whilst the oxen, unyoked, are quietly munching their hay, the men produce their gimlets, pierce the casks, and drink freely enough of the generous ruby fountain that springs therefrom. These wayside halts are often admirable subjects for pictures, especially on moonlight nights in some wild place amongst the hills, under giant chestnuts centuries old, when the men have lighted a fire, and grouped themselves about it in their long *limousin* cloaks, and moonlight and firelight play together with their contrast of cold and warm colour on the creamy white of the oxen and the bronzed complexions of the men.

The *chars* and *tombereaux* are used for all heavy work in the country, and are taken over the worst old Gaulish roads, which have remained just what they were two thousand years ago ; and since what will go on a bad road will always go on a better one, the improvement in the highways has not led to any alteration in these carts. The effects of improvement are to be seen chiefly in the rapid conveyances used with horses, which are built in constantly increasing quantities. Every farmer except the poorest has his high-wheeled spring-cart, and now the richer farmers are beginning to set up handsome four-wheeled phaetons, with coach-builder's finish. The changes in vehicles are, however, closely bound up with social matters which we shall have to study in a future chapter; for the present, it is enough to note that the highways have themselves created much rural circulation, a circulation all the more active that there is no such thing as a toll-bar.

CHAPTER IV.

Country society, our expectations about it—Our metropolitan habits—English and French customs about calling—Unpleasantness of the French system to a new comer—We do not adopt it—Decline of hospitality in rural society—Exceptions to the rule—Causes of the decline—Facility of former hospitality—The state dinner—An open house—Cultivated neighbours—Absence of a cultivated tone in general society—The ladies—Separation of the sexes—The neighbourhood very aristocratic—Comparison with an English neighbourhood—Effect of the *de* in France.

THE reader who is accustomed to think of human society as the most important of all considerations in choosing a place of residence, will probably wonder at me for thinking about it so little, and for attaching more importance to a hill and a trout-stream than to the inhabitants of the land. Here, then, let me explain what were our feelings and expectations on the subject of society, and why we treated it as a question of no importance. We had been long since spoiled for true provincial society by much frequentation of the most intelligent people in London and Paris. My wife was born in Paris, and had lived there in a particularly intelligent set ; amongst people who were either already distinguished in some great pursuit (politics, literature, science, or art), or else belonged to the active-minded class from which distinguished men emerge. I was not born in London, but had lived quite long enough there at intervals from the age of twenty, amongst people devoted to intellectual or artistic pursuits, to have acquired metropolitan ways of thinking about society, and to be pretty nearly of Julian Fane's opinion that London was the only place in the world (I would except Paris, however) where one could talk about anything worth talking about. We had kept up our old London and Paris friendships, and in our experiences of pro-vincial life we had always found that the only society worth having was that of people who really belonged to a metropolis, though they might pass much of their time, or even the greater part of it, in the country.* We were therefore, and are still, in a state of complete indifference about genuine provincial society ; we had not its habits of thought, and although we might use its words, we did not really speak its language. Farther experience has confirmed this view of the subject. It is well for any one who studies something that deserves to be studied, to avoid, if he can, the two kindred vices of self-conceit and contempt for people who study nothing ; but it is utterly impossible for him to shut his eyes to the fact that his pursuits have unfitted him for a quite uncultivated society. Even if he himself is unaware of the truth, the people who really compose that kind of society will soon make him perceive that he is

---

* This of course refers to intercourse for improvement or amusement simply, and not to intercourse where affection is con-cerned. Affection is sufficient in itself and better than anything else, but it is evident that affection is not to be considered when you settle in a district that is new to you, and where you have no

not one of themselves. *They* feel it and know it if he does not. It is scarcely possible for him even to say that the weather is fine without, in some subtle way, making the difference felt; and, if he does not avoid uncultivated society, the result is sure to be the same in the end, for uncultivated society will avoid *him.*

Was it our plan, then, to live in utter solitude? No, not quite that either, but rather to take thankfully whatever good and equal human intercourse might be brought within our reach. We had friends already much nearer than Paris who would come and stay with us; others from Paris and England would do the same; we ourselves were not bound down to the farm like rooted trees; and then there remained the chance, which might be considered a certainty, that amongst the surrounding population there would be a few companionable beings whom we should find out, by that mysterious mutual attraction which sooner or later brings people together when they are able to understand each other.

Whatever is done in England is sure to be the opposite of what (in the same kind) is done in France. In many little customs this is a matter of simple indifference. The French, for example, when they meet another carriage in driving, take the right side of the road; the English take the left. In this instance the only important matter is that there should be a rule; and the two rules are equally good. But in many other things the two opposite rules are *not* equally good. For example, if a stranger settles in a new neighbourhood in England, the custom is that the surrounding families

F

already established there, shall call upon him, if they think that he ought to be admitted into their society. This seems to be a very good custom, because it saves the stranger from all appearance of pushing, and at the same time preserves the established families from the unpleasantness of having to reject advances. In France the custom is exactly the reverse. The new-comer has to make all advances; to go and call at all the houses where he would like to be admitted; to convey to the inhabitants of these houses, as cleverly as he can, what are his claims upon their consideration—that he has aristocratic connections, an estate, a lump of money, or some sort of position or reputation. Is it possible to imagine anything more odious to a sensitive, self-respecting person? The odiousness of it is much increased by the fact, that all claims except visible wealth, and a fixed, well-ascertained title, are merely local, and lose their value when you go into a new neighbourhood. The loss of value is very considerable a hundred miles from the place where those claims are generally known; but the transfer from England to France makes them evaporate altogether, like ether in a badly corked bottle, leaving pure nothingness behind. Let us suppose, for example, the case of an Englishman with the title of baronet and some really considerable literary reputation, a reputation equal to that of our present poet-laureate. In England the two things would be of great social value; transfer them to rural France, and they are worthless. Nobody in this country knows what a baronet is; nobody has heard of Tennyson. Or imagine the position of one of our great Lancashire or Yorkshire squires, representing a family which has held the same estate from the dawn of English history, and has had its share in the events of seven centuries, transferred to some French rural neighbourhood, and paying calls on the small counts and marquises round about! "Who is this man?" they would say; "he has no title; c'est un *roturier*, a creature of ignoble birth; he has not the *de*." How is the caller to explain who and what he is, to sound his own trumpet, be his own herald? There remains, it is true, the alternative of the letter of introduction; but this is not always procurable: and who would like to go about begging for people's acquaintance with a recommendation in his hand? We were both quite of one mind about this matter of calling, and stayed quietly in our new home, without going from house to house to request the honour of knowing the inhabitants. Some time afterwards there came a family from Paris, who had inherited an estate in the neighbourhood; and they, of course, followed the usual French custom. The lady, who dressed with the greatest taste, put on her most irresistible toilette, and set off with her husband to all the noblemen's houses round about. We did not envy her that piece of work; and, when we knew the results, we were less inclined to envy than ever. Some of the personages did not return the visit at all; others came with a cool determination to snub the audacious new-comers in their own house, just sitting down and getting up again in the most distant and icy manner. The lady in question thought she had some claims to consideration. Her father had been a senator, and had bequeathed a good estate, now divided amongst eight children, but her husband had been a wine merchant in Burgundy, and *his* father an ironmonger, so the stain of trade was indelible and could not be got over. They stayed a year or two; but we predicted they would go back to Paris, and so they did, leaving behind them a charming new house with large and beautiful gardens, all in the best possible order, and the announcement "To be Let" on the prettily gilded gates.

For our part, as we never made any advances, we never had to submit to any mortifications. Our neighbours even began, of their own accord, to pay us little attentions, which made it necessary and right for us to call upon them in acknowledgment. One old squire somehow heard that my wife was not quite satisfied with the quantity of fruit she had for preserving the first year; so he sent a most polite note, to beg that she would use his garden (a richly productive one) as her own. Three rather large landowners round about us let me know that, if I wished to shoot, I was welcome to do so on their property. Finally, people began to call upon us in the English fashion, before we had called upon them. We had our own notions of self-respect, but we were not wild animals; and so it came to pass that, after a time, we had as many acquaintances as we had time or inclination to cultivate.

It will not be out of place to give here a slight general sketch of some peculiarities in this rural society which appear to be worth mentioning. We were struck at the beginning by the decline of easy hospitality in comparison with what we knew to have been the customs of the preceding generation. People did not seem to ask each other to dinner much. In England the dinner invitation comes as a matter of course when you have reached a certain degree of intimacy, but now in this part of France it seems as if people could get beyond that degree of intimacy without ever sitting together at the same table. Neighbours whom we came to know quite well, and who would put themselves to much trouble to oblige us, never invited us to any kind of feed, and declined when we invited them. Nor did they appear to receive each other more except when the guests were near relations. There appeared to be a good deal of hospitality amongst relations, but the only person outside of the family who profited by it in these cases was the *curé*. Some time later we became acquainted with four or five families who in this respect were exceptions to the general rule, and very brilliant exceptions too, so it is only just to mention them. For example, there is one country house where, if I present myself towards evening, they are quite disappointed if I do not dine and stay all night, and there is another where, at whatever hour of the day I may happen to arrive, I am expected to stay either to déjeûner or dinner. The true explanation of these peculiarities has been given me more than once by the inhabitants themselves. In former times everybody was hospitable, because it was not the custom in those days to go much beyond the ordinary habits of the house when guests were to be received—so little indeed, that no perceptible inconvenience was created. For example, instead of the oil-cloth which is common on the dinner-tables of the small squires and *bourgeoisie*, the guests would be honoured by the exhibition of a clean white table-cloth, a bottle or two of good wine would be brought out of the cellar in addition to the *vin ordinaire* of every-day life, perhaps even a bottle of champagne, and the ordinary dinner would be enriched by the addition of a single *plat* with, perhaps, some sugary thing at dessert besides the usual fruits. The housekeeping reader will see at a glance that, although these things with a few flowers and half a dozen candles are quite enough to give a festal appearance, they cost very little money, and hardly any additional trouble. A lady would be told that there were to be guests half an hour before dinner was served, and all these things would be immediately added to the every-day meal. She had no anxiety about results, she expected the dinner to be, not criticized, but enjoyed, and, as the guests brought the same happy temper to the little feast, it always passed off merrily. Now mark the lamentable change! The absurd luxury of the Second Empire, a luxury as essentially vulgar as absurd, introduced into the remotest corners of rural France that sure killer of true enjoyment, the state dinner. Instead of making the guests' dinner merely the habitual meal of the household, with a little addition of poetry in cookery, wine, flowers, and candles, the new system was to upset all ordinary habits, in order to imitate for a single night the ruinous extravagances of Parisian stock-brokers. Men of moderate fortune then began to hesitate about giving dinners, and ladies who had felt so perfectly comfortable and at home under the old rational system now began to feel all those mental torments which were so humorously portrayed by Hood in "A Table of Errata," that pathetic and sympathetic outpouring of the feelings of a hostess which ends with the stanzas :—

> "How *shall* I get through it ?
> I never can do it ;
> I'm quite looking to it
> To sink by-and-by.
>
> "Oh ! would I were dead now,
> Or up in my bed now,
> To cover my head now,
> And have a good cry ! "

People who lived themselves in the richest country for good eating and drinking in all Europe, the vine-lands of Burgundy, began to think that they were not up to the right level of extravagance unless they had half their feasts sent down from Paris by the railway. The dinner, instead of being a merry repast, became a complicated solemn ceremony, in which mysterious rites had to be observed, and a long series of dishes exhibited and reviewed. With the state dinner came the elaboration of the toilette, as evils never come alone, and good honest wives of small squires persuaded themselves that it was in the interests of civilization that they should look like *gravures de modes.* Now there may be regions of society in which the state dinner is in its right place. An English duke, it may be supposed, can hardly receive ambassadors and princes without submitting to the infliction, and con-stant practice may make it endurable in his case, and finally almost pleasant ; but the state dinner, let me be permitted to observe in serious earnest, is a monstrous evil, in our class of society. It is the destruction of social intercourse. It compels people to live alone because their tables are not splendid, although the food they eat every day is good enough for any rational human being. I need scarcely say that the ordinary living of all fairly well-to-do people in Burgundy is abundant and varied; that the cookery is excellent, the wine good ; that peaches, pears, melons, grapes, apricots, and other fruits are to be gathered fresh in their season, sun-ripened and mellow, just before they are set upon the table ; whilst the lady of the house is generally quite well able to look after every detail, and cook everything herself if the servants are not clever enough.

All these things have been said to me by the people themselves who suffer from the new state of things, but they feel that it is beyond their power to get back to the happier ancestral ways. The arrival of one ceremonious family in a neighbourhood is enough to break up the old easy hospitality. It happens in this way. The new family gives a state dinner and pays state calls in *grande toilette.* Then the old inhabitants think that, if they are to give dinners at all after that, they must be state dinners also, and, as this involves too much cost and trouble, they give as few as they possibly can.

There is, however, one very familiar old English institution which I have not yet found to exist in France, I mean that dinner which is not stately but only stupid —that dinner where there is nothing particularly good to eat, but where a dismal silence prevails, interrupted only by fitful attempts at getting up a conversation made desperately by the host himself, or by some true and devoted friend of his who compassionates his miserable situation. It is unnecessary for me to describe such a dinner in detail, because every English reader is sure to have a clear recollection of it. Whatever may be the faults of the French, neither shyness nor taciturnity are of the number, and when a little society is brought together for festal purposes a spirit of good-natured loquacious enjoyment gets possession of all present which would overcome even the timidity of an Englishman.

I know a house, far up amongst the hills of the Morvan, where the old hospitality is kept up in the old way, perhaps because it is so far from a town. There the grand dinner is altogether unknown, but the table is always covered with good things from the owner's farm, garden, or estate, and open house is kept for all comers all the year round. I have been there to dinner or déjeûner more times than it is possible to remember, and have hardly ever found myself to be the only guest. Every day there is a little party to déjeûner, meeting there by accident or invitation, and whoever the guest may be, whether he be some noble landowner or a poor man without anything to recommend him but his own abilities and conduct, the host's warm kindness meets him like a ray of sunshine on the threshold, and cares for him continually till his departure. I have seen several men who had more or less the true instinct of hospitality, but have certainly never met with an instance in which the instinct was so perfectly sustained by culture and developed into so beautiful an art. There are hospitable men who are glad to receive guests and most willing to give them good things, but who, either from absence of mind or a difficulty in adapting themselves to the feelings of different people, are awkward in their attempts to make the individual guest feel himself something more than a unit in a certain number. There are hosts, too, who spoil everything by compelling the guest to take a share in some amusement that bores him—by fixing him, for instance, to a whist-table when he does not care for whist, or making him shoot when he is not a sportsman. From all such defects our friend is perfectly free. The guest feels that his comfort and pleasure are incessantly cared for, but that his liberty is respected, and not merely respected, but approved in its exercise, and defended. The host is an ardent and successful sportsman, and there are plenty of guns in the house for those who care to shoot, but nobody is expected to shoot unless he likes it.

It would certainly be a mistake to settle in any rural district with the hope of finding much intellectual culture there, and I have already very plainly said, at the beginning of this chapter, how little we expected or hoped for. It turned out, however, that a few of our neighbours had studied something seriously at some former period of their lives, so that there remained with them a residue from early thinking and working which never quite evaporates. One of them had in early manhood studied painting in Paris under Delacroix, and might have been a good artist had he not belonged to a rich family, and possessed two or three pretty estates with all their attendant temptations. He became a capital shot, but a bad painter. Still, he had been initiated in art, and whatever else he did in the course of the year he never missed the *salon,* but made all other engagements yield him a few weeks in Paris during May or June, where he lived again in the fairy-land of art, at least as an intelligent spectator. Another of our neighbours had been an enthusiastic ornithologist in former times, and had a little museum in his house, which contained a *complete* collection of all the birds that either breed in this part of the country or visit it. Here, too, was something interesting, and it happened, besides, that our ornithologist had studied painting, pos sessed a small library, and was a friend to artists and authors.* Two painters, one of whom is well known, had studios in the city, and spent a part of the year there, bringing back Paris with them in their thoughts and talk. Afterwards, I found out an excellent botanist and entomologist, who had a remarkably fine collection, and who initiated me into the botany of the neighbourhood much more rapidly than I could have learned it without the help of a living companion. Then I discovered an antiquary or two, one of them a very distinguished student of Gaulish and Roman antiquity, whose acquaintance the reader will make more particularly in other chapters. There are also two good Greek scholars in the neighbourhood, and good Latin scholars are more numerous. One of the latter, who is a noble of high degree, gets up very early and works away

* I shall have more to say later about our ornithological friend, who had many claims to consideration besides his liberal pursuits.

energetically every morning at one of the Latin authors, like a student preparing for an examination. There is even a first-rate amateur violinist, but he has been afflicted for some years past with a morbid anxiety to hide his talents, and practises by himself in a cellar with the doors barred. What a pity that a good performer should be so anxious to keep sweet sounds to himself when so many bad ones afflict their friends with endless screeching and scraping !

The presence of a few cultivated individuals does not, however, give a cultivated tone to society generally. It is difficult ground to tread upon ; but, at the risk of being thought unchivalrous, I shall venture upon the remark, that if the ladies were to read a little more, conversation would probably gain by it. Ladies in this part of the world are divided into two distinct classes : the home-women and the visiting-women,—*les femmes d'intérieur*, and *les femmes du monde.* It is very difficult to unite the two characters in one person ; those who pretend to do so are generally worldly ladies, with an affectation of homely qualities. The character which predominates here, even amongst rich people, is the homely house-keeping character. Nothing can be more respectable, and I hope to do full justice to it later ; but it is difficult to talk long with a lady who thinks of nothing but housekeeping, and never reads anything but the cookery-book. The housekeeping provincial lady is, however, a superior person to the dressy "femme du monde," for she has substantial qualities which no sensible person will undervalue ; she makes the lives of her family tolerable on a small income, and comfortable **on** a very moderate one, so that, although she may not read clever books or take a share in clever talk, her life stands on a firm basis nevertheless, and there is compensation. The "femme du monde" talks more, and has a pretty external varnish, but she reads nothing except the little illustrated weekly papers which depict the changes of fashionable attire, and all that she knows is the current gossip of the neighbourhood. If you are well posted up in that gossip, and can take your share in it, a conversation may be maintained; but, if not, the talk drops and the situation becomes painful. This accounts for the separation of the sexes which travellers have so often remarked in France. There is not any acknowledged custom which separates them, like the English custom of leaving the gentlemen to their wine after dinner; but a fatal influence collects all the men in one place or group, and all the women in another. If by chance a cultivated woman comes amongst them, she is better appreciated by the other sex than by her own, and has rather a difficult part to play amongst ladies. They soon find out that she is not one of themselves, and, although they may not be unkind enough to do anything intentionally to make her feel it, she will have need of some caution and dexterity to keep safely within the very narrow limits of their knowledge; and we all know how easy it is to give offence by the unguarded display of anything like mental superiority. We discovered one very superior woman, surrounded by the kind of society which I have just been trying to describe, and found her cautious in an extreme degree, as if anxious to keep her brains well hidden. Such a life is as unfavourable, in one direction, as the too brilliant existence of a Madame de Girardin in another. In one case the faculties of a superior woman are subjected to the incessant stimulus of unlimited adulation ; in the other they are steadily repressed.

It happens that the neighbourhood here is singularly aristocratic. This gave me a good opportunity for comparing French with English feeling on the subject of caste, for I have intimately known the neighbourhood of a town in Lancashire where the aristocracy was more than usually strong. There can be no reason why the name of that town should be concealed, and it will be more convenient for the reader that it should be mentioned ; so I will give it here, not doubting that any inhabitants of the place who have lived long enough there to know it as it was twenty or thirty years ago will confirm my description of the old English spirit which prevailed there. Burnley is at present known as a large manufacturing town, and people in the south of England have generally the very erroneous impression that there are no old families in the manufacturing districts ; yet Burnley is almost surrounded by large estates which belong to old aristocratic families, and on several of these estates there are great country houses such as Towneley, Ormerod, Huntroyde and Gawthorpe, whilst there are several more within a radius of a few miles. Here, then, was an aristocratic society according to our English notions ; but, when I compare it with French aristocratic society, I find that, notwithstanding all that has been so fluently written about the strength of the caste spirit in England, and the absence of social distinctions in France, the genuine feudal spirit is stronger in this department than in Lancashire. There is not in Lancashire, or there certainly was not when I lived there, any bitter hostility between classes, nor any inevitable political opposition. Of the four houses mentioned above, two were liberal and two conservative, and in the middle and lower classes people were liberal or conservative, either from fidelity to a family tradition or else from personal conviction. Nor did it always inevitably happen that people's religious and political views were fastened together inseparably according to a conventional rule. Some who belonged to the Established Church were liberal, and dissenters were not unfrequently conservative. The gradation, too, from the aristocracy to the people was one of almost imperceptible degrees. Some families belonged to the aristocracy and to the middle class at the same time ; they had intimate friends in both, and therefore knew intimately all that passed in both. No doubt public opinion settled everybody's position in a definite way, but, notwithstanding the English proverb "a line must be drawn somewhere," the division was not an impenetrable wall of adamant; it was a thin porous partition, through which there was a constant interchange between the elements on one side and the other by a social *endosmosis* and *exosmosis*.

In France the condition of things is very different. For a hundred years there has been a bitter warfare between classes, and to this day the hostility continues. Much of the evil is attributable to a word of two letters—

the little prefix *de*, which divides society into two
camps, formed of those who have the *de* or have been
clever enough to assume it, and of those who have
it not.   But this is a subject which deserves a chapter
to itself.

CHAPTER V

I AM sorry to begin this chapter with an observation not entirely favourable to my own countrymen ; but, as they always take such observations in good part when they are without malice, it is probable that they will bear with me on the present occasion. What excites my wonder most about English ideas concerning French people is, not that they should be inaccurate (for ideas about foreign nations are always inaccurate), but that they should be on many subjects *exactly* the reverse of the truth—that what is red should be believed to be green, and what is purple, yellow. The English conception of French ladies is, that they are incapable of attention to household affairs ; the exact truth is, that their minds are narrowed by a too close and too minute attention to housekeeping. The English believe that nobility is of no consequence in France, and that all classes are jumbled together ; the exact truth is, that nobility is much more frequently mentioned in French conversation than in English, and much more constantly present in French people's thoughts, and that in France there is a *noblesse* as there is in Germany, Spain,* &c., whilst in England there is not a *noblesse,* but only a peerage, the descendants of which become for the most part commoners.

It is not wonderful that many French people should fraudulently usurp the *de,* for the social value of it is almost incalculable. Happily the preposition *of* has no such value in England ; if it had, there would be the same eagerness to decorate names with it, lawfully or unlawfully. The strangest thing is, that it does not seem to make very much difference whether the *de* is borne legitimately or is a fraudulent and notorious usurpation. It is like current coin, you are respected for possessing it, whether you came by it honestly or not. When you have boldly assumed it, no one can call you by your real name after that without a good deal of moral courage, and there is not a Frenchman alive who would dare to refuse the *de* to a lady who had it printed on her visiting-cards. There lived a certain lady who had the good fortune to inherit three or four different estates from wealthy and childless relations, all strictly in the *bourgeois* class, to which she herself by birth belonged. These estates came to her at intervals of a

---

* Ford expresses the distinction most truly and pithily in his " Handbook:"—" Señor de Muñoz is the appellation of a gentleman. Señor Muñoz that of a nobody " That is *precisely* the difference.

few years for her comfort in an early widowhood, and as she was clever and ambitious, the increase of fortune suggested a corresponding improvement in rank. This she very gradually effected by successive changes on her visiting-cards, without needing the help of any royal patent. She had one of those names which may be ennobled by simple division, as Delacroix may be turned into de la Croix; so this was the first step. When this no longer attracted attention, she slipped in a title, in an abbreviated form, but now she prints Madame la Marquise in full. What gentleman would refuse this consolation to a fashionable, rich, and interesting widow, as ladylike as any marchioness need be? There are not a few false nobles, it is said, within a few miles of us, but nobody refuses them the *de* except the notary on certain occasions when the false signature is not legally acceptable, and then the bearer of it has to sign the old plebeian name which his simple fathers bore. Even on these occasions, however, he adds the assumed appellation in brackets, as, for example, " Canard, Jean (de la Canardière)." It is all very well when this happens in private, between the notary and the pseudo-noble, but it is unpleasant when there are witnesses. At a fashionable marriage the notary, a straightforward man who could not endure a sham, called out in a loud voice to a false noble by that brief plebeian name so persistently laid aside, " Monsieur Pichot, ayez l'obligeance de signer *votre nom !* "*

---

* This incident really occurred within a few miles of my house, and I could give the real name if it were necessary.

The false noble, even when he has ventured beyond the *de* and created himself viscount, has still some grounds for hoping that his title may ultimately become a true one. Official recognition may, by a process surpassing the dreams of alchemy, transmute his pinchbeck into the purest gold. If the Government of the day thinks he will be useful to it, say in a *sous-préfecture*, it will not insult him by withholding the assumed title in the official document which appoints him. After that recognition he *is* noble. There is always, too, the slow but sure consecration of time to be calculated upon, even when official recognition does not come. A false title, steadily kept up for two generations, is nearly as good for social purposes as a genuine one. On one point all false nobles may live without the slightest anxiety, there will never be any official exposure of their assumptions. There have been threats of such an exposure from time to time, but no government, not even a Legitimist government (for the loudest Legitimists in the country are the false nobles) could carry out such an exposure without injuring its own friends.

All this has been said before by other observers, but there is a converse of it which I believe has not yet been noticed. As, on the one hand, the pseudo-noble easily gets his assumed rank confirmed, either officially or by usage, when he has a fair extent of landed property and a château, so, on the other hand, there is a constant process of degradation going on by which true nobles are deprived of their nobility. The reader has, perhaps, witnessed that most painful of all ceremonies, the public degradation of an officer. His epaulettes are torn

off and flung down, his gold lace and buttons ripped or
cut away, his sword taken from him and broken. It is
pleasanter to be shot than to undergo such a ceremony
as that. But there are degradations ultimately quite as
effective which are accomplished silently and invisibly.
A true noble may have all the known vices, he may
lead the most worthless and the most immoral life, but
so long as he can keep up a certain style of living,
either on his own money or other people's, his title will
not be refused. The crime which ensures his degradation is the loss of external gentility, with an honest
effort to earn his own bread. There are many descendants of the true old *noblesse* who are pursuing humble
occupations. They keep small shops; they are joiners,
saddlers, or smiths. The joiner who works for me is a
gentleman of ancient descent, and the fact is well known
to the local antiquaries, but he does not use the *de*.
This led me to take note of the names borne by the
poor, and I soon found amongst them names of the true
old noble families, in every instance shorn of the *de*.
I had a good opportunity for observing this kind of
degradation actually taking place. I knew a young
gentleman whose great-grandfather had been ennobled
by royal patent, but whose father had been ruined by an
unlucky attempt to increase his fortune, and had died,
leaving his young children penniless. My friend had
struggled bravely in the most severe adversity to get
himself some education. He entered the army as a
common soldier, but was soon made sergeant, and afterwards sergeant-major. Losing no opportunity of im-

proving himself, he became a good man of business, with a great deal of practical scientific knowledge. When I knew him he was foreman of a schist mine, and a thoroughly able, efficient man, both with head and hands. He did all the surveying; he kept the accounts; and he executed all the finest and most difficult smith's work himself. He spoke and wrote quite correctly, and had the feelings and conduct of a gentleman. One thing he clung to persistently, he would not abandon the *de*. His friends observed this, and were careful never to miss it, but there was a very general disposition to drop the *de* in speaking of or to him, and it was very generally dropped. I well remember how a middle-class man, recently enriched, sneered bitterly about that *de*. "Depuis quand la noblesse va-t-elle travailler dans les usines?" he asked with perfect scorn. "A man may be really noble," I answered, "and yet poor," on which my *bourgeois* laughed and shrugged his shoulders. Then came the war, and the poor nobleman, though a married man, enlisted voluntarily as a common soldier. He was soon promoted for his merits, and, in the comparatively short time that the war lasted, he rose first to the rank of captain, and then to that of commandant,* besides which he received the cross of the Legion of Honour, for distinguished bravery in the

---

* In the French army a captain commands a company, as in England; a *commandant* commands a battalion, which is composed of four companies : there are four battalions in a regiment, and consequently four *commandants*.

field. "Now," I said, "we shall see whether *les bourgeois* will refuse the poor lad his *de !*" Alas! he never came back to enjoy his honours and receive our congratulations! He got safely through that terrible retreat over the snows of the Jura, when Bourbaki's army was driven into Switzerland, and after passing through a thousand dangers, when we thought him safe at last with the hospitable Swiss people, in their happy neutral land, he was struck down suddenly by an attack of small-pox, and died of that cruel disease.

When first I knew France, a good many years ago, I retained for some time the prevalent English impression, that *noblesse* was no longer of any importance, and this idea was confirmed by one or two French noblemen, who told me so themselves. It did, indeed, seem that titles did not signify very much when people in good society dropped them in speaking to each other, and when the general public so frequently omitted them in speaking of titled people. Since then, however, I have seen reason to modify this first impression. The old nobility tell you that " il n'y a plus de noblesse en France, la noblesse ne signifie plus rien aujourd'hui." But this is simply a French exaggeration due to regret for the past and a sense of diminished importance, as people tell you they are ruined when their fortunes are not what they were formerly. No doubt the importance of nobility is much less than it was under the Légitimist sovereigns ; no doubt, the hope of restoring a past lustre is the reason why the nobility wanted a Legitimist revival under Henri V. But it is not accurately true that the *noblesse* is dead,

and titles of no value. The reader may remember
Stuart Mill's acute remark, " that where there is the
appearance of a difference there *is* a difference." He
may also remember how Sir Arthur Helps acknowledged as a philosopher the importance of honours.
Now, a title, or simply the *de*, is of consequence,
because it creates a distinction ; and, although the distinction may not be so important as that between a
peer of England and a commoner, it is a distinction
still. A French title has no political value, but the
social difference between " une famille noble " and
" une famille bourgeoise " is enormous. You frequently
hear such expressions as " il est noble," or " il porte
un beau nom." There are three distinct classes, under
one of which you will be placed and ticketed, whether
you will or not : *noblesse, bourgeoisie,* and *peuple*—just
as, in England, you *must* travel in one definite class on
the railway.

The time of life when it becomes of most importance
to a Frenchman that his name should be adorned with
the *de*** is the time when he determines to marry. At
that period of his life it often enables him to get a
rich heiress, without the least trouble on his own part,
by the simple process of requesting some third person
to be ambassador and ask for her. The father of the
young lady is deeply impressed when he hears that

* It may be well to observe that there are noble families which
have not the *de*, so that the " particule " (as it is called) is not
essential to nobility. French people, however, almost universally
believe that it is essential, out of pure ignorance, and in these
matters a general belief is quite as good as a fact, for rank is a
matter of faith and not of sight.

such a *beau nom* is offered to her. The girl is called, let us suppose, by one of those mean and vulgar names which are so common in the French *bourgeoisie*, and the opportunity of changing it for something sonorous, which proclaims aristocracy every time it is uttered, is an opportunity not to be lightly neglected. When a young gentleman is called *Monsieur de la Rochetar-péienne*, or Rock-anything-else, provided only that the name fills and satisfies the ear with a properly noble cadence, his chances in the matrimonial market are incomparably superior to those of the simple *bourgeois*, some plain Mangeard or Mangematin. When I look around me and take note of the heiresses and other young ladies who (or whose parents) have, in the choice of a husband, nobly preferred a *beau nom* to wealth, I see that, notwithstanding the matter-of-fact spirit of which the French are so commonly accused, there is a fine sense of the romantic in them yet. Nor does anybody seem to care in the least about the genuineness of the " beautiful name," if only it passes current. I know every field of a good estate which passed, along with the hand of a very ladylike young woman, into the possession of an officer, whose family was plebeian a few years ago, but boldly climbed into the *noblesse* by adorning itself with the *de*. I happened to be dining some time since at a distance, and met two very awkward, underbred, and ignorant young men who belonged to a "noble family" in their neighbourhood. Our host said to me privately, " They are only make-believe nobles, their grandfather bore a very plebeian name, but assumed the grandly·

sounding one they are known by to-day." Everybody in the country confirmed this, but the grandfather, who seems to have had a good ear for the music there is in names, had wisely chosen a particularly imposing one. Now there was a well-to-do young woman, a few miles off, a young woman with £24,000 ; so one of the two young gentlemen thought he might as well have the money, not having much money of his own, and made application accordingly. He was at once accepted, and he would have been as surely rejected without the magic of the *nom.* A gentleman who is now dead had two daughters (no other issue), and an estate worth about £50,000, besides which one of his daughters had £16,000 from another re lative. They were very fine handsome women, well educated, and perfect ladies, but they were not noble, and bore only a plain short name. A Frenchman in such a position is almost sure to give his daughters to men having the *particule*, and these two ladies were ennobled accordingly by marriage. Another of our friends, a country squire in very easy circumstances, had a very intelligent and beautiful daughter. Being a married man, I often saw the young lady in her own home,* and thought that she would be a prize for somebody—some rich man most likely, with broad lands *au soleil* and a château. We speculated some-times on her destiny, and at last we learned that she had been promised by her parents to a poor clerk in a bank—a clerk earning sixty pounds a year. The marriage took place in due course ; but the mystery of

* A young bachelor would not have seen much of her.

it was explained by the young gentleman's name, which had the true ring of nobility—indeed a novelist could not have invented a more high-sounding one.

The most convenient and simple way of assu.ning the *particule,* when it does not belong to you, is this. You buy a little property somewhere in the country which has some old and romantic name—there are thousands of such properties in so old a country as France. Let us suppose, for example, that the name of the property is Roulongeau. Here I may mention a real instance, as an example of how the thing may be done. A friend of mine, a notary, came into possession of a ruined castle, which we will call Roulongeau, and which was handed over to him in payment of a bad debt. Here was a capital opportunity for self-promotion into the ranks of the nobility. The notary was too honest and self-respecting a man to avail himself of it, but what he *might* have done very easily is this,—he might have begun in the usual way by signing himself by his old name, with the territorial designation in brackets after it, thus :—Machin (*de Roulongeau*), which has quite a modest appearance, because it only looks as if this Machin wished to distinguish himself from other Machins, to avoid confusion. The reader sees how easy the upward progress becomes when once this first step has been taken. The brackets are dropped first, then Machin is abandoned as unnecessary, and so you have Monsieur de Roulongeau, which sounds all the more respectable, that there really was such a family in the middle ages. After that a rich marriage is easily arranged, and why not revive the old barony? Three generations are enough to accomplish the whole evolution ; but it needs some courage at first, and a steady persistence afterwards.

The English reader is not unlikely to condemn the false *noblesse* with great severity, and to reflect with complacency that there is no such thing in England, where truth is respected, and where people would not consent to bear titles not their own. I certainly shall not attempt to defend the false *noblesse*, for the assumption of a false title is, in plain English, a lie, and a lie that is repeated every time the false nobleman signs his name or presents his visiting-card, whilst he acquiesces in a lie every time that he answers to his assumed title when it is given to him by another. But now let me be permitted to say something, not in disculpation of all these liars, but to show that there is a great deal of ordinary human nature in their conduct. In the first place, the advantages to be reaped from the lie are very great—they may be incalculably great ; and, in the next place, not only is there very strong temptation, but there are great facilities, as we have seen, and there is really nothing to fear in the way of evil consequences. There is nothing to fear from any French government, and there is nothing to fear from society. So far from expelling the false noble from human intercourse, people give him a rich girl for his wife, and are rather proud of his acquaintance. The genuine nobility hate him at first, but hatred is not more difficult to bear than contempt, and before he assumed the *de* he was despised as a *bourgeois* and *roturier*. Besides this, the old families have a strong reason for recognizing him as soon as they decently can ; and the reason is this, the man who assumes a title engages himself thereby to be a defender of orthodox opinions. He is sure to be ardently *bien pensant;* it is a part of the character he has to perform. He is sure to be a willing and eager servant of Legitimacy and Ultramontanism, and to put his time and money at their disposal. It would be unjust to insinuate that all the nobles who went to fight for the Pope were false nobles; many of them certainly belonged to well-known ancient families; but that was just what a young pseudo-noble might most wisely do, and (if courageous and enterprising) would be likely to do. To embrace that service in the "holiest cause on earth," perhaps to win the most sacred of earthly knighthoods, was a consecration which would have reconciled all the Legitimist families to the usurpation of a name.

After studying the false *noblesse* of France, it is interesting to turn to England for comparison. There is no false *noblesse* in England, but neither is there a true *noblesse* in the continental sense. The difference between a small political peerage and a *noblesse* is infinite, and the external similarity is misleading. All the sons of a peer are legally commoners whilst the father is alive, although they may have courtesy titles, and the sons of his younger sons have not even courtesy titles, but lose their nobility altogether. In a country where a *noblesse* really existed it would not tolerate or endure the idea that the majority of its descendants should be degraded to the condition of *roturiers;* it would distinguish them from the people to the latest generation as a noble caste. Now, if such a caste existed in England, as it really does exist, not only in France

but in many other continental countries, would English
truthfulness resist the temptation to get into it fraudulently, if there were every facility and even encouragement to do so? Consider that there is nothing in the
world which men prize so much as social distinction;
they prize it far more than wealth or independence,—
indeed they value wealth in most instances only as a
step towards social distinction and a means of attaining
it. There appear to be few scruples of conscience in
England about stealing other people's coats-of-arms.
The thing is done openly every day. There are heraldic
draughtsmen and engravers who get their living by
encouraging the practice. When there is not the
faintest reason for supposing that the people who
write to these draughtsmen are descended from some
ancient family of the same name, they assume its arms
without hesitation. But not only do English people
assume arms which do not belong to them, they even,
in these days, assume the names of aristocratic families
by the simple process of inserting an advertisement in the
newspapers; the arms follow as a matter of course, and
the transformation is complete. The reader will answer
that, although these practices are unhappily very common
in England, still there are many truthful, self-respecting
people, who would not condescend to them. It is to be
hoped, indeed, that so there are; but, in justice to the
French, let me observe, that there are also great
numbers of Frenchmen who have to resist the far
stronger temptation to assume the *de*, and who *do* resist
it manfully, from a feeling of honour and self-respect.
One such, a friend of mine, when negotiating a matri-

monial alliance, was urged to ennoble himself in the usual way by taking the name of his estate, but firmly refused to do so, at the risk of breaking off the negotiations. There is a great deal of this sound, right sentiment amongst respectable middle-class families, who think that, as their names were good enough for their fathers, they are good enough for them.

Sometimes people get ennobled in spite of themselves, and have to resist it. This occurs as follows:— Your name is not so generally known as that of your place of residence, or else it may be *too* generally known. In either case the peasantry will be likely to call you by the name of the estate you live upon, putting the *de* before it. This is how the *de* really originated in the middle ages. As our English name is a puzzle to the peasantry, the market-women always call my wife Madame de (the name of the estate we live upon) simply for their own convenience. There are two wealthy families in the neighbourhood, which have numerous descendants who by the division of properties have been scattered about on different estates ; so the easiest way of distinguishing them is to put the name of the estate after the patronymic, with the *de* between ; and this is often done, not by the families themselves, but by other people.

It may close this chapter appropriately to say that the author has had to contend against what others so often seek. Much to his irritation, people elevated him to the peerage by bestowing the title of " lord." This was especially frequent in official communications, I mean on papers which came from the authorities.

There is something very exasperating in an annoyance which is repeated year after year, so at last I got quite out of temper about my title, and wrote very angrily to the people who applied it. However, it turned out that they were not very much to blame. The title was duly registered in some official book at the prefecture, how and why I know not, and so I am a lord in France if not in England. There is one comfort, however. Nobody hereabouts thinks that *lord* means anything in particular, so that I have no annoyance to apprehend in the way of snobbish adulation.

CHÂPTER VI.

About money matters—Big houses—French incomes—Examples
of moderate and more important incomes in the author's own
neighbourhood—Large estates—Division of estates—How
families survive the division—Probable permanence of the
present French law of inheritance—Small establishments in
great houses—State maintained in former times—Romance of
the old châteaux—Their influence on the mind—Stuart Mill's
experience—Lamartine and Chateaubriand—Economy and
retirement in great houses—The *bourgeois* temper—Its favourable side—Skill of the *bourgeois* in finance—His readiness to
sacrifice time for small gains—Provision for families—Example
of an " avaricious " man—The *bourgeois* in adversity—Two
examples known to the author—Heroism of the *bourgeois*
temper—Its bad effects in excess—Meanness and self-satisfaction.

As nobility was the subject of the last chapter, it is a
natural transition to talk of wealth in this. The French
used to believe that every Englishman was rich, and
the English believed that all Frenchmen were in a condition resembling beggary. Neither view was precisely
accurate. The plain truth is, that very large incomes
are rare in France, but that comfortable incomes, enough
for a gentleman to live upon with a little care and
economy, are very common.

Mr. Macgregor, in the first of his canoe voyages,
observes, whilst paddling in France, " Pleasant trees and
pretty gardens are here on every side in plenty, but

II

where are the houses of the gentlemen of France, and where are the French gentlemen themselves?" The answer to this question is, that whether a house is large or small, it is a gentleman's house if it is occupied by a gentleman. The *Rob Roy* canoe was not a large yacht, but there was room in it for one who has always acted like a true gentleman.

Perhaps, however, we are using the word in two different senses. Perhaps Mr. Macgregor may have used it in the common acceptation, which is that of a man who keeps up a large establishment, with from ten to a hundred domestics, and everything else on a great scale. In this sense there are not very many gentlemen's houses in France, but there are more good incomes than a passing traveller would be likely to suppose.

There is a difference between French and English habits in estimating wealth which must be noticed before we proceed farther. In England it is thought *bon genre* to speak of everything under £2,000 a year as more or less mitigated poverty; and many people who have nothing like that income, nor yet the faintest prospect of ever either inheriting it or earning it, assume a tone of contempt when speaking of the moderate incomes which are reckoned only by hundreds. I remember meeting a German in London who lived in a state of irritation on this subject. "It seems to be thought bad taste in England," he used to say, "to recognize any of the necessities of people with moderate means, and even the writers in your periodicals talk as if they, and all their readers, had £2,000 a year each." In France the idea of wealth begins with the first savings, and you meet sometimes with such a phrase as " *il est riche de mille francs de rente*," meaning that the person in question has an amount of capital which yields him £40 a year interest. The Frenchman has greatly the advantage in the mental enjoyment of a moderate fortune. I had an English friend who, with £900 a year of his own and £600 a year with his wife, constantly talked of his poverty, and really felt very poor until that pitiable state of things was remedied by a large legacy, whereas a Frenchman would have compared his £1,500 a year with nothing, and felt himself as rich as a little Rothschild.

Many people in this neighbourhood have from £500 to £1,000 a year from land, after all deductions ; and this represents a considerable capital, as land here yields a low interest. Incomes of £2,000 a year do not seem to be much more uncommon than they would be in an English rural district of the same kind. It is difficult to learn the exact truth about the largest incomes in any district, because they are always exaggerated by popular report; but the following figures have been given me either by personal friends of the families, or else by men of business who knew the stewards or lawyers who managed the estates. According to these accounts one marquis had £7,000 a year a few years ago, but has diminished it since by losing a million of francs in a bad speculation. A certain marchioness has an estate which formerly brought in about the same income ; but there have been debts, which she is steadily paying off by the strictest economy,

H 2

so that the property will soon be what it was before. I know a certain château which is surrounded by a park large enough to be worth a clear £1,000 a year to its owner, and that is what it brings in; there are pro perties at a distance bringing £7,000 a year more to the same proprietor. There is also a family wealthier than any of these, the members of which, in order to avoid the inconvenience of division as long as possible, keep all together in a little colony, with one very well-managed and complete establishment. A lawyer who lives not far from the château where this happy family dwell when they stay in these parts, and who knows their man of business, affirms that the general family income is £24,000 a year, and, if this is not an exaggeration, the completeness of the establishment is accounted for. Besides these instances I know two large estates containing respectively seventeen and sixty farms, but do not know precisely the income derived from them. There are also some large industrial and commercial fortunes either in the district or in connection with it, but it is impossible to estimate these with any accuracy.*

There must be wealthy people in a country where families appear to survive for generations the division and subdivision of their properties. There is a certain family here which has increased into quite a clan, and, as the descendants have multiplied, the estate, of course, has been divided. Yet they are all well-to-do people,

---

* The common estimates of these industrial or commercial fortunes range from a few thousand pounds to more than two millions of pounds.

every one of them ; they all have snug country houses, they all keep horses and carriages. There is another family, not noble, of which just the same may be said. However many cousins there may be, they grow up with comfort about them as if they had downy soft pods, as beans have, made on purpose for them by the beneficence of nature. The condition of a French family, at this particular stage on its road to poverty, seems to be very pleasant and affectionate, except when the sharing has not satisfied all its members. They go and shoot on the divided bits of the ancestral estate, each as guest of another ; they have a frequent interchange of family hospitality. The resources of a single estate seem to be almost as multipliable as potatoes. I knew an old bachelor, who died, and after his death his land and money were divided amongst three families of heirs. All those three families throve happily on that single fortune ; they dressed well, they drove about, and were always asking each other to dinner.

In a hundred years the division of properties will have accomplished its work more thoroughly, and many families which are wealthy to-day will have become very small proprietors, and either sunk gradually into the condition of peasants or else into that of shop-keepers or professional people in the towns. The law of division was at the same time the most ingenious and the most powerful attack upon the *grands seigneurs* which could possibly have been devised. It made the younger sons accomplices in the destruction of thei house, and the more willing accomplices, that the de-

struction is not visible in its full extent to a single
generation. Some old families maintain themselves
a little longer by the device of living all together
under the paternal roof, but there is clearly a limit
to family clubs of this kind. There is not the faintest
chance of a revival of primogeniture, for it is one of
those customs which, once done away with, can never
be artificially restored. It is the corner-stone of an
aristocracy, when the aristocracy is not merely a caste,
but a body of powerful families—it has no other *raison
d'être*. The great majority of French people who have
talked to me on the subject are contented with the
present state of French law, which seems to them just
to the children, whilst it leaves a certain liberty of preference to the father, who may make the share of one
of his children larger, within fixed limits.

I have often wondered what will become of the great
old châteaux when the division of properties shall have
gone a little farther. Even now they are often out of
proportion to the establishment which can be maintained in them. I know one, a very extensive place,
with magnificent stabling for forty horses; you pass
thirty-six empty stalls, and find four horses ultimately
in a corner, the present strength of the establishment.
A place of that kind seems to call for the old scenes
of hunting and hospitality, when there was a famous
stud, and a famous kennel too, and when the guests
came in state-coaches with six horses. One of those
guests of the great time, just two hundred years ago,
say, that seven such coaches-and-six entered the court
of the château together, and besides these there were

five guests in the house who had coaches-and-six, but had left them at home—total, twelve coaches and seventy-two horses had all been present. The number of domestics, too, was far greater in those times than it is now. Every great noble imitated on a smaller scale the numerous *personnel* of the sovereign. At the present day two or three servants may be found, by seeking, amongst the empty chambers of a great house, but it is rare to meet with what a rich Englishman would consider a complete establishment ; these changes of custom give the great *châteaux* rather a desolate air, so that I have heard people declare that they would not live in them, and some are all but abandoned, the family coming down from their snug *appartement* or detached house in Paris to spend a month or two in the shooting season. Sometimes you find some quiet widow lady or rural-minded gentleman, who lives in one wing or one tower of the ancestral residence, and has the rest to walk about in on wet days. People who like a house to fit its owner like a coat, and be neither too big nor too small, think that there can be no comfort in one of those great old houses, unless the owner can afford to keep it full of people like a public inn ; but it always seems to me that there must be a deep charm, for any one romantic enough to feel it, in the silence and space of such a dwelling, when you live there with but a few servants who are far away from you in their own quarters. Our small modern houses provide no perfect protection against noise ; we hear *something* of all the noises that are made by children, or servants, or loud talkative people ; but how **peaceful**

arc the chambers of a vast old château, how easy to
choose amongst them some safe retreat for study! It
would be delightful, in such a place, to select one noble
room for a studio, another for a library, a smaller one in
some turret for a *sanctum*, a private den, well defended
against noise and interruption; it would help the
imagination, also, to have the range of all the other
rooms and corridors. Stuart Mill thought that his
visits to Ford Abbey were an important circumstance
in his education. "Nothing," he says, "contributes
more to nourish elevation of sentiments in a people
than the large and free character of their habitations.
The middle-age architecture, the baronial hall, and the
spacious and lofty rooms of this fine old place, so
unlike the mean and cramped externals of English
middle-class life, gave the sentiment of a larger and
freer existence, and were to me a sort of poetic cultiva-
tion, aided also by the character of the grounds in
which the abbey stood; which were *riant* and secluded,
umbrageous, and full of the sound of falling waters." *

* There cannot be a doubt that the position of Lamartine and
Chateaubriand, as descendants of old noble families which had not
yet parted with their great ancestral residences during the youth of
those writers, was a most important circumstance in their education,
and gave both of them a certain grandeur in their ways of estimating things, which pervaded their writings, and remained, to the
end, most strongly opposed to the small-minded *bourgeois* spirit.
From the autobiographical records which Lamartine and Chateaubriand have left of themselves, it is quite evident that the poetry of
the ancestral houses was strongly felt by them even in their youth,
and remained as an influence to the end. Had they been born
simply as remoter descendants of the families they belonged to,
without ever living in the old houses. the effect would have been
almost entirely lost

This may be a digression, but it leads to something closely connected with our original subject : the decline of wealth in an aristocracy, when it has not yet gone too far, is not without its (rather melancholy) advantages and compensations. There is a certain period in the decline of a family by the division of estates when it is disposed to retirement and a wise economy, nor is any place so good for this as the great old château with its memories and associations. Such a time is assuredly better for the mind than a time of extravagance and festivity. There is many a great house in France, where the people in possession are thinking little of themselves and much of the next generation, where they live soberly and quietly, that the old place may not be sold. And yet, with the present law, the old places *must* be sold at last, from the disproportion between the big house and the fraction of an estate. I know a family personally, the head of which has perhaps £3,000 a year and an ancient title, but he has also nine children, who will therefore have about £300 a year each. The château will have to be sold.

It is not, however, the richest people who contribute most to the wealth of a state ; and, although we have given the aristocracy the precedence in this chapter, it is not they who pay the taxes, subscribe to the national loans, and make the railways. The thrift of the middle classes is the financial strength of France, a strength which was never fully understood till the recent great events revealed it. I shall have more to say, later, about the *bourgeois* temper in its unfavourable aspect.

It is, of course, directly hostile to culture and to all elevation of sentiment, it is our own familiar and repulsive English Philistinism in a far more decided and developed form. Regarded, however, as we are regarding it at present, simply from the financial point of view, it is admirable. The genuine provincial *bourgeois* knows all about material values, knows the cost of everything he uses, follows the variations of price in eggs and butter with the same keen interest which he gives to the financial column of the newspaper, understands—not superficially but thoroughly, from top to bottom, and all round—everything which can affect his fortune, and sails towards material well-being as an accomplished yachtsman makes for the distant haven, eating into the wind whenever he can and never losing the faintest breath of it which may help him. The delight of his life is in the minute exercise of this skill, which he has developed into a delicate art. His incessant attention to facts and laws, in regard to which imagination is useful only in so much as it may supply hints to foresight, gives him a firm footing in life and keeps him cool alike in prosperity and in adversity, if by chance he ever falls into adversity, which is not likely to happen. We know a family of the kind which was enriched by two considerable legacies, after having lived very economically on a small property of their own; and we remarked that, instead of launching out into extravagance when they got richer, they became, if possible, rather more careful than they were before. Another very important *bourgeois* characteristic is the readiness with which the true *bourgeois* will sacrifice his time and give steady labour for a small addition to his income. I knew one who had £400 or £500 a year from property, and whose only son was a railway-guard. The idea of relinquishing the income derived from this occupation did not appear admissible, and the young man was not fit for anything else. I know another who has nearly, but not quite, the private income mentioned above, and who is a clerk in the post-office at £80 a year. The ill-paid teachers in the public schools have often private fortunes more or less considerable, and yet submit to the daily drudgery of teaching. One who is known to me by sight has £500 a year of his own, and teaches, to earn £60 or £80 in addition. Any one who knows the French *bourgeoisie* well must have met with many such instances. The most remarkable case I ever met with was that of a young man whose mother could easily have allowed him £600 a year, and who, I believe, did make him a good allowance ; this did not prevent him from being a clerk in the Court of Accounts at Paris, where for small pay he sacrificed his liberty to the most minutely wearisome of all imaginable drudgery. On one occasion I talked about this to an experienced friend, who himself had made a handsome fortune, and he answered, "One or two thousand francs may not be a large sum of money ; but when such a sum makes the difference between a surplus and a deficit at the year's end it becomes of enormous importance and well worth the sacrifice of liberty." that was a financier's statement of the case, and it contains a truth which no reasonable person will deny ; but what astonishes me in the French *bourgeoisie* is, not that they should accept ill-paid clerkships, &c, to escape a deficit, but that they should accept them when there is no reason to apprehend a deficit. There are many instances in which this is done without the slightest idea that there is anything heroic in the sacrifice, purely in order to put by a dowry for a daughter, or to give a son a better start in the world. English writers often sneer at the meanness of the French *bourgeoisie*, and certainly no English writer can detest their Philistinism more heartily than does the author of this volume; but there is a side to their close looking after money which deserves more credit than it gets. The first object of their ambition is to owe no man anything; the second, to make such provision for their families, that in case of misfortune in health or business they may not be cast naked upon the world. Surely these are respectable purposes; surely it must be a good thing for any nation when these purposes are steadily kept in view by the majority of its inhabitants! One of my *bourgeois* friends talked to me very frankly on this subject, and said what is worth repeating, and what is not to be denied. "All my life," he said, " I have had the reputation of being exceedingly avaricious, because I have been careful about money, and have never been willing to let my substance be squandered by idle people for their amusement. Now, please consider how far I have deserved this reputation for avarice. I have saved money, it is true ; but it has always been for others, not for my own pleasures. You know how simply I dress and live, and how few indulgences I give myself." Here let me observe that the argument may be fairly considered weak, for the most avaricious people dress and live the most simply. But when my friend asserted that he had saved for others, it was most true. He had been in his own person a sort of general insurance company for the benefit of all his relations, and of his wife's relations too. He began life with nothing ; when he had made money, one of the first things he did was to present a snug little property to his father, which gave him a retreat for his old age and the means of passing it comfortably. My friend's wife, with his hearty approval, made handsome yearly allowances to her poor relations. He did the same to other relations besides his father. He had two daughters, one of whom married a barrister. A very short time after their marriage the barrister was stricken down by paralysis, and so prevented from pursuing his profession. On this the "miserly" father-in-law stepped in, and made him an allowance of £400 a year, that the misfortune might be less severe. Besides these aids to relations he had often assisted friends ; " but," he said, " I will not lend money to be spent in luxuries. I did so, foolishly, once or twice when I was young, and found it only encouraged idleness, so I shut my purse to genteel applicants who are anxious to keep up their gentility. If I had not been what is called a miser, I should have been unable to help my poor relations in their need." All this was true; the "miserly" man had, in fact, been little else than a beautiful contrivance of Providence for distributing wealth wisely to those who needed it, and the more he gave the more he prospered, yet the private household expenses of himself and his wife are still fixed at £360 a year, and this includes £60 for a little tour.

The genuine *bourgeois*, uncontaminated by aristocratic or artistic ideas, invariably saves money, however poor he may be. If rich, he saves more money ; if poor, he saves less ; but every year will show a balance in his favour unless there has been some great misfortune. Even under misfortune he will try hard to balance *doit* and *avoir*, so that there may be a sou in favour of *avoir* at the year's end. His coolness in prosperity is equalled by another kind of coolness in adversity. He does not lose his wits and do foolish things, either from the folly of despair or the intoxication of success. The genuine *bourgeois* in adversity is difficult to find, for if any creature naturally avoids adversity it is he ; but now and then, in the course of many years, you *may* find one so situated, as you *may* see a cat drop from a tree into a pond. I remember two instances, one of a man who had lost his fortune in an enterprise which he was not qualified for ; the other, of a cashier of a bank who lost his sight, or nearly so, and could not earn any salary after that. The first had a very beautiful, ladylike young wife and two children. He got a small clerkship in a public office, and he sought and found a small lodging at a rent of ten pounds a year. Here the couple established themselves, and many a pleasant evening have we passed with them. Of course they had no servant ; but the lady did all the housework that she could do ; and her husband helped her when he came back from his office, and in the early morning before he went there. Seeing that, instead of despising them for their way of life, we respected them for their courage, they received us with perfect frankness, and after some time they asked us to dinner. The lady was an excellent cook, and as exquisitely clean as she was beautiful, so the reflection occurred to me, whilst she was busy over her bright pans and little charcoal fires, that we were served as rich people are *not*, and that this was the true poetry of dining. But there was not the slightest extravagance, even on these occasions, when the temptation to a momentary extravagance was so strong ; the dinner consisted of one or two good dishes and a salad, with a bottle of drinkable common wine and a *petit verre* after, this last of common white *eau de vie du pays*, a cheap brandy with a flavour of its own which some people like (I do), but which others may excusably not like. " We are very poor," our host said to me one day, " as you see, but we have one bit of pride left to us yet. We do not owe a farthing to anybody, we pay our way honestly month by month, and at the year's end the balance will *not* be against us." It was probably in consequence of this satisfactory feeling that our friends were so cheerful in their narrowed circumstances. They were as merry as rich people ought to be—but are not.

The bank cashier could not find any other occupation after losing his sight ; but his wife had a very small property in the country, with a snug little house upon it. Here they settled down, to pinch and screw themselves into solvency. They had this advantage in rustic life, that they might dress as badly as they liked, it being the French theory that, *à la campagne*, you may wear any old clothes which you happen to possess. And they *did* wear old clothes, which became very much older before they had done their work! During his life in the bank, the husband had acquired a good deal of financial knowledge, so he sold most of the little property and invested in shares, changing his investments very judiciously from time to time. They declined all invitations, and gave none; they lived chiefly on potatoes with the skins on, roasted in hot wood-ashes; they ate plenty of chestnuts, too, of the cheapest kind, when they were in season. Their breakfast (the English reader will scarcely believe this, but it is a fact) consisted of one small piece of dry bread for each member of the family, including the three children, and nothing to drink to it. If this is not counted as a meal, they had two meals a day, with an interval of seven hours between them, to get an appetite in. They fasted most religiously all through Lent, when they ate lentils, but they did not observe the feast days with the same devotion. A relation gave them a rickety little old pony-carriage, so they bought a donkey to drag it, and this was the only extravagance we were ever able to detect. "They will pull through," we said at the beginning; but after some time we said, "they will save money!" And not only did they make both ends meet, but they actually contrived to save dowries for their two daughters!

·This immediate acceptance of the unpleasant necessities of adversity, with the resolute determination to rise out of it by economy, are the heroic side of the *bourgeois* temper. The true *bourgeois* has the courage to say, "I cannot afford it," and the still higher courage to refuse himself the social consideration which is accorded to a showy way of living, in order to provide with prudence for a distant future. We ought to respect such a temper instead of treating it with ridicule, but unfortunately it happens that it is too frequently, almost necessarily, accompanied by a concentration of the mind upon minute pecuniary details which is death to all its higher and nobler faculties. If it were possible to take the resolution to be economical and have done with it, as we take a third-class railway ticket instead of a first, and think no more of the matter, then the mind would be left free to act and to grow, but this is not the state of the case. The *bourgeois* lives in a ceaseless striving to save money in minutiæ, which employs all the energies of his intellect. His maxim is "*il n'y a pas de petites économies,*" meaning, not that a small economy is useless, but that what looks like a small economy is a great one. A neighbour saw me putting markers into a book that I was reading—little bits of gummed paper which I have by me for the purpose. This excited his curiosity. "Who prepares these gummed markers?" he asked. "I prepare them myself." "What, do you buy gum at the chemist's? why, you might economise that by keeping the gummed margins of your sheets of postage-stamps." The economy here would be perhaps twopence a year.* The reader will perceive how this *incessant* attention to small economies

---

* I was obliged, in self-defence, to enter into an argument to excuse my extravagance, by showing that the markers were only gummed a little on one end, and could be written upon on both sides, so as to give convenient indications of the contents of the page, whereas the gummed stamp-paper would only take writing on one side; besides which, I had not gummed stamp-paper in sufficient quantity always at hand.

will come in time to absorb the whole mind of a man.
It becomes like an induced disease, and as the drunkard
must have his dram, so the saver is anxious every morning until he has prevented some outlay, or got something for less than its value. If it stopped there, if it
stopped at the destruction of the higher mind, the evil
would still be great ; but so long as men live honourably
in the lower mind, however poor and small the objects
they live for, they are only commonplace, not despicable.
This evil, however, reaches deeper. After starving the
intellectual faculties, it withers the moral sense. Pushed
to a certain point, it overrides all considerations of
delicacy, all obligations of kindred, all feelings of duty
and honour. There are many instances of this in
Balzac, instances which seem incredible, but I have
seen things in real life which are quite as monstrous.
There is a couple in this department who, by incessant
efforts to over-reach all their relations in matters of
inheritance and money, have finally isolated themselves
so completely, that not one of their relations will visit
them. To this they seem perfectly indifferent. Their
line of policy may have cut them off from family intercourse, but it has increased their wealth, and life for
them has no other object. Here lies the moral danger
of that economical spirit which reigns in rural France.
In its excess it becomes capable of incredible mean-
nesses. It is so ignoble, so disgusting, that anything
seems better, even the foolish ostentation of a Lamartine,
playing the prince in the East, or the childish carelessness of a Dumas, incapable of retaining money. Much
of the mad extravagance, or wild generosity, of the
cultivated classes in France is nothing but a reaction

from the meanness which they see so frequently that they are revolted by it.

The misfortune is that there does not seem to be anything in the laws of the universe which can ever make the thoroughly ignoble person dissatisfied with his own way of living. His life is so harmonious in its ugliness that the very harmony has a certain charm, as it has for example in the toad, that model of nature's good taste in carrying out an idea consistently. He is always perfectly contented with himself, which nobler people never are, and he meets with nothing to disturb his self-satisfaction. On the contrary, every day's experience confirms it. He buys shares, or property, and perceives that, as his investments increase, people treat him with more consideration. The longer he lives, the more does he see reason to congratulate himself on his entire belief in money. All that he wishes to have done money can do for him, all that he wants to procure money can procure for him. Virtue! knowledge! what do these vain words mean? His one conception of virtue is solvency, and the only knowledge he cares for is the science of getting rich. Scholars and artists, dreamers of dreams they cannot realize, dissatisfied with the world as it is and feeling their impotence to make it better, have higher aspirations and sometimes higher pleasures, but they have never his perfect assurance. They are carried away by their balloons in the rarefied air, in directions not to be foreseen; *he* goes with his feet on the earth in the familiar dirt and mud, and needs no mariner's compass to find out where he stands.

CHAPTER VII.

THE manners and customs of country folks in France
may interest the reader sufficiently to carry him through
a chapter on the subject. I shall say nothing just now
about the peasantry, because they live in a world of their
own, with its own uses and traditions, which must be
studied separately. The noblesse and *bourgeoisie*, on the
other hand, have very similar customs, at least when
their pecuniary circumstances are nearly alike.

In the country the Frenchman is generally an early
riser. A near neighbour of mine, seventy-five years old,
invited me one day to see something in his garden ; and

this led to a comparison of our habits. "Of course you are an early riser," I said ; "all your countrymen are so, except in large towns." "No," he answered, "I am not an early riser." "The expression is very uncertain, but clocks are more precise ; will you tell me what are your hours ?" "Most willingly; I get up at four in summer and six in winter ; in the spring and autumn it is some-where between the two." This would be considered early rising in England generally, and in any large French city, but it seems only the ordinary course of things to a rustic squire in this neighbourhood. Still my friend was a little earlier than other people in the same class, without being aware of it. They generally get up at five in summer, or thereabouts, and at seven in the depth of winter.

The English breakfast is entirely unknown in France, and at the risk of offending every English reader I will venture upon the observation, that the institution may very well be dispensed with. Happily for the French-man, he is not under the slightest moral or social obliga-tion to eat anything until he has earned an appetite. The English breakfast, in the middle classes, is in fact kept up as a means of persecution. You are made to sit at table, to eat eggs, or tongue, or a slice of cold meat, and to drink either tea or what is by courtesy said to be coffee, and if you rebel, and refuse to submit, you are treated as one worse than an infidel. It is at once inferred that you are a dissipated man who has destroyed the coats of his stomach, or else a feeble creature only fit for the life of an invalid. Nobody will believe that you are simply a rational being that does not like to be

compelled to eat until it is hungry.   One of the delights
of living in France is that you may do as you like about
breakfast.   Ladies generally have a basin of *café au lait*
with a piece of bread, which they first break into it, and
then fish out bit by bit with a spoon.· All the doctors
are against *café au lait,* which they affirm to be indi-
gestible and the source of unnumbered evils; but ladies
laugh at science except when it suits their fancy to do a
little doctoring themselves, and then they overwhelm us
with their learning.   Most of the men in this neighbourhood take nothing whatever in the morning,—an abstinence which does no harm to strong men, especially if
the *déjeûner à la fourchette* is not served too late; but if
the interval is too long a feeling of exhaustion comes
on, which leads to a habit worse than the English breakfast itself, or *café au lait* either, namely, *le vin blanc.*
This is very common in country towns.   The victim
begins by taking half a glass of some light white wine
to keep himself up till *déjeûner.*   He gradually increases
the dose, and finally drinks half a bottle.   This is the
general limit, but some go farther, and drink a whole
bottle.   It is curious that this habit should be so pernicious as it is, for the wines are generally good and
sound, and only heavy as Burgundy generally is, or
what a sherry-drinker would call very light ; but the evil
is, that the stimulus is poured into the empty stomach,
and that the peculiarly exciting powers of white wine
are left to operate directly upon the nervous system,
which has no food to defend it.   There is also the great
evil that the votary of white wine lives *constantly*
in a state of alcoholic stimulation.   He begins with it

in the morning, repeats it at meal times and between meals, and continues it in the evening till bed-time. You will seldom, however, find this habit amongst country squires. If the interval before the *grand déjeûner* seems too long, they take food of some kind just as they feel inclined, each man by himself, no matter where or how. One of them earnestly recommended a basin of soup to me as the best thing for this purpose, especially if one goes out early in the morning ; he said it had the advantage of sustaining well, without spoiling the appetite or offering any difficulty in digestion ; *cafe au lait*, in his opinion, was objectionable because it stopped digestion, and chocolate he did not like because it was heavy and heating. I found afterwards that others were of his way of thinking, and that the believers in soup were generally healthy and reasonable men, so I became a believer in soup myself, and am so still. It ought to be either *soupe grasse*, or *soupe à l'oignon*, with plenty of bread in it. After a basin thereof, a healthy man is able to work in full vigour, mentally or physically, from five o'clock in the morning till ten or eleven. A Frenchman hardly ever uses tea, the national beverage of England ; he looks upon it as a sort of medicine, which may be safely administered, in a weak state, to them that are afflicted with the colic, and although he likes coffee, and knows how to make it, he will not drink *café noir* when fasting.

In the country the *déjeûner à la fourchette* is the great meal of the day. Readers who know French cookery and customs from the practices of the hotels will in some respects be liable to wrong impressions about the

way of living in private houses. The dishes in the
hotels are much more remarkable for number and
variety than for good quality, the object of the variety
being to hit the taste of all the guests, so that every one
of them may find one or two dishes to his fancy. In
private houses the tastes of all the family are known
beforehand, and so even are those of friends who often
join the home party, so that every house comes in time
to have its own round of dishes, much more limited
than the long *menus* of the hotels, and generally much
better cooked. You often hear Frenchmen complain of
their own hotels just as English travellers might complain of them. They often say that hotel living is not
wholesome, that the variety is too great, and that the
cookery is not so strictly cared for, with reference to
health, as it ought to be. My own experience has always
marked the difference between the two kinds of living
in the most decided manner. French hotel life does
not suit me, but I have never been unwell after dining
or staying in a private house in France. Those who
understand these things tell me that in the hotels due
care is very seldom taken to keep dishes separate, that
sauces get mixed together, and that utensils, in the
smaller hotels at least, are not kept strictly to their own
special purposes, so that you get that *general* sickening,
well-known *goût de graillon*, which nothing less robust
than the stomach of a commercial traveller can endure
without rebellion. In a private house which is not
below the average of the well-to-do classes, you escape
these evils because dishes are kept apart and there are
plenty of well-cleaned utensils ; besides which, as the

number of dishes is much more restricted, more care is given to each, and a more perfect skill is attained by constant practice. The admirable vigilance of French ladies in everything that relates to housekeeping makes you safe and comfortable even in houses where the servants are rough and inefficient. If the lady of the house is at home you will dine well, but if she is absent that is not quite so certain.

The ordinary custom at *déjeûner* is to have a dish of meat, a dish of vegetables, and dessert, in a small family, but when there are a good many plates to fill there will be two dishes of meat. Dessert is never omitted, and in a country of fruit like France it is often both good and cheap. Melons, as the reader is probably aware, are eaten at the beginning of the meal, with pepper and salt, and a very pleasant beginning they are when they happen to be good.

The wine drunk during meals is always some cheap *vin ordinaire.* An Englishman wonders at first how rich people can be induced to drink such poor wine at all, but after some experience he discovers that *vin ordinaire* is one of those common things which are better in their place than more expensive things, just as bread is better for constant use than plum-cake. There are, however, very different qualities of *vin ordinaire*, and the skill of the master of the house is never put to a more serious test than in the choice of this common wine, the merit of which is not to bear a distant resemblance to *bon vin*, but to keep the appetite alive (*bon vin* cloys it), and to bear mixture with water. A good *vin ordinaire* is not preferred to a higher class of

wine simply from economy ; if the two were at the same
price, the judicious Frenchman would choose an *ordinaire*
for use until hunger was satisfied. A bottle of better
wine is always produced at or before dessert if there is
a guest ; but this is generally omitted when the family is
alone, unless there is some excuse for the indulgence,
such as a birthday, a *fête* day, or the return of a member of the family from a distance. In summer, white
wine is often served at *déjeûner* and drunk with seltzer
water, with which it makes a very refreshing beverage,
perhaps only too stimulating to the appetite. Coffee is
hardly ever omitted after *déjeûner* even in the most
economical families ; it is generally excellent, but not
invariably. In houses where care is taken about coffee,
it is roasted in very small quantities at a time, and very
moderately. The burnt black coffee of the *cafés* is
generally only fit for peasants at a fair, the true con-
noisseur despises it, and takes the greatest precautions
to secure the unspoiled aroma. It is very probable that
there may be some natural connection between the
wine and the coffee ; the wine seems to call for the
coffee, and perhaps physiologists may know the reason.
The wine drunk varies from half a bottle to a bottle at
each meal, for each man ; ladies drink less, and seldom
go beyond the half bottle. In hotels a bottle is the
regular allowance. Men often drink their wine pure,
but ladies never do, except a little at the end of the
repast. The quantity of wine drunk in France sometimes appears excessive to modern Englishmen, though
it would not have astonished the contemporaries of
Sheridan and Pitt, whilst Americans rather suspect you

of a tendency to intemperance if you drink anything but iced water during meals. I have never perceived that a Frenchman was less sober after his bottle of *vin ordinaire*, nor is there any reason to believe that it injures his health or shortens his existence ; but if he drinks much wine at meals he ought to abstain rigorously from drinking between meals, and the wisest Frenchmen are often very severe with themselves on this point. I know several whom nothing would induce to infringe their rule, and who never enter a *café*.

The *déjeûner* is generally served between ten and eleven in the country, so that there is a fine space of time before the six o'clock dinner, both for digestion and work. Country gentlemen usually occupy themselves about their own estates until *déjeûner*, and drive off after it to see friends or attend to business at a distance. The only inconvenience about the French *déjeûner* is that on days when you go to shoot, or for a long excursion, there is some difficulty about settling whether the meal is to be served earlier or later than usual, for eleven is an inconvenient hour in these cases, and the English breakfast at eight is more suitable. There is also an' objection to the French system on the ground of too great similarity between the two meals. In England this similarity is very happily avoided ; breakfast, lunch, and dinner, in the upper classes, or breakfast, dinner, and tea, in the middle classes, are perfectly distinct in character. The objection to the French system always seems to me most evident in rich men's houses, because there the *déjeûner* and *dîner* are in reality two dinners, and, although the interval between

them is long, it is tiresome to go through an important
ceremonious banquet twice in the same day. The
ordinary habits of the smaller country gentry correct
this, however, for the *déjeûner* is almost always the important meal, whilst what is called dinner is lighter and
simpler, very often consisting of nothing but an omelette
and salad when the family are by themselves, or a *soupe
maigre* and a bit of cold chicken. "Tea" is quite
unknown as a repast, and this may be considered unfortunate, for tea would avoid the repetition of wine; but
there is not the faintest probability that the French will
ever be persuaded to adopt the English custom. Unless
they see a bottle of wine on a table they think there is
nothing to eat. The impression of misery and insufficiency which is produced on French minds by the sight
of an English tea is highly curious, and quite independent of reason. Although there may be much more
upon the table than they can eat, they suffer from an
uncontrollable sense of starvation. The reader may
perhaps remember a scene in Mrs Oliphant's story of
"Innocent," where an English lady, at Venice, pities
the Italian girl for dining so wretchedly on thin wine,
oily salad, &c., and thinks how much better it would be
to have "a comfortable tea." Precisely the same feelings are excited in the French mind by the sight of
an English tea-table. It is one of the most curious
instances of difference in custom that the Chinese
beverage should have become so thoroughly national in
England, whilst our nearest neighbours scarcely know
the taste of it. They always say it agitates them and
prevents them from sleeping, however weak it may be;

and this is really the effect upon constitutions which have not been inured to it by practice.

In the country, French people go to bed very soon, often at nine o'clock or a little after. One of our neighbours was always so sleepy after dinner, that with the very best intentions he tried in vain to be sociable. There is a common impression in England that the French take no exercise, because they are to be seen in the cafés in large towns, but in the country they are often out all day, which accounts for the sleepiness in the evening. They are generally fond of gardening, working very steadily with their gardeners at certain interesting seasons of the year. Almost all country gentlemen shoot during the season. Here, of course, the English reader smiles, because French shooting is a standing joke in the English newspapers, where you find ancient legends about the *one* hare which was supposed to haunt a particular neighbourhood, and animated the *chasseurs* with vain hopes, year after year. Stories of this kind are generally borrowed from the French satirists themselves, who do not spare their brethren, and who find a fair pretext for their inventions in the absence of game round the large towns. In this neighbourhood there is not so much game as on a well-preserved English estate, but there is enough to afford a reasonable excuse for much walking with gun and dogs. There are plenty of partridges, a good many rabbits, and some hares, besides snipe and woodcock. I know more than one country-house which in the season is kept very well supplied with game by the master's gun, and where the cook sends hares and rabbits to

table only too frequently, dressed in various ways.
There are more partridges, however, than anything else.
The exact truth is that a good shot, who is at the same
time an untiring pedestrian (and there are many such in
the neighbourhood), will generally make a bag, if not a
very full one. There is nothing comparable to the
grouse-shooting of Scotland, though that in its turn is a
delusion and a snare in comparison with the far finer
grouse-shooting of Lancashire and West Yorkshire.
But a genuine sportsman does not estimate the pleasure
he seeks by the quantity of game which he kills. He
enjoys the ramble in quest, the life out of doors, and
the exploration of the country in detail ; he enjoys the
scenery, too, in his own way, though not perhaps with
the cultivated taste of a landscape-painter. I certainly
cannot see why French country gentlemen should always
be laughed at by English journalists. They are often
excellent shots, and capable of enduring much fatigue.
As to the foppery of the French sportsman, I have
not yet detected it in this neighbourhood, where men
generally go out in simple grey clothing, and have
nothing especially picturesque about them except the
old-fashioned netting and fringe on the game-bag. If
a journalist chooses to sneer, he can, however, generally
find an opportunity for doing so. When a man goes
out shooting in a pretty costume he can be laughed at
for dandyism, but when he dresses plainly he can be
called shabby. Marshal MacMahon, who still, notwithstanding his elevation, preserves his old habits as a
French country gentleman, goes out shooting all day
long in the simplest guise. Plain in his way of living

(when he can escape from official ceremony), he enjoys nothing so much as a vigorous walk of five or six hours after partridges, dressed in his old clothes, and with an old grey wide-awake on his head.

It seems too, if we consider all things fairly, that the sportsmen of this neighbourhood ought to be safe from the sneers of Londoners, if only on account of the nobler sports in which they share, which are not to be had in England. It is certainly not an exaggeration to say that there are hundreds of wild boars in the forests of these regions. In a single week's hunting, on the slopes of one wooded hill only, twenty-eight wild boars were killed, and the space of ground hunted over was but a small fraction of the vast forests accessible to the sportsman here. There is a valley within twelve miles of my house where the wild boars are so numerous that they are a serious inconvenience to the farmers, and although they keep generally to their hill-forests they come nearer to us occasionally. A very fine one crossed a field once close to my house in full daylight, and several others have been hunted within a distance of two miles. In another district, not close to this, but very easily accessible from here, no less than ninety-eight wild boars were killed in a single season. Now this is not precisely child's play. These boars are not tame pigs like those which are kept for the amusement of the Emperor of Germany ; they have not had their tusks sawn off; they have not been kept in paddocks and styes ; their days and nights have been passed in the wild forest, and when they are brought to bay they will fight to the last extremity. Let us respect ourselves in respecting others. It is not for Englishmen, who have never encountered anything more terrible than a hare or a fox, to laugh at brave Burgundians, who have faced the boar in his fury.

Where boars are numerous, wolves are seldom seen ; but there are wolves here in some parts of the forests which the wild boars avoid. The reader may be aware that there is an official institution intended to exterminate the wolf, but which really operates for his preservation. Certain country gentlemen are appointed *louvetiers,* and it is supposed to be their duty to fight against the wolf in the interests of mankind and civilization. What would happen if such an institution existed in England, if there were wolves in the British Islands ? The appointed exterminators would find that the hunting was very amusing, and would think it a pity to deprive themselves of it in future by the total extinction of the animal. For the enjoyment of wolf-hunting there must be wolves. The exterminators would deal with them as our Yorkshire squires deal with foxes, killing some of them, no doubt, but with quite an affectionate feeling, and having meanwhile a most tender care for the preservation of the race. This is exactly what happens in France. The wolves are hunted occasionally, but without the slightest desire to deprive posterity of the same noble amusement. Most of the country gentlemen in these parts have hunted the wolf, and are ready to hunt him again. Surely this may be considered manly sport. Lastly, there are deer, really wild in the great forests, and not taken to the rendezvous in a cart. They are not very numerous, .

except sometimes in special localities, but still they exist, and are killed occasionally. The mere knowledge that they are to be met with gives a certain poetry to the woods, as every sportsman knows.

Few country gentlemen ride on horseback now. I know two or three young ones who ride often and well, but that is nothing in proportion to the numbers who have carriages and never sit in a saddle. A notion seems to have gradually implanted itself in the French mind, that to be seen on horseback is not quite consistent with the dignity of mature years. The excellence of the roads, and the great improvements in the build of carriages have put " all the world on wheels." Former generations owed their skill in horsemanship to the bad narrow roads and rough bridle-paths which were then the only means of communication. It is now becoming rather ridiculous to be seen on horseback in France for elderly and respectable people, though young men may ride with impunity if they can. The feeling is something like that about velocipedes in an English country town. Young men may run about on them—*c'est de leur age*—but elderly magistrates, clergymen, and lawyers may not. This disuse of the saddle is really a misfortune, for it deprives country life of one of its greatest charms. There are still a good many narrow and picturesque old tracks through the woods and over the hills, which may be perfectly explored on horseback, but are entirely inaccessible to carriages, and it is delightful to follow out these, with all their rich unforeseen variety of small discoveries, giving a new interest every hundred yards

K

When the young men *do* ride they ride boldly but not always elegantly, at least according to our English taste. I remember one of them, a young officer who had behaved with much courage during the war, and who invited me one day to take a long round with him on horseback. Our road lay at first in the pretty lanes, but after a few miles we quitted these and followed a wild rocky track in the heart of a great wood. The perfect recklessness of my companion's horsemanship amazed me. The worse the road became, the wilder his riding. At length we arrived at some very steep and stony hills, with ribs of rock lying across the way ; so my young friend thought it just the place for a gallop, and set off. Not being disposed to follow at the same pace, I soon lost sight of him, but on reaching the top of a hill, perceived him lying with his head on a lump of granite and his foot fast in the stirrup, his horse standing quite patiently. " He is killed," I thought, " but if not, this will be a lesson to him." He was not killed, however, and the lesson profited little, for, once in the saddle again, he dashed away as wildly and reck-lessly as ever. It was his boast that he could ride anything, and certainly he did possess one of the most objectionable animals I ever mounted, a grey mare, very mild in aspect, but whose one idea of progression consisted of alternate kicking and rearing. He kept her, I think, merely to exhibit his own superior horse-manship, for he did get her along somehow, which nobody else could.

In the country, the men are not afraid of a long walk. One of my neighbours would go fifteen miles and back

with no other companions than his walking-stick and
a little dog, though he had a carriage ; and I know
another who sometimes does his forty miles in a day,
and very often twenty.   I also know a surgeon who has
a practice which extends over a large tract of hilly
country, thinly inhabited, and yet he will not keep a
horse, but prefers walking, as more convenient for short
cuts.   His average day's pedestrianism will be between
ten and thirty miles.   My boys often go to stay with
some young friends of theirs in a wild out-of-the-
way village, and during these visits they make daily
pedestrian excursions, in which the master of the
house often joins them ; these excursions often extend
to fifteen or twenty miles by the time they get back to
the village.   I remember meeting a friend of ours, an
old gentleman, not yet enfeebled by time, who had
given us a rendezvous at a certain large pond or lake
amongst the hills.   It was at least forty miles from his
own house, but he came on foot, and brought three
young men with him.   They had slept one night on
the way, and rambled through a wild country botanizing
and geologizing.   They went back by another round,
exactly in the same manner, guiding themselves by the
ordnance map and a mariner's compass, a necessary
precaution in crossing broad patches of forest.   There
is a great deal of this vigorous temper in the real
country, but in the small towns the men become
physically indolent through sedentary occupation,
and the habit of spending their leisure hours in the
cafés ; so that after thirty they are disinclined for exer-
tion, and require some definite excitement, such as

K 2

shooting, to overcome this disinclination. There was
very much the same temper in English country towns
until the volunteer movement did something to correct
it. I can very well remember that townspeople in
England used to speak of a walk of two miles into the
country as if it were something formidable.* If you
want to be free from interruption, a distance of two
or three miles will defend your privacy perfectly.

Amongst the manners and customs of the squires
in France, which ought to be specially noticed in a
book intended for English and American readers, is a
certain general simplicity and roughness in their belong-
ings. During the last few years, however, a rapid
change has been taking place, and the old simplicity of
rustic France is silently but swiftly giving way to a sort
of English finish in everything. This change, I think,
is much to be regretted, not so much for artistic reasons,
not so much because the old life was more picturesque
than the new, as because the polish which is now pene-
trating into country houses is of a kind which greatly
increases the cost of living without improving either the
minds, or the manners, or the health of the people who
inhabit them. The reason why country life in France
used to be possible on a small income, was its remarkable freedom from social pressure in expense. Even
ten or twelve years ago this freedom was still pretty

---

* This remark does not apply to Londoners, who often walk
considerable distances. In small towns people get the habit of
small distances, everything is so near to them, and so it comes to
pass that the inhabitants of small towns are the worst pedestrians
in the world.

nearly absolute, but now it is becoming gradually more and more restricted, and it is only too probable that there will be little of it left in twenty years. In dress, equipage, and furniture, the smaller squires spent their money, or did not spend it, precisely as they pleased, looking simply to their own means and their own real wants, without the slightest reference to any authoritative public opinion outside their own gates. If one man had a fancy for a pretty carriage, he indulged it ; but if another did not care for prettiness in carriages, he had some shabby old conveyance which his father had used before him, and nobody thought of criticizing it. So in dress, it was an acknowledged principle that everybody might dress as he pleased "*à la campagne,*" and gentlemen wore comfortable old grey clothes, or the cheapest light summer ones, without thinking about fashion, whilst ladies dressed very simply at home, and kept their toilettes for visiting. Houses were left very much in the rough ; not much money was spent on iron railings, painting, papering, and gilding ; carpets were all but unknown, and only the best rooms had polished floors, the others being of brick or plain deal. In one word there was little *finish*, or little of it was exacted by public opinion. If a small squire, on looking over his accounts, found that he could not well afford to have his carriage painted, or to buy new harness, he could put off the expense quite indefinitely, and nobody would make a remark. I knew one, by no means poor, who had made preparations for iron gates and railings, but finding that they were costly things, left his stone walls and gate-posts without them till the day of his

death, nor would he ever have his shutters painted—a
false economy, but it was his fancy. I have often slept
in a squire's house where the whole furniture of my
carpetless room was not worth five pounds—in England
such a room *could* not be offered to a guest. Yet why
not? a sleepy man may be as happy there as in one of
the state bed-chambers at Fontainebleau. This kind
of independence used to be very strongly and (to an
Englishman's taste) disagreeably exhibited in the often
indefinite postponement of papering and painting the
interiors of houses, so that they had none of that
freshness and cleanliness which we commonly find in
England. I admit that this is unpleasant to the eye,
and that the English system is much more agreeable;
but to paper and paint a house from top to bottom is
very expensive, and if public opinion allows you to put
off the evil day it is sometimes a convenience. These
liberties are now becoming much more restricted
There is hardly a squire in this neighbourhood who has
not bought a pretty well-finished new carriage within
the last few years, and when the neighbours all go in
pretty carriages it is difficult to keep up the old lumbering ancestral vehicle. A good many people have
now very elegant broughams or landaus with two
horses, which would not look out of place in the *bois de
Boulogne.* Finish and elegance are invading the houses
also. My next neighbour has just been spending a
good deal of money on handsome iron railings and
gates, whereas his place in former times was thought
sufficiently well defended when a rough wooden fence
kept the cattle out of the garden. He has also papered

and painted every room in his house, and had joiners to make the shutters fit better, to put new banisters on the stairs, and new wash-boards round the rooms. This is quite in the modern spirit, and what he is doing everybody else seems to be doing more or less thoroughly and completely. I was at a château last autumn where the old tiled roof had been entirely replaced by one of neat blue slate, whilst a new façade had been erected and a new *perron*, or external stair, the *perron* alone costing 40,000 francs. The insides of the inconvenient old country houses are altered and remodelled according to Parisian ideas. Many new houses are built with the utmost neatness, and the well-kept, well-varnished carriage passes up a smoothly-sanded drive, and is housed at last in a model coach-house with a canvas cover to protect it from the dust. In one word, the French are becoming *cossus*.

Perhaps the reader may not know precisely what it is to be *cossu*. The word comes from *cosse*, a pod, and a man who is *cossu* is a comfortable well-protected man, reminding one of beans in their downy envelope. Rich English people have been as *cossus* as possible for a very long time past, but the French are only becoming so, and the process is not yet quite complete. It is very pleasant to be *cossu* when you can easily afford it, but there is this great evil about it, namely, that those who have already entered into the podded state despise those who have not, and often become so proud that they exclude them altogether from their society. Knowing this, and not liking to be sneered at and despised (for who likes that ?), those who were perfectly contented with their old plain way of living feel a sort of obligation to leave it for more elaboration of luxury, and in order to do this they stretch their means as far as they will bear stretching. Then the *liberty of spending* is gone, and a state of things is brought about like that which exists in England, where public opinion settles how people are to live upon all different scales of income, leaving hardly any margin for spending according to tastes and character. Now what I deplore in the recent changes in France, is the loss of the ancient liberty. Six hundred a year, in rustic France, was real wealth twenty or thirty years ago, because public opinion exacted nothing from anybody, and people might economize on what was indifferent to them in order to spend upon what they delighted in. One man's hobby (I am alluding to real instances, and could give names if it were of any use) was his library; so he collected books, and could do so, because he was not eaten up by horses and servants; another could collect antiquities, because he would not keep a carriage; another liked travelling, and made excursions all over Europe from the north of Sweden to Naples, a fourth had a taste for scientific agriculture, and established a model farm, which was of the very greatest public service. It is easy to laugh at hobbies, but some special beloved pursuit is just the stimulus to energy which is needed in country life, and it cannot be followed to good effect without spending money upon it. But now comes Mrs. Grundy, or her French relative, whoever she may be, and compels all these intelligent men to spend money on things which do them no good.

which give them no pleasure, which only vex, annoy, and irritate them ; till on making up each annual budget they clearly perceive that there is no margin left for any noble or worthy spending, now that they must needs be *cossus.* Surely, amongst the various kinds of liberty, one of · the most precious is the liberty to spend and *not* to spend. In one most important particular, the old liberty is still maintained, you are free to keep as few servants as you please. Everybody who knows England is aware that there is, in the upper classes, a very strong social pressure about servants. The social position of an Englishman depends very much upon the number of servants he keeps, and it is not possible for him to enjoy unequivocal consideration without a complete establishment. It is not at all unusual for the northern English squires to keep twelve or fifteen servants ; I know some houses where the number is nearer thirty, and where you may see quite a congregation of domestics every evening at prayers. There is a house in Yorkshire where there are a hundred servants when the family is at home. Whether useful or not, they are considered necessary to dignity, and as in such matters everything depends upon opinion, they *are* necessary. In France nobody inquires or cares how many servants you have. We had an intimate friend in Paris for many years, who enjoyed a position which would have been utterly impossible in England with so small an establishment as his. He received some of the very greatest people in Europe, and you could never dine or spend an evening at his house without meeting some important personage—either a prince, or an ambassador, or a minister, or a great financier, or some one famous in literature, science, or art; in a word, it was one of those central houses where simply to be present was to see and hear the men who (before the rise of Germany) had most influence in continental Europe. Well, our host kept no carriage, and only three servants! I know that in London there are quiet literary men's houses where you may meet very great people who go there from a sympathy with literature, but our French friend was not a writer, he was an ex-minister and ambassador. Nor was the moderation of his establishment due to poverty, it was a matter of taste with him; he did not care to be troubled with carriages and servants. This, however, is a digression, for he lived in Paris. Let us, then, look *round my house.* At a distance of about ten miles from us there lived a friend of ours who enjoyed one of the most completely agreeable positions to which a continental gentleman can aspire. He had a good estate, was well known for his public spirit and activity all over the department, had been for many years *conseiller général,* was *officier de la légion d'honneur* (the rank above *chevalier*), knew everybody of importance, and lived on equal terms with the proudest old noble families. The strength of his establishment was as follows :—1. A gardener. 2. A man-servant, who groomed the horse, cleaned the knives and boots, rubbed the floors, and drove the carriage. 3. *One* woman-servant, who did the cooking and the rest. There was a lady in the house, our friend's daughter, who dusted things in the morning —a degree of bodily activity which did not prevent her from being one of the most perfect ladies, in mind and manners, that we ever had the honour to know. If the reader will think of any English county that he knows, and try to realize what sort of a position a public man could have in it who kept only one woman-servant, he will feel the contrast. It may be well to remember, also, that the average English county is, as nearly as possible, half the size of the average French department, and that, whilst the town population is denser in England, the rural population is denser in France. The plain truth is, that an English squire with such a small establishment as the one I have just described could aspire to no position in his county, and would be despised in his own parish. He would be a nobody.

I can imagine some practical English lady reading this, some lady who has a dozen servants, and finds them only just enough for the elaborate housekeeping which custom requires of her, and she will say: "But how *can* people manage with so few servants ? how can the dinner be cooked ? how can guests ever be received ?" The answer is, that the small establishment is sufficient for the needs of the household, because every one in the family has some special house duty, and also that on occasions when more servants are absolutely necessary, they are added for one or two days at a time. Every house has its reserve forces in the neighbouring villages. Servants who know the ways of the house have got married and have settled at moderate distances, in the next village perhaps, or the next but one. After that, they form the reserve force of the small squire's establishment, and are always delighted to come back to it on important occasions. Very often this temporary increase of the establishment is periodical. It is often weekly, and nothing is easier than to invite your friends for those days when the reserve is called in. There are also professed cooks in the towns, who know all about the most elaborate banquets, and one of these will relieve your mind entirely. He (or she) will look after all the details and govern your regular and reserve forces and auxiliaries, so that the lady of the house may sit in the drawing-room with a tranquil mind until the beginning of the feast. But, in all this, convenience is the only consideration. Nobody ever seems to keep servants for the maintenance of his dignity; nobody is compelled to keep them by social pressure. It is this liberty which seems good. I may add that, although servants are very useful, it is not desirable to have too many of them. A great establishment is a constant care. Intimate conversation in England betrays an incessant worry about domestics, which cannot leave the mind so free either for work or enjoyment as it ought to be.

CHAPTER VIII.

Secrets of French economy—French sentiment about self-help contrasted with that of the Scotch Highlanders and the Arabs—Stories told by Dr. Macculloch—French disposition to make use of everything—Gastronomical curiosity of a curé and notary—Objection to mutton and Jerusalem artichokes—Arrangements about household work in the middle classes—Indulgences in the ideal—Devotion and fancy work —French and English servants—The relation between master and servant in the two countries—Strong attachment of French servants—Portrait of a gardener—Portrait of another servant—His various good qualities—A perilous result of carelessness—Want of delicacy of perception in women-servants—Intelligent activity of mistresses—Servants useful for rough work—Affectionate treatment of them by mistresses—Contemptuous manner of proud French people towards servants—Modern French tendency rather towards American than English habits.

THE secret of French economy, of the "cheapness of living," which English people have always associated with continental existence, lies in the liberty to do as you like in the first place; next, in the industry and activity of the people themselves in the middle class; and lastly, in the peculiar character of servants in the rural districts. The value of liberty in matters of expense is obvious. It permits you to begin by renouncing all expenditure for what is indifferent to you, which at once sets free all the money that would have gone in obedience to other people's ideas, and leaves it at your own disposal. It also allows you to postpone many expenses from one year to another, until it is quite convenient to meet them.

The industry and activity of the people themselves are closely connected with the absence of pride. The contrast between certain races and others in regard to the sort of pride which scorns self-help is very striking, and it is worth remark that a certain form of nobleness appears to be almost incompatible with the watchful activity of really effectual self-help. The Highlanders of Scotland and the Arabs of Algeria have both a certain sentiment about self-help which is far from the English feeling, and still farther from American or French feeling upon the subject. The Highlander will no doubt work a little when absolutely compelled by what, to him, appears an unavoidable necessity ; but he takes no delight in his work, and feels degraded by it. He will submit to any amount of inconvenience rather than apply himself heartily to remedy it. Dr. Maccul-loch tells a story of a church in Glen Never which was separated from many of the parishioners by a stream which often became an impassable torrent. The materials for building a bridge were on the spot—rocks and fir-trees in abundance—but no bridge was ever built. The people were often detained for several days on one side the torrent or the other, but rather than set to work bridge-building, they had always preferred to wait for the water to subside. The same writer mentions a rocky shore near a laird's house where boats could not land in rough weather without injuring themselves, whilst the laird and his men had to jump into

the water and get wet, the men drawing the boat up
the rocks, " to the destruction of her sheathing." The
same men might at any time have built a small pier,
but they would not, and the inconvenience, had lasted
four centuries and a half. So about food and its preparation. The Highlander lives on the barest necessaries,
and will not stir to procure an addition to them. Dr.
Macculloch found a profusion of lobsters and crabs
close to a laird's house where such delicacies were unknown. He gave the laird a crab-pot to catch them,—
came back a year after, and found that it was in possession of the hens, and had never been used. Another
Highland friend made no use of the salmon which
yachtsmen from the south were catching close to his
residence. He had possessed a net " twenty years ago,
but it was full of holes." There are many other such
anecdotes in Macculloch's book, and all who know the
Highlanders can, corroborate them. I well remember a
family afflicted with scurvy from the use of salted food
and the absence of correctives. An English friend of
mine planted salad for them close to their house, but
could not induce them to adopt it; they preferred the
scurvy.

This indolence is closely connected with a certain
pride—the kind of pride which will not condescend to
ignoble anxieties and occupations. Macculloch was a
geologist, and found that a Highlander would willingly
carry his gun, which was a weapon, and therefore noble,
but would not so willingly carry his hammer, which he
handed to a boy. The same temper is found in the
Arabs ; they delight in everything that is warlike, they

scorn everything industrial Both Highlander and Arab have a certain grandeur and nobleness. I never met with a vulgar Highlander ; but vulgarity is very prevalent in the industrious Lowlands. The Arab is not vulgar, the Frenchman often is.

The French character is exactly the opposite of that Highland character which we have been describing All those minor cares which the Highlander despises are the habitual occupation of the practical French mind, which applies itself with incessant activity and ingenuity to the solution of the problem, how to make the most of the world as man finds it ; how to get the most and best food, drink, clothing, out of it, and every sort of practical convenience. Many generations of clever and ingenious people have left behind them an accumulating tradition of practical skill in the art of living, the result of the whole being the French life of to-day—the most complete life in the world which can be had for a moderate expenditure. The Highlander lives on the simplest food, and does not know how to make the most of the resources of his own bad climate. He grows nothing in his garden but cabbages, though he might grow other vegetables and some fruits as easily. He will not touch the pike in the lochs, though it is so easy to catch them. The Frenchman grows everything he can, and values eatable animals which the High- lander would not taste. Two excellent instances of this temper are the use of vine-snails and frogs, the first a particularly nourishing kind of food, as substantial as beef-steak, the second a particularly delicate food, like chicken. The disposition to try to make use of everything is often very curiously illustrated. For example, there is a very common, too common, weed which invades the ponds, to the vexation of the proprietors. It is called in botany *Trapa natans*, but the people here call it *cornueile*, or *châtaigne-d'eau*. The fruit of it is a sort of farinaceous nut, very easily overlooked as a possible article of diet ; but the French peasants have not overlooked it. The culinary curiosity of the national character is very generally known. Some extreme instances of it have come under my own observation. There was a certain *curé*, in a very out-of-the-way place amongst the hills, who had a taste for natural history and for shooting at the same time. He and the village notary used to go out together, and they killed all sorts of creatures—wild cats, owls, foxes, hawks, and every description of what gamekeepers call vermin. Neither the *curé* nor the notary had any prejudices against this thing or that ; so they always cooked their game without reference to the species, and acquired by that means a most extraordinary range of experience. Only two days before writing this page, I was rambling with the above-mentioned notary by the banks of a little stream, when I espied a water-rat, and asked if he had ever eaten any. "Oh, yes !" he answered, with the air of a man who remembers something agreeable ; "it is excellent !" That reminded me of a gardener we had some time since, who lived in a cottage in the garden and arranged about his own keep. He was a great hunter after water-rats, and always ate them ; not at all in the humour of a man whose poverty consents against his will, but in the humour of the angler who has caught a trout and thinks how delicious it will be at dinner. This readiness to use things stood the Parisians in good stead during the siege, when many of them had to live upon rats and cats, and did so with perfect appreciation of whatever qualities such meat may possess. Horse-flesh, as the reader knows, is now an important article of diet in Paris. The only inveterate prejudices that I have ever met with, in these parts, were against mutton and Jerusalem artichokes. The common country people will not touch mutton, though it is used in the towns, and is of the best possible quality.* When we came into the country, and consumed Jerusalem artichokes, we were pitied as imitations of the prodigal son who ate what was given to the swine. There are large fields of that vigorous root for the cattle, and hence the prejudice. Gooseberries are despised too, and never boiled green, whilst rhubarb is all but unknown ; but, notwithstanding these few exceptions, the fact remains, that there is a general willingness in the middle classes to make the most of everything. They take trouble very cheerfully about household affairs, and willingly, in rather poor families, divide much household work amongst themselves. The father will do the gardening and groom the pony ; his wife will be the cook ; his daughters will keep all the linen in order, and

* A lady, who came from a distance, gave mutton to her washerwomen, which produced an immediate revolt. The women were indignant, and said "Everybody knows that mutton is dirty meat." It is a well-ascertained scientific fact that there is something in mutton which is poisonous for certain constitutions, and it is highly probable that some instances of this kind have produced this traditional prejudice against it,—a prejudice which (of course) makes no distinction of cases.

make their own dresses. On certain occasions all will work heartily together—as, for instance, when the garden has to be watered in dry weather. It is easy to sneer at such arrangements; but the result of them is, that in such families the daughters live at home till they are married, and they have dowries, whilst, if such self-help were not practised, the daughters would have to go out as governesses or sempstresses. A governess would probably be a more cultivated young lady than these are, but it may be doubted if she would be happier. The father gains two satisfactions from his way of living; he is free from anxiety as to the future, and in the present he keeps his daughters with him. In England, a man in the same pecuniary and social position would live up to the edge of his income, and very probably die in debt, not because things are much dearer in England, but because people have not the same habits of self-help. I have no wish to imply that such habits are absolutely universal in rural France, but they are the rule. The exceptions are not often due to any bad cause, but rather to a certain indulgence in the ideal, which is often the sign of superior natures. This indulgence amongst rural . French ladies runs invariably in two channels—devotion and fancy-work. We know examples of ladies in remote villages whose time is pretty equally divided between these two occupations, to the neglect of their households, of course, which are left to get on as they can. The time given to religion in Protestant countries is limited, but in a Roman Catholic country it may be quite unlimited. English custom requires a lady to go to church on Sunday and say her prayers morning and evening on the other days of the week ; but this is not a perceptible loss of time, even to men of business.   In France, there is the daily mass, which all devout women attend when they are not too far from the church ; and there are also many special meditations and readings to be attended to, according to the different religious seasons, besides occasional " retreats " into some convent, when the ladies become like nuns for a week together.   The constantly changing interests and very strong contrasts of the Christian year, according to the Church of Rome, are, of themselves, enough to absorb the attention almost entirely.   It may seem to the reader an odd observation that this extreme spirit of devotion is often associated with the habit of doing fancy-work, but it is so. There must be some psychological connection between the two, a connection which may be discoverable in the meditative exercise of ideality.   It may be said that fancy-work is a poor product of the ideal faculties, and so, indeed, it is ; but feeble and uncultivated powers cannot be expected to produce anything better.   Besides, the Church herself encourages fancy-work, accepting it and exhibiting it in her services. Suppose the case of a young lady who has the charge of all the ecclesiastical vestments belonging to the church in her village.   She keeps the keys of the drawers which contain them,* and looks after them with love and pride.   Such a charge cannot but elevate fancy-work in her imagination, and make it

---

* The quantity of things may be imagined, when I say that in one instance the chest of drawers cost £48, and is quite a simple piece of joiners' work in a place where joiners' wages are very low.

seem almost sacred. She and her sister are always either occupied with their religious duties or with such minor forms of art as embroidery, crochet, patchwork, &c., &c. The consequence is, that their home is very badly kept,—so badly, that the wonder is how any creature but the spiders can endure it; the garden is neglected, the kitchen ill provided, and the table not served as it ought to be.

The difference between French and English servants is one of the most striking contrasts in all Europe. In England they form a caste apart, with its own feelings and principles—a caste which lives in a state of jealous watchfulness and readiness to resist encroachments, contrived with a determination to maintain an unwritten law, and, whilst maintaining, to strengthen whatever in it is favourable to the independence of the caste, if, indeed, a class of persons employed in domestic service can enjoy anything but a very relative independence. In France this spirit seems to be entirely unknown, unless perhaps amongst rich people's servants in the capital. So far as I have been able to observe, the feeling of French servants in the rural districts is quite personal,—I mean that it relates only to the personal connection between the particular master, Monsieur M. or N., and the particular servant, Jean or Jacques. Neither of them appears to be in the least aware that the servant has any rights, but, if they do not get on comfortably together, they separate. When a good understanding is once formed between them, they both try to keep it up by mutual frankness, and it generally lasts a long time, often till one or the other dies. In

England there is hardly any communication between servants and their masters, and they generally know little of each other. If the master attempts to break down this reserve, then the servant will maintain it in self-defence and from a sense of propriety, for he remembers the division of classes. After having been accustomed to French servants, it has happened to me more than once, in England, to address English ones as if they had been French, forgetting for a moment the difference of usage in the two countries and the still profounder differences of feeling, but I have always been quickly recalled to a sense of English propriety by the expression of surprise on the servant's face, an expression which seemed to say, " If you, sir, forget your station, I have self-respect enough to remember mine." It is not that in France we are accustomed to behave in any unbecoming way to servants, but the manner used in speaking to them is not distant or cold. A French servant likes his master to make some appeal to his good feeling and intelligence, and he is generally ready to answer such an appeal with a lively and willing obedience ; but a haughty master will not get very much out of him. The tone generally adopted towards servants in Burgundy is that of intelligent but not jocular familiarity ; and the best way to be well served is to show that you thoroughly understand what has to be done, whilst you appreciate all proofs of skill, and respect industry and endurance. When there is neglect, a clear and detailed criticism is the best thing, for the people are generally intelligent enough, though ignorant. They are sensitive to praise, which ought to be given freely from time to time when it is merited. With kind and considerate treatment they become so strongly attached, that it is impossible to dismiss them, and then they only leave you to be either married or buried. We know an instance of an old servant who was dismissed for some reason, but quietly reappeared in the house on the following day as if nothing had happened, saying that it was no use sending her away, for she would not go, and she would work without wages rather than be turned out. In most of the houses we visit we always see the same domestics, whom we know by name, and always greet by name, with a hearty *bon jour*, which is cordially returned. One of our neighbours had a gardener, who fell into weak health and at last died. When dying, he expressed a wish to be remembered to his friends, whom he mentioned. I was one of the persons mentioned, and was deeply touched, on receiving the message of kindness from the dead, by the thought that in so solemn a moment he had felt confidence in my sense of our human brotherhood, and had believed that his farewell would be valued by me, as it was and is. This little incident shows the relation between classes ; it shows how little the domestic thinks himself excluded from sympathy by his servitude. Yet he is uniformly respectful, though in an easy and rather informal way. His manners express something of this kind, if it is possible to translate such a subtle expression as that of manners into words. They seem to say, " I will not forget the distinction between us, and will serve you heartily so long as you treat me kindly, but I am not in the least afraid of you." The only servant I ever had

to find fault with about his manners was an old gardener called Pinard, a dreadfully talkative man, who was
always patronizing us, and had an inordinately high
opinion of his own abilities. He reminded me very
much of an intolerable Irishman I once knew, for his
manners were much more Irish than French. He was the
most obstinate, pig-headed creature imaginable, and the
greatest liar on earth, inventing stories without a word
of truth in them—long stories which he narrated circum-
stantially with a strong southern accent, which gave
them an irresistibly comic effect. Some notion of his
impudence may be gathered from the following little
specimen. He knew the Marchioness de MacMahon,
because she had employed him formerly; so, according
to his own account, he charged her to convey some of
his own wise advice to her uncle, the President of the
Republic, on his acceptance of office. This may have
been one of his inventions, but it may also have been
true, for his impudence was quite equal to such an
occasion. We had to be continually putting him down.
He had a patronizing way of calling me *mon ami* till I
stopped him, and when he was particularly satisfied
with himself he would pat us on the shoulder quite
affectionately. The reader, no doubt, wonders how we
could put up with such a being, but there was a reason
which inclined us to the utmost possible forbearance.
With all his faults, old Pinard was the best servant, so
far as work was concerned, whom we ever employed.
He worked so thoroughly well, and at the same time so
very expeditiously, whilst he kept at it so steadily from
morning till night, that the result was always a new

astonishment to us. It is not at all an exaggeration to say that he did three times as much as ordinary ser-vants do ; but at last an incident occurred which occa-sioned a sudden outburst of his impudence, and he was ordered off the premises in five minutes. It was a relief to be rid of him, for his gushing civility was un-pleasant at the best, but we regretted his fine working powers and his incessant industry. One thing wounded him deeply ; we discovered that he did not prune scien-tifically, so we forbade him to exercise his unskill on our fruit-trees, and borrowed a very clever man from a neighbour, who pruned admirably. When the clever pruner came, Pinard hid himself in the tool-house under pretext of repairing something, but in reality to watch his rival through the open door. This he did for some time in silence ; however, at length he could endure it no longer, and put his face out, pale, almost green, with jealousy. Then came such a torrent of bitter criticism as no master of the pruning-knife was ever before sub-jected to! At first we only laughed, and let Pinard relieve himself, believing that such a relief might be necessary to his mental and bodily well-being ; but, as there were no signs of abatement, we found employ-ment for him out of sight of his rival. One of his most remarkable peculiarities was his great readiness in assuming knowledge about everything. He had always an answer ready. We have two fine specimens of the bird-cherry-tree (*Prunus padus*) which is usually a shrub six or eight feet high. Ours (I have just mea-sured them) are *thirty-two* feet high, and strong in pro-portion, with a great quantity of dense foliage. The plant is so seldom seen in this luxuriant development, that our specimens embarrass everybody except botanists, so I asked old ‚Pinard what they were. The answer came without an instant's hesitation, "Those trees, sir, are *English plane-trees !*" There was a fine temerity, I thought, in addressing this reply to an Englishman and a landscape-painter.

A very precious man to me was François. He did not stay with us regularly, but came whenever he was asked to come, and stayed many weeks at a time, especially in the summer weather. I never knew a more thoroughly trustworthy, hard-working fellow, and he was skilful besides, being a wheelwright by trade, and quite capable of making or repairing a hundred things which we have about us in the country. François was the admiration of all the girls, for his handsome face and fine, tall figure, and he got married at last, and set up for himself in an independent fashion, before which, in the war time, he was taken for military duty, so it is now some years since he worked for me, but I shall ever remember his good, ungrudging service. He would get up when it was light, and work till it was dark in the evening, without haste, without rest, and always maintaining the same pleasant, cheerful temper. He worked just as well in our absence as when we were at home, at least in things that he understood. This man reminded me very much of the little demons in the fairy tale who were always asking for more to do. Sometimes, to quiet him, I ordered him to go and sit down somewhere and smoke a pipe. His manners were as good as those of old Pinard were insupportable, the only deficiency in him being a want of skill in gardening, where Pinard was a proficient. He would have been an excellent camp-servant for an expedition in some thinly inhabited country. I set him to build me a hut in a wood, and he did it with great rapidity and perfect skill, not requiring any over-looking of a minute kind. He was very strong and courageous, but as gentle as a woman, and I never saw him lose his quiet self-possession, even in danger. I often used to think how very different François was from the fixed conception of the French character which prevails in other countries. All his good qualities were of the kind which we are apt to consider peculiarly English. His caution reminded me very much of Yorkshire. Whenever I told him anything that he had not had the opportunity of verifying for himself, his answer never went beyond an admission that it *might* be so—never implied certainty on his part that it *was* so. The form of reply was always the same, " Ça se peut bien, Monsieur ! " He always spoke slowly, and after mature deliberation, marking the deliberation by the phrase, " J'ai pensé." For example, " J'ai pensé, Monsieur, que, si nous faisions les rayons comme vous m'avez dit hier, il ne nous resterait peut-être pas assez de bon bois pour faire une porte." And it always turned out that, when he began anything with " j'ai pensé," what followed was just the accurate truth about the matter. Notwithstanding his professional accomplishments as a wheelwright and rough joiner, François was always quite willing to turn his hand to anything that had to be done, though his skill did not always equal his willing-

ness. It is, of course, always so with a country ser-
want who has to do many different things, he cannot do
everything well. But François had the great advantage
over most others, that, if not always skilful, he was
never careless, and the more he distrusted his own
knowledge the more careful he became. He spoke a
simple kind of French, but very pure, without mixture
either of *patois* or vulgarisms. Of course he knew the
patois of the country, but kept it separate for use, when
necessary, with the peasantry. In this he resembled a
Scotch Highlander, whose English is kept separate
from his Gaelic. I never heard François swear, and I
never once heard him make use of certain expressions
which are quite common, even amongst the *bourgeois*,
but which are offensive to good taste. He was always
polite, but in a plain, easy way of his own, and he
behaved exactly in the same way to people of all classes.
There was a fund of quiet humour in his character,
which showed itself mostly by a peculiar twinkle in his
eye, when he heard of something ridiculous. He
talked little, but sometimes, when we worked together
at the hut or a boat, he would tell me a story, always
marked by a touch of humour and accompanied by
that twinkle of light in the eye.

I rather think that in this neighbourhood the men are
generally more careful than the women, and require less
looking after; but I remember one instance of carelessness which is worth telling. We had a young wild
thing to drag a light pony-carriage, so she took fright
occasionally, and more than once she smashed the little
carriage to pieces. After each of these accidents she

was so wild that it was impossible to harness her to
ar y ordinary vehicle, but I had a rough two-wheeled
machine to carry a boat, consisting simply of a pair of
very long shafts, and axle, and two wheels. Cocotte,
the little mare, was harnessed to this in her worst times,
and driven till she got tired and reasonable again   On
one of these occasions I told a man to grease the axles
before we started, and being busy writing did not look
after him myself, but simply came out and took the
reins when all was announced as ready.   Away we went
like the wind, and, after a drive more resembling an
antique chariot-race than anything in ordinary experience, we came back home again.   I then discovered, to
my horror, that, after greasing the wheels, the man had
forgotten to put the linch-pins into their places, and had
left them on a stone in the farm-yard.   It is wonderful
that we did not lose a wheel—if we had lost one, the
consequences would have been serious, and the man
himself would have suffered most, for he sat on a board
with his legs dangling, so that they would certainly have
been broken.   I, too, was to blame for not having followed the injunctions of a certain French hostler, who
used to say, " Passez la revue, Monsieur, passez toujours
la revue, et examinez tous les détails avant de monter
en voiture."

Female servants in this part of the world are
generally good-tempered, and become strongly attached when they are kindly treated ; but, although
they have nice quiet manners which would lead you
to think that they had some refinement of perception,
they are incapable of that delicacy of observation

which is necessary to a good cook, and even to a trustworthy housemaid. They come generally from peasants' houses, where there is nothing that can be called cookery, and where everything is so rough and strong that they can do but little harm by knocking things together accidentally. Whenever there is any refinement in house matters in the country in the middle classes, it is sure to be due to the intelligence and activity of the lady of the house herself. The ladies are almost always more or less scientific house managers, and able to do everything which a servant ought to do, with far superior intelligence and skill. *La Maison Rustique des Dames*, by Madame Millet-Robinet, exhibits this scientific activity in its full perfection, and the extensive sale of the work in France has done much to form a class of ladies who apply to everything which concerns the management of a country house exactly the same spirit of scientific intelligence and well-directed personal energy which an educated and zealous officer will give to the welfare of his men, and to the duties which he and they have to perform together. Nothing can be more admirable than this temper and intelligence in the ladies. They go through their household duty without having the weakness to imagine that anything can degrade them which is of importance to the health and well-being of the family, but they generally complain that the women require incessant looking after, that, when they have done a thing a hundred times well under the eye of the mistress, they will do it badly the hundred and first time, if the mistress happens to be absent.

The peasant-girls, they say, can never be taught to cook, except under constant direction, neither can they ever be trusted to wash valuable china or glass. One reason for this is probably that people keep so few servants, and so it is impossible to establish a sufficient division of labour. These peasant-girls will break a thin wine-glass, and miss the right instant for removing a pan from the fire, but for rough hard work they are excellent. They will dig the garden, wash the carriage, harness the horse, fetch water, carry weights, and all in the merriest, most good-tempered way, so that the harder they have to work, the more you hear them laugh and sing; but refined work is not their speciality. They are often extremely clean about their persons, and maintain a general decency of appearance which blooms on festival days into the *coquetterie* of a village belle. They wait very nicely at table, which may seem rather contradictory to what has just been said of their incapacity to learn things requiring delicate observation; but their good waiting is due to their natural politeness and great willingness to offer little attentions. Once in a house where they are kindly treated, they become attached to it, and will not think of leaving until they get married. Ours never leave us until their wedding-day, when the bridegroom comes, preceded by a fiddler all in ribbons, and takes them to the village church, after which they still belong to us as reserve forces. I have sometimes seen an old servant come to pay us a call, and quietly set to work just as if she had still been in our service, without being asked. Mistresses often treat them quite affectionately, and it does not spoil them, but the contrary. I have more than once seen a lady kiss the servant on leaving a house, and kind regards are sent to servants in letters just as if they were members of the family. This seems more human than the cold English way of ignoring the existence of servants or the possibility of their having any feelings; but when French people are very proud, which sometimes happens, they adopt a distinctly contemptuous manner towards servants, more disagreeable than English coldness. The *tu*, which is used from affection to children, is sometimes used from contempt to servants, by persons who affect to preserve the traditions of the *ancien régime*. This *tu* of contempt has always seemed to me perfectly monstrous, and if I were a servant I would not remain in a house where it is used. People who employ it have always at the same time a tone of contemptuous familiarity, a thousand times more unbearable than the distant reserve of the rich Englishman. On the whole, I think the French ways of treating servants best in small establishments, where there is no pretension; but, when there is any pride of state, the English system, of complete separation between the class which serves and the class which is served, may be more agreeable to both parties. French people tell me that, in great establishments in France, a class of domestics exists which has not the qualities of those simple-minded country servants whom I have just been attempting to describe, but then there are so few great establishments. The increase in the expense of living which has marked the last ten years is reducing

establishments still farther, and many respectable pro
fessional people, or small proprietors and fundholders,
who live where rents are high, are now trying the
experiment of doing altogether without servants.
The tendency in France is not towards English, but
towards American habits; the Frenchman does not
dream of some perfectly appointed English house,
with a trained domestic for each duty, but rather of
some ingenious machine at home, and a restaurant
next door, which would relieve him from the costliness
of *bonnes*. Let us hope, however, that the *bonne* will
never be totally extinguished, whatever she may cost.
It may be possible, though difficult, to invent a machine
which will do her work, but it is not possible **to pro
duce fidelity and devotion by machinery.**

CHAPTER IX.

WE have said nothing hitherto about the manners and customs of a little French town, and yet the town has its own life, which is very distinct from that of the country houses eight or ten miles away, and well worth studying on its own account.

It is almost a proverb amongst French people that *la vie de petite ville* is ruinous to men—or, rather, for I have a difficulty in finding a precise equivalent for the French expression about the matter—that it arrests the development of energy and paralyzes ambition. This kind of life is not generally, or often, ruinous in the sense of producing spendthrifts, for those who share it live generally within their means, but it has an evil effect in making men stop far short of their possibilities.

A little French city easily becomes a lotos-land of good eating and drinking and incessant small-talk for men who are either independent in fortune, or who have professions which will keep them without being very assiduously pursued. *La vie de petite ville*, is for men so situated, the very realization of that contented felicity which philosophers have so often dreamed of and so rarely enjoyed. It is so very complete in itself, it satisfies so entirely all wants both of body and mind which the average Frenchman feels, that he readily becomes attached to it, and sinks in it all ambition, all vain striving after wealth or fame, all eagerness to travel in other lands, to study other languages, to concern himself with things remote in either space or time. It is an existence incompatible with greatness, but most conducive to the happiness of the passing day and hour. A stern and strenuous moralist would condemn it for the absence of noble effort, but he ought, if consistent, to condemn equally the self-indulgence of people who live comfortably on their own means in England and elsewhere, and have no higher aim than the satisfaction of their own tastes, although their tastes may seem more exalted simply because they are more expensive, and include more locomotion, and the search for more various impressions.

The sort of little-town-life which I shall now attempt to describe is best enjoyed by a bachelor with a private fortune of about £300 a year, and a profession which increases it a little, whilst it just affords enough serious occupation to give zest to many hours of leisure, and keeps him in frequent communication with mankind, and gives him a knowledge of their affairs. He may be a barrister or a notary, for example, not encumbered with much practice, yet having just so much to do that the profession may have at least an ideal importance in his life, and save him from the *ennui* of a complete *désœuvrement.* He ought to be fairly well educated, so as to enjoy in an indolent way the conversation of the most intelligent idlers in the place; for although there is not much industry in the little society he lives in, neither, on the other hand, is there any blank stupidity, and although the conversation is generally light enough in manner, it often runs into arguments which require considerable information in the friendly combatants, so that a perfectly ignorant talker would find himself excluded. I dwell the more willingly on the intellectual side of little-town-life that it is generally ignored by foreign critics, from the total absence of pedantry in the speakers. They do not meet for intellectual purposes, and they often pass whole evenings together without talking anything better than the gossip of the neighbourhood, but every now and then they become an animated, and by no means uninteresting, debating club. At these times they are very like the talkative inhabitants of some old Greek city, with the difference that such French talk is merely critical in a provincial town, and has no influence on the course of affairs.

The long warm summers and the pleasant surroundings of a rural French town have aided in the formation of these habits. There are the avenues to walk under—fine avenues of elm, or linden, or oriental plane-tree, the green seats to rest upon and talk, the *cafés* close by, with their tables and chairs outside on the broad *trottoir*, the club-rooms upstairs, with their open windows and balconies, from which you have perhaps a view of hill or wood, or winding river. Then there is nothing particularly disagreeable in the little town itself—no coal-smoke, no rows of especially ugly houses, but the old streets are quaintly picturesque, and the new boulevard is bright and gay, so that one can walk pleasantly anywhere. And the country is so near, all round! In a quarter of an hour you have passed the old walls, and are in it, amongst the gardens. There are gardens, too, in the heart of the little city itself; the doctor walks in his garden, and plucks a peach, between the visits of two patients; the banker's counting-house is in his garden, and he walks about amongst his flowers, which refresh his mind with other thoughts than that eternal money. Little-town-life, all through the summer, is much more endurable than existence in the heated capital; there are so many shady nooks, so many bowers of greenery with little tables and chairs, and it is so easy to put cooling drinks upon those tables, and lounge away the hours upon those chairs! There, with unlimited Strasburg beer, and abundant tobacco, the Frenchman enjoys the height of his earthly felicity, in the soft air of a southern summer evening.

So far there is no harm done. It is possible to work very hard all day, and then spend the evening in a garden with sociable friends, drinking good Strasburg beer, without injury either to health or fortune. Many a man keeps himself strictly within the limit, dedicating the day to business and the evening to conversation. But little-town-life becomes dangerous when sociable people take to meeting very much in the day-time. Suppose, for instance, that a little circle of friends meet together every afternoon at the *café* to take absinthe before dinner, or bitters, as a preparation. Many do so; many meet between four and five o'clock, and sit drink-ing and smoking till six, when they go to dine. Evi-dently it would be better for their health to take a walk. But these are not by any means the worst examples of what little-town-life sometimes leads to.

The extreme instances of these sociable habits in their full development are the men, who, on getting up in the morning, go straight to a *café* for a glass of white wine, which means half a bottle, or sometimes a bottle. Whilst drinking this, or immediately after, they smoke one or two pipes or cigars. The conversation lasts some time, they take a little turn, or if they have any-thing to do before *déjeûner*, perhaps they may decide to do it. It is possible (we are supposing an extreme case) that absinthe may be considered needful to pre-pare the system for the work of digestion, which is a reason for returning to the *café*. The *déjeûner* itself is a great gastronomical piece of business, if the man is an epicure ; and during the course of it he will drink his bottle of wine. Then he will return to the *café* for his cup of coffee and little glass of pure cognac. After that he smokes, talks, lounges, does a little business of some kind, is surprised to find that it is already four o'clock, and time to meet his friends at the *café* again to drink beer, or absinthe, or bitters. Dinner comes **next**, and during dinner another bottle of wine is absorbed. After that meal, our friend returns to the *café*, and talks, or plays billiards, cards, or dominoes till eleven, smoking most of the time and drinking Strasburg beer.

We will leave out of consideration for the present the gastronomical part of such an existence, which is not the least anxiously cared for. The reader perceives that the habits just described keep a man in a state of perpetual alcoholic stimulus. One drink has not exhausted its effect before it is succeeded by another, and this from eight or nine in the morning till eleven o'clock at night. A series of small *customs* have so arranged themselves as a tradition from other *bon-vivants* who have gone before, that by simple conformity to these a man may be *constantly* alcoholized. The reader is not to suppose for a moment that such a Frenchman as I am now describing is ever drunk, in any degree perceptible to other people. He has always so perfectly the control of his reason that it even becomes doubtful whether he feels any pleasure from his drinking. Perhaps he feels no other sensations than those of the normal physical life, but the white wine, absinthe, red wine, coffee, cognac, beer, bitters, red wine again, beer again till bed-time, have become necessary to prevent him from sinking into mental dejection or physical prostration. The effect upon health, provided only that the slave of these habits does not smoke incessantly, and does not take absinthe more than once a day, is imperceptible in strong men for many years, and at the worst only seems to necessitate an annual trip to

take some kind of waters. It is probable that a delicate or studious person would soon find that this way
of life did not suit him, and, if wise, he would establish
private rules for his own guidance. Many do so and
take a certain limited share in little-town-life without
ever going beyond. Either they are never to be seen
in a café during the day, or else you will never find
them there in the evening. Others are members of a
club, and visit it once every two or three days. Others,
again, and these by no means the least sociable, never
enter such a place as a club or a *café* at all, but meet at
each other's houses on fixed evenings, when some very
mild kind of drinking goes on, and cigars are offered,
or pipes produced, but both are used in moderation.
The natural sociability and cordiality of Frenchmen
make little-town-life very charming when you happen
to get into an intelligent set. Even its worst faults
are due more to sociability than to love of tippling.

The effect on health of these habits is so imperceptible to an outsider that it is difficult to take it into
account unless one reasoned as temperance lecturers
always seem to do by taking the destruction of health
for granted, as an inevitable consequence, and then
reasoning from it as an admitted postulate. Of course
when health is destroyed by these habits it is an argument against them in those particular instances, and
you may even go farther and say that there is a possibility of danger to those who do not yet feel themselves
affected, but the destruction of health is not a certain
consequence. The evil which is certain is the enormous
waste of *time.* Little-town-life naturally leads to this.

The day is broken up .by pleasant little *causeries* at the
café, under the linden-trees, anywhere, and the whole
of the evening is given to billiards or conversation. It
is simply impossible to pursue a profession or any private study seriously without very strictly limiting one's
contact with a society of this kind. The great labours
by which many Frenchmen have distinguished themselves were not compatible with little-town-life. It did
not produce Littré's Dictionary.

Before leaving this subject altogether it seems necessary to say a few words about *cafés* and clubs. The
café, when used and not abused, seems to me one of
the most valuable of continental institutions. It offers
the easiest, cheapest, and most independent way of
enjoying the most intelligent society in a town. You
order a cup of coffee, or a glass of beer, and are free of
the place till eleven at night, with as good a right to be
there as the oldest *habitué*. It is this independence of
each person present which makes conversation better
worth listening to in a *café* than it usually is in drawing-rooms, where there is too much deference to the
lady of the house for opinions to be frankly expressed ;
or in dining-rooms, where the host exercises a too
preponderating influence. In the *café* your own chair,
and a few inches round it, are your private territory,
from whence you can express your real opinions with
the most absolute freedom. Good manners may sometimes lose by this independence—contradiction may
sometimes be more sharp than polite, more energetic
than considerate ; but amongst men who like to be able
to say what they really think, and to hear the real

opinions of others, the independence of each speaker gives a great value to conversation. It is a mistake to look upon *cafés* merely as drinking places or billiard saloons. In France they exist for conversation, and the best conversation in the country is to be found in them by those who know where the most intelligent groups are accustomed to meet. It is just possible that the reader, if not himself used to continental ways, may believe that what is called "good society" is not to be found in these places, where any working man may sit down and smoke his pipe. You certainly will not, in a provincial town, meet any one in a *café* who considers himself a particularly great personage—you will not meet the bishop there, nor the prefect, nor the head-master of the *lycée*, nor the chief justice, nor will you meet any great nobleman either; but you may meet the cleverest professional men, and if you are one of the many who esteem rich men's opinions as more valuable and instructive than the opinions of those who are not capitalists, you may be enlightened by the wisdom of a banker who has his million of francs, or a country squire who has its equivalent in arable land and forest. Those whose too great dignity of position excludes them from the *café* are not the wiser for their exclusion, but miss a good deal of acute free criticism which might be of use to them, and make them not live quite so much up in a balloon. The advocate of temperance will object that there is a great temptation to drink in such places. There may be temptation, but there is hardly any pressure. An acquaintance will invite you to share his bottle of beer when it is just uncorked, but if you decline he will not press you, nor will the master of the establishment ever ask you to order anything if he knows you. A teetotaler might order his cup of coffee, and have all the conversational advantages of the place. It is, however, not to be denied that the agreeableness of *cafés* often proves too strong an attraction for Frenchmen, so that at last they cannot be happy anywhere else, but continually fly back to them and idle away all their time there.

Clubs exist all over France ; they are often connected, for convenience, with a public *café* in this way :—The club-rooms are over the *café*, the keeper of which supplies waiters and refreshments to the members of the club, who by this arrangement escape from the inconvenience of having to keep servants and lay in provisions of their own. This system works quite perfectly, and permits the comfortable existence of very small clubs—a matter of some importance, as under the present laws a club is much more independent if it consists of less than twenty members—a large one being always subject to dissolution at the will of the prefect. There are often a good many clubs in a provincial town, each composed of people who can get on together amicably. A certain unanimity of sentiment is much more essential in a French club than in an English one, because the Frenchman goes to his club for society, the Englishman for silence. The French club, is in fact, nothing but a *café*, to which only certain known persons are admitted, just as the *café* is a club to which everybody is admitted. One French club, well known to me, was suddenly split into two parts by a difference of opinion about the propriety of illuminating on a public occasion, and nearly half the members quitted it in a single day. In clubs which exist for conversation it is impossible not to talk politics, and political divisions in France are too serious for opposite parties to get on together on the common ground of simple politeness. Thus in our city we have a legitimist club, composed of the nobility and a few legitimist commoners, and two republican clubs, one composed of professional men, chiefly lawyers, and the other for the most part of tradesmen. The reader will easily understand that it would be impossible for a republican to remain long a member of the legitimist club, because he would either have to affect acquiescence in legitimist talk or else live in perpetual hot water. One of my legitimist friends very kindly offered to have me elected, although well aware how little I agreed with him; but whilst you may have intimate and even dear friends whose opinions are strongly opposed to your own, and associate with them quite easily by mutual delicacy and forbearance, it is not so pleasant to be with people who are restrained by no considerations of friendship from saying everything that is evil of the men and measures which seem to you most worthy of approval, whilst they resent every attempt to defend them. After that I was elected honorary member of a moderate republican club, composed, as I have just said, chiefly of professional men, but including one or two bankers, country gentlemen, &c. Nothing can exceed the kindness and cordiality which have always been shown to me by the members of this club; indeed I hardly know how to give a complete idea of it to the English reader without entering into details which would afford to an ill-natured reviewer an opportunity for a sneer about gratified vanity. The reader knows what the French phrase *très entouré* means. When a deputy has made a speech in the Assembly which is much approved of by his friends, they crowd round him to shake hands. The same thing is done in a club when the members wish to make an honorary member particularly welcome on his occasional visits. I have often observed, too, that they will leave off a game which interests them if he does not join it, in order to make a circle round the fire to talk about something which interests *him*. Besides this, a theory was broached in our club, and for a long time steadily maintained in practice, that an honorary member ought to be entertained at the expense of the others; that is, supplied with unlimited cigars and Strasburg beer, or whatever else it pleased him to accept. A club of this kind is, in fact, as its French name implies, a *circle*—almost a sort of family circle. The talk is always good-humoured, and there is no end to it; but an Englishman's feeling after a while is, that it is a pity so much wit and insight cannot be ballasted with just a *little* more earnestness. The incessant laughing at everything, and at everybody celebrated enough to be talked about, is tiresome to an Englishman, who cannot help wondering how his French friends can live always on these champagne bubbles. We may easily, however, fall into a very natural mistake about the real temper which underlies this perpetual *persiflage*. We should be stupid to take it literally. It is a glittering play of light on the surface of opinion, but it is not opinion. There is a wit in our club who amuses us by his knack of making contemporary French history seem ludicrous, and he has especially the art of professing a profound satisfaction with things that are most unsatisfactory, till one begins to think that he must be Mephistopheles himself; but although the form of his criticism seems absurd, the ideas which lie behind it are those of a really able man, who judges of events with far more genuine wisdom than many a solemn-looking *homme sérieux*. The only sure way of estimating the good sense of people is to notice whether they are aware of the real tendency of events, whether or not they know in what direction things are going; and it is not always the solemn and pompous people, it is not even the serious and earnest people, who have this faculty in perfection.

Ladies object to *cafés* and clubs as a great evil in little-town-life. No doubt, from their point of view, it must seem an unkind desertion when their husbands are too regular in their attendance at such places, but the men are really very excusable. French provincial ladies who are what is considered to be thoroughly *comme-il-faut*, live so entirely outside of everything which interests educated French laymen, that it is difficult to express opinions in their presence without either going beyond the limits of their knowledge or else incurring positive disapprobation. Men like to talk together about politics, law, trade, &c., and when they are rather clever they like to indulge occasionally

in a little science or philosophy. If ladies could and
would take their fair share in masculine talk, on equal
terms, and not simply put a stop to it by the deference
and attention which they constantly expect, the sexes
would not be so much separated. The distance between
them is greater in France than it is in England, partly,
perhaps, because there is more ceremonial politeness, a
very serious evil when it reaches a certain point, for
men cannot talk freely when they may not contradict
without elaborate precautions. Frenchmen contradict
each other point-blank, it saves time and offends nobody ; but if (as is always likely to happen) they have
the misfortune to dissent from some decided feminine
opinion, there are ceremonies to be observed before
the dissent can be expressed, if indeed it can be
adequately expressed at all.

Ladies have much less influence in little-town-life
than they have in the capital. They have their own
little clubs, that is, they meet for charitable purposes,
and they visit each other a good deal ; but they see
little of the masculine portion of the community, except the priests. Ladies get up early, and the first
thing they do is to go to the daily mass at their parish
church, after which they look after household affairs
till *déjeûner*, and in the afternoon either sit quietly in
their drawing-rooms or else pay a call or two, when
they have not some work of charity to attend to. It
is exactly contrary to the truth to accuse them of much
eagerness about gaiety and amusements. Balls are
extremely rare ; as for the theatre, it is true that such
a building exists, but ladies seldom go there, except

perhaps twice a year to a concert. There is very little festive visiting of any kind. I cannot imagine what the ladies would find to interest them without the varied ceremonies of the church, their own works of charity, and a little small-talk. The reader perceives how impossible it is that a lady who takes the whole tone of her thinking from the clergy of the Church of Rome should be able to judge of great contemporary persons and events with any degree of fairness. The whole condition of her mind is so opposed to the modern spirit, that the things which seem to us laymen most right and just appear iniquitous to her. We can hardly talk about any contemporary event without, in some direct or indirect manner, wounding her susceptibilities. We make a remark on the reception of Garibaldi's Tiber scheme by the Italian parliament —here are half a dozen grounds of offence together. First, the lady, not having read the newspapers, does not know that Garibaldi is at Rome, and is displeased to learn it, because his presence there is an insult to the Holy Father; secondly, she does not like to be told that there is an Italian parliament in Rome—there *ought* to be nothing there but the perfect ecclesiastical government; thirdly, it is dreadful to think that the presumption of wicked men goes so far as to meddle with the Holy Father's own river whilst he is languishing in prison, cruelly held in bondage by that monster of all wickedness, Victor Emmanuel. We in our innocence may have forgotten all these things, to concern ourselves simply with an interesting engineering problem; we are wondering if the projected works at

Fiumicino will pay interest; one of us has been there and knows the spot, he has also seen an inundation of the Tiber, and has his opinion on the possibility of avoiding other inundations by deepening the bed of the river. The lady perceives the direction of our thinking, and disapproves of it. Now suppose that the conversation turns to something at home. Littré has just been received at the French Academy; we are glad of it because we know what a genuine, unpretending, wonderfully persistent and persevering labourer he has always been, and what gigantic services he has rendered to other labourers, were it only by his unrivalled dictionary, but the lady has been told that he is an enemy to all religion (which is not the truth), and considers his admission an insult to the Church. Or suppose, again, that we talk of contemporary politics, of the establishment of self-government in France, which has our good wishes for its success, she sees in our desire for the regular working of a sound representative system nothing but a deplorable error. All her political reading has been in such little books as Mgr. Ségur's "Vive le Roi," in which he condemns the representation of the people in parliament as *la Révolution*, "an immense blasphemy and an abominable theory, the impudent negation of the right of God over society, and of the right which He has given to his Church to teach and direct kings and peoples in the way of salvation." Her theory of government is simple and poetic. A king by right divine should be upon the throne, he should be armed with all power, and exercise it under the wise direction of the Church.

So when we talk of future parliamentary legislation, she both blames and pities us as men who encourage others to follow a path which can lead to no good, and as being ourselves not only deceivers but deceived Do what we will, it is impossible for us to touch upon any important subject without trespassing against the authority of the Church, which disapproves of all our works and ways ; she feels this by instinct, even when she cannot clearly define it. Is it surprising that men should meet together in their clubs and *cafés* to talk over the things which interest them in their own way, without incurring moral disapprobation ?* They want an atmosphere in which practical subjects can be discussed in a practical way, in which the deepening of an Italian river, the construction of an Italian port, the reception of a philologist at the Academy, the election of members of Parliament in France, can be examined from a layman's point of view.

French novels have encouraged the idea that Frenchmen are always occupied in making love to their

---

* The Pope gave Mgr. de Ségur an apostolical brief in favour of his little work " Vive le Roi." In this he expressed exactly the shade of feeling and opinion which is most prevalent amongst provincial ladies : —

" En effet, ce ne sont pas seulement les sectes impies, qui conspirent contre l'Église et contre la société, ce sont encore tous ces hommes qui, lors même qu'on leur supposerait la plus entière bonne foi et les intentions les plus droites, caressent les doctrines libérales que le Saint-Siége a souvent désapprouvées. Ces doctrines, qui favorisent les principes d'où naissent toutes les révolutions, sont d'autant plus pernicieuses peut-être que de prime abord elles paraissent plus généreuses." The last sentence is just in the tone of a rather kindly-disposed French lady when thinking of the pernicious opinions professed by her masculine acquaintances neighbours' wives. One of my friends who lives in our city asked me a question which I will repeat here, with the answer. He said, "You are a foreigner who has lived many years in France, and you have observed us, no doubt, much more closely than we observe ourselves, whilst you have means of comparison with another nation which we have not. Now please tell me frankly whether our wives seem to conduct themselves worse than English ladies in a neighbourhood of the same kind." I said, "It is just like an English neighbourhood ; one never thinks about the morality of ladies, it is a matter of course." This is a subject, indeed, which it seems almost wrong to mention even here, though I do so for the best of purposes. There exists in foreign countries, and especially in England, a belief that Frenchwomen are very generally adulteresses. The origin of the belief is this,—the manner in which marriages are generally managed in France leaves no room for interesting love-stories. Novelists and dramatists *must* find love-stories somewhere, and so they have to seek for them in illicit intrigues. These writers are read greatly in foreign countries, and as the interest of the story turns generally upon a passion for a married woman, an impression is thereby conveyed that such passions are the main interest of French life. It is also, I believe, perfectly true that there is too much of such passion in the luxurious and idle society of Paris, which is much better known to foreigners than the simpler and more restricted, yet in the aggregate incomparably more numerous, society of the country. All these influences together have produced an opinion in foreign countries which **is** most unjust to the ordinary provincial French lady, whose qualities and faults are exactly the opposite of what the foreigner usually believes. She may have unpractical views on politics, and not see the beauty of representative government, but she is thoroughly aware of the difference between morality and immorality. She may be uncharitable to Garibaldi and Victor Emmanuel, and have exaggerated ideas about the especial sanctity of Pius the Ninth, but at any rate she knows the Ten Commandments as well as if she were a Protestant, and keeps them. Besides her religion, she has too many home occupations for indulgence in amorous intrigues. Her time and strength are chiefly absorbed in managing a house with half or one-third the number of servants which English experience would prove to be necessary. She is like the skipper of one of those insufficiently manned vessels which have attracted Mr. Plimsoll's attention ; he does not simply command, he works, and so does she. It is hardly possible, after witnessing for many years the simple and laborious kind of life which these women lead, with that constant burden of petty cares and duties which they bear so bravely and cheerfully, to avoid feeling indignation at the absurd and monstrous calumnies which are received by foreigners concerning them. There can be but one excuse for such calumnies, an impression produced by a certain class of literature, and intensified by international ill-will. The reader who cares to have just opinions will only believe the truth if he simply takes it for granted that the virtue of the ordinary housekeeping French lady is no more questionable than that of his own mother and sisters. There are a few exceptions, so there are in England—the Divorce Court proves it.

The place of women in provincial French society would be stronger if they saw more of the men, and it would be better for society generally if the sexes were not so widely separated. This will become possible if ever women come to share the modern spirit, instead of condemning it as something wicked. It is indeed positively realized by a few superior women, such, for example, as Madame Edgar Quinet, but they are rare, and in country towns they would probably be misunderstood. It is not necessary that women should dazzle us by brilliant intellectual display, but it is desirable for us and for them that they should be able to enter into the hopes and ideas of laymen. The provincial French lady of to-day is a very respectable person, often, indeed, much more than respectable ; for the ideal she strives to realize is, in its perfection, truly admirable. But she is like the angels in Murillo's picture in the Louvre called "*La Cuisine des Anges.*" Those angels represent her very completely in their combination of a religious ideal with the fulfilment of the commonest household duties. The picture represents the two sides of her life, and might very well be entitled "The Allegory of the Good Frenchwoman." Two gentlemen enter on the left. They look surprised and out of place, and as if they did not know what to say. One feels that they will go to talk their own talk elsewhere, and are only temporary visitors here.

CHAPTER X.

The Author founds a Book-Club—How he managed to keep in the
Background—Friendly Suggestion of the Sub-Prefect—How
the Sub-Prefect was looked upon by Members of the Political
Parties—Wonderful Results of his Intervention—Withdrawal
of Legitimists and Republicans from the Club—Division of
French Society—English and French compared—Amenities
of Parties in Cromwell's Time—The French Revolution not
yet over—Contending Ideas—The Legitimist Theory of Govern-
ment—The Republican Theory—Bonapartist Opinions—Pre-
mature Establishment of the Republic necessary to get Popular
Education—Death of the genuine Royalist Sentiment in France
—Strength of Sentimental Loyalty in England—An Instance
of it—French Princes estimated only on their Merits—The
Count of Paris—He visits the Author's Neighbourhood—
Legitimist Enthusiasm in the Upper Classes—Free Elections—
Honest and Demoralizing Governments—Present State of
Feeling in Parties—Needs of the Country and Hopes for its
Future.

IN the last chapter we had a talk about *cafés* and clubs,
which leads me to give a true and faithful account in
this present chapter of how I founded a book-club, and
what became of it.

The idea occurred to me that there were enough
well-to-do men in the neighbourhood to make a club for
the circulation of books and reviews—all French, of
course ; for not a living human being in these regions
knows enough of any other language to read it with
any facility or comfort.

A foreigner does best, in my opinion, to put himself forward as little as possible in anything. He is looked upon by his friends amongst the natives rather as a guest than a member of the family. He is treated with great politeness, often with the greatest kindness (at least, I have found it so) but still he may do well to remember that he is not a citizen, and that a certain reserve becomes him. Thus, whenever I want to get anything done in these parts, my way is to keep entirely in the background, and set the scheme in motion through one or two private friends, under whose auspices it is brought to the test of practice, the public in general not having the remotest notion that " ce Monsieur Anglais " is at the bottom of it.

So it was with the book-club. I began by suggesting the idea to three men who belonged to three entirely different sections of society, and each went to work in his own sphere, with so much success, that in about a month we had a surprisingly long list of subscribers, when all the three lists were added together.

I now drew up a set of rules, very like the rules of such book-clubs in England, when one of my private friends asked where the club was to be established, and who was to be secretary to it. Evidently, we must have a room somewhere for the library, and a clerk to give the books out, and keep an account, and get the books back again (most difficult of duties !) from members who kept them indefinitely.

A most tempting solution was immediately offered by a friend who was also a member. This was no less a personage than the Sub-Prefect. It happened that in the courtyard of the Sub-Prefecture, close to the entrance-gate, there was a neat little building one story high, which served as offices for the clerks. There were several small rooms in this little building, so the Sub-Prefect showed me one of them, not occupied, and said, " Would not this do capitally for the library ? —you shall have it for nothing, and we can save the expense of a clerk, for one of my clerks shall keep the accounts and deliver and receive books. He has plenty of leisure moments, and he may just as well occupy them in this way."

Nothing could be more perfectly adapted to the needs of the nascent book-club than this most amiable proposal. The place was so delightfully accessible ; the building looked so clean and nice (it had some pretensions to architecture) ; then it was close to the gate, no house had to be passed through to get at it ; the clerk was there all day, and such a civil, intelligent, attentive clerk, that we might have sought a long time for the like of him ! " I will have shelves put all round the room for the books," said the Sub-Prefect, for it was part of my scheme that the books belonging to the club were to accumulate and form a library in time. In my innocence I thought we could at least accept these charming facilities for the first year or two, after which we might set up more independently, if necessary. Another consideration was, that I liked the Sub-Prefect personally. He had always been very civil to me, and I did not wish to refuse his amiable proposal. He was certainly one of the most intelligent men in the place, so that there was a certain attraction to the Sous-

Prefecture, as, when he happened to be at leisure, we went and smoked and chatted together in the garden.

All this only shows that a foreigner may live for years in a country, and be little better than a fool about it after all.

In those days we were living under the Emperor Napoleon III. Our Sub-Prefect was a Bonapartist, of course, or he would not have held that official position. Political reasons had never prevented me from being on friendly terms with any one whose acquaintance I liked to cultivate, and this made me forgetful, for a moment, of the intensity of political hatreds in the country where I now lived. This man and I had never once talked politics together; we had found plenty to talk about in other pursuits or amusements, so that he was not associated with politics in my mind. Not so in the public mind, however. The Legitimists all abominated him as the representative of a low usurper; the Republicans at the same time hated and dreaded him as the instrument of a tyrant who was ready at any time to repress liberty by the most arbitrary exercise of force, ready to cast them into prison or banish them to a deadly climate if they stirred hand or foot in the cause that was dear to them. When political differences are so profound as reach down to the nature of the government itself, official position does not command respect. In a country where the system of government is settled and accepted, an official is recognized by all as a legally appointed person. In France, under Napoleon, the prefects were respected only by the Bonapartists; the Republicans looked upon them as paid spies; the Legitimists despised

them as men who took a share in the booty of a successful thief.   Under every French régime the officials
are hated by the partisans of the other régimes, and
this hatred goes to such a length that men cannot tolerate each other enough to meet as gentlemen on some
neutral ground of literature or art.   Of course, I knew
that a Bonapartist Sub-Prefect would be an object of
political animosity to other parties, but I was innocent
enough to hope that this animosity might be forgotten
in relation to literature.   There was my mistake.   I
accepted the Sub-Prefect's offer, he put a joiner into the
room, who soon shelved it round, the clerk opened a
new account book for the concerns of the club, and I
congratulated myself on having concluded a most convenient and inexpensive arrangement.

Then came the storm!   The representative of the
Legitimists, who had promised to subscribe (a very ardent
Legitimist himself, and appointed agent of Henri V.), at
once told me in the most decided manner that neither
he nor any other member of his party would ever consent to fetch their books from the *Sous-Préfecture*, and
they all withdrew in a body.   Then the representative
of the Republican members of the club met me in the
street and said, " It is all over the town that the books
are to be kept at the *Sous-Préfecture*, so all the Republican
members have withdrawn their names from the club."
Now there were seventeen Republican members, which
in a small country book-club may be considered rather
an important contingent.   There may have been a dozen
Legitimists.   The next question was, who remained with
us ?   Had we a remnant strong enough to carry on the

scheme? There were a few Bonapartists, and a few
men of not very decided political colour who liked to
keep well with the authorities. Some books were
bought, and the club maintained a precarious existence
for perhaps eighteen months, after which it died of
inanition. Other sub-prefects have succeeded my friend
the Bonapartist, but I have never sought their assistance for the foundation of any more book-clubs.

This little history may give some faint idea of the
extreme division of French society as a consequence of
the events which have agitated the country during the
last hundred years. The English reader will no doubt
think of his own country, and congratulate himself that
Englishmen can meet on the common ground of literature, as cultivated men and gentlemen, without carrying
political animosity into everything. Mr. Disraeli can
subscribe to the Byron memorial, and Lord Derby to a
statue of John Stuart Mill ; our political chiefs of
opposite parties can profess respect for each other
without hypocrisy, and even meet in the same room
without turning pale, or pinching their lips, or chal-
lenging each other to fight duels. But how divided the
French are ! How they clench their fists, and shout,
and gesticulate, and jump, and scream in the National
Assembly ! How suspicious and uncharitable they are
in private life ! English people would never act so
under any circumstances. Would they ?

Let us not be quite too sure of this. The truth seems
to be, that so long as no fundamental questions are
touched, Englishmen behave very nicely ; but it is not
so certain that, if the most important questions, those

which divide men most, came to the surface, they would maintain perfect tranquillity of manner. Speaking of a sitting in the French National Assembly in March, 1872, the *Graphic* said in conclusion : " We may congratulate ourselves that in the British House of Commons such a scene would be impossible. With us, a member, however unpopular his opinions may be, is sure to receive a patient hearing." This was curiously put to a practical test in the same month, when Mr. Auberon Herbert supported Sir Charles Dilke's motion for an inquiry into the employment of the Civil List. A German who was present, the London correspondent of the *Allgemeine Zeitung*, said that a large number of honourable members " formed into a dense group in the background, set up a frightful howling, crowing like cocks, bellowing like cows or oxen, neighing like horses, braying like asses, barking like dogs, and mewing like cats—in short, a whole menagerie seemed to have broken out into a maniacal orgy." We all know that the House of Commons prides itself upon being, *par excellence et avant tout* an assembly of English gentlemen, who exhibit to England and the world the model of that gentlemanhood which foreigners do not understand. Now as we see that the members of this assembly, who sit so high above us, and are an example of manners for our study and imitation, actually bark, bray, neigh, howl, crow, mew, and bellow, when the question of monarchy is touched upon at its extremest out-skirts, we ought, I think, to regard Frenchmen with some indulgence if they do not always disguise their sentiments when their monarchical or anti-monarchical feelings are,

not merely tickled rather unpleasantly on the outside
by asking a question about a Civil List, but wounded
to the very quick, and that in the very sorest places.
If we go back to the times, now happily distant, when
England was distracted by disputes on fundamental
questions, to the times when there was a strong Catholic party, and a strong Absolutist party, and a strong
Republican party, we shall not find that our ancestors
used courteous epithets in speaking of each other. The
Royalists did not call Oliver Cromwell the Lord
Protector, they called him Noll, contemptuously, when
in their most civil moods, and the prettiest name they
could find for his followers was " Roundheads." On the
other hand, the Roundheads called, the Royalists " malig-
nants." It was not pretty, but it was very natural.
They could not abide each other, they hated each other,
as a gamekeeper hates vermin. Even so in these latter
years Frenchmen have hated Frenchmen when they
belonged to different camps. You cannot reasonably
expect a Republican, whose dearest friends were im-
prisoned, or exiled, or shot by the agents of Louis
Napoleon, to think only of his amiable qualities (they
say he could be very amiable in a drawing-room). A
Legitimist, on the other hand, remembers the death of
Louis XVI.—remembers, too, very probably, that his
grandmother had her head cut off, or that the family
estate was confiscated—so that he does not quite like
liberty, equality, and fraternity as understood by the
democratic party. The Bonapartists have had much
less experience of persecution than either of the other
two great parties, and yet they seem always to have

dreaded the possibility of a future application of it to themselves. On the whole, it must be admitted that political differences are very serious when society is living in a condition of suppressed civil war, with the recollection of civil war in violent outbreaks, and the anticipation of similar outbreaks in the future.

It is utterly impossible to give any conception of the present state of rural French society without some allusion to politics. The history of the book-club is a good illustration of this. There was an attempt to treat French society as if politics did not exist, and the reader has seen what were the consequences—he has seen how political opinions had their revenge.

When we look at the Milky Way our natural impression is that we are at an immense distance from it, and we are no doubt at a very great distance indeed from the suns which produce that luminous cloud upon our sky. But astronomers tell us that our own sun is really one of the stars of the Milky Way, and also that every fixed star we can see separately belongs to it. We ourselves are therefore in the Milky Way, and so is everything in our sky that we can see separately and distinctly.

So it is with the greatest political event (or series of events) in modern history, the French Revolution. To simple minds the French Revolution is at a distance in the past. They have read of its excesses in 1793, and the orthodox histories used to speak as if it came to an end at the happy restoration of Louis XVIII. Historians who wrote books of that class were afterwards rather embarrassed when the restoration did not prove to be permanent, and they had to speak of subsequent revolutions. Then whatever foreign opinion happened to be unfavourable to France assumed that the country was in an absurd and indescribable condition owing to the fickleness and unreason of its inhabitants, but did not see the one broad fact that all the convulsions which have taken place since 1793 are part of the same thing, the Revolution. It is a mere illusion of perspective to imagine that the Revolution is at a distance behind us. We are in it, as we are in the Milky Way. Some may think that we have as little chance of getting out of it as we have of getting out of the Milky Way, but I cannot agree with this opinion. In my view the French Revolution is really a transition from government by one order of ideas to government by another order of ideas. There is still enough vitality in the old ideas to make the establishment of the new ones impossible without conflict ; and the conflict has been a long one. It has lasted nearly a hundred years, if we look only at the surface of things ; but it has lasted still longer, if we look below the surface. It is not over yet; the youngest of us are not likely to see the end of it. But the new ideas are gradually gaining ground, which, if they lose from time to time, they always recover. It is a great error to suppose that the Revolution has no permanent gains. In reality, something permanent always remains ; some positive and lasting gain, not to the rulers, but to the general population of the country. The advance in general well-being, in practical civiliza-tion, has been much greater, and especially more con-tinuous than a superficial observer who did not live in

France, and was not acquainted with matters of detail, would ever be likely to imagine. A well-known English newspaper said two or three years ago that " after cen turies of agony and self-torture, France is simply the France of the middle ages, and no more." It would be just as exact to affirm that England is the England of Henry II., and no more.

The two orders of ideas which are still contending together may be fairly stated as follows :—On the one side you have the partisans of government by an authority independent of the nation, and on the other the partisans of self-government through elected repre- sentatives. Between these two is a third party, advo- cating government by authority, but claiming to derive the authority from the people in the first place. These three parties are known, all the world over, as the Legiti- mists, the Republicans, and the Bonapartists. The dif- ferences between them are, as we see, not superficial, but absolutely fundamental. No compromise is possible, nor any real reconciliation. The point of departure is distinct in each of the three. The Legitimist tells you quite frankly that a · nation has no right to choose its ruler, that the ruler is appointed for it by divine provi- dence, in the person of its legitimate sovereign, who may or may not, at his own good pleasure, call councils to assist him in the work of legislation and administra- tion. He is responsible to nobody on earth ; he is responsible only to God. The strength and liberties of the nation belong to him, to do with them what his royal will may dictate. This is really and truly the Legitimist theory, as it has been stated to me by ardent and active members of the party. After asserting the theory in this decisive manner, a Legitimist is usually careful to add that in all probability the government which he desires, if it could be established, would be as liberal as any. He will generally tell you that Henri V. would be a most liberal monarch, and would never withdraw those popular gains of the Revolution which the ordinary Frenchman values. This may be very true, and still the principle of legitimacy is to yield nothing in theory of the absolute authority of the monarch, and to derive that authority from a source outside the nation. The principle is a perfectly intelligible one, and there is much to be said in its favour. It is acted upon to a considerable extent, even in England. For example, Englishmen in general believe it to be a good thing that persons in authority should be appointed by some power outside the people they have to lead or govern. An English military officer is not elected by his own soldiers ; a clergyman of the Church of England is not appointed by his own congregation ; a judge is not raised to the bench by the votes of the criminal classes. We can see clearly enough that a king whose authority came to him from a source outside the nation would be more independent if the source of his authority were itself sufficiently august. In the legitimist theory it is so ; the only difficulty is to get people to believe in the divine origin of the royal right. The tone of all recent utterances of "le Roi" shows clearly that *he* believes in it. " I am what I am ; you must take me for what I am, or not at all ; I can yield nothing of my right ; I can make no bargains, for my right is inalienable." This is the spirit and tenor of those letters which, in reality, renounced a throne. There was a strong possibility of a restoration at the time of the fusion, and our legitimist friends disguised nothing of their thoughts and hopes. "The king will grant liberties," they said ; "he will permit parliamentary and constitutional government, but he must be trusted absolutely." They were most indignant against the "timid and ungrateful distrust" of certain more prudent Royalists, who wanted promises and guarantees. "What! cannot they trust their king ? Do they imagine that it can be compatible with his dignity to make bargains for a throne which is his own already?" We all remember Chambord's final answer—that strange document which seemed to belong to another age and another world than ours.

It is not possible to imagine a stronger contrast to this theory of government than the republican theory. The Republican does not believe in divine right ; but he, too, has a faith, for which he, or his predecessors, have been willing to undergo not a little persecution and suffering in past times, and which, even in these days, when the Republic is nominally established, cannot be professed in fashionable society without incurring a loss of social position. The republican belief is that the nation has a right to govern itself through its representatives. This idea is very familiar both in England and America, so that I need not trouble the reader with much commentary upon it ; but there is the distinction between France and England, that in England the chief of the executive and the senate are hereditary, which

French republican theory does not admit. For the rest, I believe that English opinion is generally nearer to moderate French republicanism, which is self-govern-ment, than it is to legitimacy, which is irresponsible absolutism. But I well know the difficulty of trans-ferring opinions from one country to another. For example (a very curious example), there are a very great many Bonapartists in England, with regard to French affairs, although there is nothing in English royalty bearing the remotest resemblance to the government of a Bonaparte. The explanation of this appears to be that the English Bonapartists think it a good thing for the French to be governed despotically, though they would not like to be governed so themselves, just as we think it a good thing for boys to be sent to school, though we should not like to be sent to school ourselves. I happen to be on very intimate terms with some French Bonapartists, and can tell the reader exactly what they think. Their opinion is, that the common people require to be governed by despotic authority; that they are wholly unripe for real representative government, but must be deluded by the semblance of it; that there may be houses of parliament, provided they have no power, or, at least, if there is an executive strong enough to veto their decisions.

So far as I have been able to ascertain, the real ground of the Bonapartist party is distrust of universal suffrage, accompanied by disbelief in the divine right of the legitimate sovereign. The idea of legitimacy is antiquated, but it is not, in the least, immoral. No dishonesty whatever is involved in it. The Count of

Chambord has acted in the most straightforward manner, and so have his adherents, except in the minor tactics of party. I mean that they have always enunciated their doctrines clearly, though they may have had recourse to occasional political expedients (which have always failed). The Republicans, too, are clear enough. They frankly state that they aim at representative government, by means of elected deputies. There is nothing immoral in this either ; it is an idea which has been approved of by some of the most honourable men in the world. But the Bonapartist theory is really, in one respect, immoral, for it would establish a government on popular support, and then paralyze the action of the popular will. All Bonapartists whom I have ever heard in the frankness of intimate conversation express the most perfect contempt for the political capacity of the people. "They are utterly unable to govern themselves, or even, of themselves, to choose capable representatives ; therefore they must be governed with a strong hand." This is the theory, but how to replace the Emperor when he has been displaced by such an event as Waterloo or Sedan ? By an appeal to universal suffrage, in which appeal the enlightened Bonapartists do not tell the people their true opinion of the popular capacity. I agree with the Bonapartists so far as this, that the people are not yet ripe for self-government. Clearly, they are not ripe. Very many of them cannot read at all, and few of the more educated are able to read with sufficient facility. The establishment of a Republic without popular education is unquestionably premature But now see the dilemma in which France finds herself. The republican party is the only party which will favour education ; it is even the only party which will not impede and resist it ; so that to get the people taught, the Republic must first be permanently established. The Bonapartist theory is that the people are politically incapable, and had better remain so. The legitimist theory is, that they have no need for political knowledge or capacity, since the sovereign, in his wisdom, will choose faithful administrators of his power. Of the two, the Legitimist is the more honest, because he makes no appeal to universal suffrage.

English readers will have a difficulty in realizing the nature of the one great obstacle which prevents the establishment of royal government in France. The obstacle is the death of the sentiment upon which royal families depend, or to which they owe their peculiar influence. An Englishman, and yet more an Englishwoman, cannot, without a great effort of imagination, conceive the total absence of such a sentiment, and the only way to do so is first to become *conscious* of the full power of the sentiment itself. Think of the difference between a direct command from the Queen, and an order or request from Mr. Gladstone or Mr. Disraeli ! We should all obey the first with a certain enthusiasm, with a certain emotion— the enthusiasm and emotion of loving loyalty—which no prime minister, however able and eloquent, could by any possibility excite in us. I will venture even to go a step farther than this, in a book addressed as much to an American as to an English audience. I will say, that many Americans (in my belief a very large majority of men and women in the United States) have a certain sentiment towards Queen Victoria very different from their sentiment towards President Grant. I believe that if Queen Victoria were to ask almost any American to undertake anything for her, he would undertake it (supposing the request to be reasonable) with a certain sentiment akin to loyalty, and not very distantly akin, earnest and convinced Republican though he might be. In England, notwithstanding the representative system of government, sentimental loyalty is as strong as ever. A wonderful instance of it occurred lately in the well-known incident of Miss Thompson's picture. The Prince of Wales said a word for it at a dinner, and the next morning Miss Thompson awoke to find herself famous, with a money-earning power multiplied by twenty. Nobody supposes that the Prince is a great art-critic; he has never pretended to be one; but he kindly expressed his liking for a picture which pleased him, and such is the power of royalty in England, that the painter of that picture instantaneously became the fashion, and wherever her pictures were to be seen they attracted the densest crowds, whilst the right of engraving two of them has been sold for twice as much as all Lord Byron's copyrights. This case is the more remarkable, that the influence was not exercised by the sovereign, but only by the heir to the throne. Such an incident could not possibly occur in France. There is not a prince of any family who could set so strong a current of fashion in a certain direction by the expression of his opinion about art or anything else. Nobody ever cared what the Emperor thought about art ; people used to say (I believe quite truly) that he was utterly ignorant of the subject ; and M. Charles Blanc coolly presented Troyon's name amongst a list for the Legion of Honour, though the Emperor did not like Troyon's pictures, and had said so. He signed the decree, and observed with resignation, *Il parait que décidément je ne me connais pas en peinture !* The Emperor's " Life of Cæsar" created no enthusiasm whatever, but was spoken of perhaps a little less favourably than if the author had been a private person. Prince Jérome Napoleon, a man of real ability, never got any credit for his abilities, except from a small circle of clever men who knew him quite intimately. The general public greatly underestimated him in every way, and believed him to be both dull and cowardly. The members of the Orleans family never get any more credit than they fairly earn as private persons. The behaviour of the Duc d'Aumale at Bazaine's trial got him a reputation for a manly sort of good sense ; but then he fairly deserved it. The Comte de Paris is very little known indeed, and although he is the heir presumptive to the legitimate throne, very few people take any interest in him. I remember a visit of his to our own neighbourhood just before the fusion—just before his journey to Frohsdorf. I thought I knew the people pretty well, and yet their unfeigned indifference amazed me. Suppose that the English royal family were to lose the throne in a revolution, and then suppose that the Prince of Wales of that time were to be admitted to England

again as a citizen, after an absence of many years, and
were to visit some ancient city, such as Chester or York,
not at all *incognito*, most certainly he would not be
regarded with indifference. At the very least he would
be a great historical curiosity, as the man who might
have been King of England, and who might even yet
be king if circumstances turned in his favour. Well,
the Count of Paris came amongst us, and people
scarcely turned their heads to look at him, heir though
he was of all their ancient sovereigns. He had no
reason to fear being mobbed ; he could walk everywhere
at ease, like any simple *bourgeois*, perfectly protected
from annoyance, not by public consideration, but by
public indifference. He was accompanied by a friend
who had an estate in the neighbourhood, and as the
two were crossing the square they met a councillor-
general. " Monsigneur le Comte de Paris ! " said the
prince's companion. " Why, what on earth are *you*
doing here ? " said the councillor-general, taken rather
by surprise, and uttering exactly what he thought. He
might have been more polite, but he just expressed the
general feeling. The townspeople knew who the prince
was, but did not care, and only wondered what could
have brought him amongst them ; as for the country
people, it is the simple truth that they really did not
know what his title meant, or who he was, or what
position he occupied in the country. He went to visit a
mine one day, and it happened, a few hours later, that I
visited the same mine. " You have had the Count of
Paris to-day," I said to the owner of the place. " Yes,"
he answered ; "he went all over the works, and when

he was gone I explained to the miners that he was heir to Louis Philippe, but they said he was no prince at all because he gave them nothing to drink." Active hatred would be a much more favourable sign for a royal family than this complete indifference. Hatred bears some relation to love ; it is the shadow of love, or the complementary colour of love, but indifference is the hopeless death of both love and loyalty. That tour of the Count of Paris was generally believed to have been undertaken with a view to test the popular feeling—to see whether there were any embers of Orleanist loyalty yet alive in the provinces. Shortly after his return to Paris, the next thing we heard of him was that he had gone to Frohsdorf, and that there was no longer any Orleanist party at all. The end of Orleanism caused no emotion, partly, perhaps, because public feeling had been a little hurt by the readiness with which the princes had claimed and accepted a large sum of money at a time of great national distress. Legitimacy was much stronger than Orleanism in the sentiment which it excited, and would have been irresistibly strong had its adherents been more numerous. There was a good deal of legitimist enthusiasm in the upper classes at the time when MacMahon assumed the Presidency. I well remember how most people who aspired to some social position decorated themselves with *fleurs-de-lis* in one form or another. The mystic flower dangled from gentlemen's watch-chains, and ladies wore it on their lockets. Still, it is impossible to say how much of this was really loyal sentiment, and how much the assertion of caste

and social position. The false nobility were very
forward in little demonstrations of this kind, to separate themselves from vulgar republicanism. The
Government always looked with a kindly eye on
legitimist demonstrations, and nobody was ever punished for displaying the *fleur-de-lis*, whereas people
were punished at once and severely for selling pot
figures with the cap of liberty. I always wondered
whether the royalist sentiment really existed, in its
genuineness, amongst the professed Legitimists themselves. I do believe that some of them felt it, but
certainly not all of them—perhaps not very many of
them. Orleanism was never a faith at all ; it had not
the necessary conditions for a faith ; the Orleanist
royalty had never been more than a royalty of convenience. On the other hand, the Republicans had faith
in the good of popular representation, and faith in
popular rights, which may account for the steady progress of their cause. They had undergone incessant
vexations, and small or great persecutions. Even after
the nominal establishment of the Republic, men were
looked upon by the upper classes as enemies to social
order if they ventured to advocate free elections. Men
of good social position, who declared themselves on
the side of representative government, lost caste by it.
On the other hand, I have heard, not once nor twice,
but frequently, the most outspoken hopes that if once
an absolutist government were established, the elections
might be put under official influence, and compelled to
yield results in conformity with official requirements.
" If the elections are free they will be bad ; in France,

the Government must make the elections; it is the only way to secure good results." This used to be said in the most undisguised manner.

The reader need not apprehend, in a work of this kind, any elaborate discussion of political questions, such as might be appropriate in a series of long review articles, with plenty of room for detailed arguments; but I may say that in my view the most demoralizing of all governments is the government which is really one thing whilst it professes to be another. A downright honest despotism may be terrible, but it is not disgusting or demoralizing. The captain of a ship is an honest despot; he does not profess to govern on representative principles, but his authority does not demoralize. A country may be governed like a ship; there may be a captain of the whole country who says, "My will is law," and punishes disobedience as disobedience is punished on shipboard. At the other extremity of the scale you have the honest popular government, which is founded, not upon the will of the captain, but on that of the inhabitants of the State—the government in which the executive only attempts to execute the will of the country, and resigns office so soon as it finds itself in opposition to it. But between these honest governments lie the varieties of dishonest ones, in which there are elections; but elections under official influence, with official candidatures, or else an underhand system of favouritism, by which the candidate of one colour is allowed to do all he can to advance his interests, and the candidate of another colour is hindered as much as possible. If there is anything in modern French politics which is thoroughly disgusting to a modern Englishman, it is the cool cynicism which often expresses a tranquil confidence in the corrupting powers of the authorities. The open official candidature was revolting enough, but there is a kind of candidature which is even more revolting than that—the candidature which is not openly official, but which relies upon official assistance of an underhand kind. It is, however, becoming every year more difficult for a French government to get elections done according to its own fancy. The electoral body has of late begun to perceive that it can have its will, if it has only the resolution to exercise it, and the elections become less and less controllable by the Government of the day. It may even be asserted that there is a growing tendency to vote for the candidate who is known to be disagreeable to the Government. This is not a good thing in itself, for the Government ought not even to have influence enough to cause the election of the candidate whom it dislikes ; but the consequence may be total abstention from interference on the part of the authorities, as it is becoming evident that their own interest advises it. In one department, the municipal elections and those of the *arrondissements* have been more and more republican on every successive occasion, in spite of great clerical and aristocratic influence. A direct interference of the authorities would produce radical or communal elections.

The present state of feeling (1875) in different

parties is briefly this: The Legitimists say the country is going to perdition, and express the utmost moral disapproval of MacMahon, whom they look upon as a selfish betrayer of their trust; the Bonapartists are discouraged for the present, but express a firm belief that, in spite of appearances, Prince Louis Napoleon is destined to be Emperor some day; the Republicans believe that representative institutions are gradually establishing themselves, or that the force of circumstances is gradually establishing them. Perhaps a foreign resident may have a chance of forming a more independent and more just opinion than many of those who are in the heat and dust of the conflict. My hope for France is, that a system of regularly working representative government may be the final result of the long and eventful Revolution, and that this form of government may give the country certain measures which it very greatly needs. A thorough system of national education is one of them, a real religious equality is another. These would never be conceded by a French monarchy of any type with which past experience has made the country familiar. It is something to have what the country has acquired already. It is a great thing to have, for the middle classes, so vast and (on the whole) so admirable an institution as the truly national French University, which, though often sneered at, both at home and abroad, has done much for the general enlightenment of the country, and is still continuing its work. It is a great thing that in a country where the great majority of citizens belong, at least nominally, to the most intolerant religion in the world, different, and even opposite, religions should be under the protection of the State, and subsidized by the State; although this may have the curious practical consequence that the State pays hostile sectarians for attacking each other from their pulpits. But these concessions are not broad enough for the wants of the present age. It has become desirable, not only that the middle classes should be taught Latin, but that the peasantry should be taught French, and not left in a state of ignorance like that of their own oxen. It has become desirable, too, that diversities of religious belief should be allowed to establish themselves openly in diversities of worship and practice, independently of State interference, and outside of the four categories which are alone recognized by the State. The only hope for these things, and for many other things which the country needs, and is beginning to feel that it needs, lies in the establishment of a *bonâ-fide* representative government; and as in France there is not the faintest reason to expect that the country will ever be blessed with a Queen Victoria, and a succession of monarchs reigning, but not governing, the only chance of real representation lies in the Republic. The present constitution may not be perfect, but I do seriously believe it to be by far the best constitution the country ever possessed, and the one most in conformity with its needs. One of its greatest merits is to provide for changes which are legally foreseen, and by that means doing much to avoid the danger of illegal revolutions. The French are said to be impatient. In politics they are scarcely, if at all, more impatient than the English They have patience enough, at any rate, to endure an unpopular ruler for seven years, and it may be doubted whether Englishmen would do more. Besides, a President could scarcely, in the nature of things, have had time to become thoroughly unpopular before the third year of his term of office, which would only leave four years of endurance for the country. He may even become more popular. MacMahon is decidedly better liked than he was at first. He will never get the reputation of being a clever man ; but there is a sort of simple dignity about him which pleases, and inspires a certain respect and confidence. He behaved well, too, and very unlike a tyrant, in rejecting the suggestion that he should appoint a certain number of senators by an exercise of personal authority. He has shown on one or two occasions a good deal of moral courage, and has conveyed the impression that he is a person to be relied upon. It is much in favour of the new institutions that the two first Presidents should have been both considerable men, though of such different orders. The country has been so deeply divided by tragic events in the past, by tempests of rage and bloodshed, that any immediate reconciliation between parties must be considered hopeless ; but it is by no means impossible that some time in the next century these deep divisions may be remembered by Frenchmen as we remember the events of the '45, or even the remoter contest between Parliament and the Crown. There

will be divisions still, as there are sure to be in
every healthy State where politics are openly discussed;
but it may be reasonably expected that political
hatreds will not be more deadly than they are to-day
in England, between ordinary Liberals and **Conserva-
tives.**

CHAPTER XI.

The Peasant World—A Modern Scythia—Tradition and Rumour
—Notions Current among the Peasantry—Slight Influence of
the Priests—Strange Notions about the Pope—Origin of
these Ideas—The Peasant Vote—Aristocratic Influence—
Republicanism and Bonapartism among the Peasantry—
Independence of the Rural Population—Bonapartist Propaganda—Cheap Republican Newspapers—Security of Property—The old French Noblesse—Its Oppressive Rights—
Royal Oppression—Present State of the Peasantry—Their
Ignorance—Their Intelligence—Their Good Manners—Want
of Patriotism and the Reason for it—Absence of Historical
and Geographical Knowledge—Absence of High Sentiments
—Rigour of Custom—Frugal Habits—The old Rustic Language—Specimens of Poetry—Rustic Singing.

IN the present chapter I intend to say something about
a class of persons of whom Englishmen generally know
hardly anything, and yet that class is the very bone
and muscle of France. I intend to say something about
the peasantry.

The peasant-world is a world by itself, and a very
vast and important one. How small and insignificant,
in the number of human lives which are dedicated to
them, are the pursuits of art and science in comparison
with agriculture! The farmer is everywhere, the artist
and man of science only here and there in the great
towns, or if in the country, isolated like swimmers in
the ocean. M. Renan speaks of states like France as
vast Scythias with little spots of intellectual civilization,

P

scattered over them at wide intervals. Our habits of life, our newspapers and railways, which bring the little points of light together, make us forget the width of the intervals and the millions of people who live in them. From the intellectual point of view, France is a Scythia with very small colonies of Athenians to be found in it here and there. The true Scythæ are the peasantry, the Athenians are the little groups of culti-vated people in the towns or the isolated ones in a few of the country-houses. In this chapter I propose to travel with the reader in the real Scythia, not with a comfortable travelling-carriage full of books and news-papers and luxuries which keep us still in Athens, but on foot amongst the Scythæ themselves. We will hear them speak in their own language, and see them leading their own life.

First, on the intellectual side, what is their condition, what do they know, believe, or think? A certain pro-portion of them are able to read, but few can read easily enough to do it for their pleasure, or for long together. The book and the newspaper have practically no direct influence upon peasant-life. In place of these, the peasants have two currents of communication, the descending current which flows from one generation to another, and the spreading current which flows out in all directions at once, as an inundation covers a wide plain. The first is Tradition, the second is Rumour. The two words are of course wholly unknown in the true peasant's vocabulary, but he will generally mark the distinction in the way he begins what he has to say.

1. *Les anciens disent que,* &c.—this is Tradition.
2. *On dit maintenant que,* &c.—this is Rumour.

The first answers to the history and poem of the cultivated class; it is their Henri Martin, their Michelet, their Victor Hugo. The second is the peasant's sub· stitute for *Le Temps, Le Siècle, Le Moniteur.*

The existence of tradition amongst uncultivated people is familar to everybody. We all know that there are traditions, and we have a general conception of the manner in which they are handed down from one generation to another, in the talk of the winter evenings. This has been so beautifully expressed in three of the most perfect stanzas Macaulay ever wrote that I cannot resist the temptation to enliven this page by quoting them :—

> " And in the nights of winter,
>   When the cold north winds blow,   •
> And the long howling of the wolves
>   Is heard amidst the snow;
> When round the lonely cottage
>   Roars loud the tempest's din,
> And the good logs of Algidus
>   Roar louder yet within ;
>
> " When the oldest cask is open'd,
>   And the largest lamp is lit ;
> When the chestnuts glow in the embers.
>   And the kid turns on the spit ;
> When young and old in circle
>   Around the fire-brands close ;
> When the girls are weaving baskets,
>   And the lads are shaping bows ;
>
> " When the good man mends his armour
>   And trims his helmet's plume ;
> When the good wife's shuttle merrily
>   Goes flashing through the loom ;

> With weeping and with laughter,
>   Still is the story told
> How well Horatius kept the bridge
>   In the brave days of old."

This is tradition; this is the way traditions are handed down amongst an unlettered people in the talk of the winter fireside. But Rumour holds her court in the market-place. The markets are the newspapers of a great unlettered peasantry. It is said that the news of any important occurrence will spread all through the poorest classes of India, with a rapidity which seems utterly unaccountable, and that it is not inaccurate. What I have seen of the French peasantry leads me to accept, without surprise, the rapidity with which news is said to reach every peasant in India, but what is said about its accuracy surprises me. In France the peasantry all know the same piece of news at the same time, but the piece of news is almost invariably a myth. What the peasants are saying and thinking in one department of France at any given time, they are saying and thinking in other departments a hundred leagues away, though there may be no obvious communication between them. The notion which gains currency is generally some notion utterly unimaginable by cultivated minds, and as remote from the truth as any misrepresentation of modern personages and events possibly can be; but a notion which is believed by millions in a country of universal suffrage may be worth the attention even of the enlightened. English people fancy that the minds of the French peasantry are entirely in the hands of the Roman Catholic clergy, but this is very far from being true; the peasant-mind seems to be almost entirely self-poised, self-centred, and to exist according to some laws of its own being, which for us are so obscure as to be almost inscrutable. I have often talked with priests on this subject, and they tell me that they are utterly powerless against the rumours which are the news of the peasantry. An excellent instance of this is the succession of notions unfavourable to the Pope, and to the whole priesthood, which pervaded the French peasantry some years ago. Evidently the priests did not set these notions in circulation, and they were as unable to contend against them as if they had been part of the phenomena of the weather. During the Franco-German war, the priests were universally believed by the peasantry to be agents of the Prussian Government, and whenever any priest tried to collect a little money for parochial purposes, it was believed that he sent it to Prussia. I need not say that such a suspicion was unfounded, but I may point out that it was exactly the reverse of the truth, for the priest was much more anti Prussian than the peasant himself. The priest had theological reasons for hating Prussia, which subsequent events have proved to be perfectly well founded. In this instance I venture to think that I can trace the delusion to its source. The belief that the priests were Prussian agents had been preceded a year or two before by another idea, to the effect that the Pope aspired to the French throne, and was only prevented from making himself King of France by a timely measure of precaution on the part of Napoleon III., who sent troops

to Rome to keep the bellicose Holy Father quiet.
This was the peasant's explanation of the re-occupation
of Rome by the French.   As the Pope wanted to make
himself King of France, he would naturally ally himself
with the Prussians, who were also enemies of France.
But we are not yet at the true origin of the notion of
Papal hostility to France.   The myth did not make the
Pope unpopular, it was his unpopularity that made the
myth.   What, then, was the first cause of his unpopularity ?   It is directly traceable to a certain trick about
franc-pieces, which was executed by the Papal treasury,
and certainly showed considerable ingenuity in the art
of profitable coinage.   There was a monetary convention
(still existing) between France, Italy, Belgium, and
Switzerland, by which the silver coinage of the four
nations acquired a common circulating power.   The
Papal State, which then enjoyed a nominal independence, did not join this convention, but the Roman
mint inundated France with franc-pieces bearing the
benignant effigy of his Holiness.   For a considerable
time, by the indulgence of the French Government,
these pieces circulated at their nominal value of a franc,
but as the Roman mint found the trade profitable, it
went on producing the coins in unlimited numbers, so
that at last the French Government was compelled to
announce that they could not be received by officials for
more than their real intrinsic value as so much metal.
Shopkeepers immediately followed the same rule, and
the Papal franc suddenly fell, all over France, to the
value of ninety centimes at the utmost, whilst many
would not receive it all, as it was no longer legal tender

Thousands of peasants had these Papal coins in their possession, and the peasantry feel a measure of this kind more keenly than any other class, both because they attach a greater value to small sums of money than other people do, and also because they hoard sums in actual coins. A peasant is always likely to have more silver by him than a squire. Well, the peasants found themselves suddenly losers of two sous on every Papal franc in their possession. If the Roman mint had deliberately contrived a means for making the French peasantry hate the Pope, they could not have contrived it more ingeniously. The very association of the Pope's portrait with the loss of two sous was enough to make him detested. The peasant contemplated the portrait at the very instant when the tax-gatherer or shopkeeper retained the two sous, and remembered that benignant ecclesiastical visage ever afterwards, just as we remember the face of some swindler who has cheated us. The peasantry knew no delicate distinction betwen the beautifully clever financial operations of the Roman mint and the honesty of the Pope himself—the two sous were lost for ever, and that was enough. After that the great peasant-world was ready to believe anything about the Pope, provided only that it was unfavourable enough. He wanted to be King of France. He was the ally of Prussia. All his priests were enemies and traitors. The reader may perhaps wonder how it came to pass that the spiritual functions of the Pope and his clergy were not sufficient to protect them from such a depreciation in the popular esteem, and it might be an interesting speculation to inquire whether a loss of ten per cent. on silver coins would be enough to make the Irish peasantry anti-Papal in a few days ; but, however this may be, I know that in eastern and central France, the religious influence of the clergy was quite unable to check the current of rural animosity. This question about the religious influence of the clergy will have to be considered more carefully a few pages hence ; for the present it is enough to note that the mysterious notions which pervade the peasantry are just as likely to turn against the clergy as against any other class. If we look to the other great power which has hitherto been supposed to command the reverence of peasants, the aristocracy, we shall find that it is not more safe, and that its influence, though often real, is always precarious. During the last three or four years the rural aristocracy have found it impossible to command the peasant-vote in the elections. The rural noblesse is composed almost entirely of people who, whatever may be the differences of opinion amongst themselves, are perfectly unanimous in hating the Republic, and in the determination to strangle or smother it if they can. They make every effort to influence the peasant-vote, and yet the peasants voted for Republican candidates, in constantly increasing numbers, until the Government of Moral Order·used its influence against the Republicans, through the mayors which it appointed for the purpose, after which the peasant-vote began to show a tendency in favour, not of Legitimacy, but of Bonapartism. The Legitimist aristocracy has done its very utmost during the last three or four years to secure the great peasant-vote, upon which everything depended, and we see with how little success. I can very well remember the time when the writers in certain English newspapers, who knew the French peasant no better than they knew the inhabitants of another planet, used to say that it was impossible to found the Republic, because both the nobility and the priesthood were against it, and nobles and priests would, of course, control the rural elections. It was not "of course" at all. In our neighbourhood the aristocracy and priesthood are both exceptionally strong. There are many rich nobles, and our ancient city is a cathedral city, with great ecclesiastical establishments. The clergy are universally anti-Republican, simply because they know that a Republican government will never restore the Pope to his temporal throne, and that it is likely to establish secular education and religious equality in France. The clergy are Legitimist, but in the absence of Henri V. they prefer a Bonaparte to the Republic. Our aristocracy here is as Legitimist as it can be, and on the whole it is a wealthy aristocracy, even yet. If the theory that the peasants obey the clergy and noblesse were a true theory, our part of the country ought always to return Legitimist candidates at elections, but what is the fact? The fact is that it always returns Republican candidates. Even in the very local elections, such as those to the *conseil-général,* the peasants exhibit this independence. You may go into remote places amongst the hills, where priest and noble may be supposed to rule absolutely, and yet find the peasants voting in opposition to them. There is a

hill-canton an hour's drive to the north of me, a place
lost, as you would think, amongst the deep valleys, with
the quietest of quiet villages for it *chef-lieu*, and at the
last election there were two candidates for the *conseil-
général.* One was the eldest·son of a monarchical nobleman of very high standing, a great proprietor in the
neighbourhood, representative of an old family, a man
of great ability and equally great ambition, who had
rendered very considerable services to the public ; the
young man himself was agreeable and popular, tall and
good-looking, an officer of Mobiles, greatly liked by his
men, who are all from his own neighbourhood. That
is just what in England would be called a strong candidate in a country-place, a popular young man with all
the influences, including the clericals, to back him.
The other candidate was a retired notary, living in the
middle of a hill-village—a moderate yet most decided
and energetic Republican in principles, and detested by
the clergy, both for his religious and political views.
This notary had never, even under the Empire, made
any secret of his opinions on any subject. When it
came to the voting, the young count, with the priests
and aristocracy to back him, got 700 votes ; the notary,
with the priests and aristocracy against him, got more
than 1,200.

The importance of the peasant-vote has led the
political parties to try different ways of influencing it.
The Legitimists use direct personal influence generally,
through priests and ladies, and the latter are excellent
political agents, because they go about in the cottages
and farms on missions of charity, or for mere neigh-

bourly kindness. The priest is a good political agent too, because he is always at his post, and always going about his parish, where every voter is known to him. We have just seen that the priest cannot make the peasantry do exactly what they "ought" to do, but the priest is nevertheless (as Prince Bismarck knows) the most persistent of political agents, and when he dies another succeeds him immediately. There are about 50,000 priests in France, and at least 100,000 active Legitimist ladies, all doing what they can to make the peasant *bien pensant*, though not very successfully. There is something heroic in the obstinacy with which the peasant-mind resists these male and female armies of persuasion. With regard to Orleanism, the difficulty is that the peasantry cannot clearly understand it. They do not know who made Louis Philippe king, or why he was made king ; they do not know who Philippe Égalité was, nor anything about him. Orleanism and its *raison d'être* are, from their nature, amongst those things which the uncultivated mind is always necessarily puzzled about. Many English people who can read, and consider themselves much cleverer than French peasants, are hazy about Orleanism, and could not give a clear account of it, whereas the nature of Bonapartism is quite plain to them. Bonapartism is plain also to the French peasant, and so is Legitimacy, but he cannot make out the pedigree of the Count of Paris. There has never been an efficient Orleanist propaganda amongst the peasantry, but the Bonapartists are very active amongst them, and know very accurately the nature of the peasant-mind. They have managed to get it very generally believed that Napoleon was betrayed at Sedan, and that he was a very good and capable sovereign, deceived to his ruin by treacherous subordinates in the pay of Prussia. This idea is now quite generally accepted by the peasantry, and it is only partially false ; for the truth is, that Napoleon was ruined for having trusted to incapable and untruthful subordinates, though they were not precisely traitors as the peasant understands treachery. As the reader is already aware from the newspapers, the Bonapartists employ photographs and printed cards as their means of making the Prince Imperial well known in the cottages ; their agents have worked in our own neighbourhood, and not quite unsuccessfully, for the peasant accepts the portrait willingly enough, and it makes him remember that the Prince exists—in exile. The results of these efforts have been visible in the increase of Bonapartist votes at the elections. The Republicans have done what they could on their part to influence the peasantry, but the strong-handed recent administrations have been so resolutely against them that they have worked with the greatest difficulty. Bonapartist mayors and Legitimist landowners might exercise all kinds of local influence with impunity, but let a Republican try to influence anybody, and the mighty hand of authority was down upon him at once. A vigorous attempt was made to establish little cheap Republican newspapers, treating of rural topics, such as might interest the peasantry, and including in each number a dose of plain intelligible Republican doctrine. The idea was good, but there were very great practical difficulties. In the first place, few peasants can read a newspaper, and fewer still will incur the expense of purchasing one. Then it unluckily happens that a newspaper is just one of those things which awaken the jealousy of authority in France, which always has its eye upon them. A cheap little Republican paper was like poison to the Government of Moral Order, which conceived that it had a mission to extirpate the virus. The writers, too, in these little journals had not the wisdom of serpents, if they had their stings. They were not prudent, they gave full expression to those feelings of indignation against powerful enemies which it would have been wiser to moderate. Half France being under the state of siege, nothing was easier than to suspend and suppress the journals and fine or imprison the journalists. Yet, notwithstanding all these impediments, the spread of Republicanism amongst the peasantry is one of the most striking, and one of the most unexpected, of recent changes. It is conservative Republicanism, of course, for the peasant is always conservative ; but it is only the more likely to last. A destructive Republicanism could only be a momentary aberration in the peasant's mind, and would be opposed to the whole tenor of his habits. Conservative Republicanism is quite in harmony with his habits. He is very independent in feeling, he likes to be free from the pressure of a powerful nobility, he has traditions of the dreadful time when his forefathers had to quit their own fields and leave them untilled, to slave for the noble or the king ; of the time when they had to be up all night through to beat the castle moats with long rods to prevent the frogs from croaking and

disturbing the repose of the *seigneur.* He remembers
still, through his traditions, how in the old times the
land belonged to the feudal baron, who had power to
compel the inhabitants of the villages to work for the
embellishment of his own grounds, so that the peasant
had never a week that he could call his own. These
recollections give him a decided inclination towards
modern ideas ; but one thing has until recently prevented
him from becoming Republican. His aim is to possess
land, and he has been told all along that the Republic
means the abolition of the rights of property. During
the last few years, however, he has made the discovery
that property may be secure under a Republican form of
government. He sees great *bourgeois* who have good
estates, and yet declare for the Republic, and then he
thinks, " If they are not afraid for their property, why
should I be afraid for mine ? " Once let the French peasant be completely delivered from the fear of the dividers
of spoil, " *les partageux,*" and he becomes Republican
very easily, from hereditary dislike to the domination of
the noble. Nobody has profited more than he by the
changes which have transformed the country, nobody
has less reason to wish for a return to the past. He was
a slave, and is a freeman ; he was a pauper, and is well-
to-do ; he was as powerless as his own geese, and now
holds the elections in his hands. Ignorant as he is even
yet, these things are becoming every day more plain to
him, and eloquent indeed must those persuaders be who
can make him believe that the old times were better
than the present.

It may be worth while to give two or three pages to

a slight sketch of the different conditions of the French peasantry in the old times and the new, and the more so that, in our own day, reactionary Frenchmen are always ready to tell you that the old oppressive rights were merely forms of taxation which modern govern· ments have transmuted into money. A foreigner is especially liable to be told that the feudal oppression was nothing but a reasonable taxation, as easily borne as the imposts of a modern government. It need not take me long to show how false and disingenuous this theory is.

The old French noblesse was a compact though extensive caste, as distinct from the *roture* as the whites in America from the negroes, and enjoying the most offensive powers and immunities. Many of its privileges were simply intolerable. For example, most Englishmen who have travelled in France must have observed the remarkable frequency of large pigeon-cotes about old castles and mansions, often in the shape of a round tower, detached from the rest of the building. The large detached *pigeonnier* has become so associated by tradition with the idea of the French *château*, that to this day, when a man wants to give an air of aristocracy to his house, he builds one of these pigeon-cotes. Well, there is nothing wrong in keeping pigeons at your own cost, but until the 4th of August, 1789, there existed a lordly right, execrated by the rural population, called the "*droit de colombier.*" By reason of this *droit*, the *seigneur* had the exclusive right to keep pigeons, and his pigeons, which were inviolable, had the right to stuff themselves at pleasure with the corn of their owner's

neighbours. It is the *droit de colombier* which explains
the existence of those enormous detached pigeon-cotes.
Not long since, in driving over a property belonging to
a certain French marquis, I observed a large isolated
round tower in the middle of a field, and was informed
by my companion that this venerable edifice owed its
existence to the oppressive *droit de colombier*. There it
stands, a monument of those oppressions of the past
which we of this generation do but too easily forget.
Besides his pigeons, the *seigneur* enjoyed a privilege
called "*droit de garenne*"—that is, the right of keeping
an unlimited rabbit-warren, the numerous population of
which fed on his neighbours' produce. Lastly, he had
an exclusive right to all other game. The peasants
detested these vexations, and were relieved from them
in 1789. That relief has been permanent. Before proceeding farther in the enumeration of the old grievances
of the peasant, we may observe that these two "rights"
were scarcely of the nature of taxation, as it is understood in modern times. Modern taxes are levied upon
individual members of a community for the maintenance of public interests in which all who pay taxes are
supposed to have a share. These feudal rights were
not in support of any public interest at all, but simply
for the pleasure of the *seigneur*. Well, if not taxation,
were they rent? A defence of them might possibly be
set up on that ground. It might be said that they were
manorial rents. There are, however, two objections to
this view,—first, that the loss to the peasants was not
accurately defined, as rent is, and secondly, that it was
not strictly limited to the manor, for the *seigneur's*

rabbits and pigeons might prey on his neighbours' land, whether within his manor or not, and they had no redress. The accurate definition of the *droit de colombier* and the *droit de garenne*, is the private right to establish public nuisances. However, these are mere trifles in comparison with the *corvée*. It made terrible encroachments upon the peasant's time, and for purposes which were absolutely indifferent to him. In the middle ages the *corvée* was almost exclusively imposed by the *seigneur;* but when the kings of France overruled the feudal chiefs, they imposed great *corvées* of their own. The peasant had therefore two *corvées* perpetually hanging over him, one "*seigneuriale*," and the other "*royale*." Private lords had the power to command *corvées* for the simple embellishment of their estates and grounds; they could compel the peasantry to leave their fields at the very seasons when it was most urgent that they should labour in them, in order to lay out ornamental grounds about the château, or to establish mills and baking-ovens near the château which were an oppression in themselves, for reasons which shall be given below. All this was terrible enough, but when the royal *corvée* was superadded, the situation of the peasant became such that we need not wonder at the horrible accounts of his misery which have come down to us. The King's intendants had the power to impose the *corvée* at will, for anything that might be construed into the service of the King. The intendants considered the peasantry very much as shipowners and the possessors of windmills consider the wind—a force provided by nature gratis, which it is as well to profit by to

Q

the utmost. When they wanted a road, the peasants were impressed to make it; when they wanted to build barracks, the peasants were called into requisition; when a regiment went from one garrison town to another, the peasants had to transport all the material belonging to it; when convicts had to be transported to the hulks, the peasants had to supply horses and carts, stage after stage, for the whole journey. They were taken from the most necessary labours of agriculture for all these compulsory services. They had to leave the field un-sown or the harvest ungarnered in order to give unpaid labour to the *seigneur* or the State.

I said that the mills and baking-ovens were an op-pression in themselves, so were the huge granaries of the château. All these things belonged to the terrible institution of the *banalités*. The peasant was not allowed to bake at home, his lord baked for him and fixed the price; the peasant might not keep his own grain, his lord kept it for him and charged his own price for warehouse-room. What an endless series of personal inconveniences and irresistible impositions, does this law of "*banalités*" represent! Peasants coming from a distance waiting for their turn at the bakery or the mill, not permitted to go elsewhere even in times of greatest pressure—useless to complain of the manner in which the bread was baked or the grain ground, and equally useless to complain of the price demanded! Is it not clear that a landlord who held his tenants by such a law as this held them not as tenants in our modern sense, but as serfs?

All these arrangements, the noble of to-day will tell

you, were simply "forms of taxation or of rent." If
so, they were terribly oppressive forms. They made
the-personal independence of the peasantry a simple
impossibility. Taxation paid in money does not touch
personal independence. The peasant of to-day pays
his taxes and is free. He can work all the year
round on his farm. He keeps his own grain, he
bakes his own bread; the nobleman who lives at the
château has no power over him unless he is his landlord,
and even then the power is very limited. Thousands
of peasants are landowners themselves, and independent
of everybody. They save money, knowing that they
may keep the fruits of their own industry for themselves and their children. The only remaining *corvée* is
the "*prestations*" for the repair of the country lanes,
and this is very commonly executed by the peasants
themselves, but it differs from the old *corvées* in two
respects. In the first place, the peasant is not compelled
to come and work on fixed days; he is simply served
with a notice that he has to carry a certain quantity of
stone within a certain space of time, a large latitude
being allowed for his convenience. Secondly, in case
the peasant should be too busy to do the work in his
own person or that of his servants, the option of a
money-payment is offered to him, and the money-
payment is so equitably fixed that I generally prefer it.
Finally, I may observe that the country lanes are
especially for the use of the peasantry themselves,
whilst the baron's garden was for his own pleasure.

The peasantry of to-day are, on the whole, as happy
a class of people as their forefathers were wretched,

and the improvement is simply due to those political reforms which have left the natural prudence and industry of the class full liberty to lead it to prosperity. One of the strongest reasons for the increasing Republicanism of the peasantry is their recent belief that if Henri V. came to the throne he would re-establish the old *corvées*—a very erroneous notion, of course, like all the ideas which suddenly gain. currency in the uncultivated world, but it has served the Republic well. A Royalist told me that he believed this idea had been industriously spread amongst the peasants by the Republican propaganda. Very likely the Republicans may have done their best to propagate it, and yet all such efforts would be utterly useless if there were not a tide of peasant-rumour and peasant-opinion to circulate the idea, a tide which no art, craft, wisdom, or knowledge of the instructed classes can either foresee or direct, and against which even the prodigiously strong and minutely perfect organization of the Church of Rome is utterly unable to contend.

The ignorance of the French peasantry is difficult to believe when you do not know them, and still more difficult when you know them well, because their intelligence and tact seem incompatible with ignorance. The truth seems to be that the peasant is intelligent in his own sphere, but absolutely ignorant of everything outside it. He does not feel the need of knowing more. He lives in a world so large and so visibly important, the peasant-world, that its opinion of what is necessary seems the final decision of common-sense. All men who are occupied in the principal industry of a country acquire the habit of an absolute reliance on their own standard—the firm belief in their own sufficiency. The utility of their practical work answers for them. Our own English middle-class Philistine, and the French *bourgeois*, both know that there is such a thing as culture, but despise it, and their practical success proves to their own satisfaction that culture, to say the least, is superfluous. The French peasant is not Philistine, he has not any contempt for culture, he simply does not know that there is such a thing. He does not know that science and art and literature exist; perhaps he might think them a frivolous waste of time if he were aware of their existence, but not being aware, he has no Philistine determination to be stupid, no conscious obstructiveness. A very curious result of this condition is that the peasant, in our part of France at least, always seems to have great openness of mind, and seems much less narrow than the *bourgeois*, who knows what is above him and sneers at it. Millet, the painter, whose death has recently called especial attention to his representation of rural life, has in my opinion done the French peasant less than justice on the side of intelligence. He represents him as a being in whom intelligence is extinguished under a fearful burden of honourable yet deadening toil—a being fulfilling its duties like some patient animal darkly labouring for humanity. This is not true of the French peasantry round my house. They are at the same time full of intelligence, and inconceivably ignorant. Their manners are excellent, they have delicate perceptions, they have tact, they have a certain refinement which a brutalized peasantry could not possibly have. If you talk to one of them at his own house or in his field, he will enter into conversation with you quite easily, and sustain his part in a perfectly becoming way, with a pleasant combination of dignity and quiet humour. The interval between him and a Kentish labourer is enormous. After being accustomed to the French peasants, I happened to find myself for a week in a Kentish village, and tried to make out what I could of the rustic mind round about it, but it seemed as if I encountered a thick dense wall of muddy dulness and obstructiveness. Hodge did not appear to think that any interchange of ideas between me and him could benefit either of us, and I quickly became of Hodge's opinion. Talk to a French peasant, and he will enter into your ideas if he can ; talk to Hodge, and he will stare at you.

It is a pity that so much civilization as the rustic Frenchman possesses already cannot be enriched with a little more knowledge. His ignorance is incredible. He does not really know what the word *France* means. During the Franco-German war many patriotic Frenchmen were indignant at the conduct of the peasantry, at their indifference to the invasion of Alsatia and Lorraine, and generally at the small amount of patriotic sentiment which they exhibited. But if we really enter into the rustic mind, we shall not be surprised at its insensibility to patriotic appeals. Fancy the condition of a mind which has *no* geographical knowledge! I knew an old peasant who sometimes asked me where places were, and his way was this : he would ask me to point in the direction of the place, and when two places happened to lie in the same direction, it was almost impossible to make him understand that they were not on the same spot. Rustics who are quite ignorant of geography cannot have clear conceptions about so large a country as France, which has four times the area of England, and nearly twice that of all the British Islands put together. You tell them that the war has ended in the loss of Alsatia and Lorraine. This conveys no distinct idea to their minds—why should they make sacrifices for the people of Alsatia, who were always as foreigners to them? The mind is limited to what it can in some measure conceive. The great modern States can only be imagined by the educated, and this of itself is a sufficient reason why they should educate their inhabitants. *

If the peasant cannot imagine what France is, still less does he know of foreign States. How near Switzerland is—so near that the Alps are visible at certain times from all the hill-tops in this neighbourhood! Well, the greater part of the peasantry here have never heard of Switzerland. England they have

---

* We knew a peasant-girl who was servant in a family which removed to a distance of about eighty miles, but still remained in central France. All the girl's family made great opposition to this, and wished the girl to leave her place, because they would have it that the new residence was *not in France.* Reference to the map was useless. The girl accompanied her mistress, but soon received a letter, saying that her reputation was lost in her own village, because she had gone to misconduct herself *in foreign parts.* After that, her peasant relations, who were well-to-do people, declared they would disinherit her, if she did not go back to her own country. So she quitted (in tears) an affectionate mistress to return to her native village.

heard of, but do not know where it is, and they con-
found together London and England, when they have
heard of London by chance, thinking that London is
the nation.   I knew one who thought that London was
in France, and that people might go to it by land or
water, at their own choice.   This ignorance of geography
produces the oddest effects when the peasants get hold
of names of countries by accident, as will sometimes
happen in the most unaccountable ways.   One of them
told me that he had heard there was going to be a war
between Italy and Lapland.   It was surprising to me
that he should have heard of Italy,* but still more
astonishing that he should have heard of Lapland.   I
tried to show by geographical and political reasons
that this war was very improbable, but did not succeed
in removing the apprehension of it.

The historical notions of a perfectly illiterate people
are very vague traditions.   We all know that it is
difficult to remember history accurately without going
into minute detail, and that the details themselves can
only be retained when they illustrate some particular
period which has an especial interest for us.   Our
historical knowledge, with all the aids of books, is so
inaccurate that few of us could pass an examination
in more than our favourite century, and we should be
lucky if we passed in that.   What, then, should we be
without the books?   What is the peasant, who has no
books?   Here we come to one of those subjects which

* The peasant has heard of Rome, and thinks that the Pope is
a terrible military sovereign, always likely to invade France, but
he is not yet generally aware of the unification of Italy.

always seem to me most suggestive of painful reflections. Bad as the past was for the peasant, bad as the
times were when Richelieu and the Abbé Fleury held
on principle that he ought not to read or write, when
the Dutch proverb, "*Een boer is een beest,*" was only too
true of peasantries everywhere, there were men and
deeds in those times for a great nation to be proud of.
It is therefore deplorable that the majority of a nation
should ever forget its past, or that it should have such
vague ideas about its past as those of the uneducated
classes. A French peasant, so far as I have been able to
make out, really remembers nothing of the past but its
evils, the grinding oppression of the *corvée* and the horror
of the *guerres de religion.* "Speak to a peasant," says M.
Renan, "or to a Socialist of the International, of France,
of her past, of her genius, he will not understand such
language. Military honour, from this narrow point of
view, seems folly ; the taste for what is great, the glory
of the mind, are chimeras ; money spent for art and
science is money throw away, spent foolishly." There
cannot be any noble national feeling, in modern times,
amongst the totally uneducated peasantry of a great
State, simply because they have never heard of what is
truly glorious in the past, and can have no sense of those
obligations which belong to the successors of brave and
noble persons. Renan affirms that "The noble cares of
old France, patriotism, enthusiasm for the beautiful, the
love of fame, have disappeared with the noble classes
which represented the soul of France." They have not
wholly disappeared, they exist still in the cultivated
classes, but it is useless to seek them in the peasantry

until it also is educated. M. Renan thinks that the
rural democracy is Royalist in the sense that it will
accept a dynasty of some sort, but that it is not Royalist
enough to care which dynasty; that it will make no
sacrifice for the establishment of any one of them, and
has no political idealism of any kind whatever. This
total absence of political idealism in the peasantry is
due to pure ignorance, but it has been a happy thing
for the country in preventing an extensive civil war.
France is a mixture of a little gunpowder with a great
deal of sand—the citizens of the large towns are the
gunpowder, the peasantry are the sand; if all were
gunpowder the country would explode all over, but the
sand prevents it.

The separation of the peasantry from the other classes
is marked by the most striking differences of custom.
Here let me observe that the rigour of custom is far
greater amongst the peasants than it is with the *bourgeoisie* and *noblesse.* Custom regulates everything for the
peasant with an iron rule. The customs are frugal in the
extreme, and act as an effectual sumptuary law in re-
straining any possible extravagance of the richer members of the class. There are some visible signs of the
weakening of rustic custom, but up to the present day
it still retains an enormous power in rustic public
opinion. Consider the difference, for example, between
the degree of liberty enjoyed in the middle classes in
matters of dress, and the severity of custom in the
peasantry. The *bourgeois* may wear a coat of any
colour he chooses. The peasant must wear a blouse,
and the blouse must be blue. Peasants of the same

age always wear the same kind of hat, the same texture of linen, and when they buy a cloak—in these parts at least—it is always sure to be of a brownish grey, with brown stripes, of one particular pattern. Custom, indeed, has been powerful enough to put all the class into uniform. In the furniture of their houses the peasants are equally regulated by fixed usages. The cabinet-maker's work is always of walnut, and nearly of the same design. The bed, the linen-press (*armoire*), and the clock are the three items to which most care is given. Sometimes you will find two beds, two *armoires*, and two clocks in the same room, one set belonging to the parents, the other to a married son. The women are proud of their *armoires*, which are prettily panelled, and they rub the panels till they shine. As the furniture and manner of life in the peasants' houses is always exactly the same in the same class, and as the people all dress exactly alike, and all know the same things, and are equally ignorant of everything else, the consequence must be, and is, a wonderful narrowness of experience in the class, and a corresponding mental narrowness. When rich Englishmen visit each other's houses, they find differences which stimulate and instruct. There are differences of domestic architecture. The libraries contain different books, there are different artistic and other collections to be seen, and all these things enlarge experience. But when the French peasant goes to another peasant's house, he finds exactly the same things that he left behind him at home, and nothing to enlarge experience in any way—no books, no newspapers, no varieties of education in the inhabitants. This excessive uniformity in everything is one of the main reasons why the peasant remains so decidedly the peasant, and why those members of the class who get any education never can endure to remain within it. I know a good many sons of peasants who have left the class to enter the smaller *bourgeoisie* in some occupation outside of rustic life, because the true rustic life had become unendurable to them from its narrowness and the rigidity of its customs. The only way for the educated son of a peasant to remain rustic is to become a country priest ; then he can live in relations with the peasantry which are at the same time familiar enough for him to feel no painful separation, and yet of a kind which keeps him distinct and independent, and allows him to read and think, with the infinite advantage of solitude, at will. The excessive rigour of rural custom is beneficial in a very simple-minded and ignorant class, which thus finds its path traced beforehand in everything. Simple duties, unchanging fashions, a settled rule of life, are the safety of an ignorant population, but too confining for an enlightened one. The rural French customs imply the constant practice of very great virtues—temperance, frugality, industry, patience, self-control, and self-denial. In all these virtues, the peasant acts as none but a saint or hero could act if he were alone, but he is wonderfully sustained and encouraged by the custom of his class. His character is all in one piece, and ignorance appears to be an essential part of it. No educated person would have patience to endure his monotonous toil, or the simplicity of his fare ; and the peasants themselves are fully aware of this, for they dread books and education, saying, with perfect truth, that they unfit men for steady work at the plough. Another almost inevitable effect of education is to make people appreciate and want good scientific cookery. All the educated classes in France like good eating, and the peasant, from his frugal point of view, thinks that they live most extravagantly. He is right in dreading the effects of books and newspapers on his sons. He likes to keep his sons illiterate, for he knows, by an infallible class-instinct, that the old rural life, whose virtues he appreciates and values, will be a thing of the past when Knowledge enters the homestead, with her half-sisters, Luxury and Discontent.

The books too—the clever French books, all written by University men—will destroy the old rustic language, that living chain of custom and ancient usage. What do the clever book-writing men know of the old tongue and its beloved associations with fields, and streams, and woods, and long-past summers and loves, and winters and sorrows? The rustic language varies from plain to plain, from valley to valley; there are endless varieties of *patois* in France. That spoken amongst the hills near my house is so distinct from ordinary French, that it took me a long time to understand it; and even now, when it is spoken in perfect purity, I have to listen very attentively. Would the reader like to see a specimen of it? Here is a charming little song, which we know positively to be centuries old. Some rustic composed it in the dark days of the *corvées*, and yet it is full of gaiety, and has the touch of a true poet,

The conclusion is admirable in its lively truth to
nature.   The lad calls his sweetheart and his cows at
the same time :—

> " Hô mon petiot feillot
> Lère et lo, lère et lère et lo,
> Lère et lo, hô !
> Ailon voui dézeuné
> Lo, lo, lère lo, lère et lère,
> Aipourte ton pain frô,
> Mai mie, lère et lère, lolère lère et lo !

> " Aipourte ton pain frô,
> Du coûtié du Lon-pré
> Au deçô dé Pintiô ;
> Au deçô dé Pintiô
> Ie t'y feré tâté
> Du mitan de mon gâtiau,

> " Du mitan de mon gâtiau
> Que te troúrez secré
> Mâ secré coum' o fô

> " Ma secré coum' o fô.
> Quan t' l'airez aivolé
> O ne te f'ré point de mau,

> " O ne te f'ré point de mau ;
> Ai peû te beilleré
> Quéque cou de béquo.

> " Quéque cou de béquo,
> De béquo d'aimitié
> Que ne me f'ront point d'mau !

> " Hô Piarotte, hô Piarotte
> Ven don viaz yt'chi !
> Vô lé ôte, vô lé ôte,
> Yt'chi ! tâ !
> Beurnotte,
> Fringotte,
> Métrillère,
> Metrichaude,

Corbinette,
Jeannette,
Brunette,
Jolivette,
Blondine,
      Yt'chi l tâ l
   Tâ l lâ l tâ l tâ l tâ l"

The following is a specimen of the modern *patois*, differing very little from that of two hundred years ago :—

" O diont tôs que laï milice
  Vé tiré le moué preuçaing,
  Qu'iot pôr c'lai qu'o faut qui m'mairisse
  Aitout lai feill' de nout' voising.
  O diont tôs qu'al ot ben zente,
  Qu'al ot donc' c'ment in aigniau
  Iot ben c'lai qu'iai pou qu'al me pliante
  Deux plieumes de bœu sôs mon çaipiau !

" De tôs las gas de nout' velaize
  Çaiquing l'y beille in présent :
  L'in l'y beill' de lai dentéle
  L'aut' l'y beille eune croué d'arzent
  Al dit ben que ran n'lai tente,
  Pas moîme in torse-musiau . . . . . .
  Iot ben c'lai, &c.

" Çartaing bôrjois de lai ville
  Haibillé en fignôleux,
  Tôrne alientôr de c'te feille
  Coume en mainiér' d'aimôreux ;
  O lai loisse, o lai tôrmente,
  O lai vir' c'ment in fusiau . . . .
  Iot ben c'lai, &c."

I have not space for all the song, these three stanzas are only the beginning of it, but there is perhaps as much as the reader will trouble himself to translate. It would spoil his pleasure to translate the stanzas for him, and I avoid the task the more willingly that it is by no means an easy one. Poetry is always spoiled in translation, and the perfume of these genuine rustic stanzas evaporates altogether when we attempt to transfer it to a complex and elaborate language like English. Fancy translating "cou de béquo," *strokes with a beak.* In the original, it is merely a peasant's playful way of saying *kisses;* but if, on the other hand, we say *kisses* in a translation, then we utterly miss the playfulness of the original. One or two words may be explained as a help. *O* is a general pronoun. *lot* means *it is. O diont, on dit.* There is a very lively touch in the last line but one,

" O lai vir c'ment in fusiau."

"They (*i.e.,* the *bourgeois*) turn her about like a spindle," an allusion to the waltzing in the village, in which the *bourgeois* easily beats the rustic, to the disgust of the latter, especially as the young women are at no pains to conceal their satisfaction at finding dancers who can twist them round with the proper degree of skill.

I have heard scores of such songs as these in the farms and villages, often sung with the greatest skill and taste. Many of the women have excellent voices, and manage them with much art, which has become a tradition. The music, however, is monotonous, or seems so to us. It is very often in minor keys. I have thought sometimes that it would be well worth while to collect the airs sung by the peasantry amongst the hills, for they are full of originality, although pervaded by a striking similarity of sentiment, or sentiments, for there are two classes of songs, the gay and the sad, but the first is more common. Of the two specimens just given, the reader is especially invited to notice the ending of the first, which is most brilliant. The singer calls the cows with a musical cry, and the end is a burst like the *roulade* of a nightingale. The peasants sing with great decision and confidence ; the best singers soon get a reputation in their own and the neighbouring villages, which encourages them. The constant practise of simple airs, in accordance with fixed traditional rules, permits the attainment of really considerable skill, in its own peculiar kind. I have heard women sing, with wonderful rapidity, long passages, in which the slightest hesitation or slip of memory would have been fatal to the effect, but they always got through triumphantly, with a shrill, voluble, *prestissimo* at the end, terminating in a *coup-d'éclat* like the song of a wild bird.

CHAPTER XII.

ALTHOUGH the whole of the last chapter was occupied
with the peasantry, the subject overflows into this. It
would be easy to write a volume on the mind and
habits of a class which has such decided ways of its
own, and so many interesting peculiarities. The difference between the peasantry and the *bourgeoisie* in habits
and ideas is certainly much greater than the difference
between two nations. We are accustomed, for example,
to think of the French as a cooking nation, but the
truth is, that although cookery is an elaborate well-
understood art in the *bourgeoisie*, the peasantry are
utterly ignorant of it. It is wonderful that, with so

much knowledge about food and the preparation of it
in the country towns, and in the houses of the squires,
no tincture of such knowledge should have spread itself
in the genuine rustic world, but the plain truth is that
the peasants' wives do not know how to make the best
of the materials they have, so that the rustic world
lives much less comfortably than it might live. We
knew one farmer's wife, in easy circumstances, who
systematically let her butter go rancid before using it,
"because," she said, "as the taste is stronger, less of it
is required." Sick people and children in farm-houses
are much to be pitied. My wife once actually saw
coffee given to a sick man with salt in it instead of
sugar, because salt was considered cheaper, and babies
at the breast are fed with a sort of *bouillie*, prepared in
an old cast-iron pan, that has been used for frying
bacon from time immemorial.

The great reason why cookery has never penetrated
into the rustic world, is that it seems extravagant, and
is, no doubt, in reality, a costly luxury when carried to
a needless elaboration, so that the peasantry, who are
frugal above all things, avoid it as an indulgence which
is not for them. Another reason is the indolence of the
women when they are in the house. A peasant-woman
will work very vigorously in the fields, but when she is
at home she takes as little trouble as may be, and likes
to pass her time in knitting, which is really a sort of
concealed indolence. The way of living in a peasant's
house is this. In the morning the men eat soup—that
soup which Cobden praised as the source of French
prosperity. It is cheap enough to make. For twelve

people two handfuls of dry beans or peas, or a few
potatoes, a few ounces of fried bacon to give a taste,
a good deal of hot water. The twelve basins are then
filled with thin slices of brown bread, and the hot
water, flavoured with the above ingredients, is poured
upon the bread. The bacon and peas are not in sufficient quantity to afford much nourishment, but they
give a taste to the bread and water, and a hot meal
is procured in this way at a cheap rate. Boiled rice,
with a little milk, is sometimes taken instead of soup.
If the soup is insufficient, the peasant finishes his meal
with a piece of dry bread, and as much cold water as
he likes, for of this there is no stint. The meal at
noon is composed invariably of potatoes followed by a
second dish. In this second dish consists the only
culinary variety of the peasant's life. It is either a
pancake, made with a great deal of flour and water and
few eggs, or a salad, or clotted milk. No wine or meat
is allowed, except during the great labours of hay-
making and harvest. At these times, a little wine is
given with the water drunk at dinner, and a little piece
of salted pork. At great feasts ham is served, and
beef broth, the boiled beef served afterwards without
sauce. The peasants' wives see carefully that the fasts
of the Church are observed—all economical French
people are religious enough in this—and I remember a
good instance of the lengths to which they will go.
We knew an old peasant who was not in very strong
health (he was seventy-two years old), and his conscience was not very tender about the ordinances of the
Church ; I mean, that if anybody had given him the

opportunity of eating meat in Lent he would probably have yielded to the temptation. But he had a wife who united orthodoxy with economy, and who took good care that her husband should commit no sin that would be in any way expensive. When Lent came I used to banter the old man, in a gentle way, by inquiring anxiously about his health. He always got weaker and· weaker towards the end of the forty days, and one year this weakness was so distressing to him that he committed a great crime. A pig was killed at the farm towards the end of Lent, in anticipation of Easter Sunday, but so vigilant was the eye of the mistress that nobody dared touch a morsel of the forbidden food. There was one exception, however. The old man sallied forth with a knife, cut a slice of the pig, fried it himself in open defiance of both wife and Church, and ate it boldly, like a hardened sinner, in sight of his children and servants. Whilst he was eating, he underwent a terrible female sermon. "Not only," said his wife, "are you breaking Lent now, but you have broken it all along, for every day you have cooked in the ashes two eggs for your dinner, and it's astonishing to hear you complain of weakness, after such shameless gormandizing as that!"

In the spring the peasants bleed their oxen, and cook the blood in a frying-pan with onions. They like it very much, and, although the idea seems rather disgusting, it is not more so than the notion of eating black-puddings—when we know what they are made of.

I have said elsewhere that the peasants have a profound feeling of disgust for mutton. Notwithstanding the abstemiousness of their way of life—which is really little better than one continuous fast—they will not touch mutton at all. Their feeling about it is simply the prejudice against a particular kind of flesh, which most people have in one form or another. When such a prejudice is once firmly established, the imagination makes it wonderfully strong—as, for example, in the prejudice against horseflesh, which is even less reasonable, for horseflesh poisons nobody, whereas mutton is a poison for some constitutions. Other peculiarities of the peasantry are that they never season vegetables, and their soup is so poor that at the end of a meal what remains of it is thrown into the pigs' tub, so that they never eat a *réchauffé* of any kind, hence they have an intense prejudice against *réchauffés*. A peasant-girl, when she goes as servant into a *bourgeois* family, will not touch any *réchauffé*, even when she has seen it served at her master's table, and if there is nothing else to dinner she will eat dry bread. By this prejudice, the peasantry miss one of the most intelligent economies of the middle class, for it is the simple fact that a good many French dishes are positively better when warmed a second time than they were when first cooked. This is an instance the more of the familiar truth, that human nature, even when most frugal and most humble, always associates something with the idea of self-respect, and clings to it to the last. The peasant's theory is that yesterday's dishes are for the pigs, and not for Christians.

The women of the peasant-class submit to the severity of their frugal customs without any other relief from them than the occasional feasts at weddings, but the men escape from the rule of custom more frequently, when they go to the market-town, and get a liberal *déjeûner* at the inn, which they seem to appreciate very heartily. On these occasions they get tipsy, as a matter of course, and when there is a great fair they often get more than tipsy, in consequence of successive bottles of wine and beer in the *cafés*, where they treat each other liberally, according to a theory that it is not polite to refuse, nor to accept hospitable offers without returning them. This of course makes the drinking on such occasions practically unlimited. So Bacchus has his revenge for the general abstemiousness of rural life, which is almost teetotal in the rustic homes, with bacchanalian intervals in the market-towns. I well remember hearing a farmer's wife declare that her husband (a most respectable old man, who got tipsy one day in thirty, and drank water on the remaining twenty-nine) adored Bacchus more than Venus, the Venus being herself, and a very plain homely Venus she was.* It would be better for a rustic to allow himself a little wine every day than to drink to excess occasionally, but his life would lack the great pleasure of occasional excesses, which seems to be necessary to human nature in a certain stage of civilization. The peasant observes at present the same abstinence and the same excesses in eating. Most of his time he lives as the reader has just seen, but at wedding-feasts he consumes

---

* Nothing ever surprised me more than this reference to antique mythology; how the good woman came by her knowledge of gods and goddesses I cannot imagine.

literally ten times as much animal food as an English gentleman will eat at his dinner.   I once asked a young farmer how many meals he had eaten successively in celebration of his brother's wedding.   He confessed to fifteen repasts, entirely consisting of different kinds of meat.   It is not at all an exaggeration to suppose that he would eat of five different dishes at each repast— $5 \times 15 = 75$—so that my friend ate seventy-five plates of meat to celebrate the happy occasion.   At these festivals there is not a vegetable to be seen, nor anything in the shape of sweets or pastry—the feast is purely carnivorous, an excessive reaction from the daily habits of the peasantry.   These excesses never seem to do anybody any harm, and the strict rule of daily life is accepted again quite readily afterwards, when all return to frugality and duty.   I never really understood the spirit of feasting which Rabelais and others have described as a part of the temper of the middle ages, until I saw how the French peasants enjoy what Rabelais called *noces et festins*.   A higher civilization dines comfortably and sufficiently every day, and loses the delight of occasionally indulging to the utmost a rarely satisfied appetite.   So our daily life becomes more mildly agreeable, but we lose the animating enjoyment of the feast.   Indeed, we do not know what it is to feast.   The spirit of it is not in us any more. We have found out that the sensations of having eaten and drunk too much are not the supreme happiness.

The peasant believes wine to be the universal remedy. He administers it liberally in all cases of disease, even in the most violent fevers—with what effect may be imagined. His way of treating a bad cold is to put a tallow candle in a quart of red wine, and boil till the tallow melts, after which tallow and wine are stirred up together and swallowed by the unhappy patient. For intermittent fever he beats up eggs with soot from the chimney. To cure the measles he gives hot wine with pepper and honey. Whenever any one is ill, no matter from what cause, hot wine is at once administered. A married woman, who had been a servant of ours, was so ill after childbirth, that she thought she was going to die, and so thought all her friends. They sent for the *curé*, who duly arrived and administered extreme unction. Being now, as she believed, at the point of death, and about to enter the realm of purgatory, the patient expressed a strong desire to see my wife, in order to entreat her pardon for all offences committed during her service with us. Few indeed, and of little gravity, had those offences been! On arriving at the cottage, my wife, who knows the ways of the peasants, and has just the degree of confidence in them which they deserve, strongly suspected that the patient was being quietly killed by the absurd old rural practices; so she made minute inquiries, and soon discovered what follows: 1. The woman was entirely in the hands of her relations, no doctor having been sent for. 2. The said relations had forbidden her to give milk to her child, " for fear of fatiguing her." 3. They had filled her with wine. 4. They had piled huge feather cushions on her, and quilts, till she was nearly smothered. The breasts were distended with milk, and very painful, whilst the other arrangements had greatly augmented the fever. My wife's great difficulty, in all such cases, is to prevent the people from giving wine, but she has found out an ingenious device which succeeds sometimes, and quite succeeded in this instance. She takes two or three bottles of good wine to the house of the sick person, and says they are to be administered during convalescence, but not before, and that no other wine is to be given at all. This shows an apparent deference to the popular belief in wine which conciliates public opinion, and it proves, at least, that the giver, in forbidding the use of wine for the present, does not forbid it from an apprehension that she may be asked to supply it out of her own cellar. In the instance just mentioned, a little common sense, with words of firm kindness and encouragement, saved the patient. It is a peculiarity of the peasants that they do not believe in medical science at all, and never send for a doctor till it is too late, if, indeed, they send for him even then. They generally pin their faith on some old woman who knows the old wives' remedies. My wife (though not an old woman) has really, by very simple means, saved several lives, which, in the ordinary course of rustic custom, must inevitably have been sacrificed, and this has given her a great reputation as a doctor, which she makes the most of to fight against the absurd old peasant traditions. But it is a hard fight, even for one who has visible success on her side. I remember the case of one old woman, who lived at a distance amongst the hills, and was visibly dying of exhaustion. A country doctor visited her occasionally, but gave her up. Having seen her, my wife said, "The woman is really dying for want of proper food, because nobody in the house knows how to prepare food for a weak person; but I could save her life if I had her in our own house." I said she had better try the experiment, so the woman was brought to our house. We had a daughter of hers as a servant at that time, so the patient was carefully attended to, but very strictly looked after. In a few weeks she was in very fair health, and able to walk fifteen miles. She is living yet, and quite active, but it is certain (so the doctor says) that she must have died if left to the care of peasants. From what we have seen, we are quite sure that a large mortality, amongst sick or weakly people, is caused by sheer ignorance in the peasant class—by ignorance, not by poverty, for they could easily afford what is really necessary. There is never any telling what their inconceivable ignorance will make them do. I know an instance of a woman who was affected with partial paralysis. Her friends got medicine from the chemist, and the medicine was of two kinds, one to be taken internally, the other for external friction, so they rubbed her with the potion and made her swallow the liniment, to her great internal inconvenience. Mustard plasters are now sold ready prepared, so a man in our neighbourhood bought a box of them for his wife, who was ill, and tried to make her swallow them. It was almost impossible to convince him that they were to be applied externally. "Do you think I don't know the use of mustard?" he said; "I know well enough that it is made to be eaten, so my wife must swallow these plasters." A man was suffering from an ailment which required treatment with linseed poultices, but he said that he thought they did him very little good. On inquiry, it turned out that his daughter, who had the care of him, had boiled all the linseed together in the pigs' pan, after which she took it in cold lumps, like broken stones, and so applied it to the patient. We knew another who, when she had the stomach-ache, swallowed certain remedies which had been given to her mother for varicose veins, "so that they might not be lost." The doctor is only sent for, by a peasant, at the very last extremity, and his prescriptions are never followed. I have often talked about this peculiarity with physicians whom I knew intimately, and they invariably said that it was not of the slightest use for them to give any advice to peasants. The consequence is that physicians take no interest in rustic patients, and leave them to their own prejudices, and whatever fate may be in store for them. The physician's fees, although extremely moderate, and remote indeed from the London guinea, seem to the rural mind an expense to be regretted in any event, for if the patient is cured, his friends believe that he would have come round without the doctor, and if he dies, it is plain that the doctor has not been able to save him. Our own medical adviser has a thousand anecdotes of the rustic ways, with reference to the science of medicine, which exhibit the peasant's way of thinking. One of these I select for the reader. A woman went to him for a prescription for her husband, but as she was going away, she turned on the threshold, and asked whether her husband could pull through. "Because," she added, "if he is to die after all, it will be of no use to spend five francs in medicine." She positively refused to get the prescription made up unless the doctor would guarantee her husband's life.

What the peasants really do believe in is not science of any kind, but magic and superstitious prayers. Their idea of prayer and of all religion is, in fact, very closely connected with magic. They have full faith in sorcery and in the power of combating evil by special prayers —special forms of words which make you safe if you know them accurately, when, without the knowledge of the form, you are helpless against the evil. This is so, very particularly with regard to burns and dislocated limbs. It is believed, for instance, that such an old woman knows a special prayer which will cure a burn, or make a set limb go on favourably, and when such a belief becomes current, the person who knows the prayer is in great request, but keeps the prayer itself a secret. The idea is, that there are prayers for every kind of evil, which would be perfectly efficacious if one only knew them. It is plain that the notion is more nearly allied to magic than to Christianity. Even in very grave cases, when a surgeon is absolutely required, the peasants will not send for him if they can avoid it, but they will travel many miles to fetch some ignorant old woman "*qui sait une prière.*" The simple truth is, that their minds are in a condition so wholly unscientific, that they cannot conceive the idea of science. It is useless to tell them that a physician has studied medicine and an old woman has not, for they do not know, and cannot imagine, what it is to study anything, nor are they at all able to perceive the distinction between positive knowledge and super-stition.

When a child is born it is not considered right to ask what is its sex, and if any one belonging to another class asks the question in ignorance or forgetfulness, he will not receive much of an answer, for the question is considered at the same time a violation of good man-ners and contrary to religion. It is a violation of good manners because, so long as it is unbaptized, the child is considered to be only an animal, and therefore, no credit to its father and mother ; and it is contrary to religion because, until the child has received the Divine grace through baptism, it does not truly live. The genuine peasant maintains a strict reserve in speaking of an unbaptized child—exactly the same reserve which an English gentleman would maintain to discourage ques-tioners if his wife had been delivered of a monster.

The old classical habit of putting a coin into the hand of the dead to pay Charon with, still survives amongst the French peasantry. They have forgotten Charon, and cannot tell you why they put the coin into the dead hand, but they would not omit the ceremony. A much more touching practice is that of putting flowers into the coffin of a child. They tell you their reason for this, which is, that the child must have them to play with. This, too, is a classical idea—the old idea that life of some kind continued dimly in the tomb itself.

The women go on the day of the Purification to read the Gospel to the bees, with a lighted taper in their hands. I have seen this done, and done in serious earnest, with a perfect faith that the bees could derive spiritual advantage from the reading, and were, at least so far, Christians. I need scarcely add, that there is the usual superstition against the sale of bees. They may be given or exchanged, but if bought and sold they will never prosper.

On Shrove Tuesday, the peasants have a ludicrous custom of jumping as high as they can. They believe that this makes their hemp grow. They listen to the cry of the quail with great interest, because they believe that he announces the price of wheat—but somehow there is always a difficulty in making out the figure which he announces. They are also convinced that the cattle talk together on Christmas night, at the time of the midnight mass ; but curiosity as to what the cattle may say is repressed as dangerous, there being a legend that the farmer who hid himself in the cow-house to listen heard the prediction of his own speedy demise, which took place accordingly in a few days. Thousands of peasants believe this just as firmly as they believe things in the ordinary course of nature.

The peasant mind is in such an uncritical condition that it is subject to ocular illusions, even in perfectly healthy persons. I remember a young farmer who told people that one day I was walking with his father, and made myself appear to him twice as tall as his father, by throwing some magic powder in his eyes. The old man and I were about the same height (5 ft. 10 in.), so that I must have appeared a giant of 11 ft. 8 in. The origin of the illusion, in this case, was the belief that I had magic powders, which would cause a pre-disposition to see something wonderful. Many people are believed to have magic powders, but in my case this is fully accounted for by a chemical laboratory in which I am in the habit of pursuing investigations in the chemistry of etching and painting.

In our part of France the peasants have the fullest belief in sorcery. They live in perpetual apprehension that some sorcerer may cast a spell upon their cattle, and they can tell you numberless stories of the known effects of such spells. They believe, too, that the secrets of sorcery are contained in a mysterious volume called an " Albert," and they are convinced that certain persons possess the book, though I never could see a copy of it, nor ascertain if it really existed. One of my friends, a village notary, is universally believed to have magical power and to possess an " Albert," and people actually come to him to beg him to exercise his power. On one occasion, being pestered by a peasant who would not take a refusal, the notary really did go through some ceremony in imitation of the black art.

The priests do nothing to discourage popular superstition ; indeed, it may be suspected that they prefer a superstitious state of mind to a more enlightened one. They bless sprigs of boxwood, which are a protection against evil influences. They do not deny the existence of the powers of darkness, but combat them by religious ceremonies. One of the most striking of these ceremonies is the blessing of the fields, which takes place three days before the feast of the Ascension. In the beautiful May time, the time of blossoming trees, rustic altars are erected by the villagers, and the priest leaves the church to go in procession from one to another, bearing the Holy Sacrament. The arrangements about the altars are left entirely to the peasants themselves, who erect them without any ecclesiastical or artistic direction, and the priest always accepts them just as they are with all their *naïveté*. This ceremony of the Rogations has always seemed to me one of the most beautiful of all Roman Catholic ceremonies, and it is at the same time a striking instance of the skill with which the Roman Church adapts herself to all situations and circumstances, and of her readiness to take trouble that she may win sympathy and awaken interest.

The best way to give a good idea of the Rogations will be to describe some particular instance of them from memory. Let me take the reader with me, as it were, to a certain hamlet that I know well, a place which no landscape-painter would despise. Quaint old thatched cottages surround a broad green, at least for three of its four sides, but the fourth is bounded by a clear and beautiful trout-stream, which teems with fish, and is never dry, even in the height of summer, for we are close to its perennial fountains in the forest-covered hills. Round the hamlet are green rich meadows with fine trees here and there, and beyond the meadows the land suddenly rises in steep wooded hills, about a thousand feet above the level of the green, at least to the north and west, but to the south the stream flows towards pale blue mountainous distances. It is a peaceful place, sheltered by hills, but not overwhelmed by them, nor yet too absolutely confined. Here in the heat of summer one may find coolness and welcome shade ; here the birds sing and the wild flowers grow in abundance. It seems as if one could live in such a sweet place for ever, and dream and paint in the fair meadows, and swim daily in the long deep cool pools of the stream which lie dark under vaulted roofs of half-transparent leaves.

In the very middle of the green, the people of the hamlet had erected their rustic altar. The altar itself would have been more satisfactory to Protestant senti-ment than the massive stone ones in the churches, for it consisted simply of a poor table from one of the cottages, but it was carefully hidden with a white sheet, and a box was put upon it to imitate the *rétable* or upper altar, also carefully hidden in white. On the white linen was pinned a decoration of natural leaves and flowers in a sort of rude design, like simple em-broidery. The altar was abundantly supplied with candles, and vases with flowers in them. All the candlesticks had been lent by the cottagers them-selves, so they were not splendid. The vases were the chimney ornaments from the cottages, of the kind which country people buy at fairs to gratify a love of art in its most elementary form, all painted in gaudy colours. Every house, however humble, has what is called its " chapel," that is to say, a miniature altar with a plaster cast, usually of the Virgin and Child, a couple of candlesticks, two or three pots of flowers, and some coloured religious prints on the wall, besides illumi-nated cards, surrounded with frames of embossed paper, which imitates lace. All these things are a common magazine of *objets de piété*, for an occasion of the kind I am now describing, and the young women, who are the real managers of all the preparations, select the prints, &c., which please them best. Behind the altar, and on each side of it, was a great structure of green branches, imitating the apse of a church, and towards the bottom it was hung inside with white sheets, on which were garlands of yellow flowers, and a quantity of framed prints representing scenes from the New Testament. The preparations were nearly finished when I arrived upon the scene, and as everybody in the hamlet knew me, the girls who had built the altar were very anxious that I should suggest any possible improvement on their design. I really had very little to suggest, for the whole was a piece of genuine rustic art, quite a pure and perfect expression of rustic taste, with materials that were ready to hand. It may be doubted whether a town architect would have been ingenious enough to use the materials with such good effect. Most likely he would have despised them too much. I well remember one detail. Amongst the ornaments were two sardine boxes lacquered in imitation of gilding. They were rather large and handsome boxes of their kind, and the girls had filled them with earth, in which they had stuck long branches of the bird-cherry-tree in full flower, which met over the altar very prettily. I rather wondered how the cottagers had come into possession of these boxes, for they never eat preserved sardines, but I was informed that they came from my own house, where a girl in the hamlet worked two days a week. She had perceived the availableness of the boxes, and begged them. The truth is that they did capitally at a little distance, when the sun made the lacquer shine like gold, and one could not read the tradesman's advertisement. Not only the flowers of the bird cherry-tree, but all the wild flowers that bloomed in the little valley, were pressed into requisition. The girls had an evident preference for yellow ones, because they imitated gold, and there were plenty of buttercups and marsh marigolds to satisfy this desire. White was supplied by hawthorn and cherry-blossom; red, in abundance, by the common lychnis and red lamium. There were plenty of wild pansies, too, and other flowers too long to enumerate. The last touch was put to the work only just in time, when the banners of the advancing procession flashed in the sunshine on the other side of the stream, and it soon passed over the bridge. The old priest of the nearest village came bearing the Host, and in the procession were the principal rural dignitaries, and the children of the village school. There were also two sisters of charity, and a full-bearded missionary priest. The *curé* went through the service of the benediction with simple dignity, and all the little congregation knelt upon the grass. When the service at this altar was over, the procession formed again, and its banners gradually disappeared in the winding of the little path between the meadows and the river.

Here you have the genuine rustic religion of the peasantry. They like to see the priest come amongst them, and carry the Holy Sacrament through the fields that they may be blessed, and yield an abundant harvest. The poetic sense which exists in their uncultured minds has its exercise on these occasions in the building of the rustic altar with its green bower for an apse, and its vases, and candles, and flowers. All is so closely connected with the beauty of the beautiful season that even the rude mind feels the harmony between the ceremony and the time. The year has given its first promise in the flowers, the gentle air breathes warm, summer is coming fast, and after it the peasant looks to the wealth of autumn. The sentiment of the season, and its hope for the future, are perfectly expressed in the Complaint of the Black Knight, by Chaucer :—

> The aire attempre, and the smooth wind
> Of Zephyrus among the blosomes white
> So holsome was, and so nourishing by kind,
> That smale buddes, and round blosomes lite,
> In manner gan of hir brethe delite,
> To yeve us hope there fruit shall take
> Agenst autumne redy for to shake.

As a special protection the peasants have hazel boughs blessed by the priest on this occasion, and set them in their fields as a defence against hail, which they are believed to avert.

It is not by any means easy to ascertain the exact degree of influence which the Church of Rome possesses over the peasant mind, because the people of that class are cautious and reticent in the expression of their opinions ; but a close observer may easily perceive that a strong sceptical spirit has invaded the rural districts during the last few years. At the ceremony of the Rogations, which I have just described, the only men present who belonged to the hamlet were half a dozen who happened to be preparing materials for a new bridge. They were shaping the beams upon the green, close to the altar, and they went on with their work, giving loud strokes with the axe, till the procession was almost upon them. The women protested against this as unbecoming, and did at last obtain a sort of surly acquiescence ; but the men remained with their wooden beams behind the altar, and did not join the little congregation. I made inquiry about other inhabitants of the hamlet, and discovered that they were all at their work in the fields and woods, not having thought it worth while to quit their labour for an hour, even for the most important rural ceremony of the year. The women and children were there, taking a feminine and childish pleasure in their own little arrangements of pots and candles and May flowers ; but the men in the fields and woods can scarcely have believed that the ceremony had much practical utility. In another hamlet, not a man was to be seen, except those who had come with the procession, and who might in some instances have joined it from self-interest, to stand well with a powerful noble family which owns a large property in the neighbourhood. The real feeling of the male peasant in this part of France seems to be that religion is a sort of precaution which may not turn out to be of any use, but which it is as well to take, according to the universally known proverb, *si ça ne fait pas de bien, ça ne fera pas de mal.* When the rustic sticks a blessed hazel twig in his field to preserve it from hail, he cannot feel that it is a sure preventive, because he has often seen fields lashed with hail notwithstanding hazel twigs and benedictions. But then, on the other hand, his fields have often escaped when the blessed hazel was set up in them, and at these times it is just possible that the blessed branch may have been *pour quelque chose.* At any rate, the precaution, such as it is, is one that costs very little trouble. This, so far as I have been able to ascertain, is the exact shade of mingled faith and scepticism amongst my rural neighbours. It has always been a very interesting problem for me whether the peasarts of the male sex in this region can be more accurately described as believing their religion or as not believing it. A friend of mine says that they do really believe, but have a kind of surface-scepticism which covers their belief. This is one view. The other view is that they have a surface-religion which covers a basis of scepticism as shallow water may cover a rocky bed. The peculiar feeling about unbaptized children is common to both sexes, and certainly looks like faith ; but then, on the other hand, there is a distinct vein of scepticism amongst the men which is as like the Voltairean spirit as the difference between Voltaire and an unlettered peasant will admit. It is most difficult to describe with exact truth a condition of mind which hardly ever expresses itself quite openly, and of which the peasants themselves are seldom quite clearly conscious. They believe in the efficacy of old wives' prayers for the cure of burns and dislocated shoulders, and yet, at the same time, if you tell them of a miracle fully authenticated by the clergy, they (the men) will look at each other, and smile with the most evident incredulity. For example, there is a

young lady, six miles from my house, whose family I
know. A little time since she was in a deplorable state,
partially paralyzed, and unable to walk. "If I could be
taken to Lourdes," she said, "I know I should get
better." To Lourdes she was taken accordingly, and
came back to all appearance cured. She can walk and
run—I saw her do both in my own garden not a week
since—and she now leads quite an active life. Here was
a miracle which would have excited a believing population to enthusiasm, and yet there has been no enthusiasm about it in the neighbourhood, and the men say
that it was not a miracle at all—that the young lady had
had ups and downs in her health before, and will probably have them again. This is the cool way they take
it. In the ages of real faith a person so favoured by
supernatural power would have created the most intense
excitement. People would have travelled far to see her
—to touch the hem of her garment, if, haply, some
supernatural virtue might pass from her to them. The
peasants did not seem so much interested in the matter
as I was myself. The case interested me as a remarkable evidence of the effect of imagination. A visit to
Lourdes has never restored an organ whose anatomical
structure has been changed by accident or disease, but
the influence of it on the imagination of a real believer
is often so strong as to produce a very remarkable and
beneficial effect upon the nervous system.

Another very curious test of rural religion was the
manner in which the pilgrimages were got up. The
reader is aware that there has been of late years a
great movement in France about pilgrimages, a move-

ment which has extended to other countries, so that the French holy places have been visited by many pilgrims from England, Italy, and Belgium, and even from unfriendly Germany. Very brilliant accounts have been given of the enthusiasm excited by these pilgrimages amongst the rural population of France itself. It is certainly true that many pilgrimages have been organized to Lourdes and Paray-le-Monial. We have seen them organized, and we know exactly how it is done—if the reader cares to know also, he will soon be master of the whole subject, which is not at all complicated or difficult.

A pilgrimage usually has its origin with the bishop of the diocese from which it takes its departure. Perhaps the bishop may not be exactly the first person to whom the idea occurs, possibly somebody suggests it to him, but it is he who sets the enterprise in motion as the Commander of the Faithful in his region. When His Grandeur gives the word of command to organize a pilgrimage, it is usually in the form of a very long charge, which is printed in double columns, and posted at the doors of all the churches. It may occupy as much as four pages of the *Pall Mall Gazette.* The merits of the saint or blessed personage are duly set forth, and also the great favour of the Supreme Pontiff towards all pilgrims who visit the holy shrine. The date of the pilgrimage is fixed, in proper ecclesiastical style, on the day of some notable saint. The necessary impetus is now given, and the bishop has no further personal trouble in the matter, until the day arrives, when he goes at the head of his flock. But between the charge and the pilgrimage, a feverish activity reigns in other quarters. Female emissaries go forth amongst the people, and display the most remarkable energy as recruiting sergeants. A particularly active one, whom we will call Madame Tarbi, lived very near us, so that we saw exactly how the recruiting was carried on. She made her husband hunt up recruits also, but she herself was the great source of will and energy. For this she had reasons of her own. An ambitious and agreeable little lady, she was not admitted into the *noblesse*, because her forefathers, and those of her husband, had been too honest to assume the usual false *de*, so that she was only a *roturière*, and was looked down upon accordingly. This was the more grievous to her that she lived in an old château which, though not extensive, had rather an aristocratic air on account of a pepper-box *tourelle*. Besides, although busy enough, physically, in managing her household affairs, which were always kept in excellent order, her mind was left to prey very much upon itself, for she never read anything or interested herself in anything beyond the visible life just immediately around her. A Frenchwoman in such a position easily becomes the victim of an *idée fixe*, which is to get into noble society, but noble society is a closed fortress, presenting a hard and massive front to *roturiers* and outsiders. One quality may possibly open a postern somewhere, and let the outsider in. That quality is an active zeal in behalf of Legitimacy and the Church. Madame Tarbi took care, therefore, to let everybody know that she was ardently *bien pensante*. The pilgrimages were a fine opportunity for displaying her zeal in the good cause; so no sooner had the *curé* read the bishop's charge from the pulpit, and commented thereupon, than Madame Tarbi commenced her holy work. A servant of our own happened to be in a farm-house just when Madame Tarbi called there, and from her account, the reader may judge of the arguments used. " It appears, Madame," she said to my wife in the evening, " that they are going on a pilgrimage to the country of Sainte Marie Alacoque, but it is not for that saint, it's for another that was in the same convent with her." By this other saint she meant the Sacred Heart, and this is all they know about it. The girl continued, " It's to pray for peace, and it will cost ten francs." " Well, but, Jeannette, what is the need to pray for peace at a time when we are at war with nobody?" " *Ma foi!* Madame, I know nothing about it, but Madame Tarbi said so." " At any rate, the sum of ten francs is a good deal for our farmers' wives, and there will not be many of them." " Oh, but there will! Madame Tarbi said that everybody had his name put down, and that it was better to give ten francs to God than to see the *communes* lost altogether." Madame Tarbi, who was an acute woman, found that it answered best to work upon the fears and apprehensions of the farmers' wives. The following dialogue really took place in a farm-house very near us:—

Farmer's Wife. Ah, Madame, is it then true that we are going to have a year of famine?

Mrs. H. I have heard nothing of the sort, and I see no signs of it.

Farmer's Wife. Ah, but Madame Tarbi has told us that the Bon Dieu was very angry at us, and that He had frozen the wines and the fruit to show it!

Mrs. H. Why is the Bon Dieu so angry with us?

Farmer's Wife. Ma foi! Madame, I know nothing about it, but Madame Tarbi says that it's plain enough to be seen by the frost, and that if we don't look sharp and pray together in a pilgrimage, all the good things of the earth will be lost, and we shall have a year of famine.

Mrs. H. Ten francs are not much to give to save all the crops. It is not so dear as an ordinary insurance. But who has told Madame Tarbi that the Bon Dieu was so angry with us?

Farmer's Wife. Ma foi, Madame! je n'en sais rien. She says that so long as we have no Government things will not go well.

Mrs. H. That's it, Toinette; you see you are going to make a pilgrimage to ask for a king.

Enter Farmer.

Farmer. What do we want with a king? Why cannot they let us alone? They say things cannot go on as they are doing, but we've nothing to complain of. We sell our beasts and our grain just as well as if we'd a king. It isn't the king who buys everything, is it, Madame? (*Then to his wife*) I will not let thee go to the pilgrimage, dost thou hear?

Farmer's Wife. Toinon, I durst not remain at home when the others go. What would they say of us? It never does any harm to pray to God ; and, sure enough, I shall pray for the crops, and not for the king. What does it matter to me?

Farmer. So that's why Madame Tarbi preaches to

people! She's just been to talk to François, who wasn't over-pleased. François is not a fool, he's been to Paris, and he can read in any sort of a book, so he said to the lady, " It's a queer sort of a pilgrimage, that is, in a railway. My wife once went on a pilgrimage for our little Toinot, who had the fevers, and he couldn't be cured, and we'd four girls and only one boy for a plough. Well, she did all the distance on foot, with bare feet. *That* was a real pilgrimage; but as to pilgrimages in railways, I don't believe in 'em. There will hardly be time enough to pray."

Farmer's Wife. That isn't necessary; the lady says that the intention is enough. Besides, I couldn't venture to refuse Madame Tarbi, for she sent broth to our little girls all the time that they had the measles. The poor should always submit themselves to the rich, because they may need their help at any time, and if these pilgrimages do no good, at any rate they do no harm either.

All preceding acts of kindness or patronage on the part of an influential Legitimist lady are so many levers with which she prepares beforehand a religious demonstration of this kind. A girl who came to us to sew said that she did not think there was much piety in putting on one's finest clothes, and in going about the country to eat in the middle of the fields, as one does at village feasts, but she would go to the pilgrimage all the same, so as not to lose Madame Tarbi's custom, for Madame Tarbi employed her frequently.

Nevertheless, in spite of all her skill, it seemed to us that this clever and influential lady rather deluded herself one Sunday about the sentiments of her vassals when she considered it becoming and opportune to make a speech to them all, on coming back from mass, that they might perceive what good results were to be expected from the pilgrimages by the fruits already borne by them. "You see," she exclaimed, "that God is already becoming favourable to us, since He has caused Thiers to fall, and has put in his place an honest and pious man like Marshal MacMahon. It is the beginning of the benedictions which the Divine Goodness is about to accord to us, and we may soon hope to have a Government." A general and chilling silence was the discouraging reception of this little address, for the feelings of attachment towards M. Thiers which had already taken root in the breast of the French peasant had been considerably augmented since the change of Government by the fall in the price of cattle which immediately followed the accession of Marshal MacMahon, and for which, of course, in some mysterious manner, he is held by the peasants to be responsible.

The farmer's wife who figured in the conversation quoted above came to see us a day or two afterwards to ask for some advice. She had a disappointed look, and informed us that a cow, for which she had received an offer of 550 francs when M. Thiers was President, was now unsaleable at 400 francs, and then she inquired whether Madame Tarbi would make her pay ten francs all the same if she did not go to the pilgrimage. "There cannot be a doubt of it," we answered, "if your name is written down." Then she sighed, and said, "If I pay my ten francs I may as well have some amusement." In which frame of mind she went in the crowded train to Paray-le-Monial, as a private in the company whereof Madame Tarbi was now the captain.

In addition to the means of influence just described or alluded to, there are subscriptions for. poor women who are *bien pensantes*, but have not the means necessary to pay their fare, yet who are pleased with the notion of a day's outing that costs nothing. The lady patronesses themselves find a great deal to interest and occupy them in the choice of banners with their designs, colours, and emblems, and the great questions, who will arrange them ? who will carry them ? Any reader who has once seen a party of ladies thoroughly interested and excited about a project involving some expense and display will easily imagine how delighted they are with managing the details of a pilgrimage. The whole thing suits them exactly, for it affords opportunities for display, for domination, for social success ; and all in the service of the Church, and in company with reverend ecclesiastics, including that pearl of great price, a bishop! The ladies plan long beforehand the great matter of the *toilette*, in what costume they will place themselves at the head of their respective flocks, and they compare lists in order to ascertain which lady-patroness will lead the greatest number of the faithful ; the banner itself is one of the strongest incentives to zeal on the part of ladies like Madame Tarbi, for it is only when they have been able to get together a certain number of faithful followers that the ecclesiastical authorities (wise in their generation) permit them to carry a banner at all. Madame Tarbi, after counting the number of her adherents, exclaimed with triumphant joy, " *Nous aurons une bannière !* " which, in fact, had all along been one of the principal objects of her praiseworthy exertions. But only imagine the cruel, crushing disappointment of a lady who just falls short of the number required, and has to march ingloriously, after all her exertions, at the head of a bannerless squad !

It would be an omission to quit this subject of the peasantry without some allusion to family relations amongst themselves. Between men and their wives I do not think that, generally speaking, there is very much love or affection, but neither, on the other hand, does there seem to be much distrust, or quarrelling, or conjugal infidelity. It is a common error of writers to judge whole classes by a very few specimens whom they happen to know, and I do my best to avoid hasty conclusions of this kind, but by adding together my own knowledge of the peasantry and that possessed by others who are still more familiar with them than I am, certain conclusions may be arrived at which are not likely to be very inaccurate. The reader will please to remember that the peasantry live in a mental condition of quite antique simplicity, and that they have little conception of those needs of the intellect and heart which seem to us part of the necessities of existence. They are engaged, too, in an incessant and hard struggle for plain food and simple clothing, which makes them severe for themselves and severe for those about them; notwithstanding much gentleness and charm of manner, they have little tenderness ; such affection as they feel appears to be generally connected with self-interest, but, on the other hand, this very self-interest keeps them well united. There is a strong patriarchal discipline in the farms. An old farmer with several grown-up sons, and several servants, is really in a position of far greater dignity and authority than the *bourgeois* husband, whose wife and children chatter loudly in his presence, without the slightest special deference for the head of the family, and who is looked upon simply as the money-earner. I remember one farmer who never punished any one in anger, but who did not hesitate to punish severely in cold blood when he thought the victim deserved it. One day a son of his, a fine strong young man of twenty-four, came back from a little pleasure excursion. He had exceeded his leave of absence by two days. The father, a man of seventy, received him with politeness, and said, in his *patois*, " My son, I gave thee no present at the New Year, but thou shalt lose nothing by this delay, for I will give thee thy present now." The young man stood still in the middle of the farm-yard whilst his brother took the horse to the stable. His mother came to him, and said eagerly, " Run away, lad, and hide thyself," but the young man stood firm, with his arms folded. Meanwhile the father had gone to fetch a large wooden hay-fork. " This shall be thy New Year's gift, my son !" he said, with an ironical smile, and laid it about him with all his might. The punishment was really severe. but the son stood till

the end, and as soon as it was over, went straight to
his work without a murmur, nor did I ever hear him
speak of his father without the most perfect filial
respect both in language and in tone. On another
occasion, the eldest brother, a still older man, long
past his majority, had done something to displease the
old patriarch, so on his return the father gave orders
that every man and woman should leave the house for
a quarter of an hour, as he wished to have a private
conversation with the delinquent. The conversation
was not long, but it was followed by a severe beating
with a goad. These punishments were very seldom
resorted to, but the reader perceives that the discipline
which applied them for simply exceeding leave of
absence was a severe discipline. One day a youth in
the family had been gathering some salad in the fields
for his own dinner, and served it at table. The old
man perceived this and thought it an infraction of discipline, so in a quiet but very decided manner he expressed displeasure at the incident, saying that one
of the household ought not to live differently from the
rest, but should content himself with what was provided at the common table, and he hoped such an
incident would not occur again. I knew this old man
very intimately, and I do not think I ever met with
any one who had more of what a good judge in England would consider the characteristics of a gentleman.
He had both delicacy and dignity, and perfect self-
control, and he could keep up a conversation with
ladies with much ease and politeness, his chief difficulty
being the scantiness of his vocabulary in French, which

he spoke not very incorrectly as a foreign language, his own tongue being the *patois* of the hills. He was just the opposite of a tyrant or a brute, but he considered that paternal discipline required the infliction of punishment and reproof. In the French middle class corporal punishment is never resorted to, dry bread or confinement being the substitutes, but we must remember that the peasants—the genuine rustic peasants, I mean—live in a much earlier and simpler state of society.

An incident occurred about two years ago in my neighbourhood, in which, as the reader will see, paternal authority played a very important part. There was an old gentleman whom we will call the Count, and who being in very easy circumstances, could indulge a natural disposition to eccentricity. His manners were those of a gentleman, and he was by no means a stupid person, but he had a strong preference for the society of much younger men than himself, and in a class far inferior to his own. He also liked a symposium, and would invite young farmers to come and drink with him. In former years these symposia had gone so far that the Count used to get perfectly drunk before they were over, but of late he had been more moderate and only got tipsy. Now it so happened, about two years ago, that he invited a party of young farmers to come and drink with him, lads of twenty or twenty-two years old ; there were six of them, of whom three were brothers. They drank with the Count in a private room of his, and he fetched the wine from the cellar himself. When the symposium was so far advanced that all were elated, it being then about one

o'clock in the morning, the Count went to the cellar
again to fetch another kind of wine. During his absence
one of the three brothers noticed a pocket-book on
the chimney-piece, took it and put it in his own pocket.
He, or his brothers, did as much with a ring, a watch,
and a purse full of gold. When the Count came back
he was too tipsy to notice the disappearance of these
things, and the symposium went on merrily to its
natural conclusion. On the following morning, however, he discovered his loss, remembered who had been
with him, and told the story to me personally, adding
that he did not intend to put the matter in the hands
of the police if the money (£80) were restored to him.
It soon became evident that the thief must have been
one of the three brothers. When their father became
aware of what had occurred, he called the three young
men into his presence, and sent the rest of the family
out of the house. Then he locked the door, took
down his gun, and quietly loaded it, put caps on, and
cocked it. " Now," he said, " I am ready. One of
you three is a thief. If in five minutes I am not informed which is the thief, I shall shoot two of you."
There is no doubt that he would have done it, but before the time had expired, one of the brothers said, " I
took the pocket-book." It had been buried in a field
along with the other valuables, but the lads had spent a
hundred francs of the money, which the farmer replaced at once, returning the whole without delay to
its owner.

The peasants hide their money often even yet in old
stockings, corners of cupboards with false bottoms,

holes in the wall, or in the ground, &c. Sometimes they are robbed of rather considerable sums. I remember one old peasant who was robbed of fifty pounds by a thief who entered the house in broad daylight during the only half hour in the day when there was nobody in it, and this thief was never discovered; but either the same, or another, entered the same house some time later, also in the daytime, thinking that there was nobody at home. He went straight to the *armoire*, where the money had usually been kept, and did not perceive the master of the house, who was lying ill in his bed with the curtains drawn. The farmer peeped between the curtains and (very imprudently) asked the thief what he was doing there? On this the thief violently assaulted him, and would probably have killed him, had he not heard steps approaching. During the struggle the farmer tore off the pocket in the thief's blouse, and on opening his hand after the flight of his enemy, actually discovered that he had taken the thief's purse, which he showed me the next day. The purse contained a few pieces of silver. Is not this a beautiful instance of " poetical justice" in real life? The old peasant, was rather shaken for a day or two with his fight, but the contents of the purse were a consolation.

Before quitting the peasants, I may tell an anecdote which throws some light upon their intellectual condition. A very intelligent young peasant, of a superior class, whom I knew quite well, came to see me one day on a little matter of business, and was shown into my writing-room, where there are a good many books.

His curiosity was awakened by the sight of these, and he began to ask questions. I encouraged him by kind answers, and at last he began to inquire about my own occupations, which were a very strange mystery to him. I tried to make these as plain to him as possible, showing him a printed volume and a volume in manuscript, but here I encountered a singular and insurmountable difficulty. When he held the printed volume in his hands, he said, " You have written this beautifully, it is as well written as if a bookseller had done it, but the other is not so well done, and will never be as pretty." His impression about books was that each copy was a manuscript made by the bookseller, and he believed that I was one of those booksellers who made the manuscripts, only that I was a sort of amateur, because I did not keep a shop. It was impossible to make him understand that my rough manuscripts would look neat enough in print, and equally impossible to make him comprehend that my printed works were not beautiful autographs. In a word, he had never heard of the invention of printing, or did not know what was meant by it. And yet the young man was decidedly intelligent in all matters connected with his daily life, and had about four hundred pounds of his own.

The pursuit of landscape-painting here, as everywhere else, is one of the things which puzzle the uneducated most, and there is really no means of making them understand anything about it ; their minds are not prepared to receive the idea that there is such a thing as fine art. Notwithstanding the fine natural aptitude for art which distinguishes the French race, the great majority of the French people are really ignorant of its existence, except in their little religious prints, and the pictures in the churches, which seem to them only the same prints on a larger scale, the provincial art-galleries having really done nothing to enlighten the peasants, who do not visit them. But on this subject of art I think that the total and absolute ignorance which prevails amongst the French peasants who have never heard of the Louvre, is less discouraging and less vexatious to an artist or critic than the profound misconception of art which prevails amongst the Philistine majority of the wealthier classes both in France and England. The peasant sees me at work from nature, and thinks I am a land surveyor making a map ;* but has the *bourgeois*, who passes in his carriage, a much truer conception of painting? He very rarely goes farther than the elementary notion that it is a way of making likenesses of things by means of colours, as photography is a way of making likenesses of things by means of chemicals. It is only a *bourgeois* of very rare and exceptional culture who has any conception of art as the work of the mind, and an expression of intellect and imagination.

In the course of this chapter I have selected in-

---

* Some think it is land surveying, others think it is photography. At one time I had the reputation of being a photographer, and people came to have their portraits taken. I particularly remember one very good-looking peasant girl who came into my writing-room and insisted upon being photographed. She evidently did not believe my denials, and went away at last with the idea (not flattering to her self-esteem) that I had some personal objection to herself, which was certainly not the case.

stances which seemed most in accordance with common
every-day experience; but I will mention, before con-
cluding it, a peasant who is a very remarkable exception, and who is known to me personally, for he is
a welcome guest at my house whenever he chooses
to visit it. He belongs really to the true peasant-
proprietor class; he cultivates his own land, follows
the plough himself, wears the blue blouse, and is of a
genuine peasant family. Like all the superior peasants,
he keeps his *patois* separate from his French, but speaks
both very purely, and is not, as others are, limited to a
small vocabulary. The first time I met him was at the
house of a country squire, where I happened to be
staying for two or three days. Our host said to me
one morning, " I owe you some apology for inviting a
peasant to dine and stay all night whilst you are here,
but you will find him an interesting person." The
guest presented himself in his blue blouse. His manners were the perfection of good breeding, he was quite
at ease, took a fair share in the conversation, and soon
interested me more than any other person present.
When we separated the next day, he asked my permission to call upon me, and I gave him my address, which
was at some distance from the house where we had
met. A few days later he paid his call. To my intense amazement he began to talk about English literature and English newspapers, gave his opinion about
the way in which several of the leading newspapers in
London were conducted, talked about the *Times*, the
Daily News, the *Pall Mall Gazette*, &c. In our book-
literature he had read several of our best classic authors

in the original, and some contemporaries. He had heard that I was an English author, and felt curious to know what I had written. On looking over my books, he borrowed " The Intellectual Life," " Thoughts about Art," and one or two others. He read them steadily through, and duly returned them at the end of a few weeks. The book of mine which most interested him was " The Intellectual Life," which he found to his taste. The book called " Thoughts about Art," which is a collection of essays on artistic subjects, attracted his attention also, for he takes a lively and intelligent interest in the fine arts. Reading English, he said, was one of his greatest pleasures, he liked the simplicity of our language, and the tone which is prevalent in our better literature. He greatly admired the energy of our journalism, its full information, and the surprising rapidity with which it gives an account of all that happens. If I were to say that this remarkable peasant was equal to a *bourgeois*, the comparison would be very unjust to him. The French *bourgeois* is rarely free from some taint of Philistinism, and very frequently, indeed, he is as Philistine as he possibly can be, utterly incapable of taking any interest in anything outside of the present in space and time, and always ready to laugh at everything that is above the low level of his own petty and pitiful existence. This peasant has not the faintest trace of any kind of Philistinism in his nature. His mind is broad and just, he is capable of the interests which widen a human soul, and of the admirations which elevate it, whilst he does not shrink from real intellectual labour, which the common *bourgeois* shirks and hates like an idle schoolboy.

The question which will most interest the intelligent reader just at present is, whether it is possible for such a cultivated man as this to remain in the peasant class. As a matter of fact this one does follow the plough, and lead the genuine rustic life, but there is a special reason. He abandoned the rustic life a good many years ago, and went to live in Paris, where he obtained some commercial employment. He would probably have remained in Paris many years longer had health permitted, but a peculiar form of chronic indigestion was the consequence of town air and confinement. After trying all their drugs, the doctors said at last, " It is of no use physicking yourself any more, one thing only is needed, one thing only can bring your health back again, and that is the old rustic life which you were accustomed to before you came to Paris. You must go back to the plough, there is nothing else for it, *la santé est à ce prix.*" On this my friend accepted his lot quite cheerfully, thought to himself,—

> " ergo tua rura manebunt !
> Et tibi magna satis,"

and returned to his native fields and the old life of frugality and exercise. This is how it has come to pass that we have a peasant in our neighbourhood who is such a singular exception to the general rule of ignorance. I still maintain, however, that cultivated people will not, when they can help it, remain in the peasant-class. This one has two sons—is he educating them to be peasants? Certainly not. He has sent one of them to England to learn English and study commerce, and having discovered a strong artistic gift in the other, he is now giving him a thorough artistic education in Paris as a sculptor. How very unlike the ordinary peasant's ideas about bringing up his children! How completely outside of the class-limits, the class-traditions! This is what I always maintain, that the ignorance of the French peasantry is an essential element in the continuity of their life. Educate one of them and you break the tradition of a thousand years; the continuity of the family life is interrupted, broken for ever, and past all possible mending. These breakings are now becoming more and more frequent in the peasant families. Formerly, a rustic lad who had more than common natural refinement and intelligence always went into the priesthood, and lived afterwards amongst peasants in some country parish, unless his gifts were so extraordinary as to elevate him to one of the great dignities of the Church. As a country priest, he did not really break the continuity of rustic tradition, for instead of being a hearer in the village church of his boyhood he became the officiating priest in some other village church, and instead of ploughing the fields he blessed them. His life was still bound up with all rural interests and cares, and the rule of celibacy prevented him from looking forward to another ambition for any sons of his. Thus it happened, very remarkably, that all cultivated peasants were in former times childless men, and men who drew nobody out of the class. Neither did they bring into the class any new members imperfectly trained in its austere traditions. The class therefore remained strong and homogeneous in its fixed usages, and preserved them along with that ignorance which is one of their principal safeguards. It does not need any uncommon prophetic foresight to perceive that the genuine old French peasant will be unknown in a hundred years. Even now the young men are less frugal than their fathers; and the richer peasants, with the increase of their wealth, are adopting, little by little, many of those luxuries or comforts which formerly belonged exclusively to the *bourgeoisie* and *noblesse.* The last generation did not smoke, from motives of economy, the indulgence was considered too expensive; the present generation smokes without considering the expense. The use of wine is becoming gradually more general. Children are sent to school in towns who, had they lived twenty years earlier, would have been kept on the farm to watch the sheep or the geese. These educated children will never be real rustics like their fathers and mothers; they are easily distinguishable already. If the Republic lasts, and the Republicans have their will in a system of general secular education, the peasantry will be pervaded by new ideas and by new habits also. I am far from the temper which laments the loss of what is old, merely from a romantic interest in the past. The old feudal *noblesse* was as romantic as possible, but I am heartily glad that its power is broken for ever. Nor would I sacrifice human well-being to an artist's fancy for the picturesque. The picturesque old farm-houses, with their thatched roofs, dormer windows, and delightful disorder of quaint detail, are precious indeed to artists, yet we ought not to regret their now rapid disappearance, for they are replaced by buildings incomparably better planned for human health and convenience. But there is one thing which I really do regret, and that is the impossibility—for it seems as if there were some difficulty here which amounts practically to that—the impossibility of com-- bining the self-denial of a simple state of life with the intelligence of an advanced one. There seems to be in the depths of human nature some radical incompatibility between any really heroic degree of frugality and even a very ordinary education. The uneducated French peasant has the self-denial of a stoic philosopher, and the dignity of a Hebrew patriarch; he can govern himself and govern others—the daily work of his life is a constant discipline. In the same country, under the same climate and laws, educated professional men are generally epicures. The connection between learning and self-indulgence is very strongly marked in a recent work on Burgundy by M. Emile Montégut. Just observe it in the following sentences!—"Une aisance cossue, un loisir studieux, *les charmes de l'érudition et les voluptés de la cuisine,* échurent en partage à Dijon transformé en ville parlementaire.".... "*Oh! les grasses vies de savants, et les studieuses vies d'épicuriens!*"

CHAPTER XIII.

IN the course of the last chapter we alluded to some ecclesiastical matters in connection with the pilgrimages, and this leads me to say something more about the clergy and about the position of the Church in modern France. The subject is much too complex to be dealt with thoroughly here, but a few pages ought to be given to it, for it would be difficult to find anything of greater interest or importance.

Two great forces are perpetually struggling for the mastery of France, the lay spirit and the sacerdotal spirit. The contest between them has rarely been keener than it is just now, although it is conducted

without any other violence than some occasional violence
of language, and even this bears no proportion to the
vastness of the contest, which is often either altogether
noiseless or conducted with much propriety of form.

The object which the lay spirit has in view is to
secure the political and scientific independence of laymen, so that they may manage the affairs of the State
and follow all kinds of intellectual pursuits without
asking the permission of the Church of Rome. The
object which the sacerdotal spirit has in view is to
establish such a domination over laymen that they
may not venture upon any political course of action, .
or upon any course of intellectual study, without being
authorized by the priesthood.

It is not just to represent the struggle as one simply
between belief and unbelief. If Milton had lived in the
France of to-day, he would certainly have contended
energetically against the sacerdotal party, and yet Milton
believed in Christianity. If a town full of modern
Englishmen could be transported into the midst of
France, all the Low Churchmen and all the Dissenters
would be against the sacerdotal party, the Ritualists and
Roman Catholics might be on its side, yet not all even
of these, for many sincere Roman Catholics, both in
England and elsewhere, think that it is well there should
be some limit to the power of their own priesthood.

The lay party in France has not any desire to get rid
of the Roman Church, it has not generally any of the
active hostility towards it which is felt in a Protestant
community. The lay party looks upon the Church as a
man of thirty-five may look upon his old mother who

has very strong instincts of domination. He does not want to kill his old mother, he does not even wish that she might die a natural death, but he will so manage, in a quiet way, that she shall not rule him like an infant. He may not say very much in answer to her scoldings, but he will act with the independence of manhood.

This brings me to one of those curious international misunderstandings which seem destined to be eternal. English people sometimes wonder that there is not a great Protestant revolt of the French conscience against some astounding new doctrine of the Vatican, such as the Immaculate Conception, or the Papal Infallibility. The ordinary Frenchman is not at all in that state of mind which makes such a revolt likely, or even possible. For revolts of that kind energetic faith is needed, with its sensitiveness and its determination. The ordinary Frenchman is accustomed to consider the Church as a venerable entity which somehow exists outside the domain of reason, and if she were to proclaim a new marvel every week, it would make no difference in his attitude towards her. He is not, like Mr. Gladstone, deeply moved and alarmed because the Pope says he is infallible, nor does he think it necessary to protest against the self-assertion of the Vatican. The fact is, that he does not care anything about the details of dogma; but, on the other hand, he likes so to manage matters, in a very quiet way, that the sacerdotal party may not really govern him. If that party were to become as strong as it desires to be, it would arouse a more active opposition, and then we might possibly see an exciting contest like that which is going on in

Germany. This, however, is in the highest degree improbable. A quiet kind of resistance has for many years been sufficient to secure a remarkably complete degree of personal liberty, and the same quiet resistance will probably suffice to maintain it. On the other side, the sacerdotal party carries on a warfare of the same silent kind, gaining influence, wherever possible, over families and schools; over tradesmen and professional people through their commercial or professional interests; over the National Assembly and the Government by its alliance with what are called Conservative principles and the safety of society. The sacerdotal party is steadily aggressive, the lay party is always simply on the defensive, and here lies its chief weakness. Mr. Gladstone says of the first that it has " faith, self-sacrifice, and the spirit of continuity," which, indeed, are three mighty powers; but the lay party has not much faith, and as to self-sacrifice, its object is just the opposite, namely, self-defence. Of the spirit of continuity, it has nothing consciously ; but, in fact, it is kept continuously to its own principles by the very persistence of its adversaries.

"Would it not be much better," the English reader is not unlikely to ask, " for the French to embrace some form of Protestantism, and so be fairly independent of the Vatican, and not in the false position of people who have to be constantly resisting the encroachments of a Church to which they nominally belong?" The only reasonable answer to this is, that it is useless to speculate on what would be best, since the only really interesting question is what is possible, what is in harmony with the character of the people as we find them. The English

U

or American reader might like to be told that Protestantism was making great progress, or likely to make
great progress, amongst the French people, but the
assertion would be untrue.   It exists, its liberties are
so far secured that no attempt will be made to extinguish
the two Protestant Churches, which are paid by the
State, but it has only the same kind of position that
Unitarianism has in England ; indeed a large proportion
of French Protestants, though not the majority, really
are Unitarians.   The ordinary Frenchman either follows
his own reason or else submits to ecclesiastical authority.
If he follows his own reason, he is almost always a free-
thinker, and if he submits to authority, no church on
earth appears to him so authoritative as that of Rome.
There is another and more subtle reason why the Church
of Rome is likely to keep her place.   Modern life is
miserably deficient in external pomp and solemnity,
even on those occasions when people feel that visible
ceremony is necessary.   The Church of Rome supplies
this want, and supplies it with all the skill derived from
centuries of traditional experience.   Take the occasion
of marriage, for instance.   The legal marriage is that
solemnized by the *maire*, but people do not feel that it
is enough, and this feeling of its insufficiency need not
be due to religious opinion, for a simple philosopher who
had any sense of propriety would share it.   In our village there is no public room for occasions of this kind,
so all the marriages are celebrated in the school-room, a
poor place, hung with a few maps and alphabets.   The
maire gets behind the schoolmaster's desk, ties his official
scarf round his waist, reads his little formula, asks the

woman if she will have the man, and the man if he will have the woman, after which he declares them married ; and married they are indeed in the eye of the law, but nobody present feels that this is enough. The village priest supplies what is wanting, a solemn and impressive ceremony, in a building which, at least comparatively, is noble, and can affect the imagination, a building with vaulted roof borne high on arches, and painted windows, wherein are pictured legends of the saints. The priest himself does not look like a common man prepared for a common occasion. He is at the same time splendid and dignified, like a personage prepared for some act of high importance. He goes through a long ceremony slowly, hurrying nothing and omitting nothing, and whilst it is proceeding, the bride feels, the bridegroom feels—all present are made to feel—that the day of marriage is not a common day, and that the pair who enter into the new state are not forgotten, nor neglected, nor passed over with slight notice, as if the event, so great to them, were of no consequence to others. If an anti-clerical government wished to weaken sacerdotalism effectually, its best means of doing so would be to establish imposing civil ceremonies for the great occasions of private and public life ; but to this there is the insuperable objection that no modern authority could invent such ceremonies without making them and itself ridiculous. The Church has them from tradition, and is not ridiculous. Here is one of her great forces, she can supply the need of ceremony and solemnity which exists in human nature, and she always has the means of doing so ready to hand in her own traditional usages. I have mentioned one occasion that of marriage, as an instance, but how many other occasions, private and public, make people feel the same need! There is the great subject of civil and religious burial. Thousands of Frenchmen who have hardly any faith in the dogmas of the Church would not like to be buried, or to see their friends buried, without her impressive ceremonies, simply because the advocates of civil burial have never yet been able to invent any new customs impressive enough to take their place. The priest, so splendid for a marriage, wears nothing but black and white vestments for a funeral; even the altar itself is in mourning, and crape hangs from the silver cross. And then the solemn singing, the *Dies Iræ*, and the rest? Who can invent all that? On public occasions of solemnity the priest is scarcely less indispensable. A railway is opened, people wish to make the ceremony imposing; they get the prefect to come, but who is the prefect? After all he is only a gentleman in uniform, something like court dress, with some embroidery on his breast, and a ribbon in his button-hole. The really splendid man is the bishop, with his golden cope, his crozier of silver-gilt, and his mitre all blazing with jewels. He comes with his priests, gets upon the locomotive, blesses the railway, and everybody feels that a real ceremony has been performed. When the National Assembly is opened, after each recess there is pontifical high mass, a usage which is likely to be perpetuated simply because a number of deputies in frock coats are not able of themselves to get up anything magnificent enough for the importance of the occasion. The incredible poverty of laymen in the nineteenth century in everything relating to ceremonies or public occasions, may pass unobserved in countries where the need for them is no longer felt, but the Latin races are still very much alive to the sort of poetry which strikes the eye, and ordinary life leaves a void which the Church of Rome fills very perfectly. When M. Thiers was President of the Republic, the modern poverty of costume was conspicuous in the plainness of his dress. A new costume, invented for him, would have made people laugh, but the old desire for visible splendour is not extinct, it is unsatisfied. Its only remaining satisfactions are ecclesiastical and military pomp. I believe, therefore, that the splendour of the Church of Rome, so far from being a cause of weakness for the Church, as it might be in a more northern country, is still with the Latin races one of the sources of her strength, and that the plainer and more externally uninteresting modern life becomes, the more decidedly does this ecclesiastical splendour supply a want that is felt, especially on solemn private or public occasions.

Another reason, though a negative one, why the Church of Rome is on the whole satisfactory to Frenchmen, is that she interferes so little with their ordinary habits of life. Positive religious liberty in France is not yet quite complete ; you cannot open a Dissenting chapel without being authorized, and the authority to do so may be refused ; you cannot preach in the public streets, or in the fields, if you attempted it you would most likely be put in prison. But the want of the complete positive liberty is not much felt by Frenchmen, if indeed they ever feel it, or are aware of it at all ; for they never, or only in the most rare and exceptional instances, feel any desire to preach in the fields or streets ; the sort of liberty they really do care for, and are determined to secure, is negative liberty—I mean that they would resent any interference of the clergy in their ordinary life.   In this the Church of Rome is *bonne mère.*   She has a tradition that it is wrong to eat meat on Fridays, but you can get meat on Friday in any hotel in France except those which are specially frequented by priests, and it is only in the stricter houses amongst the laity that the rule is enforced with anything like rigour.   Even amongst religious people themselves it gives way at once before the recommendation of a physician.   I have myself seen a priest eating mutton chops on Friday because his doctor said that they would be better for him than fish.   So many good things are considered *maigres*, that in any rich man's house the Friday may be looked forward to as a pleasant change ; indeed some of the most delicious repasts imaginable are served to rich people on fast-days.   There is hardly anything else in which the Church can be said to inter- fere in the course of every-day life.   A man who followed her offices very exactly might find them a fatigue, but a Frenchman is not expected to do that.   One great merit, at least, the Church has in the eyes of every Frenchman who knows the customs of Protestant countries—she does not interfere with his Sunday.   English and American travellers often imagine, when they see French- men playing billiards or going out shooting on Sunday, that they must be reprobates who knowingly disobey the Church.   It is not so ; the Church has no objection to any occupation on Sunday which does not earn money, and even with regard to those occupations which do earn it. she is not very severely intolerant. A very pious Frenchman told me that the Church did not object to literary or artistic work on Sunday; but only to slavish labour, her object being rather to protect the poor drudge, than to interfere with the liberal pursuits of the cultivated classes. Thus the only two days of the week on which the Church might be supposed to exert her authority in a special manner are days of perfect liberty for the ordinary Frenchman; so far, at least, as her dictates are concerned. He thinks that he might go farther, in the way of reform, and fare worse. He has heard (though he can never quite seriously believe it) that there are countries where a rural squire may not shoot on his own land on Sunday, and dare not use his own billiard-table, and he has a suspicion that if Protestants of the Guizot type got the upper hand in France, they might put a veto on his ordinary amusements. It is very likely, indeed, that they would, for M. Guizot had a fine spirit of domination, and a resolute hostility to heretics; but the Guizots are in a very small minority when compared with the whole nation, so men feel that their negative religious liberty is safe, and that is what they seriously care for. A traveller from a Protestant country is likely to conclude that the Church in France is weak because there is so much personal liberty, and a traveller from a despotic country might infer that the English monarchy was weak for the same reason; but both inferences would be erroneous. It is the strength and not the weakness of the English throne that the

Sovereign does not interfere with individual liberty, and it is the strength and not the weakness of the Romish Church in France that she can exist and flourish with so little inconvenience to the laity.

I have been considering the relation of the Church to the male sex, and I have endeavoured to show that there are reasons why she is not likely to be regarded with much unkindness so long as she keeps within certain limits, which are perfectly well known to her. With regard to the other sex the case is different. The relations of the Church with women are much closer and more intimate than with men. For them she is the confidant and consoler, especially by means of confession, which women delight in as a precious opportunity for talking about what most interests them in their own lives. Here, indeed, the Church does really exercise authority, for the lives of all devout women, except the few who are Protestants, are entirely under her guidance. But the authority here is not felt to be tyrannical in any way, because it is so willingly accepted. Women love the Church, their only regret is not to be able to make their husbands and brothers love her as much as they do. The interference with human life is here a source of positive strength, just as the non-interference in the affairs of the other sex is a source of negative strength. Women support the Church with the ardour of genuine conviction, and see the outer world by looking through her coloured windows.

It is from this support of the female sex that the Church derives her enormous social weight. By means of this, rather than by obtaining legal enactments, she

keeps Protestantism in a position of inferiority. Protestantism is dissent in France—tolerated, but inferior.
Legally, there is no State Church in the country, or, at
least, the two Protestant Churches, being paid by the
State, and the Jewish religion, which is paid also, are as
much State Churches as their great sister of Rome;
but socially the difference is as great as if she alone
were recognized by the State. The Romish clergy have
had the subtlety and skill to make women believe that
there is something impious in other religions. There is
a very general impression amongst them that Protestants are not Christians,* and the impression is so far
founded on fact that a great number of French Protestants, being really Unitarians, would not have been considered Christian by Dr. Arnold. As for Jews, the old
feeling of horror against them still survives in the minds
of good Catholic women. I remember an amusing
instance of this. Four young gentlemen from a great
school in Paris came to stay a few days with me, and
were invited to a nobleman's house in the country, where
there was a young lady—a model young lady according
to French ideas—with all the proper ignorances and
prejudices. She had a brother who was struck by the
idea that one of the young gentlemen had rather a
Jewish face, and this suggested to his youthful mind
the idea of getting a little fun out of the situation. He
put on a very grave face, went to his sister and told her
that the unfortunate guest was really a Jew, not only by

* In Spain this impression is said to be universal by those who
know the country, and as it is not corrected by the clergy, we may
fairly conclude that they have no objection to its existence as
a pious exaggeration serviceable to the true faith.

race but by religion. My young friends were invited for several days, but the "Jew" did not find them very enjoyable. His place was fixed for him next the young lady at dinner, but when he sat down she rose with an offended air and went as far off as possible, asking some one else to take her chair. Whenever he tried to speak to her she turned away from him with a look of horror. There were dances in the evenings; he asked her to dance, she refused point-blank, without even the usual form of politeness. This lasted three days. On the fourth, seeing that she maintained the same attitude of repulsion, he determined to ask for an explanation, and did so in plain terms. "Little explanation is necessary," said the young lady, "how is it possible for me to associate with one who has crucified my Saviour?" "I cannot tell what you mean, I never crucified anybody." "You are a Jew, and it is you Jews who did it!"

There is a way of pronouncing words which implies moral disapprobation, even when the word is used by itself quite simply. The French word "Protestant," which looks so exactly like the English word, is usually uttered in Roman Catholic families in such a manner as to convey such a sense of disapproval that it becomes a word of reproach; and young ladies, being sensitive and observant, are thus brought to associate Protestantism from their infancy with the things which are not right. There is another well-known device by which an association of ideas may be created which is sure to be unfavourable to a proscribed, or half-proscribed opinion. It may be spoken of along with something which is known to be bad, as if the two went necessarily together. Thus you may easily convey the impression that unbelievers are bad men by coupling together "vice and infidelity," and if after that you say "Protestantism and infidelity," you will convey the idea that Protestantism and vice have a very near relationship. I remember reading a book by a French bishop in which he stoutly maintained that Protestantism sprang entirely from the desire to indulge vicious passions which the Church condemned. This was not quite true or just, but I had a book by an English theologian in which exactly the same was said of freethinking, and we must remember that, to a Romanist, Protestantism, in all its varieties, is but one of the forms of freethinking.

There are certain arts by which a dominant Church may keep the weaker churches in an inferior social position, without any visible persecution. Here are one or two instances of it in little things. A few years ago it was still the custom in a great many lyceums and colleges to give the prizes for religious instruction with much pomp and publicity when the boys were Roman Catholics, but when they were Protestants the prizes were given to them in private, without solemnity of any kind. It is astonishing that a great and powerful Church should descend to such little things, but she is acute enough to perceive that nothing is beneath her attention which can exalt herself and depress her inferiors. She will even infringe the law when her own importance is in any way affected. According to French law it is not possible to delegate honours; I mean that if a bishop is absent and is represented by his vicar-general, the latter will receive only the honours due to his own rank, and not those due to the episcopal rank, even though for the time being he stands in the place of the bishop. The principle is rigidly carried out by civil functionaries. A secretary-general (*de préfecture*) may represent a prefect, but he will only receive the honours of a secretary-general. Well, it happened in 1869 that a certain archbishop was absent from his diocese on the day when prizes were distributed at the lyceum. He was represented by his vicar-general. On the same occasion were present the presidents of the Protestant and Jewish Consistories. The archbishop, had he been present, would have taken precedence of these, but the vicar-general could not legally do so. However, he insisted upon taking precedence notwithstanding the law, and by the weakness of the university authorities he gained his point. A certain bishop, whose name I know, was invited to a distribution of prizes some years earlier in the same lyceum. He asked what place he was to have, and was answered, "The place assigned to a bishop by the law," on which he refused to come. An archbishop presented a candidate for the post of chaplain in a lyceum. These chaplains are presented by the ecclesiastical authority and appointed by the Minister of Public Instruction. In this case the Minister gave the candidate a chaplaincy of the third class The archbishop protested, and demanded the second class for his candidate. "I cannot give it him," replied the Minister, "it is beyond my power to do so, the law forbids me." The archbishop insisted with great pertinacity in spite of the rule, and during the correspondence the lyceum in question remained without a chaplain. At length the archbishop's candidate was appointed, and a few days afterwards, in spite of the rules quoted by the Minister himself, he was promoted to the second class. The influence exercised by the episcopate is not, as may be imagined, confined to helping their own friends; it is also employed, often very efficaciously, against persons whom they dislike on account of their nonconformity. The principal of a certain great lyceum was a Protestant; so the bishop of the diocese used his influence to get him removed, and succeeded. An " Inspecteur d'Académie," was a Protestant, and had formerly been a pastor. Whilst holding the rank of " Inspecteur," he was imprudent enough to resume his clerical profession to some extent, for he preached a few sermons in a Protestant church. This offended the bishop of the diocese, who, like the one mentioned above, used his influence to get the Protestant removed, and succeeded.* A professor of philosophy in a lyceum not very far north of Lyons wrote some articles on the Society of St. Vincent de Paul. The clergy found out that he was the author of these articles, and had power enough to get him suspended. On the other hand, a priest published a little book very unfavourable to the French university, and particularly unfavourable to a certain college of which he was himself the chaplain. For this he was suspended by the

---

* These anecdotes are all perfectly authentic, and I have in my possession the names of the persons and places, even to the name of the Protestant church where the sermons were preached. I follow, however, my usual rule of withholding names, for the simple reason that, even when an anecdote is quite true, it may cost a good deal of time and money to *prove* the truth of it.

Rector of the academy to which the college belonged, and the Minister of Public Instruction confirmed the suspension. The bishop of the diocese met this by making the suspended chaplain a canon of his cathedral, and refused during many years to present a candidate to succeed him in his chaplaincy, which, therefore, necessarily remained vacant. Besides this, he refused to go to the college to confirm the boys, although it had always been the custom for the bishop of the diocese to do so. A well-known writer, who had a high position in one of the great professional schools of Paris, was so imprudent as to contribute an article to a review on the subject of " Catholicism." Clerical influence was powerful enough to have him dismissed with a small " indemnity." The " indemnity " for the first year was about £20. In successive years it was gradually reduced, and finally came down to nothing at all. Happily for the ex-professor, he was a clever writer, and was accepted as contributor by two or three of the best newspapers. He has been a journalist ever since.

It has sometimes happened, but rarely, that the clergy have been met by a decided opposition and refusal, even in the highest quarters. The following curious little story was communicated to me by the successor of the lay functionary whom it concerns. In a certain important lyceum there was a change of bursars. The new bursar suffered much from a varicose vein in his leg, which compelled him to pass a great deal of his time in an arm-chair, with his leg stretched on a camp-stool. When he arrived at the lyceum for the first time, he met a priest, and at once concluded that he must be the chaplain. On this the following little conversation took place between the new acquaintances :—

Bursar. I suppose that I have the honour to speak to the chaplain ?

Chaplain. Yes.

Bursar. I am the new bursar, and I fear that you will have a bad parishioner in me. My infirmity compels me to remain quiet as much as possible, and I shall be unable to attend the services in the chapel.

Chaplain. If you do not attend I give you warning that I will have you dismissed.

Bursar. Since that is the tone you take, I promise you that you will never see me in your chapel, and I shall quietly await the consequences of your denunciation.

The chaplain wrote to the Minister of Public Instruction, who at that time was M. Duruy, and in his letter he appealed to a statute of 1821 which obliges all who are lodged in the establishment to attend chapel. But the Minister answered that this applied only to functionaries who had the direction of the pupils, and that the bursar was not one of these, since his duties were limited to the control of money and material ; consequently, in matters of religion, the bursar ought to follow his own conscience. The answer was not addressed directly to the chaplain, but to the rector of the academy to which the lyceum belonged ; and it concluded by requesting the rector to remind the chaplain that the principal (Proviseur) of the lyceum, and not the chaplain, was " *seul juge de la conduite des fonctionnaires.*"

A few vigorous answers of this kind would set limits to clerical interference in university matters, but they require great courage on the part of a Minister of Public Instruction, for if once the Church finds out that he is not compliant he will have a hard time of it, and will be unable to keep his post for long unless backed by a very strong and determined Liberal Government, such as may be possible in the future, but has hardly ever yet been seen in this generation. The most effective resistance which the lay party have as yet been able to oppose to the sacerdotal has been the establishment of the University, an institution which is generally much undervalued in England, and very unjustly. It always seems to me, in reading English criticisms of the French University (which generally take the form of sneers), that the writers must have been directly under the influence of the French clergy, who dislike the University as a rival educator of youth. It is surprising how easily those views of things in France, which are set agoing by the Roman Catholic clergy for their own purposes, obtain currency in a Protestant, or at least non-Catholic, country like England. The French clergy, for example, with their usual extreme cleverness in the use of language, have of late been demanding the liberty to teach the youth of their own persuasion, and what can be more reasonable than that? An English member of Parliament was innocent enough to say, a little time since, that he thought the liberty to teach was so natural a liberty to ask for, that he could not conceive how any political party could refuse it. He seems really to have believed, though living so near to France, that "*la liberté de l'enseignment*" was what the clergy were striving for in the foundation of Catholic Universities. It is quite true that the clergy have adroitly made use of that expression " la liberté de l'enseignment," but they possessed that liberty long before. The object they have striven for recently was not the liberty to teach, but the power to give University degrees, as they liked, to good Catholic young men, as a reward for diligent attention to priestly teaching. In this project they have not quite succeeded, because the degrees are to be given by mixed boards of examiners from the State University and the Catholic Universities. Many University men regret that the entire power to grant degrees was not accorded to the priests at once, for if it had been their degrees would soon have been appreciated at their true value. The clergy certainly deserve the greatest credit for the self-sacrifice with which they devote themselves to teaching. Many clerical teachers in the seminaries receive no pay whatever, and there are orders of teaching priests (the Maristes for example) who when ordered by their superiors to undertake the drudgery of school-work will do it unflinchingly from year's end to year's end without any other reward than the sense of duty accomplished. All this is very admirable, and the clerical institutions are, in almost every instance, models of order and good management, with excellent buildings and gardens. The pupils are not a source of profit, but of loss, and yet the Church has so many means of acquiring money that she willingly undertakes the most extensive responsibilities. The one thing she aims at is to have the control of young people's minds. She dislikes parental influence, and endeavours to detach young people from it, whenever possible. In the seminary near my house, the pupils are not allowed to visit their parents during the whole scholastic year. By means of its great seminaries and colleges, and now by means of the new Catholic Universities, the Church is energetically endeavouring to crush the State University, the great lay establishment whose rivalry she dislikes above all things. Many intelligent laymen, both in the University and out of it, think that the Church, so far from injuring the University, will render her the inestimable service of stimulating to self-improvement an institution which might have crystallized into a fixed system of routine if it had never been alarmed by rivalry.

I have just said that English criticism was generally unjust to the French University. It is generally contemptuous—inconsiderately and ignorantly contemptuous. The English critic either compares the French University with Oxford, or else with some ideal in his own imagination, an ideal of what things ought to be but are not, either in France or anywhere else. Both comparisons are alike idle and unprofitable. The French University has seventy thousand undergraduates; the object of it is not to polish a few minds, but to inform a multitude. It is not seated in one old town alone, but has its colleges all over the country. It is present everywhere, so that you can never be more than a few miles from one of its establishments. It will teach a little child to read, and give a learned scholar his doctor's degree. It is entirely disinterested, the State derives no profit from it; it puts education within the reach of thousands who without its help would grow up in perfect ignorance, or with no higher teaching than that of the village school. Mr. Lowe said that it was not a University at all, but if we look to the derivation of the word, I think we must admit that few educational institutions have had such fair claims to the title. The name was given at first to educational bodies which were bound together in unity; and even English critics, little as they know about the French University, are well aware that it has unity, for they are always laughing at it because its unity is too perfect for their taste. I have disposed of the comparison with Oxford. When Oxford shall educate seventy thousand English youths at once it will be time to institute such a comparison. With regard to the dissatisfaction with a great existing institution because it does not come up to an ideal standard, I beg leave to offer some observations. It is a great thing to exist, and to work, and a wise criticism ought not to be too idealist with reference to things which are in the world of every-day reality, and do a great deal of useful labour. Most of the useful work in the world is done in places and by people who do not come up to the artistic or intellectual ideal. Nobody pretends that the French University is an ornamental institution; it was established for simple utility, and it is maintained, though not illiberally, at the lowest cost which is compatible with the work it has to do. There are no magnificent incomes, no princely residences for its magnates, and the poorer workers in it labour for little wage. Their incomes were fixed at a time when living was cheaper than it is now, and it would be simple justice to increase them. With regard to the buildings, some of the older ones, though large, are defective in their arrangements; the new ones are much better, and some of the very newest are admirable models of clever construction for their special purpose. The French University makes no pretension to wealth, its pride is to do the maximum of work at the minimum of cost; still, if the sums expended on all its colleges and lyceums were added together they would make a very formidable total. A new lyceum costs from thirty to eighty thousand pounds, which is a large sum to find for a small provincial town. There is plenty of space in these buildings for the convenience of teaching. Every class has its own room, generally lofty and well-lighted, and its own study, in which work is prepared for the classroom.* Every lyceum in France, and I believe also every college, has a room for instruction in the elements of physical science, with the necessary apparatus, which in many cases has been liberally added to of late years.

It is the fashion in the English newspapers to repeat one or two stock accusations against this University system. They delight to repeat the story of M. Duruy, who when Minister of Public Instruction looked at his watch and said that he knew what was being done at that hour in every lyceum in the country. The anecdote is true, but it is entirely misunderstood by those writers who quote it to exhibit the absurdity of the system. M. Duruy had been preceded by another Minister, Fortoul, who had a fancy for regulating every-

---

* This is of very great importance. In English Grammar Schools lessons are, or were, learned in the same room in which classes were held at the same time.

thing very exactly, and Duruy's observation about the watch was not a boast, but a little piece of " malice " directed against what he considered the needlessly minute *réglementation* of his predecessor. The English inference that because a Minister knows what the classes in the University were doing at a particular hour the system of education must be bad, is quite unwarranted, for the fact of his knowing what is done does not touch the utility of the teaching. The Archbishop of Canterbury knows exactly what chapters of the Bible are read in all Anglican churches on a particular Sunday, but this does not prove that the chapters are not worth reading, or that they are read badly. English critics represent French University teachers as mere slaves, who have no chance of making their own individuality an influence over their pupils. The assertion is grossly and ignorantly untrue ; and it is most especially untrue as regards the higher instruction where the individuality of the teacher may be brought to bear with more advantage as the work to be done requires a more constant exercise of thought. It is said that education in France can never be worth anything until every Principal of a college has full liberty to do exactly what he likes without being directed by a Minister of Public Instruction. Perhaps a Principal of uncommon discernment would, with fuller liberty, rise above the present level, but it is equally probable that many others of inferior talent and energy would sink below it. The University must have a central authority of some kind or it would cease to be a University. Some heads of lyceums and colleges are men of great attainments, but on the whole the pro-

bability is that the Minister of Public Instruction will
be superior both in attainments and in breadth of view
to the average master of a lyceum.   With a single
exception this has certainly been true of recent Minis-
ters.   The fact that the public schools are bound together
in an organized University system is at once a safeguard and a convenience.   It is a safeguard against the
educational hobbies of individual masters, and it is a
convenience, because a boy when removed from one
lyceum to another may continue his education without
a break.   The University system ensures a frequent and
severe academic inspection of public schools, which prevents them from falling below a certain average standard
of efficiency, however isolated they may be, and however remote from Paris.

The education is not so worthless as English critics
represent it to be.   It is incomparably superior to
English middle-class education, unless the latter has
been wonderfully amended during the last few years.
Its systematic character, and the steadiness of the training which it gives, with the obligatory bachelor's degree
at the end for all who enter the liberal professions, ensure
the advantages of a known method and a settled purpose.   A French provincial lawyer or surgeon having
worked steadily up through all the classes to his bachelor's degree, and taken it, is a better trained man than
the English provincial attorney or surgeon who has been
to a grammar-school and passed thence to the office or
surgery with whatever the local grammar-school might
give him.   In many cases the bachelor's degree becomes
an incentive to a higher ambition, and the young lawyer

or doctor works up to the higher academic degrees. I know one who took his doctor's degree in law, his doctor's degree in medicine, and his doctor's degree in letters. His degrees required three distinct and complete educations. You find even simple village attorneys who, thanks to the University system, are well-educated men. I know one such who is *licencié* in law and *licencié* in science at the same time. The most extraordinary instance of several different educations united in one individual which ever came to my knowledge was that of a priest who had taken his doctor's degree in letters, science, law, medicine, and theology. Not one of these degrees is honorary, each of them has to be won by passing an examination which severely tests the acquirements of the candidate.

A vast institution which thus places a liberal education within the reach of the middle classes all over the country, and does its work with sustained energy year after year, deserves more discriminating criticism than the blind scorn which will not even condescend to examine what it despises. It is impossible that so comprehensive an institution should be ideally perfect, or should satisfy in every respect the excessive exigencies of specialists. The French University has many defects, the education which it gives is faulty in many particulars, but its shortcomings are as well known to its own chiefs as to the cleverest of foreign critics. The one great evil of the system is an evil prevalent in modern education everywhere. Too many things are undertaken for all to be well done, and there is a deplorable waste of time in going half-way towards several things when it is manifestly impossible for the pupils to go all the way. "If they never arrive," as Professor Seeley said of the majority of boys in England, "what was the use of their setting out ? That a country is prosperous and pleasant is a reason for going to it, but it is not a reason for going half-way to it. If you cannot get all the way to America, you had better surely go somewhere else. If you are a parent, and think that your son is not fit to go to Cambridge, you send him into the city or into the army. You do not send him part of the way to Cambridge ; you do not send him to Royston or Bishop Stortford." French University education too often sends its pupils to half-way places like these. But in some things they go all the way. The University renders an immense service to the mental life of the nation by insisting, to begin with, that every one of its pupils shall be thoroughly trained in accurate French speaking and writing. A serious endeavour is made to awaken the attention of boys to the literary qualities of great French authors. In this way the French University really does for its own country what Professor Seeley wished that English schoolmasters would do for England—it teaches the native language and opens the gates of the native literature. This is much indeed, it is more for culture than a foreign tongue half-learned, especially in France, where the native language has a rich and elaborate grammar, which no uneducated person ever mastered. Besides French, the University teaches Latin with much thoroughness, and the consequence is that a vast number of Frenchmen can read the Latin authors without any insuperable difficulty. Geometry is well taught from good modern books in which the science is brought down to the latest date. Having mentioned these three things, I have almost exhausted the list of studies which are carried out in any thoroughness. Greek is imperfectly learned, and modern languages are learned more imperfectly still. In history, geography, and the physical sciences, all that can be done is to give abridgments, which are accurate so far as they go. These limits and imperfections are due chiefly to the multiplicity of subjects attempted. It is not possible for a boy to learn four or five languages and as many distinct sciences, all at the same time, and learn them all thoroughly. A grown man in the full vigour of his intellect could not do it even if he took the keenest interest in every one of his subjects. He would find himself compelled to throw over the majority of his subjects until he had mastered one or two, after which he might take up one or two others, if life were long enough. Why does not the University act in this rational manner? The answer is, that although the University is a great State establishment, it must have pupils in sufficient numbers to form classes, or it could not exist. To have pupils, it must offer attractions. The majority of living parents, never having really learned anything themselves, fancy that the more things are taught the more they get for their money. It is a most mischievous and foolish error, but it exists amongst uncultivated parents everywhere, simply because the uncultivated mind has not, and cannot have, the faintest conception of the time and labour required for the mastery of any single intellectual pursuit. New tasks are laid on the shoulders of the boys, but the old tasks are not removed to make room for the new ones. The burden is too great, the hours of labour are too long, the burden oppresses the mind instead of strengthening it, except in those rare cases when the natural faculties are so strong, and so elastic, and so agile, that they develop themselves happily notwithstanding. The Principal of a French college, himself a good Greek scholar, told me that he wished he could get rid of Greek in his college unless some other studies were thrown overboard. Unfortunately, you cannot get a bachelor's degree by thoroughly learning two things, but you can easily get a bachelor's degree by the aggregate of marks which results from imperfectly learning a dozen things.

This, I believe, is a fair account of the real merits and defects of French University education. Wherever too much is attempted the deficiencies will be the same, and too many things will always be attempted by educators until fathers and mothers are wise enough to perceive that things half-learned are useless. One common clerical accusation remains to be considered. It is constantly asserted that the University is irreligious because it is not exclusively Catholic, but admits Protestants, Jews, and Mahometans, with the right to follow their own faith. A great lay institution could hardly do otherwise, in this, than model itself upon the conduct of the State to which it belongs. The State is not exclusively Catholic, neither is the University. Still, the Church of Rome has by far the largest share in the religious teaching of the University, for she has a chapel and a chaplain in every lyceum and in every college. If the chaplains have not so much influence as they would like to have, it is certainly not for lack of opportunity. The real ground of the religious objection to the University is that the masters are laymen, and do not exclude heretics.

Aristocratic criticism has its own objection to the University. It is too much open to the sons of poor men, so that boys are not brought up exclusively in good society. Your son may possibly find himself in the same class with the son of a blacksmith. This objection is very terrible from the lady-mother's point of view, but the consequence of the mixture is not so deplorable as might be expected. The blacksmith's son often sets the gentleman's son the example of good conduct and hard work, which is well worth some polish of manner, and in a country where polite forms are universal, social differences are not very painfully felt. The advantage of the mixture is certainly great in after life. Men in quite different classes of society have studied together in the same college and know each other really well. This has a tendency to dissipate the illusions of exclusiveness, and to create a friendly feeling between classes, of which France has the greatest need. One of my young friends in a college at Paris told me that in his class there were boys of every rank, including even royalty, for two of his class-fellows belonged to a princely reigning family in Eastern Europe, others belonged to noble families, and others to quite poor and obscure ones. In after life this young man followed a profession which brought him into contact with all classes of society, and the variety of his early experience was of use in preserving him from two kinds of awkwardness—the *mauvaise honte* which cannot hold its own in the presence of a superior, and the pride which has never learned how to communicate rationally with people of humble rank. In this way the University has done good, and although an aristocratic Englishman would object to it as too democratic, the real truth is that its influence is an antidote to the worst evils of democracy, for it constantly tends to diminish the envy and hatred which a fierce, ignorant, and *excluded* democracy always bears to the more privileged classes. The form of democracy which the University produces is that of Jules Simon and Thiers. It gives poor boys a fair chance in life and puts them quite at their ease, never making them ashamed of their poverty as if it were a crime, and at the same time it takes the conceit out of rich ones without needlessly wounding their self-respect. A French lyceum is a public school to which a working man's son may go without the slightest apprehension that his parents will be laughed at when they come to see him, because they are not "swells," and yet a rich squire's son may go there and get all the benefits of emulation without any sacrifice of caste. Above all, the existence of so many large public schools all over the country saves thousands of boys from the dulness and sluggishness of private education, and gives them a fine stimulus to active work, not only in the rank they may win in the school itself, but in the early fame which they get in the town and department where the lyceum is situated. Everybody takes a kindly interest in the

successes of an industrious and clever lad. The public
" distribution des prix " is faithfully attended by all the
notabilities of the place, and by hundreds of other
people who, with astonishing patience, sit hour after
hour listening to tiresome discourses and lists of classes.
All the town talks about the most successful winners of
prizes, and for several days afterwards their fathers are
congratulated on every hand. It is easy to laugh at
the crowns of paper oak-leaves and gilding, at the
multiplicity of prizes, at their slight material value,
and at everything else in these ceremonies which has
that air of cheapness for which the English mind
has such an intense contempt ; but a kindly critic, or
even a just one, would feel more disposed to rejoice
in an occasion which awakened emulation amongst
boys and friendly feeling amongst men of all classes
in society.

Notwithstanding the incessant action of the University in disseminating knowledge, the ignorance of
Frenchmen, even when educated, is proverbial in Europe,
especially since their great defeat, which has lowered
the general opinion of them in every respect. I have
talked on this subject with men of many nations, and
they all agreed in laughing at French ignorance, which
indeed is often truly amazing. It is due in great part
to the predominance of the classical system in education. This system, when strong enough to be exclusive,
has in every country the effect of producing a contempt
for other knowledge rather than the openness of the
mind which would willingly receive it. " There may be
pretty enough things in your English literature," a clas-

sical Frenchman will tell you, " but you must admit that
a boy's time is far better occupied in studying the illus-
trious models of Greece and Rome, whose immense
superiority is incontestable." " It is possible that the
Germans may have some clever writers," another will
say; " but the great authors of antiquity became what
they were without knowing German, so surely we may
do without it too." Then you continually meet with the
classical theory that Greek and Latin are a training for
the mind, whereas modern languages are not a training
for the mind, but only valuable for a low kind of utility.
The head of a college told me that he knew whether a
man had studied the classical languages or not by merely
looking at his face, so visibly did they develop the
human intelligence. There is, in fact, the same contempt for modern languages, modern science, and
modern art, as that which existed at Eton a few years
ago, and a French gentleman knows about as much of
these subjects as an Etonian of the last generation.
The spirit of classicism, which leads to the pedantic
pride and learned ignorance of a Chinese mandarin, is
one of the most formidable obstacles against which the
spirit of liberal culture has to contend. It is especially
formidable because it occupies the seats of learning
themselves, which ought to be centres of light. It is
the real source of French ignorance in the upper classes.
Frenchmen are often very well informed about Roman
antiquity, and at the same time quite ignorant about
the present condition of the nations which surround
them. I know one who reads Latin nearly every day,
and never opens a newspaper. French ambassadors

know Latin, but they do not know the languages of the countries to which they are accredited.

English criticism is severe on Frenchmen for this ignorance. I do not deny or excuse it, but I think that English criticism is unfair in one respect. Englishmen seem to think that a Frenchman may be fairly expected to know as much about their country as they know about his. It is not reasonable to expect this from him. France is much more central in Europe than England, much more metropolitan, being at the same time more accessible than England, and more attractive, in the opinion of Continental nations, who fancy that there is nothing to be seen in England except factories and forges. For us to be angry with Frenchmen because they know little about our country, is therefore the same kind of mistake as that of a citizen of Leeds if he allowed himself to be angry with a Londoner because he did not know who were the notabilities of the provincial town, or what were the names of its streets. But there is another reason besides this. The history of France has been, for the last hundred years, the most exciting drama that the world has ever beheld. It is simply impossible to avoid taking an interest in contemporary French history. The dullest and most sluggish Englishman or Dutchman is roused when he hears of such events as the battle of Sedan, the fall of the Empire, the siege of Paris, and the burning of the Tuileries. In comparison with such tremendous events as these, what, to an unconcerned foreigner, can be the interest of a constitutional crisis which may possibly end by substituting one mild and gentlemanly Minister for another? If the Emperor of Germany were to land in England with half a million of men, pillage London, burn Windsor Castle, upset the monarchy, and permanently annex Sussex and Kent, whilst he inflicted a fine of £200,000,000 on the British Treasury, Frenchmen would take an interest in English news. No, the proper and fair comparison for an Englishman to make is this. He should think of some quiet State not disturbed by tremendous events, and should then say, "Do I know as much about that State as Frenchmen know about England?" He should think of Holland, for instance, and in most cases a candid self-examination would satisfy him that he really knew nothing whatever about Holland—neither its language, nor its recent and contemporary history, nor even the names of its great authors. The English are intensely ignorant even about Switzerland, which they visit so frequently. They believe Mont Blanc to be a Swiss mountain, and there is not one tourist in three hundred who knows anything whatever about Swiss politics. I wonder how many, out of the thousands who visited the country last autumn, could tell, if asked, what was the name of the President of the Federal Council?

CHAPTER XIV.

Analogy between a " Trap Dike " and the Roman Hierarchy—
Honours given to a French Bishop—His Triumphal Entry
into his Cathedral City—His splendid Social Position—Funeral
of a Bishop—A Working Bishop—Anecdotes of him—His
Lectures—Their Effect on Men—French Priests—Their Love
of Good Eating—Clever and Simple Priests—Parish Priests
in the Country—How Charitable they are sometimes—
Examples—Want of Intellectual Culture amongst them—
Popular Stories about them—The Priest and his Goats—
Attitude of the Clergy towards Popular Superstitions—A
Ghost Story—Harmony between the Clergy and Rural Ways
of Thinking.

IT is a great mistake to push analogies too far, but it
sometimes happens that an analogy is so perfect that it
cannot be pushed too far. A singularly perfect one
is that between a trap dike in geology, and the Roman
hierarchy in French society.

When, at some former period of the world's history,
fissures have occurred in the strata of comparatively
soft rock, they have often been filled up by melted
stone, which, like iron poured into a mould, consoli-
dated as it cooled. In the course of ages, the soft strata
round about it were often gradually washed away, and
then the rock which had been melted, being of a harder
nature, was not washed away by the water, but remained
in its original shape, like cast iron when the matrix has
been removed. The mass which remains is a trap dike.

Y

In the French social system of the middle ages the softer strata are the different *couches sociales* of lay society, existing on the hereditary principle. From top to bottom there were deep fissures in this society, and the fissures were filled up by something entirely different, by the ecclesiastical society, with its hierarchy existing on a principle opposed to heredity. In course of time the softer strata have been gradually washed away, but the hard casting that was formerly in the fissure now stands by itself, exactly like a trap dike.

The analogy is so perfect that you may push it farther still. In geology a trap dike is theoretically supposed to be undiminished by the erosion of water when the surrounding strata have been washed away, but the fact is that the dike itself has really been somewhat diminished also. Still, though it is diminished, we see its importance much more clearly than before the removal of what surrounded it.

Here, too, our analogy holds good, for although the Roman hierarchy has really lost some of its positive weight and bulk in France, it has gained in apparent weight and bulk by the removal of the great and powerful feudal aristocracy which surrounded it in the middle ages.

In the feudal times a bishop may have been a greater man than he is now, if you measure his positive bigness, but in those times there were neighbours of his, great laymen, who surrounded him, and prevented his bigness from being fully seen. Now that these laymen are all reduced to mere grains of sand, the bishop strikes us as the trap dike strikes the eye of a geologist.

In England, where some traces of the feudal system still remain in the laity, a baron is addressed as " your Lordship," and a duke as " your Grace." In France no such form is used in addressing a lay nobleman. Even his servants do not say " votre Seigneurie," they merely say, " Monsieur le Comte," &c., and gentlemen say simply, " Monsieur." But what a contrast when you meet a bishop! You must call him " Monseigneur," as if he were a prince of the blood, or " Votre Grandeur," which certainly expresses the idea of greatness more directly than any other form of address which human servility ever invented.

In these times even Royalty lays aside some of the insignia of its pride, and takes its part in ordinary life without visible distinction. You are not likely ever to see a King with a crown on his head and a sceptre in his hand, but you may possibly see one in a tourist's suit and a wide-awake. A French bishop, however, still wears the mitre which is his crown, and the crozier which is his sceptre, and a dress of silk and gold, and diamonds, and rubies, and sapphires.

The honours given to a French bishop are so intoxi- cating that if he becomes proud and arrogant what reasonable person can blame him? His social position is really sublime in its grandeur. It might be seriously maintained that in some important respects it is higher than that of any prince who is not a reigning sovereign. He certainly gets more worship than the Duke of Connaught, or the Duke of Edinburgh, and he is more independent of the law than the Prince of Wales him- self. Our Princes are not half-divine, they are gentlemen of high rank who do what other gentlemen do, who shoot, and smoke, and go to theatres and races, and whose most serious occupations are still of a secular character. They are very popular, very much liked, but not at all above criticism. A French bishop has the prestige of this world and the prestige of the other world at the same time. The proper attitude towards him is that of the most humble veneration. To criticize a bishop, in good society, would be thought abominable, almost an outrage. You cannot even mention him without speaking of him as your lord. To say simply "the bishop" is not enough, and the bare word by itself is never used by good Catholics, who always say, " Monseigneur." The right tone, in speaking of the bishop of the diocese, is to attribute to him all possible perfections. This is done to a surprising degree in the case of a new bishop. Some humble priest, whom nobody cared about, is suddenly elevated to the episcopate, and in the course of a single week the whole diocese will be filled with joy and astonishment that so many virtues can be found together in the same man. This belief in the extraordinary moral qualities of prelates makes their social position shine with a much purer radiance than that of Princes, of whom people generally tell scandalous stories. Bishops are also credited with great intellectual qualities whenever they enter the arena of controversy so far as to condemn heresy in a sermon or a book.

When a priest is first appointed to an episcopal see he is expected to make a triumphal entry into his cathedral city, and when several sees are united in one, he has a triumph in each of the great cities of his diocese. The honours which a bishop receives on these occasions are fully equal to those rendered to the sovereign of a monarchical country. His Grandeur is received at the railway station by the Prefect and all the civil and military authorities, by all his clergy, by all the schools, by all the religious houses which are not cloistered. He is robed by reverent hands in his full pontificals. He goes to the cathedral in a gorgeous procession. All along the route the streets are decorated with flags and wreaths. Huge garlands swing across from the opposite houses. The soldiers present arms. The cannon thunder. All ordinary business is suspended. Through a bare-headed respectful multitude the procession winds its way slowly to the cathedral, banner after banner, troop after troop of the faithful, the new bishop blessing as he goes. He enters, the huge bells shake the towers, and then all the pomp and all the splendour of architecture, vestments, ritual, all the influences of music, all the art and skill of the most consummate histrionic arrangements are employed to give the utmost conceivable importance to that one man as he sits for the first time on his high throne, under a canopy of plumes and velvet, magnificent as a Mikado, and yet visible, which the Mikados of old Japan were not. Silver censers are swung before His Grandeur, and the sweet intoxicating perfume of the frankincense rises, grateful to his nostrils. From that day, to the end of his life, he will never, in his waking hours, put off the dress or lay aside the dignity of a prelate. An Emperor may forget his rank when he walks, dressed like a country gentleman, about his parks and farms, but a bishop has always a bishop's costume and that decided episcopal demeanour which permits no one to take him for anything less than what he is. His Grandeur has a permanent court, and the very phrases used in speaking of him have a courtly sound. Thus a bishop does not receive a visit, that is not the phrase, he "grants an audience." The house he lives in, which is sometimes magnificent, and always spacious, is called a palace, just as his gilded chair in the cathedral is called a throne. People kneel to him, as if he were a king, to receive his episcopal blessing. He is such a very great personage that the Minister of Public Worship, who is his legal superior and can give him orders, dare not venture to do anything of the kind, unless by begging the Pope to give the desired command, and when the Minister writes to the bishop it is in forms of humility and veneration. Even the Chief of the State himself, though he be an Emperor, as Louis Napoleon was, cannot control a bishop who chooses to set him at defiance. The utmost punishment that can be inflicted upon a prelate for disobeying the civil power is an expression of disapproval, which does not affect him in the least or tarnish one jewel in his mitre. He enjoys the utmost license of language; he may say in public that your opinions are held by you from a desire to indulge carnal passions, and you have no redress; but if you speak disrespectfully of his opinions, he can have you put in prison for "outrage against the religion of the State." All books approved by him circulate freely, even though they may contain the most unjust and calumnious attacks against large bodies of his fellow-citizens ; but when a book displeases him, as, for example, Mr. Gladstone's recent writings about Vaticanism, the bishop has influence enough with the Government to have its circulation restrained by withholding the hawker's stamp. His power over his own clergy is great indeed, and all, except the *curés de canton*, who are *inamovibles*, have good reason to be afraid of him. Their rank in the world, relatively to his own, is like the rank of a common soldier relatively to that of a colonel, so great are the distinctions of the hierarchy. He lives thus in splendour * and dignity, as well as real power, until the day comes when the crozier falls from the dying hand. The funeral of a French prelate is one of the most imposing sights that can be imagined. It answers to his public entry into his cathedral city.

* It may be objected that a French bishop cannot live in splendour because his income is too small. His official income is only a few hundreds a year, but it is doubled or tripled by extras, and his court is not maintained at his expense, except his private servants. It must be remembered, too, that he is always a bachelor, and that his house is rent free, and furnished. His splendour, however, is rather sacerdotal than worldly, and sacerdotal splendour can be kept up without much running expense when once the first expenditure for jewellery and costumes has been incurred, as the costumes, unlike those of a king's household, are not affected by changes of fashion. The most expensive things that a bishop wears are often given to him by his admirers. When he has a private fortune he often lays out large sums in sacerdotal vestments and ornaments. The full-dress costume of a French bishop may easily cost thousands of pounds. I know by sight a bishop who gave £1,200 for a mitre, and he was not a very rich man. I know another by sight who had a cross given to him to hang from his neck, and it cost £600. There is room for endless expense in vestments if a bishop has the means to indulge in it.

Because he is a State official, the civil and military
authorities join the great ecclesiastical demonstration,
and all the gentry of the country round about come
crowding into the city the night before. As his triumphal entry was the expression of the Church's gladness,
so his exit by the gate of death is the occasion for the
utmost manifestation of her sorrow. Then she composed her visible poem of rejoicing, and now she com-
poses her other poem of sadness and deep grief. Like
Milton, she has her Allegro and her Penseroso.

Once buried, a bishop is forgotten with the most
surprising rapidity, unless he has left some remarkable
book behind him, or established some great foundation.
All those extraordinary virtues and abilities which were
attributed to him when he took the mitre are transferred, with the mitre to his successor, who invariably
excites the enthusiasm of all good Catholics in the
diocese. The new bishop effaces the long line of his
predecessors as to-day's newspaper effaces all that have
gone before it. A living bishop is continually spoken
of, a dead one hardly ever; or if by chance a dead one
happens to be mentioned, it is with a little air which
seems to say that his day of greatness belongs altogether to the past.

This sketch of the episcopal dignity as it strikes the
eye of an outsider by its external state and grandeur,
might be in some respects misleading if it were not
corrected by the observation that a prelate may be
really humble in spite of them, for he inherits these
external things from long-established customs. It is
quite conceivable that a prelate may like to govern a

diocese with the view of doing as much good as he can in it, and yet not like the excessive prominence given to his person, and the excessive homage which he receives. There is one not many miles from my house who tries to realize what may have been the earliest and purest ideal of a bishop, and who, I think, will not be so soon forgotten as men in his station generally are. He is singularly and wonderfully unworldly, absolutely careless of those arts by which an exalted position is defended and maintained, rightly disdainful of trifles and of the time-wasting ceremonies of society, always ready to give time and strength to real work that may lead to good, and to *payer de sa personne* when an indolent prelate would either do nothing or send a substitute. A young man I knew was dying of consumption He was very religious, and in his last hours had a wish to possess some little thing that had been blest by the Pope. The priest who attended him had nothing of the kind, but reflected that as the bishop had lately been at Rome he was the right person to apply to. So the priest went and told his story. Before he had mentioned the name of the young man the bishop had put his hat on and said, " I will take it myself to him at once ; where does he live ? Show me the way." As it happened, the dying youth was a young gentleman, but he might have been in the humblest rank. The bishop did not ask who or what he was. On the other hand, great ladies were rather disappointed because this strange prelate gave so little time to society. When they called upon him he had the air of a busy man unpleasantly interrupted, and they said that he was ill-

bred. "So much the better," was his observation ;
"that is just what I want them to think ; they will
waste less of my time." " Your Grandeur will come to
my drawing-rooms," said one *grande dame.* " No," was
the frank reply, " I am too busy, and I don't much
approve of drawing-room priests, or dining-room priests
either ; there are too many of both sorts." One rainy
day he went on foot to a convent, and when he left
there was a great fuss to find the bishop's umbrella.
The sisters emulated each other's zeal. " I think I can
find it better than you can," he said with a smile, and
fished up an old cotton one. Every ladies' priest has a
silk one, as a matter of course, so the sisters had been
misled by the material. Some amusing stories of his
kindly ways ran about the diocese and made friends for
him amongst reasonable people, whilst they earned for
him the grave disapproval of proud and stuck-up people,
who believe in artificial dignity. One day he passed
a tanner's yard, thought he should like to see the processes of the unsavoury trade, and so entered and talked
familiarly with the workmen. On leaving he gave them
twenty francs to drink, which was much blamed by evil
tongues as an encouragement to inebriety, but he accompanied his present with the following little speech :
" This is to drink the bishop's health, and now let me
tell you how a bishop's health ought to be drunk. You
must not go and drink the money at the wine-shop and
leave your wives all by themselves, but you must buy a
few bottles of really good sound wine and drink it in
your own homes, and let your wives have their fair
share." It is impossible, I think, to reprove with more

wisdom, tact, and kindness, the besetting sin of the
ouvrier, which is to leave his wife alone whilst he drinks
in the public-house. On the other hand, the bishop has
the rare courage to reprove with some severity the tendency to a trifling exercise of the fancy which, especially of late years, has so much invaded the Roman
Catholic worship. Some ladies, aided by a "ladies'
priest," had made a wonderful *mois de Marie* in the
cathedral during the prelate's absence. On his return
he saw this mountain of flowers, ribbons, gilt paper,
vases, and other trifles, which are the delight of French
ladies who have nothing to do. One glance was enough.
"Let all that be removed at once," he said; "is this
place a théatre?" I rather imagine that, if he had his
way in everything, as in the matter of those flowers, the
apparatus of religious ceremonial would be simplified
in other respects also.

Being afflicted by the presence of so much religious
indifference and unbelief in his diocese, this good bishop
set to work manfully to convert as many unbelievers as
he could, by means of evening lectures in the cathedral.
These lectures were exclusively for men, and great
numbers of the unbelieving sex attended them. The
average congregation may have been about twelve hundred, all belonging to the middle and upper classes.
The general estimate was that about two hundred of
these would be good Catholics, and the remaining thousand freethinkers of various kinds, mostly deists. The
bishop laid a regular siege to rationalism, in the tone of
a man who knew what the world was, and would not
affect to be shocked by a fact so familiar as the exist-

ence of all manner of heresies. He never had recourse to denunciation, never rose into the region of mysticism, but spoke in a very clear, direct manner, and always admirably well. I never heard more perfect elocution ; indeed, I never heard any orator who so fully realized my notion of what public speaking ought to be. With the most beautiful ease of delivery, every sentence was constructed in such pure French that a literal report of the discourse might have been published, without correction, in a book. The speaker never once hesitated or went back to correct himself, and every syllable was distinctly heard in every corner of the cathedral. This great oratorical charm was intensely appreciated by the strange congregation there assembled. All present listened willingly, and went again and again. There were even, it is said, a few conversions, which means that some men were induced to take the sacrament who had not taken it for a long time. But although the unbelievers liked to hear the bishop, and both admired his oratory and esteemed his character, they used to say in the *cafés*, when the evening's lecture was over, that he had left matters exactly where they were, and had not touched the real question between the laity and the Church. The bishop had undertaken the very difficult task of converting unbelievers by means of friendly reasoning, that is to say, by reasons which did not seem reasonable to them. After that, nothing is left for a Roman Catholic bishop but an energetic affirmation of the authority of the Church, which is the most frank and candid method he can use ; so why not use it from the beginning ? Nobody can complain of him for saying, " These are the dogmas of the Church, to be rejected at your peril ;" but if once he begins to reason, he thereby incites others to reason in their own way, which may possibly not be the orthodox way.

It has been my fortune to know a good many French priests, and to be on terms of intimacy—indeed, I may truly say friendship—with two or three. They are generally most respectable men, devoted to their work, living contentedly on wonderfully small incomes, and as far removed as possible from that dissolution of manners which did so much to discredit the Church of Rome in England in the times immediately preceding the Reformation. The worst fault they have, as a class, is too much fondness for good eating, which may very easily be accounted for. Their position affords them very few opportunities for any kind of amusement or pleasure. They wear the long black cassock every day and all day, and wherever they go are obliged to be very strict in their demeanour. They are much more separated from the world of the laity than a clergyman of the Church of England is. They may not enjoy any active out-door pleasures except a grave kind of pedestrianism ; they may not go to the *café* to play billiards as laymen do, and yet they have no domestic enjoyments except a book by the solitary fireside of the *presbytère*, and perhaps a secret pipe or a pinch of snuff from time to time. We must remember, too, that the priest is often really a hungry man. He cannot say mass if he has eaten anything—the laws of the Church forbid it—and after mass he often has other work to do which postpones the hour of *déjeûner*. Then there are fast-days and the

long Lent season, which an earnest priest observes with
the greatest strictness. Now, it seems to be an inevitable law—the law of reaction, the swing of the pendulum
—that all who fast well feast well when opportunity offers.
We have seen the operation of this law in the case of
the peasantry. The priests are like the peasants in
this, except that they are careful not to get tipsy, which
the lay peasant is not. It is perfectly well known, all
over France, that if a priest is asked to dinner, the dinner is sure to be a good one. The priests are pets of
ladies who take good care that they shall be well fed.
Gourmands who are not in orders always like to meet
the clergy on that account. When the black cassock
makes its appearance the lay gourmand is content, and
says to himself, "We are sure of a good feed." There
is something really surprising in the clerical appetite on
these occasions, and in the keen gastronomic enjoyment
which is visible on the clerical countenance. One result
of it is pleasant to everybody. As the priest at table is
the happiest of men, so he is one of the most polite and
agreeable. If to his good-humour he can add, as sometimes happens, the charms of wit and culture, his society
becomes perfectly delightful.

Priests may be broadly divided into two classes, the
clever and the simple. The clever priest usually lives
in a town, and confesses great ladies ; the simple priest
lives in a country village, and hears the wearisome con-
fessions of the peasants' wives and daughters. The first
is sometimes a finished man of the world, who, were he
placed in the position of a Mazarin, a Richelieu, or an
Antonelli, might easily be the diplomatist or statesman ·

the second tends rather to the saintly than the intellectual life, and sometimes does, indeed, almost realize
the difficult ideal of Roman Catholic sanctity. The
contrast between the two lives is great indeed. The
fashionable confessor passes half his time in drawing-
rooms, and his own sitting-room is like the boudoir of a
grande dame, with all sorts of *biblos*, vases, engravings,
candelabra, bouquets of flowers, pretty needlework, and
beautifully bound books ; the poor *curé de campagne* lives
in a small cottage, which may be worth a rental of five
pounds, with one old ugly servant and a few pieces of
meagre furniture. I well remember visiting quite recently, in the course of a pedestrian excursion with a
party of friends, a curious little village perched on the
very crest of a steep hill 1,500 feet high. There was an
interesting Romanesque church, and service was going
on when we entered it. At the close of the service the
curé began catechizing and instructing a class of children, but he very kindly sent a man to us to say that if
we would go and rest ourselves in the *presbytère* he
would join us when his work was over. His home was
quite a poor man's cottage, without the least pretension
to comfort. Another messenger came from the *curé* to
say how much he regretted not to be able to offer us a
glass of wine after our ascent of the hill, but he had no
wine in the house. An English reader will realize with
difficulty the degree of destitution which this implies in
a wine-producing country like France, where common
wine is not looked upon at all in the light of a luxury,
but is considered, except by the frugal peasants, a part
of necessary food. "We are expecting," his servant

said, "a little cask of white wine from the low country, but it is a long time in reaching us." One of us observed that the *curé* must be very hungry, for we knew that he had eaten nothing yet, as he had said mass, and we thought he would have done better to get his *déjeûner* before teaching the children. "This is his *déjeûner*," the woman said, lifting a plate from a basin that she kept warm upon the hearth. It contained nothing but mallow tea. The good *curé*, who was as thin as he well could be, was, in fact, one of those admirable priests who are so absorbed in the duties and charities of their calling that they forget self altogether.. Priests of that saintly character are looked upon by the more worldly clergy as innocent idealists, whose proper sphere is an out-of-the-way village. It is said by those who know the Church better than I do, that they very seldom get much ecclesiastical advancement. Their self-denial is sometimes almost incredible. The following instances, which have been narrated to me by people who knew the *curés* themselves, will convey some idea of it.

My first story shall be about a *curé* who was formerly incumbent of the parish where my house is situated. He is dead now, but when he was alive he was not remarkable for attention to personal appearance. His wardrobe (except, of course, the vestments in which he officiated) consisted of one old black cotton cassock, and when he was asked to dinner it was his custom to ink over those places which seemed to need a little restoration, after which process he considered himself presentable in good society. This, however, was not the opinion of his brethren who were men of the world.

One day the bishop invited him to dinner, so our good *curé* went in his old cassock even to the bishop's palace itself. The priests of the episcopal court drew the prelate's attention to that cassock, and the wearer of it incurred a severe reprimand for his *mauvaise tenue.*✶ The ladies of his parish, who loved and respected him (with good reason), were much pained when they heard of this, and subscribed to buy him a good new silk cassock, to be worn on state occasions, especially at the bishop's table. For a short time the *curé* remained in possession of this garment, but no invitation came from the bishop. At last somebody told His Grandeur that the poor priest had now the means of making a decent appearance, so he invited him again. "Alas, Monseigneur," was the reply, "a month since I could have come, for I had the new cassock, but now I possess it no longer, and so I cannot come!" On inquiry it turned out that some poor little boys, who had come to be catechized, had ragged waistcoats, and could not make a decent appearance at church; so it struck the *curé* that the cassock was big enough to make several capital waistcoats for little boys, and he had employed it for that purpose, to the advantage of *their* appearance, but to the detriment of his own.

My next story, which is also perfectly authentic, concerns a priest who is still alive, and so incorrigibly charitable as to be the despair of his good sister, who tries in vain to keep him decent. He does not live quite

---

✶ This was not the present bishop of the diocese, who would probably have inquired minutely into the character of the old *curé*, and found reason to respect him rather than to reprimand him.

close to my house, but I have authentic tidings of him from a very near neighbour of his who comes to see me occasionally. One day at the beginning of winter, some years ago, a lady came to this priest's house to see him on business, but as he was absent, she had to wait for his return. The first thing that struck him on entering his room was that the lady looked miserably cold. " How cold you do look, madame !" he said ; " I wish I had a fire to warm you ; but the fact is—I have no fuel." When the lady went away she told the story to her friends, and they plotted together to buy the *curé* a comfortable little stove and a cartload of wood, which comforts were duly sent to the *presbytère*. Some weeks afterwards, in the severe winter weather, the lady thought she would go and see how the *curé's* stove acted, and whether he was as comfortable as she had expected. On this visit the following little conversation took place.

Lady. The weather is so bitterly cold, that I thought I would come to see whether your stove warmed your room properly.

Curé. Thank you, thank you ! The stove you were so good as to give me is really excellent. It warms a room capitally.

Lady (who by this time has penetrated into the chamber, which is the *curé's* bedroom and sitting-room in one). But, I declare, you have no fire at all ! And the stove is not here ! Have you set it up somewhere else ?

Curé (much embarrassed). Yes, it is set up elsewhere. The fact is, there was a very poor woman who was delivered of a child at the time you sent me the stove, and she had no fire, so I gave it to her

Lady. And the cartload of wood ?

Curé. Oh! of course she must have fuel **for her** stove, so I gave her the wood too.

It is the simple truth that the good Christian man was quietly sitting without a spark of fire all through a bitter winter, because, in his opinion, the poor woman needed warmth more than he did. The same *curé* came home sometimes without a shirt—the shirt having been given to some very poor parishioner—and, at least once, he came back without shoes, for the same reason. At one time he had a small private fortune : need I say that it has long since disappeared ? He spent a good deal ot it in restoring an old chapel which had been abandoned to ruin, but is now used again for public worship. He himself officiates there, but the neighbouring clergy still retain the marriages, christenings, and burials, so that he has nothing to live upon but the little pittance given by the Government.

The mention of burials reminds me of another *curé*, who lives within a few miles of the one just mentioned. This one does not give his shirt or his shoes, does not reach the heroism of charity, but is a fine example of humane feelings, which professional customs have never been able to deaden. He has a poor parish—I mean a parish where there is a good deal of really severe poverty amongst the inhabitants,—and he was complaining, on one occasion, of the extreme narrowness of his means. "But you have a good *casuel*," some one observed. "You have a populous parish, with plenty of funerals." "Alas!" he answered, "it is true enough that there are plenty of funerals in my parish, but how

can I charge burial fees to poor widows and orphans
who have nothing left to live upon, or to poor workmen
who have had sickness in the house till they cannot pay
their way ?"

English and American travellers on the continent of
Europe see the splendid ceremonies in the cathedrals
and the gorgeous processions in the streets, but they do
not see the obscure acts of charity and self-denial, which
are only known to the local inhabitants, and not even
to all of these. From seeing the ceremonies, and nothing else, the foreigner readily misconceives their relation to the daily life of the rural clergy, which is simple
enough in its poverty and isolation, and is often dignified by an earnest endeavour to realize the Christian
ideal.

The rural French clergy are, I believe, as respectable
a class of men, from the moral point of view, as can be
found anywhere, but they have little knowledge, little
intellectual culture. The Church discipline leaves them
scanty time for the improvement of their minds in any
other than a religious sense. They have daily service
to attend to, mass every morning all the year round,
and the daily reading of the eternal breviary, besides
special readings for special days which are always
coming round, there are so many of them in the calen-
dar. A priest who has a large country parish has a
great deal of walking to do. The one whom I mentioned as being the *curé* of a village perched on the
crest of a hill 1,500 feet high, descends and ascends that
hill every time he goes out on his parish work, which
he does every day. The books and newspapers which

the country clergy receive are not likely to enlarge their minds. They cannot go to *cafés*, which are the real newsrooms of the country, and so they are driven, out of sheer dulness, to take in that untrustworthy and scandalous but often witty paper the *Figaro*, which is sold to them at a much lower price than to lay subscribers. People must have an amusement of some kind. The country priest finds his amusement in reading the *Figaro*, and his pleasure in eating a good dinner—when it is offered to him.

As the *curé* is an isolated personage, not dressed like other people, and not conforming to their customs, it is inevitable that, notwithstanding the sanctity of his character, he should be the object of much quiet rural satire. Every village has its funny stories about *curés*, either living or dead. The following would supply a good subject for a picture.

In a hill village well known to me, where the hill-sides slope down in very rapid declivities, diversified by grassy places and stony places, there lived, a few years ago, a venerable old *curé*, who, to eke out his wretched little income, kept a few animals, and amongst the rest a couple of goats. He used to take these goats out with him upon the hill-side, and whilst they were feeding he read his breviary, but whilst he was reading the goats sometimes strayed inconveniently far, and the inconvenience was all the greater to him that he could not see very well, so that it was not easy to find them. At last, however, he hit upon a capital expedient, which seemed to reconcile completely the two occupations he wished to carry on at the same time. With two strong and rather long cords he tied one goat to one of his ankles and the other to the other, after which he sat down on the hill-side and read his breviary without much interruption from the animals, which soon knew the length of their tether. This device succeeded so well that the *curé* was rather proud of it, and might often be seen on the hill-side in this position on a fine afternoon. At length, however, an incident occurred which showed that the priest's invention might, under certain circumstances, be dangerous. Some huntsmen came suddenly over the brow of the hill with a small pack of beagles. The goats were much alarmed at these strange dogs, and set off at full speed down the steep slope, over the grassy places and the stony places, dragging the poor old *curé* after them. He was not killed, but he found that mode of travelling decidedly disagreeable.＊ The incident was not altogether displeasing to his rustic parishioners. They would probably not have gone the whole length of desiring for him the punishment of Ganelon the traitor, in the Song of Roland, but this mild form of it tickled their sense of the ludicrous, and gratified the latent malevolence with which human

＊ This good priest's successor, who is now living in the same parish, found that people complained of the length of his sermons, so he said to his old woman-servant, " When I get agoing I never know when to stop ; you should make me a sign when I have preached long enough, and then I would stop." After that the woman made her sign accordingly, and the *curé* broke off abruptly with the usual form. The effect, however, was strange sometimes, as on one occasion when he said to his parishioners, " If you do not conduct yourself better the Devil will certainly take you." Here the preacher glanced at his servant, who made the sign agreed upon, so he ended, at once, with the customary set phrase, " C'est la grâce que je vous souhaite."

nature generally regards those who are set in authority over it.

The magnificently perfect organization of the Church of Rome, with her severe and efficient discipline, has produced a gigantic instrument for influencing mankind, which would produce glorious results if it were really used for their enlightenment ; but this, unfortunately, is not her object. I have said elsewhere that the Church does not discourage rural superstition, but I might have gone farther than that, and said with truth that she positively encourages it, whilst she has no objection to that intensity of ignorance which reigns amongst the peasantry. I have been telling, perhaps, rather too many anecdotes of late, yet must tell one anecdote more, because of its deep significance, and because of the light it throws upon the relation of the Church of Rome to popular superstition.

A peasant girl, called Annette, who lived on a farm quite close to our house, was in the habit of drawing water at a well which happened to be situated near a lane. As this lane serves for a communication between several different farms, and also connects them with the high road, a good many people use it. Well, this girl was drawing water at six o'clock on a very misty October morning, when some one gave her a hearty slap on the back, said "Bon jour, Annette!" in a cheery voice, and immediately disappeared in the misty twilight. What inference would the reader draw from this incident ? He will conclude, at once, that some lad, belonging to a neighbouring farm, who knew Annette, had amused himself by giving her this greeting, and by disappearing in the mist before she could discover who he was. The vigorous slap on the back is evidence enough that the greeting came from a living human being, and not from an impalpable shade. This, however, was not Annette's interpretation of the incident. She told the story with evident accuracy as to the facts, but interpreted them as follows: The person who had said " Bon jour, Annette," was not a living human being, but a ghost, the ghost of her own father, and the reason why he came to say *bon jour* in such an unexpected manner was that he was very uncomfortable in purgatory. This made the girl quite wretched. My wife tried to reason with her, adopting the obvious line of argument that, in the first place, the greeting had nothing of sadness in it, and, in the next place, that it had been accompanied by a good slap on the back, which a living lad might easily give, but a ghost not so easily. These arguments, however, proved utterly vain. The girl remained inconsolable all day, and in the evening went to seek comfort from the parish priest. Now the priest, instead of taking the rational side, and correcting the absurd superstition of which the girl was a victim, instinctively preferred to take the superstitious side. He accepted the incident as a real visitation from the dead, confirmed the girl's interpretation of it with the immense weight of his ecclesiastical authority, and told her that as she had now plain proof that her father's soul was unhappy she ought to have masses said for its repose.

This little story exhibits the priest quite actively on the side of popular superstition; but, without going quite so far as this, a priesthood may encourage superstition in a negative way simply by not discountenancing it, and this is the most usual way in which the Romish priesthood maintains the mental darkness of continental rural populations. In every village there is a man whose position gives him great importance in the eyes of the inhabitants, who is set there to teach them and guide them, who is often the only educated person in the place, and yet this man, instead of contending against the ignorance and superstition around him, tacitly allows both to be handed down from generation to generation! There is a reason for this, of course, and the reason, in plain terms, is that the clergy dread the spirit of rationalism* and prefer any other spirit to that. Hence, whatever may be their moral and religious merits, and they are often considerable, the Roman Catholic clergy will never of themselves do much to educate a nation, and they will oppose a strong resist-ance, either active or passive, to all schemes originating with laymen which have for their object the secular instruction of the people. At the same time we cannot but admit that there is a perfect harmony between the Church and the rural French population as it is. The two suit each other exactly. The Church is truly the Church of the peasant, and speaks to him a language in harmony with his mental state. Even in the anecdote which I have just related about the girl and the ghost,

* I use the word rationalism here in the broadest sense. For example, all educated Englishmen are rationalists with regard to witchcraft, with regard to trial by ordeal, &c. In the story told of the girl Annette, my wife's explanation was a piece of pure ration-alism in opposition to the supernatural explanation of the girl herself.

the exact adaptation of the Church to the peasant-mind is curiously illustrated. My wife tried the rational method and failed completely. She did not dislodge the belief in the ghost's visit, neither did she calm the agitation of the girl's mind. The parish priest, by admitting that the visitant was ghostly, at once gained the girl's confidence, and was in a position to offer efficient consolation. Here he acted truly in the sense of his Church. She does not contradict ignorance, does not vex it by unwelcome enlightenment, but puts herself on its level, and wins its sympathy and trust, after which she consoles it just as it wants to be consoled.

CHAPTER XV.

AMONGST the many curious subjects of study which an
Englishman finds in France, not the least interesting is
that of marriage. The clergy, of whom we have been
talking lately, are made wholly independent of marriage
by the law of their order. All doubts and difficulties on
this subject are removed from their life by the inexor-
able rule of ecclesiastical discipline. The *curé* settles
down into his bachelor-existence without the feeling of
unsettledness which all but the most resolute bachelors
have in England. I well remember how an English

country clergyman said to me, " My position is very satisfactory in many respects, but I am not settled yet, you know." " Not settled yet ! Why not ? What do you mean ?" " I mean," he answered, with a little hesitation, and a faint blush on his clear Saxon face, " I mean that I am not married." If marriage is necessary to give a clergyman settled feelings, it is evident that the French priests can never feel settled as long as they live.

The real truth appears to be very different from this. When celibacy is decided by an exterior rule, like the discipline of the Church, it gives much decision and stability to life ; but people who do not live under such disciplined celibacy fancy that nothing is decided for them until they get married.

In France this feeling of instability in celibate life is even stronger than it is in England. A Frenchman looks forward to marriage as his inevitable fate at some time or other, and a French girl never looks to old maidenhood with that contented anticipation which may be seen in some English girls.

It is only after many years of experience that a foreigner really understands French customs and sentiments about marriage. There are differences, too, in the strength and intensity of those customs in different parts of the country. In Paris they are not the same as Round My House.

The usual English representation of the matter is roughly true, but not accurately true. English writers generally say that French marriages are purely matters of business, and that all Frenchmen are fortune-hunters.

The truth is that marriages are not *quite* purely matters of business, and that very few Frenchmen indeed are fortune-hunters in the English sense of the word. What is really true is that marriages in France are generally arranged by the exercise of reason and prudence, rather than by either passion or affection.

By reason and prudence—that is to say, by what the natives of the country, or the majority of them, believe to be reason and prudence. In the opinion of the reader of this chapter, or in the opinion of the writer, such "reason" may often be unreasonable, and such "prudence" imprudent.

With regard to fortune-hunting, all that can be fairly and truly said is, that a Frenchman does not generally wish to take the whole burden of marriage and its expenses upon his own unassisted shoulders. On the other hand, he seldom seeks to make a profit out of marriage. He seldom tries to throw the burden of his family on his wife. His notion is that the wife should do something to help him, but he is not very exacting as to the share she ought to take. He will not marry a girl without a dower, but he will marry a girl with a very moderate dower, the interest of which shall be just barely enough to keep herself, without considering the children. For example, thousands of young Frenchmen in the professions will marry girls with 20,000 francs for a dowry. At five per cent., this gives £40 a year interest. This can scarcely be called fortune-hunting, since it is evident that in making a marriage of this kind a man takes upon himself a burden which his wife's dowry will only partially help him to bear.

From the division of property amongst male and female children alike, it results that there are immense numbers of girls in France who have a fortune of some kind, but there are very few in proportion whom it would be a profitable speculation to marry. It would be a great mistake, in most cases, to marry even a girl with £10,000 as a money speculation, for she and her children would cause as much expenditure as the interest of her fortune would provide for. Young men in the upper classes are perfectly aware of this, yet they marry often when the girl has a much smaller dower than the one just mentioned. The girl's money is then prudently invested, and the man's own personal expenditure is rather diminished than increased after his marriage. You cannot, in such cases, fairly or justly say that the man sells himself for money, when he neither uses the principal nor the interest for his own pleasure.

The exact shade of opinion amongst young men is this. They all seem to believe that at a certain time of life marriage is a necessity, and they try to manage so that in conforming to this necessity they shall not cripple themselves entirely in their money matters. If a matrimonial arrangement can be managed in this quietly prudent way, they are generally ready to enter into it, on the conditions that the young lady and her family are not decidedly objectionable in any way. So far from being determined fortune-hunters, they very often seem to consider it inconsistent with their self-respect to look for more than a fair proportion of fortune in a wife.

In all matters of custom we must ever remember that the idea of *propriety* is associated with existing customs, however absurd they may seem to foreigners, and the idea of *impropriety* is associated with the breach of them. In matters connected with marriage these notions are always tremendously strong. To French parents in a decent rank of life, the English customs about marriage do not merely seem foreign, they seem indecorous and improper in a very bad sense. On the other hand, the French customs, which I am about to describe in this chapter, seem to them exactly what all respectable and right-thinking persons will observe as a matter of common decency and of right manners and behaviour.

The difficulty for young men is to become acquainted with young ladies in their own class. This difficulty varies in degree according to places and to rank in society. In Paris, in the upper classes, it is not insurmountable ; in the country, amongst the peasantry, it cannot be said to exist. It is strongest in what may be called the " respectable" classes in country towns and their vicinities. In Parisian society young ladies go out into " le monde," and may be seen and even spoken to at evening parties. Penniless girls in Paris often make good matches when they are pretty and intelligent, or even when they have simply a little reputation for good household qualities ; but in a country town it is extremely difficult for a penniless girl in the middle classes to get a husband at all, for reasons which the reader will fully appreciate when they have been clearly explained.

When the idea of propriety has become attached to a custom, there is always a tendency to carry the custom farther and farther in its own direction, as people wish to distinguish themselves by a greater degree of propriety than their neighbours, or as they dread more and more the terrible imputation of being indecorous, and indifferent to those things which constitute respectability and good-breeding. I may mention as a good instance of this the progressive purification of the English language in respectable society, by which very many things in which our forefathers saw no harm have been tabooed one after the other as unbecoming, until now not only what is really immoral is not permitted, but a thousand things which are not in the least immoral are forbidden as contrary to good taste. The progression of Sunday observance in Scotland from former laxity to its present minute strictness of social law, is another effect of the same cause. To keep the Sabbath strictly is part of respectability in Scotland, consequently, there has been much emulation in the discovery of new kinds and degrees of strictness, until at last the point is reached of keeping the blinds down and covering up the bird-cages to prevent the birds from singing; or delicate distinctions are established as that you may cross a loch in a rowing-boat on Sunday, but not with a sail, because although rowing is a toil sailing may be interpreted as a pleasure, which is the more sinful of the two. Many readers will be much surprised to hear me compare French customs about marriage with English and Scotch proprieties of language and Sabbath-keeping, but the comparison is a perfectly just one, as I will now prove.

The true foundation of the French marriage custom is the notion of propriety in the bringing-up of young ladies, which has led respectable people, and those who wished to be considered respectable, to refine upon the original idea of what is necessary to the pure reputation of a virgin, until at last they have arrived at that dangerous consummation, the realization of an ideal, which in a world like this is always sure to be punished by very serious practical inconveniences.

The English critic of French manners who does not really know France, but has only read about it in the newspapers, or passed through it on the railway, fancies that young Frenchmen are indifferent to the charms and qualities of marriageable young women, and think of nothing but their dowries. The English critic puts the blame of the present system on the wrong shoulders. The young men are not to blame ; they would be ready enough, perhaps, to fall in love if they had the chance, like any Englishman or German, but the respectable parents of the young lady take care that they shall *not* have the chance of falling in love.

The French ideal of a well-brought-up young lady is that she should not know anything whatever about love and marriage, that she should be both innocent and ignorant, and both in the supreme degree, both to a degree which no English person can imagine. If, indeed, I were to say here quite plainly to what a degree this innocence and this ignorance are carried in the most thoroughly respectable French families, the English reader would laugh at me, and say that it was neither true nor possible, and that I was very innocent myself for believing it to be possible.

The respectable view of matters is, that when a young lady has been kept in quite perfect innocence and ignorance, and has never had an attachment of any kind, if an arrangement can be made which will secure her material comfort in a marriage arranged for her by her parents, she will in all probability attach herself to her husband, and never know any disturbing affection; whereas if she were to form an attachment before marriage it would probably be unsuitable, and lead not only to her loss of reputation, but also to the wreck of her happiness.

It is as well to remember, what foreign critics so easily forget, that the mother of the young lady has been brought up and married in the respectable way also, and that she is always firmly convinced by her own experience that it is the path of safety.

The general goodness and devotedness of womankind come to support this view. It is the plain undeniable fact that most young women brought up and married on respectable principles make very good wives. In our part of France the respectable principle is pushed to its utmost conceivable extreme; and the young ladies become excellent wives, faithful, orderly, dutiful, contented, and economical.

The practical success of the system gives its advocates the upper hand in argument against romantic opponents who venture to argue in favour of the affections. " A woman always loves her husband," they tell you, " so there need be no anxiety on that account." And, really, they all either love their husbands or conduct themselves as if they did so, which is quite as satisfactory to the

It is only fair, in writing about French marriages, to remember that the blame resides with the parents of the young lady, and that their caution and timidity ought to be regarded with the very utmost indulgence, as it proceeds entirely from their anxiety to protect the reputation and assure the happiness of their daughters.

The extent to which the idea of virginal purity is pushed in respectable French families is one of the most striking examples one could find of a poetical and religious ideal carried out to its extremest practical consequences.

Suppose a house (I can see such a house from my windows) where there is a young lady of a marriageable age. How is a young gentleman to gain admission to that house? There is but one way for him. He must first, through a third party, ask to marry the young lady, and, if her parents consent, he will then be admitted to see her and speak to her, but not otherwise. The respectable order of affairs is that the offer and acceptance should precede, and not follow, the courtship

How, then, does Cœlebs ascertain what sort of a person is his future wife? There are two ways. First, as to her character, he makes inquiries to ascertain whether she has worldly or homely tastes, whether she understands housekeeping or spends her time in devotion and fancy work. He gets this information generally from ladies who have access to the house, but, however truthfully they answer him, they are likely enough to deceive him, unwittingly, in some respects. All "well-elevated" young French girls are simple in their dress and modest in their manners, but they may possibly have a strong though repressed desire for "la toilette," and tongues that would go like barrel-organs if once they were set in motion. Information is sometimes got through the parish priest, but he too may deceive, unwittingly, from a natural preference for girls who embroider vestments for him, and altar-cloths, and who are more attached to the ceremonies of the Church than to the duties of housekeeping. However, Cœlebs gets his "renseignments" from various sources, and consoles himself by the reflection that if he saw the young lady every day he would probably be just as far from knowing the real truth about her character and habits. "I shall find out all that after marriage," he says to himself, a reflection which may be comforting or not, according to the degree of his faith in the general goodness and reasonableness of womankind.

In order to appreciate the charms of the young lady's person, Cœlebs tries furtively to get a sight of her. There are several ways in which this may be managed ; the most usual ways are these. He finds out where she goes to mass, and attends service in company with some male or female acquaintance who knows the young lady by sight. In this way many young Frenchmen, who are not generally in the habit of going to church, become suddenly quite frequent attendants, both at mass and vespers, to the surprise and pleasure of all religious old ladies who know them. Sometimes there is a little difficulty when there are two or three sisters who are dressed precisely alike, or when some other young lady has adopted the same fashions, and I have known an instance where Cœlebs thought he had been admiring Mademoiselle B., who had been recommended to him, whereas in reality it was Mademoiselle C. whose good looks had appeared to him so satisfactory. To avoid a mistake of this kind, the best way is to go and visit a friend in the town who knows everybody by sight, on some day when there is a religious procession. All the girls are sure to join it, and if Cœlebs has a friend with a window commanding a corner road which the procession will have to turn, and a little reach of street along which it will have to pass, there will be time enough (considering how slowly such processions move) to make sure who is who, whilst explanations can be given much more easily in a private house than they can at church in service-time. Cœlebs in this way gets a glimpse of the young lady, and is satisfied or not satisfied as the case may be. As a rule, he is generally very easily satisfied indeed, especially as a few yards of distance lend enchantment to the view. Provided, then, that the young lady's nose is not like that of the late Lord Brougham, and that she does not squint too violently, and that she has not a hump-back, and is not lame, Cœlebs will most probably conclude that he has no objection, and he will send an ambassador to the lady's father and mother to request the honour of a matrimonial alliance. He has not heard the young lady's voice yet, but he will probably hear quite enough of it after marriage, so there is no immediate hurry.

This, however, is rather a *bourgeoise* manner of preparing one's mind to enter into matrimony. This peeping at church and in the street betrays a low anxiety about the young lady's person, whereas the right manner of regarding marriage, according to the opinion of good society, is to consider it as a contract between two social positions, rather than between two persons. The *quite* perfect manner of doing things is to ask, by an ambassador, for the hand of a young lady whom you have never seen ; for if you have never seen her, it is impossible that there should be any taint of earthly passion in your project, which is evidently suggested to you by considerations of worldly wisdom, and by these considerations alone. There is nothing which good society in France disapproves of so much as the passion of love, or anything resembling it ; and there is nothing which it so much respects and esteems in a young man (or an old one either) as a proper sense of what is conducive to the maintenance of social position. When Cœlebs asks for the hand of a girl he has seen for a minute, he may just possibly be in love with her, which is a degrading supposition ; but if he has never seen her, you cannot even suspect him of a sentiment so unbecoming.

I well remember a certain young gentleman who came to ask me to be his ambassador in a matrimonial negotiation—an office which I very willingly undertook. He had a small independent property and a profession ; he had also taken better university degrees than most Frenchmen think it necessary to take, and was, on the whole, a superior person, very eligible as a son-in-law. The young lady whom he wanted to marry belonged to a very respectable *bourgeoise* family, and had land of her own fully sufficient for her maintenance. She had been well educated (as female education goes), and was quite able to manage a house with order and economy ; she had plenty of good common sense, was as ladylike as it is possible to be, and very agreeable to those who knew her intimately, as we did. One detail remains to be added : she was one of the most beautiful women I ever saw in my life.

I at once concluded that my client (like many another) had been conquered by that beautiful face, and become the slave of love. I rather liked him for it. Here, at any rate, I thought, was a Frenchman who had eyes to see and a heart capable of feeling certain tender emotions which we read about in the poets of other ages, but which very seldom give their divine warmth and sweetness to the chilly, calculating times in which we live. "I don't wonder," I said, "that you should admire such an admirable young lady. She becomes more and more beautiful every day."

"Is she pretty? I have never seen her. Some people say she is pretty."

My feelings, as an Englishman believing in love, and an artist believing in beauty, were outraged by this answer ; so I rejoined with some acerbity,—

"Then for what reason on earth do you want to marry her?"

It was now his turn to be surprised. After opening his eyes in astonishment, he said, "I have reached the time of life when men take wives. I have made careful inquiries, and, from all I can learn, this young lady would make me a good and suitable wife. They say that she is well brought up, and can manage a house, and that she has good manners. I know that she has a suitable property, which is essential. There would be a

fair proportion between her estate and mine, and my
professional income would place a considerable balance
on my side."

It was absurd to expect this young gentleman to
reason otherwise than after the manner of a respectable
Frenchman. His motives were honest enough. He
was not in the least a fortune-hunter, telling lies to get
possession of an estate; he was simply a decent young
Frenchman, telling the exact truth about himself and
his motives. He had got the idea into his head on his
last birthday—he being then thirty-two years of age—
that it was time to get married, and this was the manner, at once frank and prudent, in which he thought it
best to set about it.

In England, or in any country where marriage customs were not founded upon an absurdly exaggerated
anxiety for the reputation of young women, a person
who knew both parties, as I did, would simply have
invited them at the same time, that they might look at
each other and hear each other's voices. In rural France
such an arrangement was utterly impossible. Had I
invited the young lady and her mother after telling the
latter that Cœlebs would be present, she would have
refused at once to bring her daughter; and if I had
invited the ladies without warning the mother about
Cœlebs, she would have considered the arrangement an
outrage, and would never have forgiven me. I suggested
that he ought to do as others did in similar circumstances—namely, try and get a peep at the young lady;
but he said he had not time. It might be weeks before
he could get the glimpse, and he wanted to know his

fate at once, because, if refused, he might then go else-where.

This being so, I promised to make the offer, and set off accordingly next day for the house where the beau-tiful young lady dwelt. Circumstances favoured me greatly, for I met her mamma in a quiet country lane, and very soon came to the point. In England such a mission would have been preposterous, but I knew French prejudices well enough to be aware that I was doing exactly the right thing in the right way, and that what would have seemed preposterous in England (the fact that Cœlebs had never seen the girl) was strongly in my favour, as a proof that my client had what we shall call the ideas and feelings of a gentleman. It turned out as I had expected. Mamma, by her ques-tions (which were answered with the most absolute frankness), soon discovered this, and I could see by her looks that Cœlebs gained thereby in her esteem. The answer I got was by no means unfavourable, and amounted to this—that if Cœlebs would wait two years, he would have a fair chance, if a richer and nobler Cœlebs did not turn up in the meanwhile, but that the young lady was to dwell in maidenhood until the expi-ration of that time. My client, however, was but little satisfied with this decision, and applied for another young lady, whom he married in about a month. I cannot say whether he ever saw her before their en-gagement,—very likely he did not,—but she is an excellent wife to him, and they both appear (so far as others can judge) to dwell together in the greatest domestic bliss.

It is not merely difficult, in our neighbourhood, for a young man in the respectable classes to get acquainted with a young lady, but every conceivable arrangement is devised to make it absolutely impossible. Balls and evening parties are hardly ever given, and when they are given great care is taken to keep young men out of them, and marriageable girls either dance with each other or with mere children. Children's parties are frequent enough, especially garden parties in summer, and young ladies go to them *faute de mieux*. To give the reader some faint idea of the way in which young bachelors are excluded, I will tell him a little anecdote which is perfectly true. A certain lady who had a son about twenty-two years old, and some daughters, gave a grand dance, to our astonishment. What astonished us was how it came to pass that respectable mothers would let their daughters go and dance at a house where there was a young man, but when we learned how things had been managed, our perplexity entirely ceased. The lady sent her son away for the evening, and the young ladies were divided into two bodies, one of which, decorated with blue rosettes, was supposed to represent the inadmissible male sex.

I remember a very amusing but vexatious incident which occurred at my own house. A lady and her daughter had come to spend the day. The girl was in every respect attractive, she was very pretty, perfectly *bien élevée*, very intelligent, and an excellent musician. She had also a good substantial dowry, which is never objectionable. At the same time both mother and daughter were intensely ambitious. Well, as ill-luck would have it, it so happened that in the course of the afternoon, whilst these ladies were with us, a young man called upon me, and (through the bad management of a servant) was shown, not into my study, but into the room where these ladies were. Of course they could put but one interpretation on such an extraordinary and almost outrageous incident. They must, necessarily, have supposed that I had invited the young gentleman to come to look at Mademoiselle. Dark clouds of displeasure lowered on the maternal brow, and only disappeared when I got the youth out of the room as quickly as possible, and it was explained that he had come to see me quite by accident that day. Very shortly afterwards Mademoiselle became Madame la Comtesse de ——, and the maternal anxieties were at an end.

Married people will tell you very frankly the history of their marriages, even in the presence of each other. " I only saw my wife a month before we were married," a man will tell you, and a lady will say, "I never saw my husband until we were already engaged." The general opinion amongst married people is that the more quickly all preliminaries are got through the better. The whole affair is often got through in a month. On the first of April Monsieur Nigaud may awake and think to himself, "Tiens! j'ai trente ans, si je me mariais?" but without the most remote idea of any particular lady, and on the first of May he may awake and see Madame Nigaud quietly sleeping by his side, whilst her parents are perfectly satisfied with the arrangement. The most curious thing about

French marriages is that all parties seem so intensely satisfied with the wisdom of their own decisions. They all enter into these arrangements with the determination to be deliberately prudent, so as to leave no room for regret ; and they are firmly persuaded ever afterwards that they have done exactly what was best. Can any state of mind be more conducive to contentment ?

There are very few old maids in France, except in the nunneries, but sometimes a girl will take the resolution to remain in celibacy without either taking the veil or becoming a sister of charity. When this happens, the young lady has a particularly difficult transition to accomplish. How is she to pass from the condition of a marriageable *jeune fille*, with all its severe restrictions, to the condition of a *vieille fille*, with its liberties ? The only way for her to manage this is to incur the terrible risk of being a subject for scandalous tongues, and the certainty of being the town's talk until her new position is recognized. A respectable *jeune fille* cannot go out of the house unattended, a *vieille fille* can ; but the first time that Mademoiselle (now twenty-five years old, and determined to embrace celibacy) issues forth to do a little shopping without the customary *bonne*, a thousand tongues are set agoing. Many blame her thoughtless conduct, others doubt if she is still respectable, others accept the act as a declaration of spinsterhood, but speak of the resolution ill-naturedly. On such occasions, however, there will generally be found a few good souls to protect the young lady's reputation, and in a week or two nobody thinks of the matter any more ; she may go wherever she pleases, amidst the public indifference. Still, it is a hard transition to accomplish—incomparably harder than in England, where a woman is not irrevocably an old maid till after thirty, and where a young girl may go where she likes without much risk to her good name.

I have said already that I believe it to be a dangerous thing for people to carry ideals too far towards actual realization in common life. We live between contradictions, between opposing forces, and our ideals are generally little else than a preference of one force or principle to another when we ought to pay equal regard to both of them. The French ideal of the *jeune fille* is very beautiful, it is a sort of poem, but it is carried too far for the rude realities of the world. In our neighbourhood girls are brought up with a degree of strictness of which English people have no conception. Their existence is composed entirely of religious duties and homely service, with hardly anything in the way of pleasure or variety. They get up early, work from morning till night at household duties of some kind, see hardly any society, never speak to a young gentleman by any chance, go to church very often, retreat occasionally into a convent to make themselves more pious than ever, and cultivate practically to the utmost the two virtues of simplicity and obedience. They dress plainly, never wear jewels, and if by chance they are thrown into society they never open their lips. Public opinion and parental authority weigh upon them with such irresistible power that what are quite ordinary and blameless actions in all other people are heinous offences

in them. They may not cross a street alone, nor open
a book which has not been examined, nor have an
opinion about anything. They are not really and
frankly admitted into any one branch of human knowledge. History is expurgated and arranged for them,
so are science and art, so is even theology, of which
they constantly hear so much. The wonder is that
under such a strict system they should not mope and
make themselves miserable. On the contrary, they are
remarkably cheerful, their obedience always seems hearty
and willing, their trust in their parents absolute, their
love for them great enough to bear the most exacting
and irritating parental government without a murmur.
If they have personal vanity it has no opportunity of
showing itself, for they are dressed too simply, and
sisters are dressed precisely alike, to the smallest bit of
ribbon. One quality of a negative kind they have, of
course, in perfection; they never do anything to catch
husbands, the existing social system makes that impossible.

There is not much visible evil in all this, and the
object of the training is good in intention. It is
thought that the *jeune fille* cannot be too innocent, too
virtuous, or too religious. And the fact is that the life
of a good *jeune fille* must be like that of paradise before
the fall. She has not eaten of the tree of knowledge,
she is industrious as Milton says that innocent Eve was,
and, like Eve, she talks to angels and lives in the presence of God.

The real evil of the system is the violent contrast
between such an entirely ideal condition and the reali-

ties of the world. Many French girls think the common world so wicked that they utterly refuse to enter it, and become nuns. Others submit to marriage as a part of obedience to their parents, but ever afterwards, though dutiful to their husbands, look to the priest and not the husband as the true friend and confidant. All that can be said to parents who are grieved when their daughters go into nunneries is that it is a very natural consequence of their education. The convent is the continuation of the *vie de jeune fille* in its restriction, protection, severe rule, and devout observances, in its exclusion of all men but priests. Of the life that women lead in the convents I can tell the reader but little. It varies greatly according to the orders. In some, as the Carmelites, for instance, it is pitilessly severe; in others, it approaches more nearly to the life of devout ladies in a not too uncomfortable home. There is an order of white nuns near us, closely cloistered, who are dressed like phantoms, and worship at the altar day and night with arms extended like the arms of Christ upon the cross. When utterly overcome by weariness and pain they still keep their arms in the same extended position, but fall down prostrate on their faces on the cold stone pavement of their chapel. The austerity of the Carmelite sisters, if what I hear of them is true, almost passes belief, but I hesitate about giving details which cannot be checked by my own personal observation. These ascetic lives, severed from all the interests of the human world, are the product of that too strict and too artificial system in which young girls are educated. Almost every French girl who is *bien élevée*, at one time or other passes through a period of saintly enthusiasm which aspires to the condition of a nun as the highest possible vocation.

Amongst the lower classes, the peasantry and work· men, it would of course be utterly impossible to keep up a system of this kind. In these classes girls have as much freedom as they have in England. The great institution of the *parlement* gives them ample opportunities for becoming acquainted with their lovers ; indeed the acquaintance, in many cases, goes farther than is altogether desirable. A peasant-girl requires no parental help in looking after her own interests. She admits a lover to the happy state of *parlement*, which means that he has a right to talk with her when they meet, and to call upon her, dance with her, &c. The lover is always eager to fix the wedding-day, the girl is not so eager. She keeps him on indefinitely until a richer one appears, on which No. 1 has the mortification of seeing himself excluded from *parlement*, whilst another takes his place. In this way a clever girl will go on for several years, amusing herself by torturing amorous swains, until at length a sufficiently big fish nibbles at the bait, when she hooks him at once, and takes good care that *he* shall not escape. Nothing can be more pathetically ludicrous than the condition of a young peasant who is really in love, especially if he is able to write, for then he pours forth his feelings in innumerable letters full of tenderness and complaint. On her part the girl does not answer the letters, and has not the slightest pity for the unhappy victim of her charms. After seeing a good deal of such love affairs I have come to the conclusion that in humble life young men do really very often feel

> The hope, the fear, the jealous care,
>   The exalted portion of the pain
> And power of love.

and they "wear the chain" too. Young women, on the other hand, seem only to amuse themselves with all this simple-hearted devotion,—

> And Mammon wins his way where Seraphs might despair.

CHAPTER XVI.

THE leading events of the great war with Germany
must be so familiar to every reader of this volume that
it would be useless to fill its pages with a narrative of
battles and skirmishes, and it would be foreign to my
plan to assume what is called the dignity of history, and
record stupendous events. Limited, however, as the
scheme of this book may be, there are certain aspects
of the war which come fairly within its range, and may
be treated exactly in the same manner as the various
subjects which have hitherto occupied us.

Every foreigner who lived in France during the fort-
night which preceded the declaration of war against

Prussia will long remember the strange condition of people's minds. The fever seized a few of them suddenly, here and there, and these few passed at once from the reasonable to the passionate temper. Eight or ten days before, it had been possible to discuss European politics with these very persons as tranquilly as those of the continent of America ; but now an idea had taken possession of them—the idea that a war with Prussia was absolutely inevitable, and that to think otherwise was evidence of a want of confidence in the prowess and the destiny of France. The kindest and gentlest of civilians, who did all in their power to relieve whatever misery came in their way, entered suddenly into that exalted mental condition in which the shedding of blood and the infliction of torture seem details unworthy of consideration. There were people certainly (there always are a few reasonable persons in times of national excitement), who thought that the dispute about the candidature to the throne of Spain might be settled without killing two hundred thousand men, but these few reasonable persons hardly dared to say openly what they thought. They were like heretics in some rigidly orthodox country, and had, in self-defence, to affect to share the opinions which surrounded them. In one thing all French people really agreed : they were all persuaded that their army was invincible. The prevalent opinion, too, at that time, about Napoleon III., is very well worth recording. At present (after the event) French people all tell you that the Emperor's military incapacity was notorious. Well, so it was, in a certain peculiar sense. His conduct in

the war of 1859 had convinced people that he had not
the rapid decision on the battle-field which is necessary
to a great commander, and so far he was believed to be
incapable.   But Napoleon III. was believed by his subjects to be a very safe administrator, or what we should
call a good war minister.   In this character he inspired
absolute confidence.   Men who had no love for him —
men who were strongly opposed to the establishment
of his dynasty, and who were much more inclined to
underrate than to overestimate his abilities in ordinary
matters—were nevertheless quite firmly persuaded that
he would not enter upon a great contest without the
most exact preparation of every material detail.   They
told anecdotes in illustration of his perfect foresight and
his attention to little things : how, in the departure for
the Italian campaign, the artillery (or some regiment of
artillery) were ordered to leave certain portions of the
gun-carriages in Paris, and found, to their surprise, on
arriving in Italy, that similar portions awaited their
coming, but all quite new, and fitting without a fault.
Then it was remembered how regularly the army had
been provisioned, from its departure to the very day of
Solferino.   Not only had the soldiers been supplied
with every necessary of life, but even with its luxuries,
so that they never missed their *café*, their *petit verre*, and
their cheap cigar or tobacco.   These reminiscences produced the most absolute reliance on the readiness of
the French *intendance*.   This absolutely confident temper was not without its grandeur.   When war was declared, there was not the slightest fear of invasion ;
people slept quietly in open villages and unfortified

towns, without dreaming of any possibility of danger.

The transition from confidence to anxiety came gradually, yet rapidly, during the two or three weeks that the French army had to waste about Metz and Strasburg, when it lost the chance of taking the offensive. Private letters from the seat of war spread a vague uneasiness. We knew little, at that time, of the condition of the army, but we were aware that officers were waiting vainly for necessary things. Then came the beginning of the invasion, which people would not believe.

I remember one day well. We had gone on a little excursion to see a ruined castle. I was sketching it, and an old woman came to tell me that the French army, under MacMahon, had been defeated, and that the enemy was advancing rapidly; a traveller had left the news at her cottage. We immediately drove home to learn the truth, and met mounted gendarmes galloping at full speed in the twilight. And so, for the year 1870, ended my last day's study from nature. The excitement of panic began to get possession of people's minds, and in a week from that time every peasant in the whole country knew that I had been drawing that old castle "for the Prussians." It was amazing how far this piece of information spread. It covered a tract of country forty miles in diameter, and from that day it became dangerous to be seen anywhere with a sketch-book. A French artist who lived in the town escaped from actual outrage by nothing but that presence of mind which has so often, in an emergency, been the salvation of a traveller amongst savages. He happened, by good luck, to be painting from nature in oil; and so, in answer to some infuriated peasants who accused him of making maps for the Prussians, he said, "Don't you see that I cannot be making a map, for this is oil-paint, and nobody can make a map in oil-paint." This made his accusers hesitate, and he slipped away whilst they gave him the opportunity. "If you study from nature at all," he said, "mind that it is in oil-colour; and use canvas and a portable easel; it looks less suspicious than a sketch-book." However, it seemed more prudent to limit my studies from nature to the material visible from my own windows, and a little later I found reason to congratulate myself on this excessive caution, for the popular indignation was fully roused against me, and the slightest additional provocation would have irritated it to uncontrollable frenzy. On one point only I remained attached to former habits. There was just one German in the town, whom I knew. He had sometimes come to see me before the war, but now, as no Frenchman would speak to him, he came to my house more frequently. I did what every Englishman would have done in similar circumstances—that is, made him heartily welcome every time he came, and often accompanied him back to his own home. This, of course, cast additional suspicion upon myself, for everybody "knew" that he was a spy in the pay of Bismarck. Certainly, he and I had more accurate information than our neighbours, for each of us subscribed to an English newspaper, and we knew something of the actual progress of the invasion.

There is a little detail peculiar to life in an invaded country, which the reader may realize vividly enough by the simple process of substituting one map for another. The wall of our entrance was covered with maps of the seat of war, and the progress of the invasion was marked upon them by the well-known process of sticking pins day after day as the news from the army reached us. This was done, no doubt, at the same time by military men in England, and by civilians who took an interest in military matters ; but there is a great difference in the interest of the process when it is carried out in countries that are, or are not, themselves exposed to invasion. It is exactly the difference between examining one's private accounts and examining the accounts of somebody else in whose affairs we have nothing but an external interest. To understand the peculiar feelings with which we altered the position of the pins as soon as the day's newspaper had come to hand, the reader is requested to imagine himself a resident at, let us say, Peterborough, and to be sticking pins every morning in a map of England, which pins make plain to him the steady, irresistible advance of a French army already in possession of Kent, and resolutely advancing upon London. Under these circumstances he would discover that a pennyworth of common pins would very soon make themselves the pivots of all his thoughts, and that he would gain an acquaintance with the geography of certain districts incomparably more minute than is attainable by any other known process, except that of serving upon an ordnance survey. O those dreadful n.aps! How willingly we tore them all down when peace was proclaimed at last.

My German friend was a Badener, and perhaps not very enthusiastic in favour of Prussian supremacy, though he counted on victory for the Germans. The suspicions against him grew so rapidly that in a week or two it was unsafe for him to be seen out of his own rooms. Even the most intelligent and cultivated townsmen were fully persuaded that he was a spy, but they did not wish to do him bodily harm, only to get him out of the place that he might spy no longer. The populace, more menacing and dangerous, decided that he ought to be lynched. The police told him that his life was not safe, and that it would be difficult to protect him if he stayed. On this he took the next train, and arrived safely at the Lake of Constance.

Besides this Badener an intelligent and well-educated American had settled in the town before the war broke out. He spoke French, English, and Italian as nearly perfectly as any one possibly can speak three languages, but he did not speak German, and had never been in Germany. However, as he was a foreigner, it was soon decided that he also was a German spy. We occasionally exchanged visits, but one day when I went to see my American friend I was told that he had suddenly left for Florence, and was not likely to return. He, also, had received his warning, and I expected mine from one day to another.

The most difficult time to pass, on account of the violent popular excitement, was from the early part of August to the fourth of September. About the middle of August an incident occurred which might have had unpleasant consequences. A French widow lady, a friend of ours, happened to be staying with us just then, and she was in a state of considerable anxiety about her son, for there were rumours that even the eldest sons of widows would be called to active service like the rest. She had the strongest dislike to the Imperial Government, and with good reason, in her case, for the *coup d'état* had done great injury to her friends, sacrificing the life of one of them, and driving the others into exile. Well, it so happened that one sultry August evening we were sauntering out together, and we met one of our neighbours, a man not remarkable at the best of times for much delicacy of manner, and just now quite peevish and ill-natured from the course that things were evidently taking. He had been hearing some disagreeable news, and so came straight to us and announced in a tone of triumph that all widows' sons would be immediately compelled to serve in the active army. The effect of this announcement, made so rudely to a lady who had been in great anxiety for weeks on this particular subject, may be easily imagined. A great scene took place, in which things were said amounting to treason against the Emperor, and which might be malevolently, though not justly, reported as evidences of hostility to France. Our neighbour replied, in mingled rage and bitterness, as if he had understood them in that sense, and unfortunately, just at that very moment, two labouring men passed close to us as they crossed the fields by a pathway that led to their village. There they recounted what they had heard, and recounted it after their own fashion, so in the course of the same evening it was "known" all over the neighbourhood, on the evidence of these two witnesses, how our friend had expressed her earnest wish that "*no conscript who left the village might ever come back alive.*" The reader may imagine the effect of this upon a French populace already excited beyond endurance. The women, whose sons were the conscripts in question, became like so many Furies, and incited their husbands to revenge. There were about three hundred miners in the place, who worked in the schist-mines, and as these men drank in the wine-shops that night they adopted certain resolutions.

Now there happened to be amongst these miners a young man who had lived close to me for several years, and who had worked a good deal for me at odd times. His name was Jules, and as he had been in Paris and seen the world, he was much sharper and more intelligent than the French peasant usually is when he lives entirely in the country. So he kept his own counsel amongst his comrades, but the next day, as I was sitting reading my newspaper in an arbour in the garden, I heard a rustling in the shrubs behind me, and a human head emerged from them, which I recognized as belonging to my friend Jules. His face was deadly pale, and he spoke only in a whisper. " I shouldn't like it to be known, sir, that I came here to-day, and I must slip away as I came, without letting anybody catch a sight of me, or else it might be a bad job for me, but I could not rest without coming to tell you what the miners said amongst themselves last night. I would have come sooner if I had had an opportunity, but I never could manage it without being watched. They have determined to come and murder Madame G——, and pillage your house this afternoon. I saw B—— charge his pistol, saying, ' This bullet is for Madame G——.' He will be here with the others in about an hour. I thought it my duty to tell you, so that you might get her out of the way."

Having duly delivered himself of this agreeable piece of information, Jules disappeared again amongst the shrubs, and crept along a hedge-bottom till I saw no more of him. The first thing to be done was to get all women and children out of the house, and send Madame G—— to her own home by railway. Next (like Robinson Crusoe in his castle) I got together everything I possessed in the nature of fire-arms, and prepared to resist the enemy. I was soon armed like a brigand, with everything loaded that would send a bullet. Then, with locked doors and shutters fastened, I sat waiting for the attack, having no other ally than my big dog, who at that time was fierce enough. It is a pity, after such a dramatic beginning to end without gratifying the reader with at least one homicide, but unluckily for the interest of my story, the project of attack was abandoned when it became known that our guest had departed. I am not likely, however, soon to forget the couple of hours spent in waiting for the mob, during which I tried to read, but found real life so interesting that it was difficult to give attention to a book.

Just about this time I was denounced to the authorities as a Prussian spy, but I had lived too long in the neighbourhood, and knew too many influential people, for an accusation of that kind to take effect No foreigner who had settled here recently, could have remained throughout the war ; but the upper classes, with one single exception, stood by me quite kindly and faithfully, doing everything in their power to protect me from the common people. Two ladies were so good as to go amongst the poor and try to produce a more favourable impression. An old gentleman, who was the largest landowner in the neighbourhood, and deservedly respected for the good he had done in various ways, showed himself very heartily my friend. The principal schist-master got his workmen together and made them an energetic speech, in which he said everything in favour of me that generous good feeling could suggest. Meanwhile, my wife and I went out every day for short walks and drives so that everybody might see us. The courteous French custom of salutation compelled even our worst enemies to lift their hats to us from habit, and this gave us the opportunity of speaking to those we knew, as we used to do before the war began. In this way we tided over the most difficult weeks, which were those between Weissemberg and Sedan. Strangely enough, our most dangerous enemy for the time being was an excellent, but rather simple-minded, country squire, with whom we had been on the best of terms before the war began. He went about telling people that the popular rumour was not likely to be altogether without foundation, and that I was in the constant habit of sending things by post.

which were not simply letters, and must be plans and information for the enemy. What made these suggestions the more dangerous was that the old gentleman in question was *maire* of the very commune I lived in, and so might be supposed to know more about me than another; besides which his official position gave him an engine of hostility against me, if ever he felt it advisable to proceed to extremities. But even in this case there was only doubt and suspicion, not any real malice, and after inquiry the *maire* became finally quite convinced of my innocence, and atoned for his suspicions in a manly and becoming way. He came to pay us a state call, with his wife and sons, in his carriage, all in *grande toilette*, and was as amiable as he possibly could be. No allusion was made to the unpleasant rumours that had been in circulation, but the carriage stood for nearly an hour at my door, and this was his way of telling people that I was not to be suspected any longer. He has been a good neighbour ever since, but however agreeable may be his visits in time of peace, they have not the political value of that state call in the height of the war fever.

After Sedan, the news of the birth of the Republic came to us in the oddest, most ridiculous way that can be imagined. A peasant woman whom we knew came rushing into our kitchen at five o'clock in the morning, sobbing and wringing her hands, and yelling out at the top of her voice "Elle est déchainée, elle est déchainée!" My wife, hearing this noise, went to see what was the matter, and the same phrase was repeated for her benefit, "Elle est déchainée, elle est déchainée!"

She thought some wild beast must have broken loose, and asked what beast it was. " La Ré—pub—lique ! " was the answer.

On hearing this we first laughed till the tears came into our eyes, and then cried " *Vive la République !* " and I sang with a loud voice, " *Domine salvam fac Rempublicam, et exaudi nos in die quâ vocaverimus te !* "

A very distinguished French prelate, who is now dead, told an intimate friend of mine that when the Archbishop of Paris congratulated the Emperor on a recent escape from a great personal danger, Napoleon III. answered in tones of the most solemn conviction, " My hour is not yet come, but when my hour shall come *I shall be broken like glass !* " In the beginning of September, 1870, the fatal hour arrived, and the Colossus which had overawed Europe fell shattered from his pedestal.

The same prelate visited our neighbourhood some time after the fall of the Empire, and said that having known Napoleon in Paris and seen him afterwards during the campaign, just before the movement in the direction of Sedan, he had been very painfully impressed on the latter occasion by the evident decline in the mental faculties of the Emperor. A friend of mine who visited the Emperor a short time before the war broke out, told me that Louis Napoleon had not only greatly aged, but had lost the charm of his manner, and appeared almost inanimate. This was the more painful that his corpse-like cheeks had been visibly rouged for the occasion, and as he had just left his hair-dresser, there was a perfection in the toilette which jarred upon the feelings of all present. The fault of his government, which for many years had been constantly attacked for being a "personal government," was in later times the fault of not being personal enough. The gradual ebbing of vitality translated itself by an increasing intellectual indolence, and a disposition to trust everything to subordinates, which was the exact opposite of that personal watchfulness over details that formed part of the character and habits of the first Napoleon, and was one of the causes of his success.

I may mention in this place a most curious coincidence which I believe has never been noticed elsewhere. An illustrated French newspaper, the *Univers Illustré*, gave a woodcut representing the departure of Napoleon III. from the private station at St. Cloud, and the same number contained, a little farther on, a woodcut representing the German palace *of Wilhelmshohe.* The French editor believed that Cassel would shortly become "interesting in connection with the war," but little foresaw the kind of interest which would attach to it.

When once the Emperor had arrived at his luxurious prison of Wilhelmshohe nobody thought about him any more. He was really more forgotten at that time than he is likely to be in the future, for with all his faults he will for ever remain one of the most remarkable curiosities of history. But the French, as I have said elsewhere, have not the monarchical sentiment, and Louis Napoleon had not succeeded in creating it. The last time I saw him was in 1867. His carriage came slowly down the Champs Elysées; a crowd was seated on each side the avenue, yet nobody rose, and not a hat was lifted. The feeling about Louis Napoleon at that time was a feeling of indifference, such as we have towards some old abuse which, though it may not be removed this year or the next, is certain to be cleared away before long, by the inevitable progress of events.

The autumn of 1870, during the steady progress of the invasion, was a time of much anxiety in our part of the country, because it was always probable that we should be included in the space occupied by the enemy. In one respect we were more unfortunate than the inhabitants of regions actually invaded, for we were kept incessantly, during the whole war, on the tenter-hooks of apprehension. The southern departments never seriously apprehended invasion for themselves, and felt the evil only as people feel the evils of others, except so far as it affected trade ; whilst the departments quite to the east, which were occupied by the enemy in the early part of the campaign, had to do with the invasion as a present and practical evil, and were, therefore, relieved, by its very reality, from the miseries of incessant forebodings. The reader may possibly enter into our feelings, such as they were at that time ; but he will only be able to do so by a very strong effort of imagination. Let him suppose himself comfortably settled in an English country-house, unpretending, if he will, but provided with everything necessary to the regular and peaceful course of his life and occupations —let him suppose that he has spent on this house and what it contains a good deal of money relatively to his means, and that amongst its contents are many things which he values greatly, and which, once destroyed, can never possibly be replaced. Then let him imagine that he awakes every morning for months together with the possibility before him that in a few days, or even hours, his house may be occupied by the rough soldiers of a hostile army, who will probably carry off half his things and spoil the rest, whilst it is the merest chance whether they will behave to his wife and family like gentlemen or like brigands. To leave your home in such a time is to expose it to certain pillage ; to remain in it is to run the risk, though only a risk, of yet more serious evils. The English newspapers whose sympathies were on the side of Germany during the war, described the conduct of the German soldiery in the most favourable terms, and it may be true that, on the whole, they behaved better than is the custom of invaders, but this did not much lessen our anxiety, because we knew that their conduct varied in different cases. Some houses occupied by them were left uninjured, and the householder escaped with a heavy fine in the shape of requisitions, often out of all proportion to his means ; but others saw their dwellings devastated as if out of mere hate and spite. Without going to the newspapers for evidence of this, I will give an instance nearer hand. My wife's uncle, who lived in Dijon, had a small country house on the hill-side in the middle of a large garden. This place had been his hobby for many years, so when the Germans occupied it, he did all he could to prevent them from injuring it. He supplied them with unlimited fire-wood, and promised to supply more if required, but they preferred cutting down his fruit-trees and burning the *green* wood because they knew it would vex him. They also smashed his mirrors and destroyed his furniture on purpose. Besides the prospect of these annoyances, we had before us the probability that forty or fifty German soldiers would be billeted on us, to be kept in the most liberal manner at our expense, and that at a time when provisions were at the most impossible prices, so that the cost of living was tripled. There remained yet another possibility of evil. Our house was so situated that it might very easily be included in the middle of a battle-field, and occupied by one side or the other, if not by both in succession. Under certain circumstances, not difficult to foresee, it would become of considerable strategic importance if the combat took place in the plain. In that case the walls could be pierced for rifles, the rooms filled with soldiers, and (on a small scale) a scene might be enacted round about it like the episode of Hougomont, at Waterloo. That these apprehensions were not altogether groundless may be proved by the remark of an artilleryman whose battery I visited when the war had come quite close to us. The guns were pointed, ready shotted, straight in the direction of my house. I noted the fact jestingly, on which an artillery-man answered, *quite in earnest*, "Our guns can easily carry as far as your house, sir, and this battery may turn out to be very useful if your house should be occupied by the enemy." I may also observe that my apprehensions about piercing the walls for rifles were realized in the case of one of my neighbours, whose house was turned into a military position and pierced with a hundred loopholes.

Garibaldi came into our neighbourhood very suddenly and unexpectedly one cold, wintry night. I happened to be in the town that evening, and about nine o'clock a rumour began to circulate to the effect that Garibaldi was on his way and would sleep that night at the *sous-prefecture*. About half-past nine a crowd began to collect about the railway station, and a shabby one-horse carriage came to receive the soldier of Italian independence, who was much too unpopular with the clerical party to be noticed by the local aristocracy. First came a train full of Garibaldians; the chief himself arrived much later. The men who preceded him were the flower of his little army—the "children," not to be confounded with the volunteers of all kinds who joined the army of the Vosges. They formed in the garden behind the railway station, and the first thing that struck me was the extreme inequality of their stature. I had seen tall regiments and short regiments, but never a body of soldiers in which astonishingly tall men and miniature beings, who looked like little boys, were so oddly jumbled together. The commanding officer asked me the way to the Hôtel de Ville, and then begged me to lead the regiment there myself, so we marched into the town together to the sound of the wild Garibaldian music in the dark windy night. When we got to our destination, I could see the men better under the gaslight; they were smart and tidy-looking, in new uniforms, and they had just been armed with new Remington rifles, in which they took a boyish pleasure and pride. Poor lads! how many of them died of hardship and disease in a few weeks? I thought, as I saw them lie down wearily on the straw, how delicate many of them were, only boys yet, and not robust boys either, having nothing to resist the fatigues of a winter campaign but a lively courage, and a firm faith in the genius of their commander.

He came at last, the commander, the most romantic hero of our century, the most famous human being on the planet, the leader most sure of living in the hearts of future generations, a living man whose legend is already as firmly implanted as that of Wallace or William Tell, whilst the severest historical critics of the future will be unable to deny either the reality of his exploits or the originality of his character. Who shall say that Garibaldi was not brave, disinterested, patient under suffering, a living Don Quixote, with all the fine and noble qualities with which Cervantes endowed his hero and just enough of his simplicity to be beloved for it? A living Don Quixote! I repeat in all earnestness and respect, and yet there is this difference between the two, that whereas Sancho's master tilted against windmills and effected no practical good, the Italian Quixote set lance in rest against a tyrannical dynasty and shattered it past all possibility of restoration. Afterwards it is true that he tilted against the temporal power of the Papacy and there came to grief, but if that adventure did not upset the windmill, it shook it, and the windmill has fallen since.

When this hero came amongst us and walked through the station to his one-horse carriage we saw his face very clearly in the gas-light. It was a pale, grave face, much more like that of a student and philosopher than a hero of great exploits. We cried *Vive Garibaldi !* with some energy, but he answered with a tone of extreme gravity and sadness " *Vive la République Française !* " We thought they might have given him a pair of horses and even perhaps a little glorification of torchlight and of music, but that simplicity harmonized well enough with his personal character and habits, and also with the serious anxieties of the time.

It is difficult for Protestants to realize the unaffected horror with which the clergy and religious corporations of an old French cathedral city must have heard on awakening one morning in November, 1870, that this Garibaldi, who at a distance was to them like a rock in the deep sea, or like Satan chained during the millennium, was now actually in the midst of them, and their absolute master, being invested with all the despotic authority of a general in time of war.

The day after his arrival Garibaldi held a little review, and sat in a carriage whilst his regiments marched past, for other regiments had arrived during the morning, and train after train poured thousands of men into the place. There was unfolded his own personal Garibaldian flag, an invention of his own, a very original invention too, and one not by any means calculated to reassure the lovers of tranquillity. It was all red, to begin with, red as the sanguinary Revolution, and this is a colour which the lovers of order admire only when it is worn by the Princes of the Church. On the flag were none of the devices of heraldry, no lions, nor eagles, nor any such picturings of the old illiterate ages, but a single word, in great legible Roman capitals, and the word was—

PATATRAC.*

If we had any illusions about Garibaldi they must
have been dissipated by having him so near us, and
hearing everything that the bitterest antagonism could
find to say against him.   For my part, I venture to
affirm that I never had any illusions about Garibaldi.
Men of his class cannot possibly be reasonable, heroism
is not reasonable, it is pure passion, a fire which casts
strong lights and very black shadows upon everything

* As this narrative is written for English readers it may be well
to attempt an explanation of what this strange word means.   The
form of it most commonly recognized by the dictionaries appears
to be not Patatrac but Patatras ; however, Garibaldi's form, with
the hard looking consonant at the end is used often enough by
French people when they talk familiarly and is, I think, the more
expressive, by its cacophony, of the two.   It is an ejaculation,
intended to convey (which it does very effectually by imitative
sound) the impression of confusion in falling.   For example, suppose that a Frenchman were to narrate some accident like the following, the word would come in quite naturally: " the servant was
bringing a tray covered with glasses into the drawing-room, when
his foot caught in the edge of the carpet, and *patatrac!* he fell
forward and all the glasses were broken."   What Garibaldi meant
by it was as plain as the great legible letters of which the terrible
word was composed.   He meant that wherever that scarlet banner
was unfolded there would be an overthrow of old-world institutions,
with noisy confusion and smashing.   It was a proclamation of
disorder and destruction, and the proclamation was so alarmingly
laconic that there was no room in it for any hint of a new and
better order to be erected on a world in ruins.   And when at a
later period I heard of the smashing and crashing that was effected
on so large a scale by the Communards, of the falling of ruined
palaces and streets, of the upsetting of the Vendôme column, I
said " This is Garibaldi's PATATRAC " and that word on the banner
which flapped in the November wind seemed a word of baleful
prophecy, a sinister suggestion of all the evil that was to come.

around it. Least of all can those heroes be reasonable who live in the heat of action. It may be said that Wellington was so, but had Wellington the genuine heroic temper ? Was he not rather a prudent and practical general, with very fine powers of mind and body, than a hero ? Had he not rather the firm prose of military valour than its fiery inspiration ? Garibaldi is not wise, Garibaldi is not even intelligent, whilst he is far indeed from being intellectual; but he is as perfect a type of genuine, believing heroism as the world has ever beheld. And the consequence is, that his name is immortal, whilst the names of a hundred generals not less brave than he is, and much more learned in their art than he has ever been, are as mortal as their own bodies, and destined, like them, to imminent oblivion.

An excellent instance of his utter want of tact occurred on the very first day of his residence in our neighbourhood. He held a reception at the Sous Préfecture, which was attended by a good many men and also by some ladies who had the courage to brave public opinion and pay their respects to the representative of everything that is infamous. He received them very gracefully; he has a natural kindness and softness which renders his manners very agreeable to women, but he thought the occasion a good one for having a shot at his *bêtes noires*, the ecclesiastics, and so actually lectured these ladies on their too great submission to the priesthood. This was a fault of tact for two reasons; in the first place, the ladies in question had given strong proof of their independence of priestly authority by coming to see Garibaldi, and therefore did not either need or deserve the lesson; and in the second place his observations strengthened the very authority he desired to weaken, for they alarmed all who were afraid of the opinions of society, a large majority amongst women. It was not possible for Garibaldi to make the priesthood detest him more bitterly; but it was not necessary to frighten the ladies.

Garibaldi's little army was composed of very heterogeneous materials. He said that his men were the *élite des nations*, and it is quite true that there were some very fine fellows amongst them, but there were also hundreds of rascals who ought to have been in prison, and kept there, for the safety of society. There was especially a legion of sharpshooters from Marseilles, whose conception of military discipline was that they were to do just as they liked. They were armed, of course, and with good weapons, so that no civilian had a chance against them. By a singularly injudicious arrangement these very Marseilles fellows were sent to lodge at the bishop's palace. Now there was a story current that the prelate, on his return from the great Vatican Council, had brought amongst his baggage several packing-cases filled with military weapons, to be used for no good purpose; and so, as these free-shooters found themselves at night in the very building where these weapons were said to be concealed, they thought, or affected to think, that it would be a good opportunity to ascertain the truth of the story by a strict search over the whole building. This they executed with more zeal than consideration, making a good deal of noise, and frightening the unarmed inhabitants of the building, so that one of the servants jumped out of a window and sprained his ankle. The soldiers went into the bishop's own bedchamber and made a thorough search, to his annoyance. Amongst this disturbance a small gold cross disappeared. The incident, much exaggerated, was circulated by the clerical press all over Europe, and English Protestant newspapers, with that curious facility which so often makes them serve Roman Catholic purposes, without being aware of it, repeated the story with all its exaggerations. The facts are that the bishop's privacy was invaded, and that his little gold cross was lost. Very probably it was stolen. His watch was left untouched. The only person injured was the servant who sprained his own ankle. I have no wish to excuse the Marseilles fellows, who invaded my house, also, in the night-time most unpleasantly. It is not agreeable, as I know by experience, to be at the mercy of a band of armed men who recognize no law but their own good pleasure ; and I sympathize with the bishop, because I have experienced the same annoyance as he did ; but the plain truth is these Marseilles men were simply impudent and troublesome, no more. The clerical press used the incident with its habitual skill, and continued to spread the odium of it on the whole Garibaldian army. The bishop made ecclesiastical capital out of it, assumed the attitude of a sort of demi-martyr, and told the faithful, in his pastoral charge, that the presence of Garibaldi in their midst was enough to draw down on France the maledictions of Heaven.

It is only fair to the old companions of Garibaldi to observe in this place that, although many disorders occurred which were inevitable with a force just newly got together and never subjected to any preparatory discipline, it was never, or hardly ever, the real Italian Garibaldians who were guilty of these disorders, but men like those in that legion from Marseilles, who, indeed, formed part of the Army of the Vosges, but were not Garibaldi's comrades; they had simply been put under his orders by Gambetta; and the Italian general was peculiarly unfortunate in this respect, that, since he was considered a good captain of guerillas, all sorts of freeshooters were sent to him as soon as they presented themselves. Now, of all soldiers whom I ever beheld or talked with, those French *franc-tireurs* were the most absolutely undisciplined; indeed, it was a point of honour with them not to recognize any superior authority at all. Their theory, which they themselves have explained to me over and over again, was that an officer was only one of themselves, and that they were there to harass the enemy in the way they liked best. They had not, indeed, the most remote conception of the nature and utility of discipline, or even of any unity of action. Garibaldi's enemies were careful to lay the irregularities of all these *franc-tireurs* at his door, by calling them Garibaldians, as if they had come with him from Caprera; whereas the truth was that they were Frenchmen, not forming part of the "Garibaldian invasion of France," and that they would have served the French cause under some other general if Garibaldi had never presented himself.

Not only was the clerical sentiment strongly excited against Garibaldi, but even in minds which had not much of the *odium theologicum* there existed a very strong national antipathy. There is nothing that a nation hates, said one who has known many nations, like another nation. It was felt by many Frenchmen as a slight on their national pride that an Italian should presume to offer them any assistance in the hour of their distress ; and as no French general would serve under Garibaldi, so in the public opinion of civilians there was a feeling that he was a presumptuous intruder, who felt that, because he had beaten a few miserable Neapolitans in a little enterprise that had become famous for the mere romance of it, he could conquer the great armies of Germany, before which so many French generals had been compelled to retreat in disaster. Yet at the same time (such is the inconsistency of ill-will) that Garibaldi was despised for his nationality, his followers who were Frenchmen incurred a share of this national antipathy, and the Army of the Vosges, though most of the soldiers in it were born and nurtured on the soil of France, was looked upon as a foreign army, devouring the substance of the country.*

* Even if considered simply with regard to the maintenance of friendly relations with France, the non-intervention of England in her behalf was most judicious. I am fully persuaded that if England had sent a *corps d'armée* to help the French, and if this assistance, at some critical hour, had turned the tide of war in their favour, they would have disliked the English after that assistance more heartily than they dislike them now for their neutrality. There never was much French animosity against England during the war, because the French are persuaded that England has "no army" and cannot fight on land ; they look upon her as a sort of big fish confined to salt-water. It was the Germans who detested England during the war. The German press spoke of England with contempt mingled with aversion, whilst the English press was praising Germany as the model of all that was most admirable and most moral.

CHAPTER XVII.

WE had three classes of troops in our city, the *Mobiles*, the *Mobilisés*, and the Garibaldians. When Garibaldi arrived the *Mobiles* had left, but 2,000of the *Mobilises* remained. These occupied much of the room that was to be had, and Garibaldi's army could not sleep out in the streets, for the temperature was several degrees below freezing-point. Under these circumstances, the town-hall and the court-house were lent by the civil authorities to serve as barracks, and a considerable number of men lodged with the inhabitants. Suddenly, however, it became necessary to find shelter for an in flux of four thousand more. A good many had already been so left out, and had found it hard to have to pass the night in that manner with the thermometer below zero. Under these circumstances, the civil authorities agreed with Garibaldi that rather than let the men perish in the open streets, they would let them sleep in the churches. There was nothing new in this; it has always been done by armies in time of war, and was actually done during the Franco-German war both by French and German troops. There was a great outcry about this "desecration," however, in the especial case of the Garibaldians, due to the open hostility between their leader and the clerical party.

The choice lay between the churches and the public square, between a tolerable shelter and the intolerable cold without. There was, indeed, a way of escaping from the dilemma of inhumanity or desecration. If the rich inhabitants of the town had been disposed to make a sacrifice in the cause of religion they might have saved the houses of God from defilement by receiving more men into their own. It is true that they did already lodge a few Garibaldians who were billeted upon them, but these few were as nothing in comparison with the numbers they might have accommodated had they been willing to sacrifice their own personal comfort, and to incur the loss occasioned by inevitable damage to their tastefully decorated rooms. Every one who is in the least acquainted with military matters knows how easy it is to lodge a hundred men, as soldiers are lodged in tents, requiring nothing but floor-space, and plenty of straw to lie upon. In an old French town the poor are narrowly lodged, so are the commercial people who live over the shops, but the aristocracy have spacious old houses, hidden away in gardens, with very fine big rooms in them. Had Garibaldi taken possession of these, he need not have occupied the churches.

The next question is, how did the men behave in these places of worship? The answer is, that they behaved as soldiers always do in war-time under similar circumstances. They made themselves at home, they sang, they smoked, they lit fires where they ought not to have lighted them, they burned benches and chairs, and anything else that would help to make a fire. As to the uses to which piscinæ and confessionals were applied, it is easier to conceive them, than to find terms by which they may be described with decency. All this, no doubt, grated dreadfully on the feelings of good Roman Catholics, and I do not defend it ; I only say that it is nothing but the ordinary conduct of soldiers on a campaign. When the church is their only home, they make themselves at home there in their own rude way, certainly without any respect for the sacredness of the place, but also without any especial eagerness to profane it. And notwithstanding whatever comfort might be derived from bonfires and pipes of tobacco, the clerical party may always console itself with the reflection that many a young Garibaldian met his death from sleeping in damp and insufficient clothing on the pavement of those churches. Every week there was a list of deaths in the local papers which were not due to wounds, but to bad lodging, to damp and cold, to irregular and ill-prepared food, in short, to the hardships of warfare in the depth of one of the bitterest winters ever known in a country where winters are almost always severe.*

* It is unnecessary to add that the public services of religion were suspended during the military occupation of the edifices, and

I saw a good deal of the Garibaldian army about this time. The officers, like all the officers in the Franco-German war, spent all their spare time in cafés, which were always full of them, except when they messed in the different hotels. Garibaldi's habits of solitude and his wretched health, deprived the army of what might have been a beneficial influence, since he never messed with the officers, even of the staff, but ate his basin of soup alone, and drank his glass of water just as if he had been still in his solitude at Caprera. Nothing can be more strange ; nothing, surely, more unprecedented, than such a powerful influence as his exercised with so little personal intercourse. The officers never ate with Garibaldi, never passed an evening with him, he was very rarely visible to the soldiers, and then only in the character of an invalid taking "carriage exercise." He went to bed regularly between five and six o'clock in the evening, and for days together was only visible to his valet or Bordone. Whilst the Deliverer of the Two Sicilies lay on his sick bed in a chamber on the ground-floor, Bordone, acting always

---

this is felt as a hardship in a Catholic country, perhaps even more than it would be in a Protestant one, because the churches are used every day and at every hour of the day. At last the public schools were given up to the military, which rendered the churches no longer necessary, and the clergy complained, perhaps with reason, that although the troops might have evacuated the churches entirely at this time they did not evacuate them, but left a few men in possession. The clergy said that the purpose of this continued occupation was to prevent the re-establishment of public worship, but it is only fair to Garibaldi and the sub-prefect to suggest that it may have been done in view of the arrival of fresh troops, for the army was constantly increasing.

in his name, was the active and visible high-priest of the
mysterious, invisible hero-divinity. It was he, Bordone,
and not Garibaldi, who had the control of the army and
who held the strings of the purse. Events which happened a little later proved, for evil as well as good, the
force of his relentless will. He had the talents and
faculties of a despot, the firm resolve, the calm of nerve
which could permit him to live perfectly at ease in
situations of anxiety and peril, and in addition to these
gifts he had that other terrible one which has belonged
to every *master*—the readiness to inflict the punishment
of death.

Never was little army so numerously officered as this
Army of the Vosges. All of Garibaldi's old friends
who were with him had military titles of some kind,
and the number of colonels, especially, was surprising.
The Italians had a strong taste for brilliant and picturesque uniforms, and as these were all new, the effect,
just at first, was rather that of a levée or review than
the dinginess of actual warfare. Many fine-looking
young Italians wore Garibaldi's uniform, and they had a
way of draping themselves majestically in their scarlet
cloaks, by throwing them across the breast and mouth,
and over the shoulder, which, when accompanied, as it
generally was, by a look of sufficient sternness and a
resolutely martial bearing, had the happiest theatrical
effect imaginable. There were one or two troops of
light cavalry called " Guides " employed incessantly as
scouts, and these fellows had a costume so very picturesque and becoming that it was only *too* becoming,
and reminded one inevitably of the hippodrome. They

wore the red shirt, often traversed by chains and trinkets, with a short scarlet cloak, light bluish-grey trousers, and high equestrian boots. They wore, too, a coquettish-looking *biretta* (a peculiar sort of cap) with a high feather in it, and they soon learned the art, or had it instinctively in their Italian blood, of setting this cap and feather on their heads in the jauntiest possible manner, with the evident intention of causing every pretty Frenchwoman to fall in love with them forthwith It may be remarked, in passing, that these martial Italians never could address a person of the "beautiful sex" without either a conquering or an imploring air. and the ladies professed to be angry with them for these too amorous Southern manners.

But the most remarkable peculiarity of the Italian officers was their inveterate habit of eating sweet little cakes at the confectioners'. Never since the time of the ancient Romans had that business been so profitable as it was in those busy Garibaldian days. There were two good shops of the kind in the town—at one of them a pretty woman, at the other a handsome one. What brave Italian could resist the combined attraction of sugary cakes and female loveliness? From early morning till dinner-time did these appreciators of sweetness and light (sweetness of tarts and light of ladies' eyes) throng the shops where happiness was to be bought with silver, and how after all those luscious cakes, and those glasses of cloying Malaga wine, they could go and consume a substantial dinner at the hotel I know not. Yet so, indeed, they did!

The privates in Garibaldi s army were remarkable for

their combination of blind faith with inconceivable ignorance. I did not expect them to know much, but I expected them to know something about Italy, and at least the principal facts in the history of Garibaldi himself. They were sufficiently interested in Garibaldi to risk their lives in following him, yet not sufficiently interested to make them ascertain what had been the deeds of their hero in other and greater adventures. The rule appeared to be this. If a Garibaldian, a man of the people, a man not belonging to the educated classes, had actually taken part in one of Garibaldi's former expeditions, he would know that there had been such an expedition ; but if he had not taken part in it, then he would know nothing whatever about it. I remember trying vainly to persuade a very bright-looking young sergeant, a lad who could write Italian almost correctly, and read it easily, that Garibaldi had defended Rome against the French in 1849. He maintained that Garibaldi had never been in Rome—"he had been in Naples, but not in Rome." The only chapter of his leader's history of which this youth knew anything was the famous Sicilian expedition, and of that he knew only what he had seen. He was a native of Palermo, and had joined the expedition soon after it landed. Nor was this a solitary instance. All the Garibaldians I talked with, except educated officers, were equally in the dark. It was impossible to talk with them about contemporary events, for they were in a condition not only without information, but curiously repellent of information. It was not of the least use to tell them anything, for they would not believe you.

Firmly, yet politely, they would shake their heads and say that you had been misinformed, after which they would give you a true account of the matter, that is to say, the belief which was current amongst them. These beliefs took possession of the whole army in a manner that it was utterly impossible to foresee ; but one thing was inevitable, either the belief was absolutely and inconceivably absurd, or else it took up some bit of very old news indeed, and circulated it suddenly, as an alarming telegram is circulated in London or New York.

Garibaldianism has very little to do with knowledge. It is not even the devotion to a cause. The genuine Garibaldians, officers or men, know little and care little about causes. What they feel is an entire, unreasoning, wholly uncritical faith in the absolute excellence and wisdom of one human being, their famous leader, whom they do not call " our captain," nor " our general," but " our father."

Garibaldianism is really *a new religion.*

The first time that this became plain to me was between two and three o'clock in the morning, at the outpost nearest the enemy, when I was smoking and talking with one or two old officers of Garibaldi by a blazing fire in a cottage. Others were sleeping on the straw which covered the rude floor.

"We have no discipline whatever," said the captain, "but our affection for our father Garibaldi, it is that which binds us together. It was not for the French Republic that we came here, but our father came, and so we followed him. Look at those men on that straw ?

D D 2

Where will they be in a week? In the grave, perhaps, or in the hospital. There will be hard fighting soon, and it is a hard season. Some of those fellows are well-to-do, others have not a halfpenny; the richer ones share with their poor brethren, but whatever may be the differences of social station or military rank, all the Garibaldians feel themselves equal in the presence of their father, and all are equally cared for and beloved by him."

I was just thinking that Garibaldianism was a sort of religious faith, when the speaker resumed, after a pause, and rather startled me, with the following expressions, which I remember accurately enough to write them down word for word. " Yes," he continued, " there has been no such influence exercised over the wills of men since Jesus of Nazareth was followed by his disciples. There have been other great military leaders, but they were worldly men, and their followers were actuated by worldly motives. But our poor dear father, Garibaldi, pray what has *he* to offer? The liberty to follow him— the delight of knowing that we are near him, and shall see his face occasionally, and hear the tones of his voice calling us his children—the pride of being his own, his chosen, who have shared in all his perils and have never deserted him to the last—*these* are the only rewards that the beloved father offers, or that the devoted children care for."*

---

* This looks improbable in English because Englishmen are so careful to avoid the expression of anything resembling noble senti- ments in conversation that such sentiments are very unusual in English dialogue, but my conversations with the Garibaldians were

It was the first time that I had heard the genuine enthusiasm of Garibaldianism, but I heard exactly the same things afterwards from others, and found that it was the true tone or note of the faith. Unbelievers will naturally think that the note is pitched very high, but careful subsequent observation, for which I had ample opportunities, convinced me that the faithful had really tuned their souls up to that diapason. They had even reached the point when a faith is self-sustaining. Even the oldest officers hardly ever saw Garibaldi when he was in our neighbourhood, and they certainly never spoke to him. He lived in solitude, a sad-faced invalid, an austere water-drinker, as abstemious in eating as an anchorite. Is it not strange that this idealist, with his passion for retirement, should be the idol of strong men who, in all other respects, seemed exactly like other military officers?

About this time we were often greatly annoyed by straggling bodies of free-shooters, who would demand admittance at all hours of the night "in the name of the law," which they neither knew nor obeyed. They never did any harm in the house except by causing an increased expenditure in common wine and firewood; but it was disagreeable to be called out of bed to administer to their comforts. It is unpleasant to know that you are entirely in the power of an armed man, and what can a civilian do against a dozen fellows armed with chassepots and revolvers? One night I happened to be away during one of these visitations,

always either in Italian or French—languages which not only do not check the expression of noble sentiments, but positively favour it.

and the *franc-tireurs* had conducted themselves so very authoritatively (though not badly in any other sense), that I stayed at home afterwards to bear the brunt of it. A very odd detail of their conduct that evening was that they ordered my wife to show them all my pictures. So she went from one to another with a candle, whilst these strange connoisseurs made their critical remarks. They themselves, with their interesting costumes and arms, would have made a more interesting picture than any which they did me the honour to examine.

After that I adopted a system which answered perfectly. The house was open to free-shooters all night through, but one of the company, the highest in rank, was requested to enter his name and regiment in a book. They did this quite willingly, and I believe the names written were genuine, for they behaved very reasonably after this. When you consider that it was impossible to oppose their demands for drink, it seems rather to their credit that they were satisfied with the most moderate quantities. We had very exceptional luck in one thing—not a single soldier was ever billeted on us during the whole Garibaldian occupation ; and this is the more remarkable that the next farm was occupied as a post, whilst the nearest gentleman's house in the other direction was for some time selected as the residence of some Garibaldian officers, to the despair of the excellent housekeeper, whose cup of bitterness was full when she saw them walking with nailed and miry boots on her carefully waxed oaken floors.

We were all expecting the enemy, yet he surprised us, as a host is surprised when the guest comes before the time fixed. How perfectly I remember all the little details of that day! It was impossible to write or paint—impossible to read even, for one could not help going to look out from the upper windows in the direction where the Germans were marching. Peasants who passed along the road told us that the enemy was advancing fast, and would be upon us before evening. One of our neighbours had gone to the town in the morning and left his daughter alone. The young lady had come to us, and we had invited her to *déjeûner*. Whilst we were at table her father returned, and passed on to his own house, saying that it was still doubtful if the enemy would come that day. We had just finished our *déjeûner*, when I went to pay a visit to the stable to see that everything was ready, in case we had to abandon the house and retreat to the hills. After examining every strap and buckle of the harness, and giving Cocotte an extra feed of corn, I walked slowly back to the house and looked towards Garibaldi's outposts. There was nothing to attract attention, but I continued to look, and lo! a large puff of white smoke, and then a little cloud up in the air like a balloon. "There goes a shell!" I thought, and the little cloud descended upon the city, and after several seconds a dull *boom* came sounding across the fields. I waited to see if the Garibaldians would answer, and very soon a little white cloud rose out of the town itself and took its flight towards the spot from which the first had proceeded. After that, rose several other white clouds of the same kind, and the dull booming became incessant.

The first shot that one sees fired in actual warfare

produces quite a new impression. However familiar one may have been with reviews and royal salutes, the cannon seems to have quite a different voice in war time, as I suppose that the lion's roar must be more terrible in Africa than it is in the Zoological Gardens. It is not the noise that awes us, it is the meaning of the noise.

A strong wind was, blowing that day, and the sound of the guns did not reach us in its full strength, so the ladies in the dining-room had not heard it. When I joined them again they were still in quiet conversation, wondering whether the Prussians would arrive in the night. "Ladies," I said, ceremoniously, "if you would like to see a bombardment I shall be happy to show you one from the garret window, where you will see General Werder's army, which has just arrived, and is already displaying great activity." If the reader has ever suddenly announced to the ladies of his household that a bombardment was to be seen from his garret, he will know the effect of such an announcement; if not, he may perhaps imagine it. Not much time was lost in getting to the top of the house, and as I had a good telescope I put the end of it through a broken pane and surveyed the action in detail. Everybody tells me that I saw more of the combat than any other spectator, for those in the town were prevented from seeing anything by the houses and trees, whilst the soldiers who were actually engaged had no general view of the operations. It is probable that no rustic at a safe distance had a telescope. Mine enabled me to observe not only bodies of troops but even men individually.

There was a steady line of darkly-clothed Germans on the slope of a rising ground, and before them was their artillery. The sunshine was so clear and bright, and the guns so clean that I could see them glittering. They were served with perfect regularity, and for some time continued to pour shells into the town. The Garibaldians, on their part, occupied a more elevated position, and shelled the Germans with great energy. I heartily admired the perfect steadiness of the Germans under fire ; they were as orderly as soldiers at a review, and yet they were unpleasantly exposed, being in the open field, whereas the Garibaldians fired upon them from the houses in the *faubourg*.

It is one of the peculiarities of the fair sex not to be able to see anything with a telescope, so, after some ineffectual attempts, the ladies begged me to do all the looking, and I was placed in the position of Rebecca in "Ivanhoe," when she described the siege of the castle to the sick knight who could not look upon it with his own eyes. After a while, the Germans found their situation rather too much exposed, and a mounted officer, whom I believed to be a Colonel, took his regiment behind the Paris road, which, for a short distance, runs on an embankment, and therefore may afford some shelter. His men were now protected from the rifles in the houses, but full in view for me, and I became especially interested in the Colonel himself, because he would keep riding about on his handsome black charger, climbing the embankment repeatedly and exposing himself alone on the road to see how matters were going forward, without thinking of the peril, which was great indeed, for he was a capital mark for the riflemen as he sat on his tall horse alone in the middle of the highway. "There's a brave fellow," I said, "and a careful officer; he has put his own men out of harm's way for the present, but does not care to consult his own safety. I wish him well through it all, enemy though he be." Just as I spoke he rode out upon the highway once again, rode out to meet his fate, for he fell from the saddle a dead man. The charger turned round at once and trotted back towards the regiment. I saw a soldier go out to meet the horse and take him by the bridle. The man led the horse very quietly, but neither he nor the animal was wounded.

Now and then in the ranks of the Germans there was a little temporary disturbance when a soldier was killed or wounded, but it did not affect the rigidity of the line, which was drawn upon the field like a regiment in a stiff military picture, and the artillerymen went on serving the guns as mechanically as if they had been automatons. Being now satisfied that the Germans were not advancing their positions, but showed a tendency to withdraw from those at first occupied, I left my post of observation and busied myself about our own affairs.

We had determined to remain at home in case of simple occupation, but to leave if our house seemed likely to be included in a battle-field. There was still great risk of this; the Germans actually tried to get their artillery over the river which flowed behind my house, and could not manage it. Had they known the country roads and the fords they would certainly have

come straight to the house, whilst it is likely that some troops on the French side would have met them there. In that case our intention was to drive off to a little village high amongst the hills, not likely, from its situation, to be permanently occupied by the enemy, though he might visit it to make occasional requisitions. I had a roomy sort of four-wheeled dog-cart, with a very capacious coffer stuffed to the utmost with what we were most anxious to carry away. A more difficult task was to get a certain strong iron box away into the depths of a neighbouring wood without being observed by the *franc-tireurs*, or by rustics on the lookout First I smuggled a spade into the wood, then a pickaxe, lastly the box, then dug the hole myself, and buried my treasure, within range of the artillery, but not precisely under fire, as it was not shelling the wood where I dug the hole. I made no mark in the wood, but only this memorandum in my pocket-book : —
" First great oak, after that first birch due north, then eleven yards due west of latter." By the help of this memorandum I recovered my box quite easily after the peace ; but many country people, from trusting to their memories, and not knowing the art of making an accurate memorandum, have never been able to find what they had hidden. About a hundred *franc-tireurs* passed within a few yards of me when my task was just completed. A constant stream of civilians was pouring along the high road in all manner of conveyances, going they knew not whither. All these people had been under fire for the space of half a mile (which they passed at full gallop), but nobody was

wounded. A woman, whom I knew, came in a little donkey-carriage, and when I asked if she had any news to tell, she wrung my hand and burst into tears. This was merely the effect of excitement, for she had lost nobody she knew, and had no reason to be particularly anxious about anybody near or dear to her. The men, on the other hand, seemed to take a pride in talking like military critics, and as if they were quite accustomed to combats and sieges.

The firing ceased at dusk, and the enemy had not yet taken the place, but kept his position in the suburb. Then came a brilliant, frosty moonlight, and I set off to get news of some scouts whom we had posted to bring us information of any movement of the enemy in our direction. I met with a solitary *franc-tireur*, who was dreadfully afraid of being caught and executed by the Germans. I told him he had better come home with me, which he did with some reluctance, as he said that if we were both caught I should be shot too. He had eaten nothing all day, so I made him dine with us, and whilst we were at dinner, there came a thundering noise at the front door. It was one of our scouts, who said that the Germans were on us, so the *franc-tireur* hid himself, and I went out to look. The alarm turned out to be false, and as it was a very fine evening I drove him to the next military outpost, where he might pass the night by the fire in the guard-room.

A very odd incident happened as I was returning home. A man seized my hand and implored my intercession with the enemy, that his house and its inhabitants might be spared. There was a general impression that, as I was a foreigner, and the Germans were foreigners also, we should understand each other perfectly.

Everybody remembers the line in " Hohenlinden,"—

<blockquote>" Far flashed the red artillery ! "</blockquote>

It occurred to my memory that evening when the Germans resumed firing under the moonlight, and we could see the red flashes leaping from the cannons' mouths, silent like the red blaze in a battle picture, till the thunder came upon us tardily.

Very probably the reader will imagine that we sat up anxiously all night, but the plain truth is that we went to bed soon, and slept as well as possible till the next morning. The excitement of the day had produced that weariness, so common in war-time, which enables people to sleep in perfect tranquillity, notwithstanding the noise of cannon.

The next morning we got up early. The firing had ceased. Men who had been with the Germans all night (for the enemy had occupied their houses) came to tell us that they were in full retreat.

The next time they advanced upon us, the armistice stopped them a few miles from our house. Then the peace came, and we were delivered.

Imagine some tremendous conflagration in the primæval forest, covering thousands of square leagues; it rages and spreads till at length it reaches its limit, and just outside the limit there is a little bird's-nest, with the young in it, and the conflagration ceases, and the nest is not even singed. That nest was like our house.

Imagine some fearful inundation, which devastates a hundred towns and more than a thousand farms. It rises and spreads till it goes far inland, and comes near to a little flower. It uproots great trees, and makes many a field like a desert, but that little plant is an inch outside of its course, and the waters subside, and it is just as it was before. Our garden was like that plant.

It would be easy to thrill the reader with an account of bloodshed and wounds, but *à quoi bon ?* He has had enough of such reading in 1870 and 1871. Did he ever see such a thing as a cartload of wounded ? I have, and I do not wish to see it again. Did he ever hear the moans of men and horses in their anguish ? I have, and I do not wish to hear them again.

One would hear and see these things with greater equanimity in a just and necessary war, but that huge sanguinary conflict of 1870–71 was unnecessary in its beginning by the French and its continuation by the Germans. The French Government might have maintained peace after the renunciation of Prince Hohenzollern, and the Germans might as easily have restored it after Sedan. The war was begun by French ambition and continued by Prussian ambition, with supreme indifference, in both cases, to the interests of humanity. It was, therefore, from beginning to end, a thoroughly discouraging spectacle from the moral point of view. The conduct of Napoleon was not even national, it was selfish, for, by his own admission, it sacrificed strategic to political considerations. The conduct of the Prussians was national, but without a trace of generosity or nobleness. That terrible year can have left but one desire in all just and thoughtful minds—the wish for a stronger international law by which the ambition of rulers may be kept within reasonable limits. This may be too much to hope for in our day, but let us work for it already, each with his own small influence and strength. The time may yet come to Europe when the career of a conqueror will be as impossible within its limits as that of a Sicilian brigand is already in the Isle of Wight.

FINIS.